YURI

Roxie Rivera

Night Works Books
College Station, Texas

Roxie Rivera/Night Works Books
3515-B Longmire Dr. #103
College Station, Texas 77845
www.roxierivera.com

Publisher's Note: This is a work of fiction. Names, characters, places, and incidents are a product of the author's imagination. Locales and public names are sometimes used for atmospheric purposes. Any resemblance to actual people, living or dead, or to businesses, companies, events, institutions, or locales is completely coincidental.

Cover photograph © 2013 Konradbak/Fotolia.com

YURI (Her Russian Protector #3)/Roxie Rivera. – 2nd ed.

YURI

DEDICATION

For my parents. Thank you for teaching me that anything can
be achieved through hard work.

CHAPTER ONE

I was about ten seconds away from a meltdown that would rival even the worst mayhem of a certain supermodel. Clenching my cell phone tightly, I gritted my teeth and counted backward from five before addressing the bouncer guarding the front entrance at 716, the club where I was the PR rep.

"Where the hell is the party I booked, Trey?"

The tanned muscle-head shrugged. "Yo, Dragon Lady, I just wave through the ones with the orange wristbands. No wristband? No go."

I bit back the *screw you* burning the tip of my tongue. "Yo, Trey, you know my best friend is getting married to Dimitri over at Front Door Security, right?" From the look on the bouncer's face, he'd forgotten. "Yeah, you can kiss any chance of a job there goodbye."

Head aching, I pushed into the club's noisy entrance without waiting for a nasty reply from the bouncer. Even though 716 paid their bouncers well, everyone wanted to make the jump to Dimitri Stepanov's security firm. It was starting to be a real pain in my ass.

Not only did his bouncers get first dibs on the openings at Faze, the hot new Houston night club owned by billionaire Yuri Novakovsky, but there were rumors Dimitri would be selecting some of his best bouncers for extensive training to work as bodyguards for the wealthy and elite. It was big money—and that rat bastard Trey wasn't getting a dime of it, if I had any say.

Dragon Lady? What a dick!

On the edges of the club, I searched the gyrating crowd for any sign of my lost party. I'd worked my ass off to book the group of professional football players for this weekend. Other than hip hop artists, no one spent money like professional athletes. Considering revenue at 716 was down and my job was on the line, I needed big spenders at the VIP tables.

More importantly, club goers wanted to rub elbows with celebrities. And I'd promised my thousands of Twitter followers and Facebook friends that they'd have a chance to do just that if they came out to 716 tonight. I never lied to my followers and always gave them exactly what I'd promised. Now some sort of velvet rope snafu threatened my reputation.

But as I fought my way across the crowd, I wondered if it really was a snafu. It wouldn't be the first time one of the bouncers had been working a side game to line his own pocket while hurting the club.

As a wide-eyed intern working PR at some of the smaller clubs the firm represented, I'd seen some truly shady shit. Backroom drug deals, hookers, underage drinkers—if there was action to be had, there were bouncers who wouldn't mind getting their hands dirty for some cold, hard cash.

Something fishy was going on here…and this *dragon lady* was going to sniff it out.

At the bar, I planted both hands on the polished quartz and shoved up to reach the ear of the sexy Brazilian who tended bar on Friday nights. "Where is Bobby?"

Celia pointed behind her, indicating the back of the house. This time of night, the rabbit's warren of hallways and stockrooms turned into a damn den of iniquity. Girding my loins and expecting the absolute worst, I squeezed and shoved my way to the locked door leading to the rear of the building. I grabbed my lanyard and swiped the ID card hanging around my neck through the card reader.

Inside the darkened hallway, I shut the door firmly behind me and let my eyes adjust to the even dimmer lighting. The closed door muted the thudding music and the incessant throbbing in my head eased some. Vivian, my best friend and roommate, warned me that I'd be deaf by thirty if I continued to work the club scene. Maybe she was right. Maybe it was time to give my eardrums a well-earned rest.

Steeled for the worst, I started opening doors. A couple of the rooms were empty. One was being used for some kind of weird amateur porn shoot between two girls and a guy wearing bright yellow briefs. I shut that door fast and kept moving. Another door revealed some preppy college kid scoring coke. Chains, the dealer, was a lowlife I'd specifically asked Bobby, the head bouncer, to keep out of the place.

Holding the door open, I scowled at the kid. "Get the hell out of here. *Now!*"

He dropped the drugs and almost ran me over trying to get out of there. Chains bent down to retrieve his product. The kid had left without getting back his money so Chains pocketed it.

"Baby, I bet I got something here that would mellow you out." His hand brushed his crotch.

I nearly gagged at his disgusting come-on. "Yeah? Well, I got something in my purse that will hollow you out."

His eyes widened but he quickly recovered. "Come on, sugar. Don't be so nasty. Why don't we work together? I'll cut you in on my action."

"Not interested, Chains." I jerked my thumb over my shoulder. "It's time for you to go."

He took a step toward me but I didn't move. I'd learned a long time ago never to show weakness to any man. His hand slipped to his pocket. I squared my shoulders and rocked my weight to my back foot. Even in high heels, I could still kick his ass.

"You touch me and you'll be crawling out of here with your balls in your pocket."

"*Ay, mamí*!" He laughed but put up both hands. "All right. I don't need to be told twice. I'm out of here." As he slipped by me, his eyes narrowed. "You look familiar. You sure you ain't from my neighborhood?"

The reminder of the place where I'd come from wasn't a pleasant one. "Anything is possible."

His eyes widened with sudden recognition. "Wait! I got it! Are you related to Tommy Cruz?"

I cringed at the mention of my ne'er-do-well cousin. "Yes. Why?"

He sucked air through his teeth and grimaced. "Too bad about that job he fucked, huh?"

"I don't know what you're talking about." I truly didn't. I tried to stay far away from the criminal activities of my cousin and wayward father. "Frankly, I don't care. Now go."

He looked like he wanted to say something else but

didn't. With jerky movements, he pimp-walked down the hallway. I made sure he let himself out before turning my back on him. That same crap neighborhood where I'd been raised had taught me numerous survival skills.

Three doors down, I finally located Bobby. My belly lurched at the sight of him pounding into some girl. Average height and pot-bellied, Bobby wasn't the kind of man a hot young thing like that blonde would normally bang on a Friday night. Her tiny thong dangled from one ankle. She still had her bright red pumps on and her skirt was hiked up around her waist.

Bobby's pasty white ass pumped as he gave it to her. He sounded like a damn pig as he grunted and snorted. Clearly, he wasn't much concerned about her pleasure. She looked about as excited as a girl making her yearly visit to the gynecologist.

When he finally came, he jerked and made the strangest yowling noise. There was no doubt in my mind I'd be haunted by the sound of Bobby having an orgasm for the rest of my life.

He pulled out and let the young woman drop to the floor without a care for her safety. She landed on both feet but tottered precariously. Unfortunately, I got a good look at his stumpy you-know-what. Now I was almost certain I'd never be able to have sex again. The combination of optical assaults was too much for me. Where was the eye-bleach when a girl needed it?

Bobby leered at me. "Give me five minutes to recover, Lena. I'd love to bend you over that stack of booze."

I shot him the finger. "You're a pig."

"That just got laid."

The woman flinched with embarrassment and I ached for her. "Are you all right?"

"I'm fine."

She wasn't. I hated to think that she'd degraded herself for entrance into the club but it wasn't uncommon. The girls who couldn't get into Faze tried 716. If they couldn't get in through the front door, they'd try to catch the eyes of the bouncers. Trading favors in back rooms was the currency around here.

And it made me sick. This line of work was starting to kill my faith in humanity.

Face aflame with humiliation, she tugged up her thong and pushed down her skirt. She extended her hand to Bobby, palm side up. Had I interrupted a hooker turning a trick?

Bobby reached into his pocket and retrieved a bright orange wristband. He slapped it into her hand. "Have fun."

The woman rushed out of the room, knocking into me and throwing me into the wall. I rubbed my arm and glared at Bobby. "Where the hell did you get those?"

"Get what?" He played dumb and tucked his sad little prick back into his pants.

"Don't screw with me tonight, Bobby. Where did you get those wristbands?"

"I don't know. I found them on the bar."

"Liar." The pieces fell into place. "Let me guess. Someone from Faze paid you to swap out the wristbands that were supposed to be couriered to my private party, right? They get the wrong color and get turned away at the door so they go to Faze. You keep the orange bands and sell them to anyone who wants into the VIP area by promising them they'll get to party with celebrities? Is this some huge scam?"

"Is everything a conspiracy with you?"

"What the hell is wrong with you? Don't you know how badly this club needed that party? How do you think you get paid?"

"Alls I know is that before you came here, I was making money hand over fist at the back door. I got a cut of everything that came in here. Then you went on your rampage about underage drinkers and drugs and the whores. How the hell am I supposed to make a living?"

"So that's what this is? Payback?" I scoffed at his plan. "If you ruin the club, you're out of a job too."

"I can get a job anywhere. You? Good luck getting anyone to hire the girl who drove Houston's hottest club into the ground."

"You're an asshole."

He grinned widely and made a kissy face at me. Disgusted, I spun on my heel and left the back room. Back out in the club, I tried to think of some way to salvage the night. If I could find Danny, the club's owner, and get him to okay a markdown on the pricey top shelf liquor we'd stocked in anticipation for the VIPs, we could pack the place with thirsty college kids looking for a deal. They'd spend way more than intended if there was no cover charge and a promise of cheap booze.

As I hastily did the math between the wholesale price he paid per case and what I thought my followers would pay, I weaved in and out of the dancing throng. I finally spotted Danny and got his attention by waving my hand. He wore an expression that didn't bode well for me. My stomach knotted with anxiety.

When I drew close enough, Danny grabbed my upper arm. Fear punched my gut as the painful clutch registered. I tried to wrench free but he grabbed me even harder. Before I could even recover from the shock of being manhandled like that, Danny pivoted and jerked me behind him. I stumbled forward and barely managed to regain my footing as he dragged me through the crowd to a private door. He hauled me into the hallway that led to his office.

"Let go of me!" I pried my arm free from his painful grasp and shoved at his chest. He lurched backward and slammed into the wall. As he glared at me, I rubbed the spot where my arm throbbed. "Don't you ever put your hands on me again!"

"I own you, Lena. This club made your career. I'll put my hands wherever the hell I want."

"Try it, Danny. I'll have you in handcuffs." My nose wrinkled at the scent of alcohol spilling out of his mouth. "You're drunk."

"And you're fucking pathetic. What the hell do I pay you for, Lena? Where's the party you promised me? Huh? Lately, you're all promises but no follow through." Sneering, he hissed, "You're like a high-priced whore who never gets wet. I can fuck you but it won't be any good."

I reeled back in shock at his ugly remark. It wasn't the first time he'd said something that gross to me. He had a reputation for being a real asshole but I'd learned to deal with him. Working PR for the hottest nightspots necessitated a thick skin. In this line of work, I'd grown accustomed to dealing with the verbal abuse and blatant sexual harassment. If it wasn't the club owners, it was the high rollers with their grabby hands or the musicians who thought every woman wanted to flop on her back or drop to her knees.

I always told myself that it was going to be the last time I let someone talk to me like that but the fear of losing my job, of getting knocked off the career ladder I'd fought so damn hard to climb, stopped me. A childhood living hand to mouth had left me craving the security of a steady paycheck.

But this time I'd had enough. I was better than this.

"I don't have to take this shit."

"You walk out of here and I'll make sure the firm shit-cans you. By the time I'm done telling everyone how you've ruined my club, you'll be lucky to get hired by one of the airport titty bars."

"How *I* ruined your club?" Irritated, I shouted, "I saved your liquor license by kicking out the hookers and the high school kids and the drug dealers. I brought in a new and better crowd flush with cash—but you got greedy. *You* ruined this place." I put up my hands. "I'm so over this, Danny. I'm done."

"I'll tell you when you're done!"

Rolling my eyes at his empty threat, I stormed to the door and out of the club. With every step I took, I felt the constriction in my chest ease. For weeks now, I'd been carrying around the stress of this hellhole. It was going to kill me.

After my coworker had stolen my ideas and jumped ship to work on Faze's dedicated PR team, my boss at the firm had handed me the full reins of 716. Basically, he'd given me a cup to bail out a sinking ship.

Danny was increasingly erratic and the bouncers headed by Bobby were impossible to work alongside. The bartenders were gaining a reputation for watering down drinks and substituting cheap booze for the good stuff. I had a hell of a time booking DJs after a bloody brawl broke out in the VIP area because a certain DJ and a local rap star had gotten into it over some girl. I'd specifically warned Danny against booking them both at the same time but did he listen to me?

Out on the sidewalk, I ignored the catcalls from Trey and stalked to the corner in search of a cab. I didn't doubt that Danny would follow through on his threat to get me fired. I'd been walking a fine line at the firm as it was.

This would be the last straw for my boss.

He'd been riding my ass for the last week about taking side jobs on my own time. There was nothing in my contract that said I couldn't have outside clients but that didn't stop him from accusing me of putting my own interests before the firm's. It was a bald-faced lie, of course. In the last month, I'd averaged seventy-eight hours a week for my firm clients. Not a single one of them complained about the quality of my work. As always, I received high marks and maintained my standards, even if I was running on caffeine fumes.

A cab pulled up to the curb, and I hopped into the backseat. I met the cab driver's gaze in the rearview mirror. "Where you going, sweetheart?"

God, wasn't that the question of the night! Where the hell was I going? Where was my life going? My career? I didn't have any idea and it scared me. Feeling impotent and confused, I could think of only one place. "Take me to Faze."

"The night club?"

"Yes."

I had a score to settle with Yuri Novakovsky.

* * *

Kicked back in the private section of his Houston night club, Yuri closed his eyes and relaxed. It had been one hell of a week. For the last year, he'd been putting together a pipeline project that would carry gas from the plants he owned in Russia to a spider web system that covered Europe. In the last month, tiny problems continued to crop up with what should have been an easy deal. Every time he put out one fire, another seemed to spark into a raging inferno.

Despite the stress of it all, he wouldn't trade his life for anything. He'd reached a pinnacle of success most men could only dream of and he'd done it all before reaching forty. He'd come from nothing—less than nothing—and soared to an echelon of wealth so astronomically high that there were only a handful of people in the entire world who could call themselves his peers.

But all the money in the world couldn't buy what he wanted most.

Oh, he had the yachts and the cars and the houses and the night clubs. With one call, he could have a private jet fueled and in the air to any continent he desired. Wherever he went, gorgeous women practically threw themselves at him—and he'd sampled quite a few of them.

But the one he really wanted didn't see him.

Once, he'd stupidly believed there were no doors his money couldn't open. Now Yuri knew better. There was one door that no amount of money in the world could ever unlock and it was the one door he desperately wanted to open.

"Sir?"

Lost in his thoughts, Yuri hadn't noticed his bodyguard, Derek, approach. "Yes?"

"Big V wants you to know he just let Miss Cruz through the front door. You said you wanted to be informed anytime she visited the club."

Though he schooled his expression and stayed cool and reserved on the outside, Yuri experienced a surge of excitement. His heartbeat sprinted at the idea of seeing her again. She hadn't ever come to his club alone. Usually it was Erin who dragged her along. Why had she come here tonight?

A flutter of hope invaded his chest but he batted it

away quickly. If there was one thing he'd learned about Lena Cruz, it was that she was never predictable.

"Bring her to me, Derek."

"Yes, sir."

After his bodyguard left, Yuri rose from his comfortable perch and moved to the balcony overlooking the dance floor. His searching gaze zeroed in on Lena. Even at this distance, she knocked the air right out of his lungs.

Tonight she wore a curve-hugging dress. The pale turquoise skirt and black strapless top outlined her sexy shape perfectly. Waves of dark hair tumbled around her bare shoulders. She managed to meld together the perfect mix of flirty but classy.

Like him, the men on the dance floor couldn't keep their eyes off her. A few guys tried to dance up against her but she froze them in place with that icy glare. In his entire life, Yuri had known only one other person who could send people fleeing with one look—and that was Nikolai. He knew exactly how Nikolai had developed that particular talent but Lena was more of a mystery to him.

Jake, his other bodyguard, got close to Lena. He whispered in her ear and gestured to the private VIP section. Her gaze jumped to the balcony. Instead of the smile he'd hoped to see, Yuri received only a frown. Anger glinted in her dark eyes. Something told him this wasn't going to be a conversation he was going to enjoy.

Steeled for the worst, he backed away from the railing. If there had been more time, he would have ordered a stiff drink. His gut clenched with nervousness. When was the last time any woman had affected him like this?

Lena stepped through the gauzy curtain separating this private section from the rest of the VIP area. God, but she was even prettier this close. His gaze drifted to those red, pouty lips of hers. What he wouldn't give for the chance to claim them just once!

"I thought we were friends, Yuri."

Frowning, he insisted, "We are."

"Are we?" She took another step toward him. Finger raised, she jabbed at the air between them. "When you found out how Harry stole my ideas and used them to get hired by your company, you promised me you were going to let him go. You swore to me that you didn't like to do dirty business."

"I did let him go, and I don't like dirty business dealings."

"Bullshit!" She angrily gestured over her shoulder. "I just walked through a VIP room packed with the party I arranged for 716. Someone at your club paid one of the bouncers at 716 to switch out the priority wristbands so my party would be turned away at the door and come here. That's so shady, Yuri."

He had no idea what she was talking about but believed her version of the tale. She'd never given him any reason to doubt her. "It is," he agreed. "But I didn't have anything to do with it."

"It's your club, Yuri. I realize you're just the money behind the venture but you set the tone for the employees. If they think they can get away with these kinds of tricks, they will."

"I'm sorry. I'll look into it." He could see how upset she was about being sabotaged. "Let me make it right. How much money did 716 lose tonight?"

Her jaw tensed. "I don't want your damn money, Yuri. That's not why I came here."

"Why did you come here?"

"I…" Lena's voice trailed off and her shoulders slumped. He witnessed the fight leave her and wondered what the hell she'd been through tonight. Rubbing her forehead, she dropped her gaze and shook her head. "I just couldn't take it anymore. I had to get out of that place and then I got out to the cab and I was just so angry. I wanted to come here and shout at you and tell you off for sabotaging me but—of course—you had to be totally reasonable. Why do you always have to be so damn perfect?"

He didn't know how to respond to that accusation. Desperate to lighten the tense mood, he joked, "It's a gift."

She snorted indelicately and wiped at her cheeks. When she lifted her face, Yuri's heart stuttered. Tears shimmered in her dark eyes and dripped onto her cheeks. Taken aback by her unusual display of emotion, he crossed the distance between them in three long strides. "*Yelena.*"

He stopped when there were only a few inches between them. Her perfume, that breezy scent that he'd always associate with her, called to him. He wanted to slide his arms around her and gather her close but he hesitated.

Not wanting to make her uncomfortable, he reached inside his jacket and withdrew a handkerchief. She didn't fight him when he dabbed at the wet trails on her cheeks. Looking up at him through those thick eyelashes, Lena presented such an enticing picture. He fought the urge to tip her chin and claim that sensual mouth of hers.

"I'm sorry." She dropped her gaze in embarrassment. "I shouldn't have come here. Now I'm acting like a hot mess."

"You're not," he assured her. "I'm glad you came to me." Realizing this was the chance he'd been waiting for, he snatched it. "Let's get out of here. Let's find a quiet place to talk."

Her lips parted almost immediately and he tensed in anticipation of a rejection. She stunned him by agreeing with a little nod. "Okay. Let's go."

Hope flared to life deep inside him. The night was young and anything could happen now.

CHAPTER TWO

I still couldn't quite believe I was sitting in the backseat of one of Yuri's ridiculously expensive private cars. The sexy as sin Russian billionaire sat mere inches from me. His body heat amplified the subtle citrus notes of his cologne. The seductive scent matched his personality.

Try as I might, I couldn't deny my attraction to Yuri. He got under my skin in a way no man ever had. I was really starting to understand what Erin and Benny meant when they described the instant attraction to their Russian hunks. Like his best friends Ivan and Dimitri, Yuri possessed that striking ability to be both commanding and incredibly alpha without being controlling or overbearing.

It infuriated me. I desperately wanted a reason *not* to like him. He presented too many challenges. Yuri was used to buying what he wanted and I was so not *that* girl. I'd worked hard to get an education and make it on my own. I sure as heck didn't need a sugar daddy in my life who thought he could keep me happy by buying me nice things.

Yet here I was, driving through the busy streets of Houston on a Saturday night with him. *What the hell are you doing?*

My cell phone rang and rattled around in my purse. It was the third time that particular ringtone had blared since I'd climbed into Yuri's car but I wasn't in any hurry to answer it.

"Are you going to get that? I don't mind."

I glanced at Yuri and shook my head. "No."

His eyebrows arched with surprise. "Is it someone you want to ignore? A boyfriend perhaps?" There was no mistaking the hint of jealousy in his voice.

"I'm not seeing anyone." Uncertain why I'd confessed to the sad state of my personal life, I grabbed my bag. As I muted my phone, I explained, "It's my cousin, Tommy. He probably wants to borrow money."

"I see."

He didn't, I was sure, but I let it go. My thoughts traveled back to Chains at 716. What had he said? Tommy had screwed up a job. I groaned inwardly and prayed my dad wasn't involved in whatever had gone awry.

For the last few years, my dad had been grooming Tommy to take the reins of the illicit family business. There was only one man in Houston who dealt in pricey stolen goods—and that was my father. It wasn't a fact I advertised. Like much of my family history, it was a detail I kept deliberately vague and quiet. Only Vivian knew the absolute truth of my crazy, sordid family tale. In that department, at least, she had me beat.

Not wanting to open the door to a discussion of my dysfunctional family, I asked, "So what are we doing?"

"I don't know," he admitted with a surprisingly nervous smile. "What would you like to do?"

My belly did a little somersault at the sight of his lopsided, boyish grin. "I wouldn't mind a bite to eat."

Yuri pushed up his cuff and checked his watch. My gaze lingered on the outrageously expensive timepiece. The rich chocolate-brown leather of the wrist band complemented his tanned skin. With that fleet of yachts at his disposal, I wasn't surprised that he kept a tan year-round. "Samovar is still open. I'm sure Nikolai wouldn't mind seating us."

The Russian restaurant owned by his friend Nikolai was firmly in Yuri's comfort zone. I wondered what it would be like to have him on my turf. "You know what? I have a better idea. It'll be my treat."

Interest sparked in his hazel eyes. "Your treat, huh? My goodness, it's been a long time since *I* was wined and dined."

Laughing softly, I tapped my phone screen to bring up my Twitter timeline. It took me a few seconds of scrolling to find what I needed. My favorite food trucks moved their late-night parking spots every week. This was the only way to keep track. Armed with the address, I sat forward to give the driver directions. "I think you'll like where I'm taking you."

He murmured something in Russian and I narrowed my eyes. With a wag of my finger, I playfully warned, "None of that, Yuri. Erin and Benny might find it cute when their guys do that but not me."

Yuri smiled. "You don't think I'm cute?"

Nervous, I glanced toward the window. "I'm not sure cute is the word I'd use to describe you."

"Lena?"

"Yes?"

"What happened tonight? It wasn't simply the sabotage that brought you to my club."

For a long moment, I stared out the window and watched the bright lights of the city whiz by us. Finally, I said, "I really hate my job."

"What?" He sounded so surprised. "But you're so good at it."

With a soft sigh, I turned to face him. "You can be really good at something and not like it."

"Is it PR that you don't like or is it the environment of the firm?"

I considered his query. "The firm," I decided. "It was such a great place to work when I started there as an intern and even at first when they hired me on as a full-time rep."

"But something changed?"

I nodded. "My mentor, Lisa, decided to follow her husband to Atlanta where he'd been hired as a big-time neurosurgeon. They didn't promote from within to fill her spot but hired someone from outside the company. I think the cracks started then."

"Why have you stayed so long?"

"I don't know," I admitted. "I ask myself that same question all the time. Heck, two months ago, I was having a conversation almost exactly like this one with Benny."

"And what did she suggest?"

"That I use my connections, my blog and my huge social media following to strike out on my own."

"And why didn't you?"

I shrugged. "Money. Fear."

"For what it's worth," Yuri said, "I made some of my biggest gains in wealth when I had deals on the table that terrified me. People always say to listen to your gut but sometimes you have to just close your eyes and jump, Lena."

While I mulled over his advice, he reached out to tap

my knee. Our gazes locked in the shadowy backseat. I held my breath and waited for him to speak.

"You're brilliant, Lena. You have great instincts and innovative ideas. People like you. You're funny and witty and you know how to work your contacts. Will you fall flat on your face if you strike out on your own? No, definitely not. Will you be an overnight success? No. Can you build something successful with a year or two of hard work? Yes. Absolutely."

I swallowed hard at his vote of confidence. "You seem pretty sure."

His sexy grin made my tummy wobble. "I'm never wrong."

I arched an eyebrow. "Never?"

"Never."

The car slowed and made a turn into a parking lot bustling with the late-night crowd. Some of the city's hottest chefs ran food trucks on the weekends to cater to the hungry folks coming out of the theaters, art galleries and clubs in the area. Over the last few years, I'd become friendly with Tai and Chuy, two chefs who owned a pair of the city's hippest restaurants.

When their businesses had started to struggle, I'd pitched the idea of the two of them throwing in together to buy a food truck that offered a delectable mix of their Asian and Mexican cuisines. I'd used my social media platform to push customers their way during those first crucial weeks. They'd become such a huge hit that they were about to launch a second truck that would cater to the downtown medical center crowd.

As always, I tapped on my phone's screen to update my status and location. Something stopped me. Glancing at Yuri, I asked, "Would it be a really bad idea for me to tag you in this post?"

Reluctantly, he confirmed my suspicion. "I try to be careful about that kind of thing. Houston is an incredibly safe place, and I've never had any problems here but one never knows." His gaze jumped to the window and the shadowy form waiting there. "My bodyguards wouldn't be pleased to have my location broadcasted."

I switched up my posting and made no mention of Yuri. I could only imagine what kinds of loons probably wanted to hurt him. A man with his money and his reputation in business had likely made some real enemies along the way.

When we stepped out of the car, the two bodyguards who went everywhere with him surrounded us. Yuri motioned for them to give us some space. As we joined the long, winding line for the truck Chuy and Tai owned, I couldn't help but ask, "Doesn't that feel weird?"

He glanced back at the intimidating bodyguards in their matching dark suits and with half-hidden earpieces twirling down their necks. "You get used to it."

Sadness gripped me. It couldn't be easy to live in a fishbowl, constantly followed and watched. "I'm sorry you need them."

He shrugged. "It's the trade-off for the success I've enjoyed. I'll happily accept it for all the other opportunities I'm afforded."

Yuri reached out and swept some of my hair behind my shoulder. His fingertips brushed my skin, the very touch searing me. The shuddery flutter in my lower belly accompanied an uptick in my heart rate. It stunned me how easily the man affected me.

When his gaze dropped to my arm, Yuri's eyes narrowed and anger flashed across his face. Carefully, he ran his fingertips along my skin. "Who did this to you?"

I glanced at the ugly bruises forming there and winced.

"It's nothing."

"Yelena." He used my full name, his Russian accent so thick as he emphasized the syllables. "Please don't lie to me. Did someone hurt you?"

"It was just a stupid work thing. Danny grabbed me but I got away from him. It's one of the reasons I quit."

His square jaw visibly tensed. Rage etched hard lines into his handsome face. "Has he touched you before this?"

Taken aback by his outrage, I insisted, "Yuri, I handled it. It's no big deal."

"No big deal?" He practically gawked at me. "A man grabbed and bruised you. It's unforgiveable. It's disgraceful."

Indignation welled within me. "Yuri, I can take care of myself."

"I didn't say you couldn't." His gentle fingertips moved over my sore arm. "If you were mine—"

"I'm not yours," I interjected without thinking. Almost instantly, I hated myself for it. He flinched, his cheek pulling tight for a millisecond, and dropped his hand. "Yuri, I didn't—"

"No," he said softly. "It's fine. I understand."

Desperate to make him understand and certain I'd just really stepped in it, I grasped his hand and tugged him out of the line. We were already attracting eavesdroppers and I wanted some privacy. The bodyguards shadowed us but I figured there was no losing those two.

For a few seconds, I simply held his hand and stared at him. He seemed confused and I couldn't blame him. I was throwing out mixed signals like crazy.

With a noisy exhale, I confessed, "You scare me, Yuri."

His eyes widened. Concerned, he stepped toward me.

"Have I done something to upset you?"

"No," I hurriedly assured him. "It's not like that." I searched for the right words. "You're big and sexy and powerful and wealthy and I just—I don't know what you want with me. I'm a big nobody and you're—"

"You are *not* a nobody," he interjected roughly.

I was taken aback by the emotion in his voice. Swallowing hard, I asked again, "What do you want with me? Is this just a game? Are you chasing me because you think I'm playing hard to get?"

"Are you playing hard to get?"

I shook my head. "I don't like games, Yuri."

"Neither do I." He dared to reach out and caress my cheek. "Lena, you tempt me in ways I cannot even describe. You make me want it all."

My heart thudded in my chest as his fingertips trailed along my skin. I tried to swallow but my mouth had gone dry. "All?"

Nodding, he cupped my face with one hand. His mouth curved in a sinful smile "But we can start with a kiss."

As his mouth lowered to mine, I experienced a quicksilver flash of panic. More than anything in the world, I wanted to feel Yuri's lips against mine but I was smart enough to know we were playing with fire. He wanted it all and I wanted—well—I didn't really know what the hell I wanted.

But I closed my eyes and jumped in with both feet.

Yuri's lips brushed mine, just briefly, and then disappeared. A little disappointed by the chaste kiss, I gazed up at him in confusion. A teasing smile played upon his mouth. He cupped my nape and lowered his mouth to mine. This time his kiss was more insistent, almost commanding. I whimpered a little and clutched at his arm, my fingers gripping the fabric of his blazer.

I'd been kissed plenty of times but I'd never been kissed like *this*. The tips of my toes tingled and my belly did crazy flip-flops as Yuri nibbled my lower lip and flicked his tongue against mine. It wasn't a very long kiss, and it ended much too soon

Trembling inside, I inhaled a steadying breath and stared into his eyes. I didn't know what to say. I sensed he didn't either. Instead, he dropped his hand to mine and interlaced our fingers. With a little tug, he urged me to get back into line. I noticed a couple of curious stares but most people seemed too interested in their own business to nose into mine.

I'd never been the kind of girl who enjoyed holding hands but there was something comforting in the way Yuri clasped mine now. Was this what Erin and Benny craved so much about their big, sexy Russians? Though Yuri wasn't quite as tall or muscular as Ivan or Dimitri, he still towered over me. His dominating presence made me feel...secure.

Standing here with Yuri, our hands entwined, I felt as though I could let my guard down a little. His hawkish gaze moved around the crowd, constantly assessing for trouble. Normally, I was the one doing that. Growing up in one of Houston's hardest neighborhoods, I'd been baptized by fire, so to speak.

Though I doubted he'd eaten street food in years, he surprised me by just rolling with it when it was our turn to order. We picked out a few tasty things from the menu and slid down the line. Yuri found a cozy spot at one of the picnic tables. Sitting across from one another, we tucked into our late night dinner.

"This is *very* good."

I laughed at how shocked he sounded. "Did you think

I would bring you to a total dive?"

"No! Of course not," he quickly replied. "I didn't mean—"

Waving my plastic fork, I smiled and assured him, "I know what you meant. I was just teasing."

Yuri tipped his head to the side as if studying me. "I can't always tell with you. Other people are so easy to read but you..." He shook his head. "You remind me very much of Nikolai. Even after all these years of being friends, I still struggle with reading him."

I reached for my cup of iced tea. "Vivian says the same thing to me all the time."

"Since she knows you both so well, I'll have to ask her for pointers." He picked up one of the tiny egg rolls. "I haven't had a chance to see Benny or Dimitri in almost a week. How is the future Mrs. Stepanov?"

"Wouldn't that be Stepanova?"

He laughed. "Well, not here in this country but back home? Yes. I've learned to conform but I'm surprised you knew that. Are they making you learn Russian now?"

"Vivian makes Benny and Erin talk in Russian whenever they're all together. I'm basically being forced to learn so I can contribute to our conversations."

"Is it such a hardship to expand your horizons?"

I heard the teasing in his voice. "No, I suppose not."

"How is Benny's bakery coming along?"

"She opens on Monday. The place looks fantastic. You won't recognize it."

"And your PR for the launch?"

"I've been able to line up a ton of press for her. Don't get me wrong. The fire was terrible. What Jonah Krause did to threaten her was just *awful*—but it's been damn good for business."

Yuri didn't seem very scandalized. If anything, he

seemed to understand perfectly. "People like a good underdog story."

"Yes!" I practically squealed with delight that he got it. He laughed at my enthusiasm. "Sorry." I felt a bit sheepish. "It's just that I've been saying the same thing to Benny for weeks. People want her to succeed. They want her to thrive. I keep telling her that she's like a phoenix. She's rising from the ashes."

Yuri got the funniest look on his face. He laughed hard. "That's too funny."

Confused by his reaction, I asked, "What is?"

He motioned toward his back with his fork. "Dimitri has a phoenix tattoo on his back."

"Really?"

"Yes."

"Huh." I sipped my tea. "He doesn't have any tattoos on his hands or forearms like Ivan and Nikolai. I assumed he didn't have any ink anywhere." I gazed at Yuri and wondered what he had going on under his shirt. "Do you have any tattoos?"

He held my questioning gaze. With a mischievous smile, he said, "You'll have to get me naked and see for yourself."

Rolling my eyes, I giggled softly. "I walked right into that one."

"Have I embarrassed you?" His playful tone made me smile.

"Me? Hardly. Had you said that to Vivi? She would have crawled under the table."

"If I'd said that to Vivian, I would be ducking under the table to escape Nikolai."

"He does seem to take his guardian role rather seriously." I watched Yuri's face as I made my comment. His eyes glinted with the same suspicion I had. "Of course, Vivian doesn't seem to mind in the least."

"No, I don't think she does."

"We're not going to come right out and say it, are we?"

"That Nikolai cares deeply for Vivian and she cares for him?" He shrugged. "What's there to say? You know as well as I do that their relationship is complicated in the extreme."

"To say the least," I murmured.

Changing the subject and putting an end to our speculation, he remarked, "When you talk about your work with Benny, you seem much more excited than when I've heard you discuss 716. Do you not enjoy your work in the night club scene anymore?"

I blinked with surprise. Just like that, he'd nailed the question that gnawed at me every night. "I'm bored with it. Or, maybe, I'm fed up with it." I crumpled up my paper napkin. "When I got started in this line of work, being a PR girl for a hot night club was, like, my dream. I went after it and I got it. I've proven that I have what it takes but now I feel so…so…"

"Stagnant?"

I nodded at his suggestion. "Yes. I'm not growing. I'm simply…existing."

"You need a challenge." He held my gaze. "Come work for me."

My tummy fluttered wildly at his offer but not for the reason it should have. It wasn't the prospect of the big salary and working for an international organization that made my pulse race. No, it was the prospect of working alongside Yuri every day. "No, thank you."

His eyes narrowed for the briefest moment. What was he thinking? "I'll double the salary I offered the first time."

"The answer is still no."

He sat forward and assumed a negotiating position. "You can have any office in the building downtown that you want. There would be a car and the best travel accommodations money can buy. The opportunity for bonuses and advancement are unmatched by any other company."

My lips twitched with amusement. I wondered when he'd last found himself in the losing position of a negotiation. "It's not about the money, Yuri."

He studied me intently, those hazel eyes of his boring into me and making my skin prickle with heat. "What is it about, Lena?"

I dropped my gaze to the picnic table and ran my finger around a knot in the wood. I couldn't think of a single reason to dance around my attraction to him anymore. "I *like* you."

He grasped my hand and coaxed me to meet his piercing gaze. "And I like you."

My belly quivered. Trying to get a grip on my wild emotions, I asked, "Yes but for how long? Your reputation—"

He cut me off with a string of Russian that sounded suspiciously like cursing. Clearly remembering my earlier chiding, he hastily apologized in English. "Forgive me." With a heavy sigh, Yuri said, "Look, I'm not going to sit here and pretend that I haven't played the field. Heavily," he added with a touch of regret in his voice. "That doesn't mean that I can't change."

"Have you? Changed, I mean."

"Yes—or, rather, I *am* changing. Seeing Ivan and Dimitri so happy? It's made me evaluate my own life. I have so much wealth, so many material things, but I don't have anything that *matters*."

The idea that I could be someone who mattered was

incredibly seductive. I projected a confident persona but deep down inside I struggled with feelings of inadequacy. Watching my mother walk out on me and listening to her say the awful thing she'd said on her way out the door had crushed my self-esteem. I'd managed to cobble together the pieces but the cracks were still there.

Sitting up straighter, Yuri embraced the role of successful magnate. He exuded such power and control. A bit imperiously, he informed me, "We're going out Monday night." Gesturing toward me, he said, "We're going to give this dating thing a try."

His unilateral decision should have annoyed me much more than it did. For some reason I couldn't quite fathom, I found his declaration oddly enticing. There weren't many men brave enough to tell me what to do but he hadn't done it arrogantly or coldly. I sensed he understood that even though I wanted to see where things between us might go I was too afraid, too hesitant, to say yes. He'd just taken away my control—and left me vibrating with excitement.

Clearing my throat, I said, "I need to look at my calendar."

Amusement glinted in his eyes. He held out his hand. "Give me your phone."

Wondering what he was playing at, I pulled my phone from my purse and slapped it into his hand after unlocking the front screen. He tapped away at it and then handed it back. "Now you have my private number."

I heard his emphasis on *private*. I figured I'd made it onto a short list of people with access to those digits. "Would you like my number?"

"I already have it."

"Oh really?"

His mouth curved in a devilishly sexy grin. "There's

nothing I can't get my hands on when I want it, Yelena."

When he said my full name, his Russian accent highlighting and stretching out the three syllables, I experienced the most delicious tingle in my chest. Considering what he'd said about getting his hands on the things he wanted, I gave a nonchalant shrug. "We'll see."

Chuckling, Yuri glanced around the parking lot. "That food truck serves ice cream. Would you like some?"

"Sure."

We gathered up our trash and chucked it into the various recycling and refuse bins at the edge of the eating area. The line at the dessert truck wasn't very long. We chose a cup of sweet, creamy homemade vanilla. Sharing something as simple as a paper cup of ice cream with Yuri felt somehow more magical.

"You've shown me a different side of Houston tonight," he said as we headed for his car. "I should get out more."

I considered the two guards shadowing us. Though he was alone tonight, he typically traveled with an army of assistants. "You'd have to leave your babysitters at home to really enjoy this side of the city."

He gave my hair a playful tug. "Only if you're my tour guide."

Smiling, I slid into the backseat of the waiting car. Yuri moved in from the other side. This time there was no pretense of accidental touching. The moment we were both buckled in, he grasped my hand and stroked his thumb over my skin. My gaze skipped to the tinted window. I could just make out the bright lights of the food trucks. An idea began to form.

"What are you thinking about? I can practically hear the gears turning."

"I'm thinking that Benny should find a way to partner

up with a successful food truck."

He made a humming sound in agreement. "It would be a good way to cross-promote businesses. One brand could feed another. Sharing costs might be attractive to all parties." Yuri wound wavy strands of my hair around his finger. "It's an idea worth feeling out and getting some solid numbers."

Hearing him talk business made me so hot. "Okay," I said a bit breathlessly. "That was ridiculously sexy."

He laughed. "Kitten, if you think that's sexy, I've got piles of quarterly earnings estimates in my briefcase that I'd be happy to read to you."

"Tease." I thumped his chest. "I do love a good bedtime story."

Yuri's hand moved to my knee. Our gazes clashed as his palm slowly glided along my bare skin to dip just under the hem of my skirt. "Come home with me tonight and I'll read you anything you want."

I shivered as his hand inched along my thigh. "No."

"You can pick the language—English, Russian, Mandarin or Arabic."

My lips parted with surprise. "You speak Mandarin and Arabic?"

"Passably," he said with some self-deprecation. "I'm no scholar but I can negotiate and communicate clearly. It suits my business needs."

"That's amazing."

His sensuous mouth curved with a mischievous grin. "If you think that's amazing, you should see the other tricks I've mastered."

His playfulness infected me. Gripping his wrist, I halted the achingly slow slide of his hand. "You're tenacious. I'll give you that."

"I'll give you everything if you come home with me."

"Is that a time sensitive offer?"

He held my gaze for a long moment. "For you? There's no expiration." He peppered ticklish kisses up the side of my neck and across my bare shoulder. "Come home with me tonight, tomorrow, next week or next year." He punctuated each word with a feather-light kiss. "My offer will always stand."

Inside, I trembled violently. This wickedly sexy, outrageously powerful man had just offered me the world. Was I brave enough to say yes?

Swallowing hard, I met his intense, unnerving gaze. "I've never been more tempted in my life to go home with a man." I trailed my fingers down the front of his shirt. "But I won't break that rule, not even for you."

Yuri's reaction convinced me that he wasn't playing games with me. He'd meant every word he said. Nuzzling my neck, he whispered, "I like a woman with principles." His lips skimmed my jaw. "Do I get a goodnight kiss at least?"

"Well...I suppose one kiss wouldn't hurt."

As our lips touched, we both knew this wasn't stopping at one kiss. Cloaked in the privacy of the partitioned backseat, I surrendered to Yuri's masterful mouth. His strong hand roamed my body with such appreciation. He awakened the lust and desire hidden deep within me.

Yielding to his insistent mouth, I relished the sweet sugary vanilla clinging to his tongue. Our mouths mated with such ferocity it stole my breath and left me shaking. We were lost in the wonder of our feverish kisses as the car swiftly navigated the bustling Houston streets.

Too soon, we arrived at the gated complex where I shared an apartment with Vivi. With a growl of frustration, Yuri reluctantly pulled away from me. I sensed he wanted to try his charms on me again but he didn't. Instead he swept his thumbs across my cheeks. "I'm walking you to your door so I can get one more kiss."

"Just one?"

He groaned dramatically. "You're going to kill me."

Giggling, I grabbed my purse and grasped the door handle. One of the bodyguards took hold of the door and pulled it open before reaching inside to help me out of the backseat. I noticed the way his sharp, calculating gaze scanned the parking lot. He kept his body between me and the open street.

It occurred to me suddenly that this man, this total stranger, protected me with his own body simply because I was with Yuri. I couldn't believe how well Dimitri had trained him or how far this man was willing to go to protect Yuri. Although it was crass, I wondered how much he was paid to take a bullet, if necessary. It must have been an outrageous amount.

"What's your name?"

The guard glanced down at me. "Jake, ma'am."

My eyebrow arched at the *ma'am*. "It's nice to meet you, Jake. Thank you for watching over me tonight. I appreciate it."

He nodded but didn't make eye contact again. By now, Yuri stood nearby. He held out his hand and I happily grasped it. As we stepped onto the sidewalk another realization struck me. I hadn't said anything to Tony, the driver, about where I lived or how to get here.

My gaze fixed on Yuri's shadowy profile. "You already knew where I lived. Your driver already had my address."

"Yes."

"But…why?"

"Why not?" He glanced at me. "Let's not kid

ourselves, Lena. I knew the moment I first saw you that I'd be making this walk to your front door someday. I didn't know how soon it would happen but I wanted to be prepared."

"I can't decide if that's incredibly romantic or borderline stalker behavior."

Yuri laughed and slid his arm around my waist. His lips brushed my temple. "You have such a way with words, Yelena."

His playfully sarcastic reply coaxed a smile from me. As we neared my apartment, I reached into my purse for my keys. I was still digging around for them when the door suddenly opened to reveal Vivian in a paint-stained tank top and shorts. Paint splatters dotted her bare feet and hands. Her expression turned comical and it was all I could do to bite back a laugh at the shock on her face.

"Oh!" She glanced at me with wide eyes. "I heard voices and thought you were on your phone. I didn't want you to have to juggle your keys and purse." Her gaze turned to Yuri again. "Anyway. I'll...uh...I'll just go now."

Yuri chuckled softly as she scampered out of view. "Ten dollars says she's running to her phone and calling Erin or Benny."

Smiling, I agreed. "Definitely." Feeling a bit awkward, I said, "So..."

"So this is goodnight." His fingers tangled in my hair and he dragged me close for another one of his sensual, toe-tingling kisses. When his lips finally left mine, he traced my swollen pout with his finger. "I'll see you Monday night."

I couldn't speak. I simply nodded. Yuri stepped away from me but didn't leave immediately. We stared at one another, both of us desperate to take this to the next level but fully aware that waiting would make our first time even hotter and more significant.

Gulping, I turned my back toward him and stepped into the apartment. I shut the door with shaking hands and flipped the deadbolt. Overcome by the night's strange turn of events, I pivoted toward the living room and collapsed back against the door.

My gaze met Vivian's questioning one. Curiosity radiated from her in waves. Grinning, she said, "I'm going to grab a bottle of wine and two glasses. You kick off your shoes and get comfy. I have a feeling we're going to be talking late tonight."

"Girl," I shook my head and toed off my pumps, "you aren't going to believe this…"

CHAPTER THREE

"We headed home, Boss?"

Yuri caught Jake's gaze and shook his head. "Take me to 716."

"The back door?" Jake's expression told Yuri that his bodyguard had overhead what that pig had done to Lena.

"*Da*." Yuri slid into the back seat and fastened his seatbelt. He interlaced his fingers and tried to calm the rage threatening to overtake him. That any man should put his hands on any woman was despicable enough but for that prick Danny to put his filthy paws on Lena was unforgiveable.

He finally understood what Ivan and Dimitri had experienced when faced with defending their women. The fury burning his gut stunned him. He couldn't get Lena's brave, beautiful face out of his mind. She'd spoken so calmly about being violently manhandled, as if was a common occurrence, and it pained him.

Yuri knew only too well the environment of Lena's childhood. His own had been just as miserable. At an extremely young age, he'd learned how truly cruel other people could be. He'd grown hardened and callous and angry. Luckily, he'd been smart enough to listen to a mentor who urged him to turn that anger into fuel that drove his ambition and got him out of the shithole of his youth.

Lena seemed to have done the same thing. When he'd first become enamored with her, he'd gotten her old address from Nikolai and had instructed his driver to take him through the neighborhood where she'd been raised. The place could have easily served as the backdrop for a post-apocalyptic movie set. Broken-down cars, ramshackle houses, drug dealers and whores on the street corners—it sickened him to think she'd had to navigate that hellish landscape every day of her young life.

But it also made him so incredibly proud of her. There weren't many success stories to come out of places like that and she was one of them. This mess with her current job situation was only a bump in the road. He had no doubt she would find her way around it and on to better things.

Not that she would ever work for him, of course.

He didn't like being told no by anyone, but when Lena did it, he found it oddly exciting. He believed her when she said she didn't play games. There was something enticing about taking it slow with her. He'd get her in his bed eventually but that wasn't his overall goal.

With other women, sex had always been the ultimate, final step—a romp or two in the sack and he'd send them along with some expensive gifts to remember him by. With Lena, making love seemed like a step along the path. One they would both enjoy immensely but a step nonetheless. It was everything else that he craved with her.

Their impromptu, casual date tonight had convinced

him that she'd been worth the wait. He couldn't remember the last time he'd been so relaxed and at ease with a woman. There were no expectations from Lena. She truly didn't have any interest in his money. In fact, he suspected it made her wholly uncomfortable.

He'd heard that line from other women—that they weren't interested in the cold, hard cash stacked in his bank accounts—but Lena was the first one he'd ever believed. With one swift strike, she'd taken away his most seductive power. His usual M.O., to shower a woman with wildly expensive gifts, wouldn't work on her. It occurred to him that his initial plan to fly her to New York for dinner at the city's best restaurant probably wouldn't have the same effect he desired. At best, she'd find him pretentious. At worst—well, he wouldn't think about that.

So what to do about their Monday night date?

He continued to mull that over as the car wound its way through traffic. When it slowed to a stop in the alley running behind 716, his thoughts turned darker. He wanted nothing more than to give Danny a taste of the pain he'd probably caused Lena but he recognized the risk in doing such a thing. A man like Danny would want to sue and make problems. Lena would be furious with him for interfering in a situation she considered already handled.

But he couldn't let Danny get away with manhandling her and leaving bruises on her beautiful skin.

When one of the bouncers watching the rear entrance to 716 approached the vehicle, Yuri rolled down his window. The man bent down for a better view. His eyes widened. "Mr. Novakovsky!"

"Tell your boss I want to speak to him."

"Uh—out here?"

"Yes." He rolled the window up and unbuckled his belt. Comfortable in the back seat, he waited for Danny to make his appearance. As expected, the scuzzy bastard practically ran out the rear entrance. Derek, Yuri's other guard, was waiting near the car. He stopped Danny and frisked him. From the way Danny jerked from side to side, it was clear Derek was purposely being rough with him.

The door opened and Danny slid inside. Breathless, he ran a hand through his hair. Yuri caught the scents of perfume, sex and alcohol wafting from him. Was this how he conducted business? Such a disgrace!

"To what do I owe the pleasure, Yuri?"

Yuri arched an eyebrow at the impertinence of the man using his first name. They weren't peers. They weren't colleagues. They definitely weren't friends. "I wanted to discuss some business with you."

"Business?" The weasel-eyed bastard grinned. "Why don't we take this into my office?"

"I prefer my turf."

"Oh. Well. Okay. So what's up?"

"I want to talk about a PR rep who worked for you."

"Worked for me? Oh. *Her.*" Danny sneered. "Lena Fucking Cruz, huh?" He blew out a noisy breath. "You want my advice, Yuri? Stay the fuck away from her. She's trouble with a capital *T.*"

"Really? I understood she was quite a hard worker and very capable at her profession."

Danny laughed. "Who told you that? Shit, Yuri! The only positive performance reviews Lena Cruz has ever gotten came from her blowjob skills."

Rage exploded within Yuri. He balled his hands into tight fists at his sides and barely managed to maintain control.

"If you're looking for a side piece, you can snatch her up cheap. She quit tonight. I have it on good authority that the firm is going to fire her in the morning. I wouldn't let her run PR for any of your businesses, but she's got one hell of a mouth on her, if you know what I mean."

"I don't." Yuri fixed Danny with a furious glare. "In fact, I doubt very much that you know anything about her."

Danny held up his hands. "Hey, man, don't get so defensive. You think a girl like that got out of the projects with a full-ride scholarship without sucking a few dicks along the way?"

And just like that Yuri's control snapped.

With the stealth and swiftness of his military days, he threw out his arm and caught Danny across the throat. In an instant, he had the man pinned on the backseat. Eyes wild with fright, Danny spluttered and shoved at Yuri's arms but it was no use. He had the upper hand and he wasn't ready to let go.

"Listen to me, you little shit. If I hear one whisper of such nasty things about *my* Lena from anyone, I'll know the source. Believe me, Danny. You don't want me to come back here." He shoved hard enough to make the bastard's eyes bug out of his head before releasing just enough pressure to allow the club owner to drag air into his oxygen-starved lungs. "Do you understand me?"

"Y-yes, Yu-Yuri." Danny stammered and coughed. "I'm sorry, man. I didn't know. I didn't know you were fucking her."

Yuri backhanded him. "Is that what you think this is about? That I'm jealous?" Disgusted, he slid off the man and let him sit up. "Lena isn't that kind of girl, but you wouldn't know that because all you see is where she came from and some stereotype of what *girls like that* are supposed to be. It must eat you up to know that she wouldn't give a prick like you a second glance."

Danny put his hand to his bloody nose and mouth. "You fucking Russian dick! I'm bleeding!"

"Be glad you're only bleeding and don't need a hospital." He grabbed Danny by the front of the shirt and jerked him forward for one last warning. "If you ever put your hands on a woman again, it will be the last time you have hands to use. Understood?"

Danny paled. "She pissed me off, man. Okay? But, look, I didn't mean to hurt her."

The man's justification for grabbing and bruising Lena made him ill. "That wasn't what I asked."

"I understand. I'm sorry. I won't do it again."

"You know I'll find out if you do."

"I do. I do know."

Yuri let go of Danny. He sat back in his seat and fixed his mussed cuffs. "In the morning, you're going to call Lena's firm and tell them you amicably parted ways. You'll let them know that you had creative differences but you'd recommend her to anyone. And when someone calls you seeking a recommendation, you'll give her a glowing review—a review that she deserves."

"Yes, Yuri."

"Good. Now get the fuck out."

Danny didn't need to be told twice. He bolted from the back seat and rushed to the rear entrance of his club. One of his bouncers took a menacing step toward the car but Derek and Jake stood should-to-shoulder and scared him away. When his bodyguards were safely in place, Yuri addressed Tony. "Take me to Faze."

By the time they'd arrived at Faze, his anger had nearly dissipated. Now he was ready to sniff out the saboteur among his staff. Even if it hadn't been Lena hurt by the subversion, he would have been just as upset by it. He'd seen enough of that underhanded, backstabbing bullshit during his early foray into the business world.

At Faze, it was nearing closing time. He found Araceli, the club's manager, and asked her for a private word in her office. The surprise and anger in her expression convinced him she'd had no hand in this.

"If I had to put money on anyone, it would be Jeannie, the new go-go dancer we picked up last month. Her boyfriend, Trey, is one of the bouncers at Faze. She tried getting him a job here but Dimitri wouldn't hire him. He said the guy had a bad handshake."

Yuri's mouth curved with amusement. That sounded exactly like Dimitri. "She sounds like a good place to start but let's be perfectly honest, Araceli. A girl who dances in our cages and on our tables to keep the crowd pumped isn't the one who would benefit most from taking that VIP party."

"Agreed." Araceli sighed heavily. "It could have been one of the bartenders up there on the VIP floor or one of the waitresses. Hell it could have been all of them. I saw the bill those guys racked up. The tip is going to be a tidy cut for the servers and bartenders to share."

"Then we haul them all in here and sweat them." Yuri slipped out of his jacket and rolled up his shirt sleeves. "I won't have this kind of subterfuge in my clubs. This is how stupid feuds begin between businesses. We nip this in the bud tonight."

Araceli's instinct proved true. Within four minutes of questioning by the tough-as-nails manager, Jeannie started to bawl like a baby and confessed the whole sordid mess. Trey had approached her about stealing the party to get back at Lena for cutting their side-deals with the hookers and drug dealers and underage kids. Jeannie had acted as the go-between with the bouncers at 716 and the VIP crew at Faze. The Faze team had turned down three major bookings for the VIP lounge to make sure they could accept the athletes bounced from 716.

Even though Yuri owned the club, he left the day-to-day operations in Araceli's capable hands. He knew what he wanted to do about the situation but he trusted her judgment. He wouldn't have hired her otherwise.

"They're gone," Araceli decided. "I'm keeping the two new waitresses because they're young and dumb and weren't brave enough to say no to this scheme but the others?" She drew a line across her neck. "I won't have my people acting like a bunch of high school kids."

"I support your decision, Araceli." He wasn't keen on keeping the two waitresses but her justification made it palatable. "I suppose it's a good thing we're closed Sunday and Monday nights."

"It won't be hard to fill the open spots."

Standing, Yuri grabbed his jacket and slung it over his shoulder. "Then I leave it in your hands."

"Are you sticking around Houston this week or are you jetting off again?"

"Sticking around," he said and headed for the door.

"I see." She said it as if she knew his secret. Maybe she did. Lena's appearance earlier and their disappearance together wouldn't have gone unnoticed by Araceli.

"Keep me updated on this." He tapped the door frame before leaving. Out in the cool fall night, he slipped into the backseat after telling his team he was ready to go home. It was a twenty-five minute drive to the sprawling estate he'd recently finished building on the outskirts of Houston. The large secluded lot sat in a gated enclave that housed a handful of obscenely wealthy Texans.

Though he had a rather swanky penthouse suite in the best building downtown, he found that he rather craved the quiet solitude of the mansion he'd built. Only a few rooms in the place were fully furnished and decorated and he still needed to hire a staff but he didn't mind. There was something peaceful about its emptiness and unfinished state.

In many ways, the house was much like him. Empty and unfinished but waiting to be filled. Where the house needed furniture and art and rugs, he needed one thing and one thing only to make his life complete—the love of a good woman.

His work cell phone started to ring. He fished the black phone from his pocket. It was Anna, his executive assistant. If she was calling this late at night, it wasn't good. "Yes?"

In fast-paced Russian, Anna laid out the problem. "Someone leaked a copy of the environmental report. There is a media firestorm over it. My contact on the planning committee says there's a good chance the pipeline approval is going to fail."

Yuri bit back a curse. The pipeline arcing across Europe was an absolute necessity. "When do they vote?"

"Tuesday morning."

He pinched the bridge of his nose. The last thing he wanted to do right now was jet off to Europe to schmooze and negotiate. "We'll leave in the morning."

"I'll send the details to you as soon as I have them."

Annoyed by this hiccup in his grand plans, Yuri pocketed his phone and rubbed his tired eyes. He'd thought this whole deal was in the bag but apparently not. No doubt this bump in the road was going to cost him but he'd be damned if it interfered with the date he'd already made with Lena. It would be a tight schedule flying over and back before Monday night but he'd make it work. For her, he didn't mind burning the jet fuel.

He used the rest of the drive to send emails to the team handling the pipeline negotiations and to study the quick itinerary Anna had dropped into his inbox. Of all the assistants he'd ever had, Anna was the only one who could keep up with him. Often, she was two steps ahead and prepared for any possibility.

He'd found her through a headhunter. She'd come highly recommended and he'd known within a few minutes that she was the new assistant he needed. Their shared language and background made it easy to work with her.

Though he'd intended to groom her for a move to a VP spot, she'd made it clear earlier that year that she enjoyed her current position and didn't want the stress or drama associated with a new job title. He'd supported her decision but still held out hope that someday she would want to make the jump into a position where he knew she would shine.

They passed through the gates guarding the enclave and turned down his private road. In the circular driveway, the car stopped near the fountain so he could exit. Jake slipped out of the front seat and trailed him up the steps. Derek remained in the SUV that had been trailing them all evening.

Stepping inside his home, Yuri braced for the arrival of Sasha. On cue, the massive bear-sized Caucasian Ovcharka let loose a rumbling bark and bounded down the long hallway. His warning growl softened at the sight of his master. He skidded to a stop and plopped down in a well-trained sitting position.

Yuri rewarded the shaggy beast with a good scratch between the ears. Out of the corner of his eye, he noticed

Feodor, the elderly mentor who had followed him from Russia, entering the foyer. Feodor was one of the few men Sasha tolerated and the only one Yuri felt comfortable leaving in charge of the dog.

After exchanging a few words with Feodor, he said goodnight and snapped his fingers to indicate that Sasha should follow. Fully aware of the pecking order in the house, the dog followed at his heel.

With a beast so large and ferocious protecting him, Yuri required complete obedience from the dog. In Russia, the breed was used to guard the most notorious prisons but they were also incredibly loyal and protective of their owners. Yuri found peace of mind in the idea that Sasha was always nearby.

Upstairs, he passed the long gallery wall where some of his favorite paintings decorated the space. More would be shipped in from his collections in London and Moscow. He paused in front of the piece he'd commissioned from Vivian last year. The little minx had charged him a damn arm and a leg for the painting but he'd happily paid it. There was no doubt in his mind he'd made a good investment. Someday her work would command outrageous prices.

He couldn't wait to invite her over to see where he'd placed her painting. She'd get such a kick out of seeing her piece between a Basquiat and a Galán. He'd thought it rather clever to sandwich her painting between two artists who had been huge influences on her style.

Inside his bedroom, he finally relaxed and kicked off his shoes. He dropped his watch and cuff links on their trays before moving toward his bed. Exhausted, he fell back on the plush mattress and closed his eyes. Sasha walked in circles, the tags on his collar jangling together as he searched for the perfect place to plop down on his comfortable bedding in the far corner.

Visions of Lena danced before his eyes. He wasn't sure where their relationship was going but he was all right with that. He looked forward to the journey they were taking together. These things couldn't be rushed.

In time, Lena would be his.

* * *

The annoying buzz of my cell phone rattling across my bedside table jerked me out of a deep sleep. Opening one eye, I glared at my alarm clock. Oh, Jesus! It was too dang early for this nonsense.

I grabbed my phone and glanced at the screen. My father's face greeted me. He never called this early—and it scared me. "Hello?"

"*Mi'ja?*"

"Dad?"

He let loose a relieved sounding sigh. "I was worried about you. I couldn't reach you last night."

"I was working and then I had a date." His end of the line crackled. "What's wrong with your reception?"

"Oh, it's—it's nothing, *mi'ja*. Listen, if Tommy comes around, don't let him stay with you girls."

I frowned and rubbed my tired eyes. "I never let Tommy stay here. Why would I start now?"

"Good. Keep it that way."

Something in my father's tone worried me. "Is everything okay?"

"It's fine." He hesitated. "You still have that gun I bought you for your birthday?"

My gaze flitted to the top drawer where it rested. Technically, he'd only given me the money for it and the concealed carry course I'd taken. With his record, there wasn't a gun store in Texas that would sell to him. "Yes. Why?"

"Just keep it on you, *mi'ja*."

My heart thudded into my throat. "Dad, what's wrong?"

"Nothing. It's nothing. I just—I worry about you."

"Dad…"

"I have to go. I'll call you soon. I love you, Lena."

"I love you, too, Dad."

The line went dead. I stared at my phone and replayed the bizarre conversation. Despite my father's ex-con history and his current illegal line of work, he'd always been a damned good dad to me. Unlike Vivian's father who had put her in harm's way again and again, Dad had given up the drug-dealing and gun-running for a safer criminal enterprise. His fencing operation had paid for me to attend the private high school where I'd met Vivian and Erin. As much as I hated the line of work he'd chosen, I couldn't deny that it had provided certain opportunities for me.

Not wanting to get out of bed but unable to fall back asleep, I scrolled through my list of missed calls and voicemails. Tommy had called, like, a million times. What the hell had he done this time? Whatever it was I had a bad feeling he'd dragged my dad into it.

Not wanting to deal with that mess, I hit my email inbox. Apparently word of my epic flounce from 716 had already spread. There were messages of the "you go, girl!" and the "what the fuck were you thinking?" variety. I was too tired to answer any of them, and honestly, I didn't have the answers.

Checking my Twitter timeline shocked me. A message sent out by Ty Weston, Houston's society gossipmonger and the king of an international gossip empire, tagged with my name and Yuri's handle with a pic attached had gotten a hell of a lot of retweets. Stomach knotting with dread, I clicked the link—and nearly died.

There, blown up on my phone's screen, was a snapshot of Yuri kissing me. The caption killed me. *@PRPrincess giving new client @YNovakovsky that personal touch?*

For the longest time, I simply stared at it. In fact, I was still staring at it when Vivian knocked on my bedroom door and stepped inside. She had her phone clutched in one hand and a mug of that cinnamon tea she loved so much in the other. From the look of her wet hair, she'd already been out for her morning run and had showered. Her gaze dropped to my phone. "I guess you've seen the photo."

"Yeah." I sat up and pushed my pillow behind my back for support. "Surely Ty had hotter gossip than me and Yuri kissing to peddle to his society page followers."

Vivian sat on the edge of my bed. "I don't know. That's a pretty hot picture."

I groaned. "This is crazy, Vee. Is this what it's going to be like if we date? Am I going to have to worry about dumbass people taking pics of us?"

"Probably." She didn't even try to sugarcoat it for me. "The guy is a billionaire, Lena. And he's not one of those bottom-of-the-list billionaires either. Yuri is *filthy* rich. People love to gossip about sexy, wealthy men and the women they date."

"Ugh." I put my head in my hands. "I don't want everyone in my business."

"I guess you better decide if Yuri's worth the trouble."

The answer came to me instantly. "He is."

She smiled and thumped my leg through the covers. "I knew it!"

"What?"

"Last night, you were telling me you wanted to take it slow with him but I think maybe you two have been taking it slow for too long. Like glacially slow."

I started to point out that she had no business talking to me about dancing around a mutual attraction but bit my tongue. "Look, I like him. I *really* like Yuri. I just want it to go right between us."

"You want my advice? Stop thinking about everything that could go wrong. You always do that when you meet a great guy. It's like you're ready to pounce on the first thing that goes wrong so you can write him out of your life." She squeezed my foot through the duvet. "Don't let Yuri be one of those guys. He's special, Lena. I mean, he's, like, *the one* material."

I couldn't argue with her about that. He was special. That's what scared me so much about dating him. He belonged to a world of wealth and privilege I couldn't even comprehend. What if I did something dumb? Used the wrong fork at a dinner or made some awful social gaffe that humiliated him? God, I'd just die!

My phone started to vibrate again. I glanced at the screen and saw Yuri's name. Clearing my throat, I took a deep breath and answered. "Hello?"

"Yelena?"

My belly wobbled as Yuri spoke my name in that rumbling baritone voice. "Hey, Yuri."

"You've seen the photo."

"Yes. I'm sorry. I didn't realize we were being watched."

"When you're with me, you're always being watched. Don't apologize. I thought it was a lovely photo. Not many couples have their very first kiss captured for posterity."

I could hear the teasing in his voice. "No, I suppose not. I haven't replied to Ty but I'm tempted."

"Leave it. It's not worth an online tiff with Houston's biggest gossipmonger. We're still on for Monday night?"

"Yes."

"Wonderful. I'll have my assistant, Anna, call you with the details. I have to run out of town for a few days." Regret filled his voice. "There's been a development overnight in one of my business interests abroad. I'm flying out as we speak to deal with it—but I will be back for our date."

I couldn't believe he was planning to fly to Europe and back—for me. "Yuri, don't worry about it. We can reschedule."

"Woman, you've evaded me for months. I'm not about to give you a reason to run away from me again."

A girlish giggle escaped my throat. "Okay."

"All right. Monday night. I can't wait to see you."

"Same here."

"Goodbye."

"Bye."

Feeling like a high school kid with her first crush, I couldn't stop the silly smile that spread across my face. Vivian looked so amused. "Oh my gosh! You have it *bad*."

Sliding down in bed, I clutched my phone to my chest and enjoyed the looping track of Yuri's sexy voice playing in my head. Hell, Vivian was right. I had it bad.

Monday night couldn't get here fast enough.

CHAPTER FOUR

Monday morning arrived before I was ready for it. Today we were launching the grand opening of Benny's new bakery location. As I dragged my ass out of bed at that abominable hour, I cursed bakers and their terrible work schedules. I could barely function enough to shower and gulp down two cups of coffee. How the hell was Benny going to do this every morning while baking that tiny little Dimitri bun in her oven?

The couple still hadn't officially announced their impending bundle of joy. It was still very early. I figured they were either waiting for the most dangerous period of the pregnancy to pass or for their wedding in early December or maybe both. Either way it really wasn't my business—but that didn't mean I wasn't going to be nosy about it.

When I arrived at the bakery a quarter after five, I found a nice spot in the parking lot. The whole thing had been resurfaced last week and looked perfect. I stopped to admire the mural Vivian had painted along the exposed wall of the new building. She'd brought together the artsy friends she shared a studio space with to complete the project. Every time I looked at it, I found different things to love.

Inside the bakery, the place was bustling. Benny spotted me and waved. I couldn't believe how pretty and vibrant she looked this morning. Maybe that saying about pregnancy glow was true. Dimitri sure as heck couldn't keep his eyes off her. She'd put him to work assembling bakery boxes but his loving, hungry gaze remained fixed on her.

"If he keeps staring at you like that, he's going to set off the smoke alarms!" I gave Benny a quick hug as she joined me near the entrance.

Glancing over her shoulder, she smiled at her soon-to-be husband. "Well *someone* wanted to get frisky this morning but we were already running late so I had to shut him down."

"Ouch. Denied!" I actually felt a little bad for the big blond Russian hunk. After the last few nights of ridiculously sexy dreams starring Yuri, I'd woken up frustrated and needful. Considering some of the hotly whispered stories Benny had told me, Dimitri had one hell of a libido. Right now, he looked at Benny like he wanted to just eat her right up.

"He knows I'll make it up to him later."

Laughing at her naughty innuendo, I whipped out the binder I'd put together and pulled out the laminated, color-coded charts I'd worked on yesterday.

Benny touched my wrist. "Is it true about your job? I saw your Facebook and Twitter feeds," she explained. "I asked Vivian but she said that you hadn't said anything concrete."

My tummy clenched just thinking about the awkward conversation I'd had with my boss. "They didn't fire me.

Actually, they tried to get me to stay but I just thought *fuck it*. I'm done. So I quit."

"What happens now?"

"I have no idea." My tummy tightened even more. "I really don't. I'm sort of…waiting. I've been careful with my money so I have enough to keep me going for ten or twelve months, maybe even longer if I really cut back to the bare minimums."

"I don't think you'll have a hard time finding a new job."

"I've already had a few offers." I didn't tell her that one of them was from Yuri. "I considered two of them seriously but I just keep thinking that maybe this is the push I needed to go off on my own. I can set my own hours. I can work with people who will respect me and not steal from me. I can be the master of my own destiny, you know?"

"I have faith in you." She squeezed my arm. "You'll land on your feet."

"Let's hope so. Otherwise Vivi might be in the market for a new roommate." I tapped the schedule to get us back on track. "Mark, the reporter for the Life section of the paper, is coming out with a photographer around eight. I thought we'd feature you, Marco, Adam, Celia and Lupe in that piece. Mark loves your buns—"—I winked at her as she snickered—"—so I know he's going to give you a great write-up."

"And Flora at *Hoy*?" Benny named the major Spanish language newspaper in the city. "Is she still coming today?"

"She'll be here at nine o'clock but I promised I'd snap pics from the official opening for her to use. Ada Montoya will be here around ten to shoot a package for the noon, six and ten broadcasts on the Spanish channel

54

news."

Benny self-consciously touched her face. "Should I put on more makeup for that?"

Before I could answer, Dimitri swept up behind her and wrapped his arms around her waist. Holding her from behind, he bent down and placed a noisy kiss on her cheek. "You don't need makeup. You're already so damn beautiful. Put on more makeup and I'll have to grab the bat from your office to fight off the men who will be stampeding down here."

A blush crept up Benny's neck and colored her cheeks. Dimitri dropped his lips to her ear and whispered something that only she could hear. Her eyes widened briefly and she curled under her lips as if to stifle a frustrated moan.

Normally, their public display of affection would have inspired such envy in me. It was the same thing I felt when I watched Ivan nuzzle Erin's neck or stroke her hand so lovingly. Today I felt oddly…hopeful. Tonight I would see Yuri—and anything could happen.

As if reading my mind, Dimitri loosened his embrace of Benny. A mischievous smile played upon his lips. "So—tell me about this picture."

I groaned. "Please don't tease me, Dimitri. Vivian hasn't let up since the dang thing showed up online."

He laughed. "I'm shocked. Sweet little Vivian being so mean? Never."

"Sweet? Honey, don't let that innocent schoolgirl exterior fool you. Underestimate Vivian at your own peril."

Still smiling, Benny finally found the courage to ask what I'm sure she'd been dying to know since I walked in the front door. "So are you two dating or what?"

"We're getting together tonight."

"He asked you out?" She looked so excited I was surprised she wasn't jumping up and down.

"Not exactly," I said and dropped my gaze. "He sort of told me."

Dimitri snorted with amusement. "Now that sounds very much like Yuri."

"Is he coming over this morning?" Benny wondered.

I shook my head. "There was some issue in Europe. The pipeline, I think." I'd hit the internet after he'd called me and found a few articles hinting at trouble. "He should be back here sometime this afternoon. Or, at least, that's what Anna, his assistant, told me last night in the email she sent."

Benny frowned. "He had his assistant email you about your date?"

"I know." I rolled my eyes. "Believe me. He's going to hear about that. I thought about sending him a text to let him know how uncool it was but I sort of felt bad for him. I have a feeling he's under a lot of pressure."

She hummed with uncertainty and glanced at Dimitri. He put up his hands and stepped away from her. "I'm not touching this one."

She thumped him in the chest. "You better go on then. I don't want you to feel conflicted while we gossip about your boy."

Grinning, he kissed the top of her head and left to help Marco. Benny turned back to me. She studied me for a moment before finally saying, "I think you have to establish very early in this relationship how things are going to go. He's like Nikolai. He's used to people doing what he says, when he says it. It's hard to break bad behaviors once you let them start. Look at my brother? Like—*whoa*. I should have nipped that gangster crap of his in the bud but I let it slide. Bad habits, you know?"

"I get it." I sensed she felt awkward telling me what she thought but I appreciated that she cared enough about me to lay it on the line.

"Look, I really think that Yuri has put you in a different category than all those other women he's…romanced. There's real potential here, you know?"

I nodded. "When we were having dinner the other night, I could tell Yuri feels out of his element with me. I feel the same way with him. This is new territory for both of us. I'm not playing by the same rules most of the women he's dated used and he's definitely not playing by the same rules of the guys I've dated."

"Sounds pretty exciting actually. You're both entering a whole new world filled with possibilities."

I liked the way she described the way things stood between Yuri and me. It had a hopeful ring to it.

In no time at all, the bakery got crazy busy. By the time the doors were opened at six on the dot, there was a line snaking down the street. Patrons swarmed the place, many of them old faces who had followed from the other location. Benny and some of her longtime employees stood near the door and welcomed them inside.

I was so utterly thrilled by the turnout and snapped dozens of pics. Tagging the hell out of them, I posted them to the bakery's social media accounts and my own. I watched the hashtag I'd chosen for the launch gain momentum.

By the time the first reporter showed up, the line of waiting customers had grown even longer. Benny looked a bit frazzled but one soothing caress from Dimitri settled her nerves. I stood on the sidelines and watched her interviews. All the coaching I'd done had really worked out for her. She came across exactly as I knew her to be in real life—sweet, authentic and excited about her business.

I kept an eye on the reviews on some of the major online sites and the bakery's Facebook page. There were a couple of complainers about the slow pace of the line early in the morning but overall the reviews were hugely positive. Everyone raved about the pastries and burritos and Lupe's special hot chocolate.

When Erin and Ivan stopped by for a late breakfast, I got dragged into a corner by her. With her gossipy face firmly in place, she demanded, "You better spill it. I know you've been dodging my calls. What is going on with you?"

"I quit the firm. I'm sort of, kind of, *possibly* dating Yuri. That's what's going on with me. What's new with you?"

Her mouth curved in a wicked smile. "Oh I see. We're going to play it cool, huh? That's the Lena M.O., right?"

Now I was smiling. "Pretty much."

She shook her head and laughed. "For what it's worth, Ivan thought you two looked great together in the photo. Actually, what he really said was *finally*."

I rolled my eyes. "Tell Ivan I said thank you for his approval."

"I know you're joking but those four guys?" She glanced at Dimitri and Ivan who chatted across the restaurant. "They value one another's opinions big time. It's good that Nikolai, Dimitri and Ivan like you so much."

"To be fair, our group is the same way. You relied on our opinions when you were talking about moving in with Ivan. If we'd said no, you would have reconsidered."

"Maybe," she said uncertainly. "By the time he asked me to move in with him, I was totally head over heels for him." She gazed at Ivan with such love in her eyes. "Some mornings I wake up and I can't believe how lucky I am that he risked his life to help me save my sister. I mean, I know how he looks. He's so big and scary and intimidating—but my God, Lena. That man only knows one way to love and that is totally and completely. I've never been happier."

She gulped and blinked rapidly. Regaining her composure, she said, "I want that for you. I want you to know how totally fucking amazing it is to know you have a man like Ivan in your corner."

Feeling a bit of pressure, I warned, "Let's not get ahead of ourselves. Yuri and I have only been on one sort-of date. We haven't even slept together yet."

Erin waggled her eyebrows. "Ooh! You think tonight is the night?"

"No. Definitely not."

"What if he turns on that infamous charm?"

"He tried that the other night. It didn't work."

"Uh-huh." She eyed me skeptically. "It didn't make you even the slightest bit tingly?'

"Well…"

"Ha! Knew it!"

I rolled my eyes. "You're a real goofball, you know that?"

She threw her arms around me. "And you love me!"

"Yeah. I guess." I hugged her back. Catching Ivan's amused gaze, I released her. "I think the Hulk is ready to go. I'm sure he's got a whole gym full of fighters waiting to be tortured."

"Probably," she agreed with a laugh. "I'm going to text you tonight. I want a play-by-play."

"Erin, you're impossible!"

"Whatever!" She snapped my arm with a flick of her finger. "You always want the juicy details from me and

Benny. Now it's your turn to entertain us with all the deliciously dirty bits."

She had a point. I had been awfully obnoxious about getting the scoop on the between-the-sheets action Benny and Erin shared with their men. I decided payback was only fair. "All right. Fine. But try to keep it to one text an hour. He's going to think I'm a freak if I'm running to the bathroom every twenty minutes to answer you."

"Well, we wouldn't want him to learn the truth about you until *after* he's bought you a big, snooty yacht."

"Bitch," I hissed with a giggle. Playing along, I added, "Well, if he does you're not welcome on my big, snooty yacht."

Still giggling, she waved at me and wound her way through the crowd toward Ivan. Hand in hand, they left the bakery. A short time later, Vivian popped in for a quick bite to eat and to congratulate Benny on the successful launch. Before she could leave, Ada Montoya, the news anchor for the hugely popular Spanish channel in Houston, dragged her aside for a quick interview about the mural she'd painted.

As I watched Vivian chattering away in Spanish, it occurred to me that if she was serious about making it as an artist after she finished school next May she was going to need a strong internet presence. I'd been the one to design her promo materials for her last art show, the one in the spring that had done so well, but I could see that she wasn't thinking big yet. She always downplayed her talent but I knew she was going places—successful places.

By noon, I'd squared away the last of the press I'd booked. I sensed Benny was starting to feel the fatigue of launching a new business and early pregnancy but she didn't let it slow her down. Though I worried about her overdoing it, one look at Dimitri's concerned face told me it was under control. As protective as he was of Benny, I figured he'd have her tucked away in his truck and home for a nap within the hour.

With my part in the day complete, I gave Benny one last hug and promised to run interference with any publicity issues she forwarded my way. As my one and only client, I could offer her my total attention.

It felt so weird to be home alone at the apartment in the middle of the day. For the longest time, I sat on the couch and stared at the French doors leading to the patio. I felt completely at a loss. I didn't know what to do with myself.

Napping seemed like the only real option so I stripped down to my undies and crawled into bed. After setting my alarm, I tugged the covers over my head and tried to calm my racing thoughts. I didn't want to think about my unemployed status or the very real possibility that my father was in trouble for something my dumbass cousin had done. I wanted to dream about nice things, about good things.

About Yuri.

His smiling face invaded my thoughts and calmed me. I could picture the way the little lines crinkled around his eyes and the way his grin became lopsided when he laughed. My tummy wobbled as I remembered the feel of his big, warm hand gliding along my thigh and the way his lips felt pressed to mine. My breasts ached as I grew aroused by the naughty images of where that backseat make-out session might have gone. I squeezed my thighs together to ease the throbbing there.

Not surprisingly, my dreams were ridiculously dirty. In bed with my dream Yuri, I indulged all the naughty fantasies that I'd never been brave enough to try out in real life. When I woke up to the sound of my alarm, I shook with desire. Need trembled through me and I wondered if I could deny myself what I wanted so badly.

Staring up at my ceiling, I tried to figure out what it was that scared me so much about making love to Yuri. It wasn't that I was strictly no sex without a wedding band like Vivian. I'd had three lovers since starting college. I'd cared about each of those men and they'd all loved me so it wasn't that the experiences had been cheap or dirty. They were simply unsatisfying.

Deep down inside, I worried I was broken. Here, in the safety of my own room, climaxing was easy. Once I got between the sheets with a man, I turned to ice. I enjoyed the intimacy and closeness of writhing together with a lover but there was no completion for me. There was no release. I often climbed out of bed more frustrated than when I'd slid into it.

So I'd basically sworn off sex after Price had broken up with me a little more than a year ago. He'd been a great boyfriend and we'd had a good time together but he was looking for things I didn't want. The last time I'd stalked his Facebook page, I'd seen that he was engaged. Apparently, he'd found a girl who wanted the same things he did.

I was happy for him. I was happy for anyone who found someone special to share their lives with but I often wondered if I was too damaged for that kind of happiness. Watching my mother walk out on me had done some crazy things to me. There weren't many people I let get close. Vivian, Erin, Benny, my father—they were the only people I loved and trusted not to betray me.

But Yuri? Was he someone I could trust? I honestly didn't know.

It occurred to me that keeping him at a distance wasn't going to answer that question. I'd never know if he was worthy to be added to the extremely short list of people I loved if I didn't open up and make myself vulnerable.

And it scared me. The very thought of opening myself up to that kind of heartbreak terrified me.

But, if I didn't, I would never know.

And I had to know.

CHAPTER FIVE

Dressed in my favorite new dress, I tried to find the courage to enter the restaurant. I'd just watched the valet at the downtown hotspot drive away in my red compact. It wasn't quite a beater but it definitely wasn't nice enough for this restaurant.

A quiver of embarrassment flickered through me at the idea Yuri might have seen me climbing out of the car. Sure, I'd paid cash for the thing after working my ass off my senior year of high school and I was damn proud of it—but Yuri probably spent more on one bespoke suit than I had on the whole car.

I smoothed a hand down the front of my dress. On a shopping trip with Erin last month, I'd fallen in love with the sweet little peplum number the moment I'd spotted it in the boutique. It was a knockoff of the hottest runway styles and fit perfectly in my budget. I'd even had enough left over to splurge on some slingback heels and a cute clutch. This was my first chance to wear it. I hoped it had the same effect on Yuri that it had on the valet guy who nearly broke his neck watching me get out of the car.

With my heart beating in my throat, I stepped into the swanky restaurant. The upscale waiting area was surprisingly busy for a Monday night. My gaze skipped around the seating areas but I didn't see Yuri. Had he already gone to our table?

I waited in line at the hostess station and tried to get a grip on my wild emotions. Nervous. Excited. Anxious. Aroused. My poor body was jumping from one extreme to the next.

"May I help you?" the peppy brunette greeted me with a smile.

"I'm meeting someone for dinner. Yuri Novakovsky."

Her eyes widened slightly. Obviously she recognized his name. Her gaze dropped to the laminated seating chart. When she didn't find anything there, she opened the small black book and ran her fingertip down the reservation list. "I'm sorry, ma'am. There's no reservation for Mr. Novakovsky tonight."

Confused, I whipped out my phone and quickly brought up the email from his assistant. I flashed the screen at the hostess. "These were the details I was sent."

"I'm so sorry. There must have been a mix up." She glanced at her chart again. "I can seat you or you can wait at the bar until Mr. Novakovsky arrives."

"I'd rather sit at a table."

The hostess found an open spot for us, no doubt bumping the people who had been waiting ahead of me. I felt a twinge of guilt but shrugged it off. Yuri obviously came here frequently enough that the hostess and wait staff knew him. If his name got us a table quicker, that was a perk I was happy to enjoy.

Seated in the center rear of the restaurant, I ordered a glass of wine and hoped I wasn't in for a long wait. Certain it was some sort of travel delay keeping Yuri, I tried not to worry. I scanned the restaurant to see if I noticed anyone.

My gaze landed on none other than Ty Weston, wealthy gossiper extraordinaire. He held court at a large round table. I recognized most of the faces surrounding him. They were a who's who of Texas trust fund babies including Caitlin, his little sister, and Pips Barlow Bennett, his best friend and an heiress to an oil and gas mega fortune.

Our gazes clashed across the restaurant. Ty smiled and lifted his glass. I fought the urge to roll my eyes and smiled instead. Turning away, I pretended not to notice his lingering stare. It wasn't because he was interested in me. That's for damn sure. Ty was probably the only son of a conservative senator brave enough to be openly gay and living his life out loud and proud. I had to give it to him. The guy had huge balls.

My cell phone chirped. Sure it was Erin, I grabbed it out of my clutch. It was Ty sending me a direct message via Twitter. I glanced at his table but he was engaged in a conversation with Pips.

Hope I didn't cause any problems with the pic the other day. Was too juicy to pass up. You two looked HAWT.

I hesitated before typing an answer.

Wasn't thrilled to be the focus of your tittle-tattle but I'll live.

I watched him reach into his pocket and withdraw his phone. His mouth curved in a smile. I waited for his reply to ding my inbox.

Better get used to it. Notoriety is the price of dating a man in that league.

If anyone knew what it was like to date a billionaire unable to shake the paparazzi, it was probably Ty. He'd had a couple of high profile romances with an actor and a super-rich heir from some tiny European principality.

Like me, he didn't seem to be able to make a relationship stick.

We'd been acquaintances since my first summer interning with the PR firm. At the time, he'd been an intern at the newspaper. We'd worked together on a couple of projects but then I'd caught him digging through the dumpsters behind the building the PR company shared with a law firm that specialized in the energy industry.

I'd been shocked and dismayed to see the fruits of those dirty labors show up on his fledgling gossip site. He'd uncovered a disgusting cover-up but had hurt some innocent people in the process. I'd tried to make him see that two wrongs didn't make a right but he wouldn't be swayed. After that, I'd given him a wide berth.

But, unlike a lot of people, I didn't find him malicious. Misguided? Overzealous? Yes. Malicious? Never. He was just the kind of guy who believed the truth had to be told, no matter the costs.

"Ma'am?" A waiter stood next to the table. "I hate to be so rude but would you mind moving to the bar until your guest arrives? We're running short on space and there's a party with reservations that would like to be seated."

"Oh." Feeling a bit flustered, I nodded and grabbed my wine glass. "Sure. It's no problem."

There was no way I could ignore the curious stares directed at me as I left the busy floor of the restaurant for the equally busy bar. I couldn't get a seat there so I stood in a corner and tried not to look ridiculous. Sipping my wine, I wondered where the hell Yuri was. He was nearly half an hour late.

Why hadn't he texted? I checked my phone to be sure I hadn't missed one from him. As I typed in a message for him, my phone vibrated as a message from Erin appeared. I switched to it.

Well?! How's it going?!

He's not here yet.

What?

He's not here. We're not on the reservation list.

You at the right place?

Of course!

Sorry. Just wondering. Don't bite my head off. Text him!

I did. I sent him a simple text asking where he was and if we were still on for tonight. Ten minutes later and reaching the bottom of my wine glass, I still hadn't received an answer from him so I texted Erin back.

No answer. Starting to feel stupid.

You're not stupid!

A cold chill crept up my neck. In the back of my mind, an ugly, mean voice started to taunt me. *He's playing you and you were dumb enough to fall for it.*

I shook off the irritating taunting. Yuri had been so sweet the other night. He wasn't playing around with me. Whatever that nasty voice in my head said, it wasn't true. Yuri wouldn't lead me on just to ditch me like this.

"Lena?"

It wasn't Yuri's voice that called to me but Ty Weston's. He touched my arm and drew my gaze. Smiling, he asked, "Can I buy you a drink while you wait?"

I glanced at my empty wine glass. "Sure."

Ty's hand settled on the small of my back and he guided me through the throng. At the bar, I exchanged my glass of wine for another. He asked for whiskey, neat, and took me to a pair of chairs that had opened up in the opposite corner of the bar area. He sipped his drink and ran his finger over the rim. "It's busy here tonight."

"Very," I agreed and swirled the dark, rich wine in my glass. "Are you out celebrating or is this a regular dinner spot for you?"

"Just a run-of-the-mill get-together."

"Oh."

"You're on a date?"

"Well, I'm supposed to be," I said with a nervous laugh. "He's running late."

Ty sighed and set aside his glass. Leaning forward, he touched my knee. "Sugar, if it's the man I'm thinking of, he's not coming."

"What?" I sat back and laughed. "You must be thinking of the wrong guy. It's Yuri Novakovsky."

Ty wore a reluctant expression as he plucked his phone from his pocket. He tapped at his screen and spun it around for me to see. At first I wasn't quite sure what I was supposed to see. Then it hit me like a ton bricks.

My heart stuttered in my chest at the sight of Yuri in a tuxedo with his arm wrapped around a drop-dead gorgeous brunette in a glimmering gold evening gown. Self-consciously, I rubbed a hand along the front of my knockoff dress. The silver hoops dangling from my ears and the simple bangle bracelets I'd worn looked so cheap compared to the diamonds and emeralds dripping from her neck and ears. No doubt her high heels probably cost more than Vivi and I spent on our rent every month.

What the hell was wrong with me? Had I really believed that I could ever move in *that* world? I could never be that woman. Obviously Yuri had figured it out before me.

"When was this taken?" I croaked the question as I tried to blink back the tears prickling my eyes.

"A few hours ago at a charity gala in Berlin. Apparently he was there for some pipeline deal." He hesitated before saying, "Her name is Tanya Kruger. She's a media heiress he dated last year."

Of course she was. Ty tried to pull the phone away but I stopped him. "Are there more?"

Compassion flashed in his dark eyes. "You don't need to see them."

"I do." I had to burn the images into my brain so I'd never be stupid enough to think a guy like Yuri would ever want something to do with a ghetto princess like me.

Holding the phone in my trembling hands, I swiped through the gallery. Yuri looked sexy and dashing and so damn happy. In every photo he smiled. In every photo *she* clung to his arm. Tanya—with the perfect hair and the perfect dress and the perfect face. And the perfect bank account and pedigree no doubt.

It was obvious he'd gotten a better offer while he was away on business. He could have come back to Houston to see stupid, poor, unlovable, unemployed me or he could stay there and rub elbows with Europe's wealthy and elite while a supermodel lookalike gazed adoringly at him.

I handed the phone back to Ty and lifted my glass of wine to my mouth. In three long pulls, I gulped it down. Catching Ty's eye, I said, "You must think I'm a real dumbass."

His gaze never wavered. "I don't think that at all, Lena. I think men like Yuri are used to taking what they want and discarding it when they're done. You're at a disadvantage because you didn't grow up in this glossy world of mine. You learn quickly to spot the users."

Was Yuri a user? He came across as so caring and kind. Was it all an act? I rubbed my face. "God, I'm really losing my touch. There was a time when this wouldn't have happened to me."

Ty gripped my hand. "Don't let him win. He's nothing, okay? He's just some rich ass Russian with some stupid boats."

My lips quirked in a sad smile. "I thought he was something special."

"Oh, honey." He squeezed my fingers. "Don't."

Feeling colossally stupid, I cringed at the idea of going home and telling Vivian what had happened. She would be so sweet and supporting but it wasn't what I wanted right now.

And Erin? She would be furious for me and demand that Ivan track Yuri down and kick his ass as a twisted way of restoring my honor. Knowing how tightly she had Ivan wrapped around her little finger, he'd probably do it too. Then Dimitri and Nikolai would be dragged into the mess. The last thing Benny needed was the stress of a huge bust-up in our tightly connected group of friends.

"Hey," Ty tipped my chin with his finger, "come out with me."

"What? No. I'm okay. I'll go home. You don't have to offer to take me out because you pity me."

"I don't pity you. I actually like you quite a bit. I think we got off on the wrong foot. You and me? We have more in common than you think, Lena Cruz."

I wasn't so sure about that but the prospect of a sad night in my apartment didn't seem so appealing. Tempted by his offer, I asked, "What did you have in mind?"

Grasping my hand, he dragged me out of my seat. "Well, it wouldn't be any fun if I told you…"

* * *

The relentless chirp of a cell phone dragged Yuri from a deep sleep. Confused and groggy, he rolled onto his back and tried to remember where the hell he was. Berlin. A hotel. Another night alone in a strange bed.

The cell phone on the bedside table continued to vibrate and ring. If it had been the ringtone from his business phone, he would have let it go but it was his private line, the line to which only a handful of people had access. Worried something had happened in Houston, he snatched up the phone and answered. Fully expecting Ivan, Dimitri or Nikolai, he slipped into Russian. "What's happened?"

"I to-told you! English only!"

Taken aback, Yuri bolted upright at the sound of Lena's slurred voice. The heavy, thumping electronic music in the background made it difficult to hear her. He glanced at the clock and calculated the time in Houston. It was nearly one in the morning there. "Lena? Are you okay?"

"Like you care," she snapped back.

He'd never heard such anger in her voice. There was something else coloring her tone. Pain? "Of course I care."

"Liar. You're a big, stupid, Russian liar and I'm a big, dumb Mexican believer."

He frowned and tried to make sense of her ramblings. It was clear she was very drunk. "Lena, are you alone? Is Erin or Vivian there?"

"It's none of your business who I'm with tonight." He heard male voices in the background. She came back on the line, louder and angrier. "Yeah, that's right. You want to be so nosy about what I'm doing. Who the fuck was that girl you were with tonight? Huh? Is she with you now?"

"Tanya? What does Tanya matter?"

"Apparently a lot. You dumped me for her."

"What are you—?" The pieces fell into place. Had she seen photos from the gala? Did she think he had feelings for Tanya? "Lena, it was just a charity thing. It doesn't matter."

"Charity? Are you calling me a charity case?"

Between the alcohol dimming her wits and the outrageously loud music, she'd misunderstood him. "No. I didn't call you a charity case."

"Whatever, Yuri. What! Ever!"

He flinched as she shouted into the phone. The loud male laughter in the background worried him. If she was alone and drunk with men, it could be dangerous for her. "Lena, where are you?"

"Wherever you aren't."

Pinching his nose, he tried to keep his temper in check. "Lena, please, I'm begging you. Tell me where you are."

"Oh my God! I love this song." Her voice sounded fainter. He strained to hear her. The sound of fabric rustling against the phone scratched at his ear. A few moments later, he heard Lena whooping and raucous applause.

Imagining the very worst, he shouted, "Lena? *Yelena!*"

A deep male voice came on the line. "Sorry, dude, Lena can't play right now. She's busy dancing."

The line went dead. Panicked, he tried to call her but there was no answer. Terrified that she'd gotten herself into a dangerous situation, he called the only person who could find her in a city the size of Houston.

"Yuri?" Nikolai's calm voice soothed his raw nerves.

"I need you to find Lena."

He laughed. "Let the girl sleep, Yuri. She doesn't need you calling her all hours of the night because you're lovesick."

Somehow he managed not shout at his best friend. "She's not at home. She's drunk and in a club. I'm worried about her."

There was a moment's pause before Nikolai sighed. "Let me call Vee."

The line went dead. As Yuri waited for Nikolai's call, he flipped on the lamp and slid out of bed. The exhaustion he'd been feeling from the protracted negotiations fled as adrenaline took hold. What the hell was Lena thinking?

As he tugged on a shirt and pants, he replayed her conversation. Behind the alcohol making her so aggressive, there was so much hurt in her voice. What in the world did she think was going on here in Berlin? What was her hang-up with Tanya?

He had specifically told Anna to make sure that Lena understood this was simply a way for him to get the approval on the pipeline. He went with Tanya, gave an outrageous donation to an environmental charity and in the morning her father would run positive coverage in his papers to steady the nerves of those people preparing to vote to allow the pipeline to cross German soil.

"Shit." Running his fingers through his hair, Yuri pocketed his private phone and stormed out of his bedroom. He crossed the large suite to the bedroom where Anna slept. Hating to wake her so early after all the work she had done, he knocked loud enough to get her attention. "Anna?"

It was more than a minute before the door opened. Rumpled and sleepy, she hugged her robe around her willowy frame. "What's wrong?"

"Did you speak to Lena about cancelling our plans?"

"Yes. Well." Her cheek twitched and she made an apologetic face. "I sent her an email. Between running interference with the council and trying to track down a tuxedo and getting the cash freed up for the donation, I didn't have time for a phone call. Why? Was it important?"

Yuri groaned and wiped a hand down his face. "She's incredibly important to me."

Anna looked surprised. "I'm sorry. I didn't realize she was—I mean, I thought she was just another one of them. If I had known—"

"Yes." He lifted a hand to stop her. His stomach knotted so painfully he thought he might get sick. The stupidity of what he had done threatened to drop him to his knees. He had been so focused on this damn pipeline that he'd put everything at risk. Now there was only one thing to be done. "Get me on a flight to Houston as soon as possible."

Her eyes widened. "But it's—"

He cut her off. "I know what time it is. Leave our private jet here for the rest of team. Find me another one. Hell, I'll take a commercial flight if that's the only thing available."

"Yes, sir." She hesitated. "And the pipeline deal?"

"Jameson is my VP for a reason. If he can't seal the deal, he can find a new job." Harshness edged into his voice. He had no one to blame for this mess but himself. "I'm sorry. I shouldn't be so short with you. This is my fault."

She didn't argue with him. "I'll get it handled."

"Thank you." His phone started to ring as he crossed the living area and ducked into the bedroom. "Nikolai?"

"We've found her."

Yuri sagged against the closed door with relief. "Where is she?"

"Vee tracked her down using the internet. Apparently

she's been posting pictures all night on a club run with someone called Ty."

Yuri groaned even louder. Could this night get any worse? "He's a gossip columnist." Certain Nikolai didn't care, he said, "It doesn't matter. Can you get her?"

"I'm waiting for Vivian to get dressed. I'm not about to try to bring Lena home myself—especially if she has that damn gun in her purse."

Yuri reeled with shock. "She carries a gun?"

"Can you blame her? With a father like that she needs it."

Yuri's brow furrowed. He had only done a cursory peek into her background. Clearly he needed to delve deeper. "Be careful. I don't want this to turn into a bigger mess than it is."

"Vee and I can handle this." Nikolai's voice trailed off and Yuri heard Vivian's soft voice in the background. When Nikolai returned, he sounded unhappy. "You owe me big, Yuri."

"Why?"

"Because I'm going to have to bribe my way into Houston's most notorious gay bar," he grumbled. "This girl had better be worth it."

"She is."

"Are you headed here?"

"As soon as I get a flight arranged, I'll be on my way."

"I'd suggest you spend that time coming up with an apology. Flowers and diamonds aren't going to cut it this time."

The line went dead and Yuri tossed his phone onto his bed. Quickly, he washed his face and brushed his teeth. There wasn't time for a shower but he hopped into clean jeans and a shirt. He was tossing things into his suitcases when Anna knocked on his door. "Come in."

She stepped inside but stayed near the open door. "You're on a private jet leaving in fifty-five minutes. The car is waiting to take you. Jake and Derek will be in the lobby in ten minutes. I'll have Tony waiting at the airport in Houston. I've emailed the details."

Yuri glanced at his watch and made the calculations. It would be noon Houston-time before he arrived. He hoped Lena could sleep off her hangover by then. They needed to have a serious talk, one that required her to be sober.

"Thank you, Anna."

"Is there anything else I can do?"

He started to say no but remembered something Nikolai had said. "When you have a chance, I want a full background dossier on Lena. Concentrate on her parents."

Surprise colored her face but she nodded nonetheless. "I'll get it done as soon as possible."

"Thank you."

"I'm sorry for whatever problems I've caused tonight."

"You didn't cause them. This was all me."

He prayed Lena would forgive him and give him a chance to try again. Thankfully, he had a trans-Atlantic flight to figure out a way to make this right.

CHAPTER SIX

It had been the longest flight of his life. Now sitting in the backseat of his car, Yuri rubbed the back of his aching neck. He had a few short minutes until they reached Lena's apartment. He still had no idea what the hell he was going to say.

On one hand, he was irritated that she had jumped to such a nasty conclusion. Did she really think so little of him? Did she honestly believe he could be so cruel?

On the other hand, he had seen the glossy photographs posted to his company's social media pages. They didn't look very innocent. Though he considered Tanya a friend, it was clear from the expression on her face that she thought differently. It wasn't difficult to understand how Lena had arrived at her conclusion.

He could only imagine how hurt she must have been to sit at that damn restaurant waiting for him. He still didn't understand how she had missed the email from Anna but it wouldn't be the first time correspondence had disappeared into the online ether. How she'd ended up with Ty Weston still confused him. He hadn't even realized they were friends. It occurred to him there was a lot he didn't know about Lena Cruz. Hopefully Anna's dossier would fill in those blanks.

Picking up his phone, he tormented himself again by scrolling through the photos on her timeline. She'd been a very busy girl last night. The photo of a half-naked, tattooed male dancer licking lime and salt off her neck drove him crazy. It had been snapped at a gay bar but the way the man looked at Lena told him he wasn't playing for the home team. The man looked like he wanted to flip up her skirt and fuck her right there on the bar.

The photos of Lena knocking back shots with a group of friends would have been amusing if he hadn't been so worried about her. He cringed at the idea of how much alcohol she must have imbibed. Only the knowledge that Vivian would never leave Lena in danger soothed his raw nerves. If there had been any question of Lena's health, Vivian would have demanded Nikolai take them to an emergency room.

But Vivian's text from earlier had assured him that Lena was home and in her own bed. The short, snippy tone of Vivian's message told him he was on her shit-list. Getting off of it wouldn't be easy. She was so damn loyal to her friends. It would take a miracle to convince her not to hate him for hurting Lena.

The car pulled into the parking lot of the complex. He exhaled slowly before unlatching his safety belt and climbing out of the backseat. Derek stood at the ready and glanced around the quiet complex. "You want me to come in, Boss?"

Yuri shook his head. "I should probably do this on my own."

"I don't know. If Lena wings you, Dimitri is going to have my ass." The bodyguard said it with a joking smile but it didn't ease Yuri's anxiety any.

Yuri clapped Derek on the arm and walked toward the building. Jake followed him down the sidewalk but stayed back from the front door, giving Yuri some privacy. He was suddenly very glad he'd had a non-disclosure agreement inserted in their contracts. Lena was probably going to tear into him when she came to the door.

Gathering his courage, he knocked three times and stepped back so he could be seen clearly through the peephole. He heard the deadbolt flip and his heart raced. The door opened to reveal a frowning Vivian. For a long time, they stared at one another. Finally, she sighed dramatically and stepped aside. "You'd better come in."

"Thank you." He entered the apartment but didn't dare go farther than the entryway. Glancing around, he noticed the bohemian décor. Everything looked so cozy and welcoming. Unfortunately the look on Vivian's face wasn't.

"You're a real jerk." She addressed him in Russian. "I don't know why you led her on like that but it was cruel and mean. I've never seen her cry like that. *Never.*"

Yuri winced. "It wasn't like that, Vivian. It was a mix-up. An honest-to-God mistake."

"Well, don't tell me! Tell her."

"Will you see if she'll speak to me?"

Vivian glanced at the hallway. "She's going to be a real beast with that hangover but I'll see if she'll talk to you."

Vivian left him standing there and disappeared into the room on the left. He strained to hear but their voices were muffled by the half-closed door. When Vivian came out some time later, she gestured to the couch. "You'd better get comfortable. It's going to be a while."

He didn't think he could sit still so he paced instead. Vivian grabbed some books from the coffee table and stuffed them inside her backpack. "Are you leaving?"

"I'm not sticking around for this shouting match."

He knew enough about Vivian's family history to understand why she was sensitive to couples yelling at one another. "I'm not going to yell at her."

"I wasn't talking about you." She hefted her bag onto her back. "Just a fair warning—Nikolai is in a really bad mood after last night. He was groped and kissed and had his ass smacked by about five different drunk guys before we got Lena out of there. It was mayhem."

"Shit." Yuri closed his eyes and wondered if this situation could get any worse. With Nikolai's background, he could only imagine the awful memories being groped and manhandled had dredged up for his friend. "I am sorry that you two were dragged into this."

She stared at him for an unnerving moment and then left without a word. It was another five minutes before Lena finally emerged from her bedroom. She looked like hell but he wasn't about to tell her that. Her dark hair was pulled into a low, messy bun. A rumpled cotton camisole and stained, ripped yoga pants completed her ensemble.

Her angry gaze seared him. Gulping, he took a step toward her but no more. "Yelena, please, let me explain."

She held up a hand. "I need coffee and something for this damn headache before you start with the groveling."

A flutter of hope invaded his chest. "Where do you keep your coffee?"

"You can manage that on your own? Are you sure you don't need to email one of your assistants for help?"

The barb hit its mark. "I'm sorry. I shouldn't have left it to my assistant. I wasn't—"

She put up her hand again. "I said coffee and pain killers first."

"Right." He followed her into the kitchen. While she

dug around in a basket for some acetaminophen, he found the little cups for the coffee maker. She hadn't been far from the mark with her assistant come-back but he did still remember how to make a cup of coffee.

While she washed down the tablets with some water, he made two cups of coffee and carried them to the dining room table where she waited for him. He found a spoon in a drawer and a bottle of flavored creamer in the refrigerator

Sitting across from her, he watched her stab her spoon into the sugar bowl on the table and dump the heaping scoops into her steaming hot cup. She splashed in a liberal amount of creamer and stirred the syrupy sweet slurry. He wasn't sure how anyone could drink coffee that sweet and sipped his cup of strong black coffee.

"I suppose you expect me to say thank you for sending Vivian and Nikolai to rescue me from that den of iniquity."

His lips twitched at her description of the rowdy gay bar where she'd been partying. "No. I was simply worried about you. I heard all those men and I was terrified you would be taken advantage of or hurt."

"I don't think there was much chance of that. Now Ty?" She drank some of her coffee. "That's a different story."

"I didn't realize you were friends."

"My relationship with Ty is complicated."

"Like ours?" he asked the obvious question.

She stared down into her cup. "Do we have a relationship?"

"I was a complete jackass."

Her surprised gaze jumped to his face. She stirred her coffee. "Go on."

Amusement tugged at the corners of his mouth. "I should have called you personally. I should have told you that the negotiations were going badly and I needed to make an appearance at that charity gala to prove that I was serious about addressing the environmental concerns associated with the pipeline. I should have told you about Tanya."

"Yes, you should have, Yuri. You *really* should have told me you were going out with an old girlfriend."

"She means nothing to me, Lena. She's simply an ex-girlfriend with connections I needed to get the deal done."

"That's harsh."

"It's the truth."

"And me? Are you after me for my connections?"

"I'm only here for you, Yelena Cruz. *Only you.*"

She ran her finger around the rim of her cup but didn't drink. "I was so humiliated. I just sat there waiting for you like some big dummy and you were off in Berlin having the time of your life with some rich, beautiful model girl." She made a disgusted sound and buried her face in her hands. "The people at the restaurant probably think I'm some psycho stalker with delusions of dating you after making them check the book and get me a table."

"Then we'll have to put in an appearance there later this week to prove that you're not a psycho stalker with delusions of dating me."

She frowned at him. "It's not funny, Yuri. You really hurt me."

The vise-like grip on his chest tightened. "I'm sorry. I never meant to hurt you. I never meant for you to feel like you weren't important to me." He reached across the table and grasped her hand. "Because you are important to me, Lena."

She stared at his hand. Eventually, she rotated her wrist and clasped his fingers. "This is your second chance, Yuri. Don't fuck it up because I won't give you a third."

"Understood."

She sipped her coffee. "Are you hungry?"

"Famished," he answered honestly. "I ran out of Berlin before sunrise and couldn't eat on the flight."

"God, now I feel so guilty."

"Why should you feel guilty? I'm the one who screwed everything up."

"Yeah, but I'm a terrible cook." She bit her plump lower lip. "You're famished and the best I can offer is, like, toast or a bowl of cereal."

"Cereal is fine."

"You're sure?"

"Positive."

She slid out of her seat. He let his hungry gaze roam the sloping plane of her belly as she reached up to grab cereal boxes from a high shelf in the small pantry. Her top rode up on her stomach and revealed more of her silky skin. He caught another tantalizing glimpse as she dragged down bowls. She carried her armload of boxes, milk and bowls to the table. When she came back with spoons, she smiled at him as he pushed aside the boring, bland bran cereal with raisins for the box with the cartoon captain emblazoned on the front.

"What?" He returned her grin.

"Vivian is always on my case about eating this sugary stuff but it's so addicting."

"When I was a kid, we dreamed about eating something other than thin oatmeal porridge." He shook the crispy, sweet cereal into his bowl. "The first time I had real money of my own, I gorged myself on so much junk food. I puked for an entire weekend."

She smiled at him with understanding. "I was raised on food stamps so junk food rarely made it into our grocery carts because the budget was so tight. It wasn't until later, after my dad got out of the pen and was working, that we had extra cash for luxuries like name-brand cereal."

Yuri splashed milk into his bowl. He didn't know if it was all right to ask about her father so he erred on the side of caution and didn't bring it up. They ate in silence for a few minutes. Finally, she said, "You can ask. I'm not embarrassed."

Yuri held her gaze. She had the most honest brown eyes he'd ever seen. "Why was he in prison?"

"Which time?"

"The first time?"

"Drug trafficking."

"And the second?"

"Gun buy gone wrong."

"And the third?"

She shook her head. "There wasn't a third time. He cleaned up his act. Well. Mostly."

"I see."

She laughed and dunked her spoon into her bowl. "Of all the guys I've dated, you're probably the only one who can even comprehend what it means to have someone you love in prison."

He thought of the gut-gnawing worry he'd experienced every time Ivan or Nikolai had gone inside for a stretch. "It's not easy."

"No, it's not."

"Do you see your father often?"

She nodded. "Once or twice a month, he takes me out for lunch or dinner. We're not as close as we were when I was in school but I guess that's just part of growing up."

"I wouldn't know." When she snorted with laughter,

he clarified, "About the parent part, not the growing up part. I think I've mastered the growing up part."

Finished with her cereal, she pushed her bowl to the center of the table. "Did you ever look for your parents?" His head snapped up and her eyes widened. Instantly, she apologized. "Oh my God! I don't know why I asked that, Yuri. I'm sorry. Just forget I said something so insensitive."

"It's not insensitive. Honestly, I was simply surprised by the question. I haven't thought about my parents or who they might be in years. And, yes, I did look for them once. I didn't find any promising leads so I let it go. I didn't see how anything good could come from it."

She caressed his fingers. "I'm sorry."

He shrugged. "That's life. I can't complain. The orphanage was hell on earth but I survived and came out stronger on the other end. I wouldn't be where I am today without the experiences of my childhood."

"I suppose that's the positive outlook on your situation."

"It's the only one I'll indulge." He realized she hadn't said anything about her mother. "What about your mother? Does she live nearby?"

Lena's expression hardened. She stood and grabbed her empty bowl and his. With her back toward him, she said, "My mom walked out on us when I was nine. I tracked her down when I was seventeen but she was already dead."

The anguish in her voice cut him deeply. He was on his feet in the blink of an eye and crossing the kitchen. She still had her back to him as she rinsed the bowls in the sink. When he slid his arms around her waist, she stiffened. He dipped his head and kissed the side of her neck. "I'm sorry. I didn't mean to upset you."

She relaxed in his arms. Her wet hand grasped his forearm. "It's okay. You didn't know."

He kissed her neck again and then her cheek. She giggled and pulled away from the ticklish peck of his lips. "Stop," she said and pushed at him. "I'm all gross from my wild night."

The scent of her perfume was mixed with the faint smell of alcohol and cigarette smoke from her night of endless clubbing but he wouldn't call it gross. "You're fine."

"I'm not. I need a shower."

"So do I," he said, certain he wasn't his freshest either after trekking across the Atlantic Ocean to reach her.

She turned slowly in his arms and gazed up at him. He lost himself in the dark pools of her eyes. When she licked her lips, his cock started to throb to life. A little nervously, she said, "Our shower is pretty big."

"Is it?" He nuzzled her neck and pressed his lips to her skin. He delighted in the sight of goose bumps blossoming there.

"And Vivian is gone for the afternoon."

"Yes, she is."

She pushed on his chest and stared up at him. "This is only a shower, Yuri."

"Only a shower," he agreed.

But that didn't mean he wasn't going to try to convince her that it was finally time for them to take that next step.

CHAPTER SEVEN

My belly wobbled violently as I led Yuri down the hallway. He'd paused long enough to text his handlers and then dropped his phone on the kitchen table. When we stepped into the bathroom, he caught my uncomfortable expression in the mirror. "What's wrong?"

I stared at his reflection. "It's weird to think your bodyguards and driver are just sitting out there waiting."

He shrugged and grasped the bottom of his shirt. "It's not the first time they've done it."

His words hit me like a splash of cold water. They drove home the point that I was simply one more in a long line of conquests.

Seeing the hurt on my face, he reached for me. "I didn't mean it like that. I meant that they have to wait for me to conduct business all the time."

"Uh-huh," I said, unconvinced.

He rested his chin on the crown of my head as he gathered me to his chest. "I swear, woman. I've never stepped in the shit so many times in my life. You leave me flustered."

"Me?"

"You." His hand swept down my back. "I'm not going to stand here and pretend I'm a choirboy, Lena. I've had a string of relationships, most of them very short, but I've always maintained certain boundaries. I've never slept over at a woman's home and I've never brought a woman into my homes."

I had seen pics of hot women doing the walk of shame from his downtown penthouse. "But your penthouse—"

"I'm not talking about my penthouses." He kissed my cheek. "I'm talking about my homes, my private houses in London, Moscow and here."

I leaned back so I could see his face. "You have a house? Here?"

He nodded. "It's about half an hour outside of town. I'm taking you to see it tonight."

"Is that so?"

His lips touched mine briefly. "Yes."

As I wiggled out of his embrace and adjusted the water temp, I tried to figure out what his willingness to break those rules of his with me meant. Was this his way of telling me that he was looking for something long-term? Was he open to a committed relationship?

An even better question to consider? Was I ready for all the things he seemed to be offering?

I turned around—and almost choked. Yuri had stripped out of his shirt. My appreciative gaze roamed every sexy inch of his tanned skin. Unlike Dimitri and Ivan who were built heavy and thick like fighters, Yuri had the leaner physique of a swimmer or runner.

And I could not stop staring at him.

My fingertips practically burned with the need to touch his hot flesh. I wanted to ride the smooth, hard planks of his rippled stomach and sweep my palms over the ridged muscles of his well-defined pecs and biceps. I needed to feel his steely heat.

Unable to help myself, I reached out and traced the tattoo in the center of his chest. The dark ink sat low enough to be hidden by his shirts. I traced the Cyrillic letters in the knotted scrolling artwork. I had sat in on enough of Vivian's Russian language lessons at our kitchen table to recognize the first initials of Ivan, Nikolai and Dimitri's names.

My gaze lifted to his. "Your brothers?"

He grasped my hand and dragged my fingertip along the intricate ink. "We may not have the same mother or father but our bond goes deeper than blood."

"After seeing how far the four of you will go to support one another, I believe it."

Yuri's other hand cupped my chin. He gazed down at me with such concern. "You don't have to worry about competing with them."

I frowned. "Why in the world would you think I'm worried about something like that?"

His anxious expression relaxed. "Other women have. It's always been one of the top complaints—that I care about them more or I put them first."

"Well," I said carefully, "I don't want to think I'm dead last on your list of priorities but I also understand that the four of you have known one another for decades. I would understand if you had to drop everything to help one of them."

He brushed his fingers over my cheek. "I realize I fucked up last night and made you feel like you weren't a priority but that isn't going to happen again. You come first."

Even though he was being serious, I caught the mischievous glint in his eyes at the double entendre. I lightly whacked his arm. "Behave, Yuri. This is only a shower, remember?"

"Only a shower," he whispered and kissed me. Gathered in his strong arms, I surrendered to the sensual press of his lips. When his tongue touched mine, I tasted the fruity sweetness of the cereal. He didn't try to take the kiss any deeper and left me throbbing with arousal and wanting so much more when he dragged his mouth away.

Only a shower. The thought circled round and round in my head as I slipped out of my ratty yoga pants and top. I felt the slightest bit of embarrassment at coming out of my bedroom wearing them but I'd been so annoyed by Vivian's interruption and his arrival that I hadn't much cared. Now I cringed a little at the idea that he'd seen me in such an awful outfit with my hair a mess and the reek of my long night clinging to me.

"What are you thinking about now?" Yuri tilted his head to study me. "Your expression looks almost panicked."

I shook my head. "I'm sort of annoyed with myself for letting you see me like this."

"Like what?" He slid his arms around me from behind and engulfed me in his warm embrace. "Naked? Sexy? Hot?"

My toes curled against the tile as the hard length of his cock brushed against my bottom. When I felt the tip of it touch my lower back, my eyes widened. He was *big*. I had suspected he would measure up, so to speak, but *this* was so much more than I'd expected. I squeezed my knees together as the ache between my thighs begged to be assuaged.

Remembering his question, I finally managed to answer him. "I meant in that terrible outfit."

"I didn't notice."

I smacked his hip. "Liar."

"Okay," he said with a laugh. "Maybe a little bit."

"I promise I'm not usually such a mess in the mornings."

"I would be perfectly happy to wake up to find you wearing absolutely nothing in the mornings. Think of all the laundry it would save."

I stepped out of his embrace and into the shower. Yuri shadowed my moves. I didn't dare glance over my shoulder to get a look at what I was sure would be quite an impressive package. I worried that what little resolve I had would snap the moment I spied it. Instead I shoved my face in the shower spray and let the hot water spill over me.

Yuri's hands caressed my naked curves. I'd showered before with a boyfriend but this felt different. For one, we hadn't gotten busy under the covers yet. I felt like we were doing everything out of order. We hadn't even had one official date but I was pretty sure that drunken phone call last night qualified as a breakup. This morning felt like we were dancing around makeup sex without, you know, the actual sex part.

When I reached for my shampoo, he brushed my hand out of the way and took the bottle from me. "Let me."

I glanced back at him and nodded. No man had ever washed my hair. He took his time massaging the fragrant suds into my scalp. Eyes closed, I relaxed back against Yuri. Somehow he made the simplest thing so incredibly sexy and intimate. By the time he finished washing my long tresses, my tummy wobbled and my clit pulsed incessantly. I kept my trembling fingers interlaced in front of me and tried to get a grip on my wild emotions.

With gentle pressure, he coaxed me to turn around and face him. Carefully, he guided me under the spray. He threaded his long fingers through my wet hair as he rinsed it. When he cupped my nape and tugged me forward, I moved without hesitation. His lips found mine in a shockingly tender kiss.

I couldn't understand the way Yuri affected me. All the weeks of tension and sneaked glances came to a head there under the warm rush of water. I wasn't sure where this was going or what would become of our relationship but I had to see it through. I had to know if it was possible for me to be in a normal, loving, long-term relationship—and Yuri was the only man in the world brave enough to walk along that path with me.

"The things you do to me, Lena," he whispered against my lips. "You threaten my control like no other woman."

"Maybe control is over-rated," I daringly replied.

His fingertips grazed my cheek. "I thought this was only a shower."

"Then maybe you should help me get squeaky clean." Even as I spoke the bold words, I felt the ripples of anxiety rocking my core. Was I coming on too strong? Was I pulling off the sex kitten vibe? Did this make me pathetic or too easy?

His sinful smile told me everything I needed to know. Grabbing the bottle of body wash from the caddy mounted on the wall, he flipped open the top and squeezed a dollop onto his palm. The scent of coconut and verbena blossomed in the steamy interior of the shower. Yuri rubbed his palms together, creating a thick froth, and smeared the creamy suds all over my skin.

"Do you mind smelling frou-frou?"

"Judging by the bottles on this wall, I don't think I have much of a choice." His amused gaze jumped from my shower caddy to Vivian's.

"Sorry." I gathered some of the scented foam from my

skin and swept my slick palms over his ridiculously sexy chest. "We don't have male guests here."

"Never?"

I shook my head and continued to wash his corded arms. "Vivian doesn't believe in pre-marital sex and I respect that. When I've dated someone, I kept my trysts confined to my boyfriend's place."

Our gazes held for a moment before he said, "Looks like today is a day of firsts for both of us."

His hand glided along my spine. I gasped when he grasped my bottom in both hands and gave it a playful squeeze. His forehead dipped to mine as his hand rode the curve of my hip and slipped down toward my bare mound. My heated gaze melded to his as his fingers stopped so very close to their final destination.

"May I touch you?"

Burning up with need, I breathed heavily. "Please."

At the first touch of his fingertips against my sex, I nearly fainted. My heart stuttered wildly and my belly did crazy somersaults. I licked my lips and pressed my flattened palms to the tile behind me.

"Open your thighs for me."

His whispered order made my head pound but I hurried to comply. Ever so gently, he parted the folds of my secret place with his soapy fingers. A sudsy fingertip swirled around my clit. My knees threatened to give out as he drew torturously slow circles around the throbbing, aching bud. "*Yuri.*"

"Are you going to come for me?"

Oh God. If only it were that simple! "I want to but—"

"No," he interrupted with a tap to my inflamed clit. I shuddered with the intensity of his gaze. "Are you going to come for me, Yelena?"

"Yes." The breathless, shaky answer left my lips on a

pleasured sigh. Those magnificent fingers of his framed my clit and moved side to side around the stiff nub. My eyelids drifted together as lust overcame me.

"Look at me," he urged, his voice husky with desire. "I want to watch your face while you come."

Gripping his wrist, I kept my gaze glued to his while those skillful fingers manipulated my swollen clit. Our shared breaths mingled as he pushed me closer and closer to the edge. My thighs tensed and my toes curled. I relished the frantic frissons of white-hot delight spearing my core.

And then it happened.

"Yuri!" His name fell from my lips on a stunned a cry and echoed in the small bathroom. "*Oh!*"

"Come," he commanded. "Come for me."

And I did. I came so hard my knees knocked together and I started to slide down the tile. Yuri was quicker, stronger, and caught me before I could fall. Chuckling, he kissed my neck and cheek. "Are you all right?"

"Not really," I murmured with a little laugh. "Oh my God." I clutched at him and pressed my cheek to his chest. "I haven't ever been able to have an orgasm that easily."

He tangled his hands in my hair and tilted my head back for a passionate, demanding kiss. "I meant what I said earlier. You always come first."

"And you?" I nipped at his lower lip. "When do you come?"

"With you, after you, whenever you'll have me."

I reached between our bodies and grasped his rock-hard shaft. The soapy suds clinging to his steely length slicked the slow downward stroke of my palm. "I think I'll have you now."

"Kitten..." He kissed me again, crashing our lips

together in a needful mating of tongues. His low groan ricocheted off the tile as I worked my hand up and down his thick, long cock. When my other hand slipped down to cup his sac, Yuri let loose a string of Russian curse words, the kind I'd only heard Vivian use when she stubbed a toe. His grip on my waist tightened as I sped up my stroking hand. He said my name with a growl. "Yelena."

His eyes flashed open a second before I felt the splash of his blazing hot seed on my belly. My name escaped his lips on a whisper as he came hard. When the last drop left him, he claimed my mouth in a kiss so erotic that it left me dizzy.

Yuri dragged his fingers through the pearly white essence dotting my brown skin. "So fucking beautiful," he murmured before kissing me again. He captured my gaze. "Let me stay with you."

The vulnerable glint in his eyes surprised me. I caressed his jaw. "You can stay—but I should warn you that my bed is pretty small. There's no five-star luxury here."

He grinned. "There's something quaint about roughing it. I'm sure I'll survive."

"Uh-huh." I mockingly rolled my eyes and turned toward the pounding spray to rinse the evidence of our shower tryst off my skin.

Yuri enveloped me from behind. His lips ghosted across my ear. "If this is *only* a shower, I'm sold on your version."

I laughed and reached out to shut off the water. "Well, you did fly all the way from Berlin for me. I suppose it was the least I could do."

His bark of laughter made my tummy flip-flop. That boyish grin of his brightened his whole face and made him seem younger and less stressed. I ran my fingertips down his cheek. The rough stubble rasped my skin. "You should do that more often."

He took my hand and kissed my fingertips. "Do what, Kitten?"

I tried to ignore the way his pet name made me shiver inside. "Smile." I gestured to his wet hair and his relaxed posture. "I like you this way, without the bespoke suits and the army of handlers and the glossy photo-ready hair and face."

"It's a character." He rolled his shoulders. "It's what investors expect of me. Hell, it's what most women expect of me."

Not for the first time, I experienced the strangest sensation of *knowing* Yuri. Sometimes I felt like we were more alike than either could imagine.

"I know what it's like to play a character. I've been playing a role since I was a teenager. Fake it 'til you make it, right?" I dragged back the shower curtain and reached for one of the neatly folded towels on the shelf. I handed him one and took another for myself. "People see this polished, educated, well-spoken professional but deep down inside?"

The shadow of his painful past crossed his handsome face. "You feel like a fraud? You feel like an actor playing a role? Sometimes I find myself in the middle of a gala or some political event and I'm rubbing shoulders with the elite and wealthy and I just think—" He stopped himself and cleared his throat. "I don't belong there. No one there understands what it means to be me."

My eyes grew hot and I glanced away from him. He confessed all the things I'd been feeling for years. "I understand, Yuri."

"Yes, I know you do. Earlier you said I'm the only

man you've ever dated who could understand what it's like to have a loved one in prison. Well, you're the only woman I've ever known who can understand what it is like to claw your way out of hell and into a boardroom."

The heady statement hit me with its truth. He was right. He'd escaped an orphanage where the boys were starved and neglected. I'd escaped a neighborhood where hookers turned tricks next to my school bus stop and drug dealers lived next door. By twelve, I'd dodged more bullets than most soldiers would on deployment.

Yuri slid an arm around my waist and hauled me tight to his chest. "The other day, Dimitri told me that he believes fate brought him from Russia to Houston, to that tiny apartment over Benny's old bakery. He believes that she was made for him. I'll admit that I thought that to be the silliest thing I'd ever heard but now…"

Gazing up at him, I asked, "But now?"

He brushed his fingers through my wet hair. "Now I'm standing here with you and I'm telling you things I've never told anyone and I feel like…" His voice trailed away as he searched for the right words. "Maybe Dimitri was right."

No man had ever said anything so romantic to me. I desperately wondered what I could say that would show him I was feeling the same thing but he traced my lower lip with his thumb and smiled down at me. In that moment, I realized that I didn't have to say anything. He *knew*.

Silently, we finished drying off and gathered up our discarded clothing. Inside my bedroom, I cringed at the mess on my desk and the pile of dresses draped over the chair in the corner. "Um—don't mind the mess."

"It's fine." He pretended not to care but I sensed he was fighting the urge to pick up the piles of books and shift aside the pyramid of high heels blocking the closet. Not bothering to slip back into his boxers, he crashed down onto my bed and dragged the top sheet over his chest. With an arm over his eyes, he said, "I can't remember the last time I was this tired."

Patting his foot, I said, "I'll be right back. I'm going to make sure the coffee pot is off."

He made a humming sound of acknowledgment. By the time I'd slipped into a robe and secured the belt, Yuri had passed out completely. I stared at him for the longest time. I couldn't believe a man who regularly made the rich lists was sleeping on my rumpled Target sheets. As tall as he was, he took up most of my full-size bed. I was probably going to have to fight him for space when I got back.

After turning off the coffee pot, I spotted his phone on the table. Guilt seized me as I thought about poor Jake and the other bodyguard and his driver waiting out there while he slept. If they'd been in Berlin with him, they were probably dead tired.

Feeling self-conscious, I made my way to the front door and peered out the peephole. I spotted Jake's familiar form leaning against the opposite wall. I flipped the locked and opened the door. He snapped to attention and took a step forward. Even with his sunglasses in place, there was no mistaking his concerned impression. "Miss Cruz," he said with a nod. "Is everything all right, ma'am?"

"It's fine. Um…" I clutched my robe a little tighter. "Look, Yuri is asleep and I just wondered if you guys wanted to come inside and get comfy? I'm sure you're hungry and tired. There's no reason for you to be stuck outside while he naps."

"Oh." Surprise colored his voice. "Well, we aren't

supposed to—"

"Please?" I turned up the charm. "I feel like such a bad hostess having you outside in that car. Come in. Have something to eat. Nap. You know—whatever."

Jake finally accepted. "Thank you. We'll be right in, ma'am."

"You can drop the ma'am. It's just Lena."

"No can do, ma'am. When you're with the boss, you're Miss Cruz or ma'am."

I didn't know how to react to that so I let it go. "I'll leave the door unlocked. Make yourselves at home."

Back inside the house, I returned to my room and found my cell. I didn't have the energy to look at the collateral damage from my night of drunken tweeting and Facebook posting. I typed a quick message to Vivian and got pulled into a conversation with her.

Yuri's bodyguards and driver are kicking it on our couch. Don't freak when you get home.

Oookay. Kinda weird but I'm cool with it.

Sorry. I should have asked first. Also—Yuri is sort of sleeping in my bed.

Sort of?

No, he is. I promise he isn't staying the night. I know how you feel about overnight guests.

Oh geez! It's fine. It's Yuri. Sister Vivian says to get some rest and quit bothering me while I'm in class! ;)

Smiling at her Sister Vivian joke, I dropped my phone on the bedside table and slid into bed with Yuri. He woke briefly when my foot brushed his. Reaching for me, he said, "Come here, Lena."

I happily snuggled up against his cozy warmth. Wrapped in his arms, I relaxed and let sleep take me. This was strangest start to any relationship I'd ever had but damn if it didn't feel promising.

CHAPTER EIGHT

"I don't think I've ever seen anyone type that fast."

I glanced over at Yuri as we drove to his estate outside Houston. My thumbs paused over my phone's touchscreen. "It's a learned skill. You should practice more."

He shook his head. "I hate cell phones. I'm old enough to remember what it was like to not be tethered to the outside world twenty-four hours a day, seven days a week."

I rolled my eyes at his age remark. "Please, you're not *that* old."

"I'm older than you. I'm older than Ivan and Dimitri. Hell, I was a teenager when you were born."

"And?" My eyebrows arched expectantly. "Is that a problem?"

"I don't know. Is it?"

"It's not an issue for me."

The worry lines around his mouth visibly relaxed. "Then it's not an issue for me. Now—what are you doing?"

"Trying to salvage last night's cringe-fest," I said with a grimace. "When I was getting dressed and packing my overnight bag, it occurred to me that an apology for getting blitzed and making an ass out of myself was just going to draw more attention to *me*."

He narrowed his eyes with interest. "So what's your brilliant plan?"

"I'm tagging these photos and adding funny, witty captions. I'm drawing attention to all the fantastic places I visited last night. Clearly, I had a damn good time. I'm sure my followers will too."

His lips pursed as he leaned over for a better look at my screen. "Clearly."

I laughed and considered the dancer. The low-slung leather pants hugged his spectacular ass so nicely. "Don't be jealous."

"There's a lot I'm willing to do for you but wearing leather pants isn't one of them."

I giggled and finished typing in the last caption on my photos. Switching to Twitter, I came up with a few quick lines including the night's specials at each club and set them to post throughout the evening.

"Will you get paid for those?"

I shook my head. "I don't have any kind of understanding with the places I visited last night. I'm pretty sure Ty gets paid to promo most of the gay hotspots in town. I wouldn't cut in on his action."

"Not even after he dragged you out and let you get drunk and take all those wild pictures?"

My gaze flicked to Yuri's face. "He was trying to be a good friend by helping me forget how craptastic I felt last night. Things just went a little too far."

"A little? You drunk-dialed me and ended up dancing on a bar sandwiched between two sweaty, half-naked men."

"Are you really going to sit there and chastise me? What am I? Five?"

He glanced toward the window. I watched his jaw tensing and relaxing. "I don't want to lecture you but you put yourself at risk last night. If Vivian and Nikolai hadn't found you and brought you home, you could have been hurt."

I wasn't sure what annoyed me more. That he was giving me a verbal hand-slap for being a bad girl or that he was right about the precarious position I'd been in last night. Annoyed, I crossed my arms. "Yeah, well, we all make mistakes."

His warm hand grasped mine and his serious, somber gaze searched my face. "You have to be more careful, Lena. When you're with me, it's complicated. There are people out there who would see you as a target for all types of schemes. If you want to go out and have fun, go out—but do it at Faze where I know Big V or Kelly will keep an eye on you or let me arrange a bodyguard to keep you safe."

My eyes widened. "A bodyguard? Yuri, come on! Nobody is going to bother me. I don't have anything they could possibly want."

"You are important to me. People will look at you and see dollar signs. It's an ugly fact that goes along with dating me."

I heard the regret in his voice and placed my other hand over his. "That's okay. I'm willing to deal with it."

Smiling, he lifted my hands and kissed my knuckles. Hand in hand, we rode the rest of the way in silence. When we pulled through a gated entry, I got my first clue that this was an incredibly exclusive enclave. Ivan and Erin lived in a fabulous gated community but this place?

Holy hell. It was jaw-dropping.

The huge mansions were set far back from the main road and accessible down private lanes. Most were hidden by lush trees but a few had visible facades. We turned down a paved road and drove almost two minutes before I got my first look at Yuri's home.

My jaw dropped. The place was massive. "Jesus, Yuri. Do you think you have enough space in that museum?"

He looked chagrined. "It's a little bigger than I'd initially planned."

"I don't even want to imagine what your electricity bill is like in the summer!"

"After seeing Vivian's sticky notes on all the light switches, I'm tempted to invite her over to let her label all of mine too. I bet I could cut twenty percent off my bill if I could get my staff to turn off lights when they leave a room."

Considering the size of the house, a twenty percent cutback would probably be more money than I earned in an entire month. "Do you have a large staff?"

"I haven't hired a full staff yet. There's only Feodor at the house full-time."

"Feodor?"

"He's an older man that I've known since I was a boy. He used to run my Moscow house. I don't spend much time there anymore so I brought him here to take care of this new place. Other than Feodor, there are the bodyguards who live there full-time. Tony and a couple of other drivers on contract come by every morning. I also have a handful of housekeepers and landscapers on contract with a staffing company. Eventually, I need to find the time to sit down and find permanent staff."

"So you're not living here all the time?"

He shook his head. "When I'm in Houston, I spend

most of my time at the penthouse downtown. It's centrally located to my business interests and closer to the airport if I need to leave at a moment's notice."

Hoping I didn't sound too pathetic, I asked, "How often are you in Houston?"

"Typically? Three weeks out of the month. I travel to London and then Moscow the first week of every month to handle business affairs there."

"Oh."

"We'll make it work." He brushed a few wisps of hair from my eyes. The intimate touch made my tummy swoop. "You could always come with me."

I started to turn him down by reminding him that I had to work but then I remembered that I no longer had a job. Other than keeping my blog and social media platform active for the advertising money, I had nothing going for me. "That's a tempting offer."

"Have you ever been to London?"

I shook my head. "The farthest I've traveled is New York on the east coast and Seattle on the west coast."

"Do you have a passport?" When I nodded, he smiled and gave my hand a quick squeeze. "Then you will come with me next week."

Taken aback, I hurriedly protested, "Yuri, I can't just drop everything and fly to London. I mean—that's *expensive*."

His fingertip touched my lips, silencing me gently. "It's my treat."

I tugged his finger away from my mouth. "I don't want this to be a pattern. It's one thing if you buy dinner or take care of the tab for a date but paying for me to travel? It makes me feel...conflicted."

"Why?" He seemed genuinely confused. "It's my money. Why shouldn't I spend it on trips we would enjoy?"

I rubbed my face and tried to find the right way to explain things. "Look, I've *always* paid my own way. Once I turned eighteen, I stopped letting my dad pay for things too. Every single hour of class and every penny of my rent and living expenses have come out of my pocket since then."

His strong fingers curved along my cheek. "And I respect that. I respect the hell out of you for everything you've accomplished and for doing it on your own terms." He nuzzled my neck and peppered ticklish kisses along my sensitive skin. "Let me spoil you, Lena."

How could I say no to that? As if sensing my capitulation, Yuri claimed my mouth in a teasing kiss. He caressed my belly through the thin fabric of my dress. His whispered words buffeted my ear. "Say yes, Kitten. Say that you'll let me spoil you the way you deserve."

My gaze flitted to his. If any other man had offered such a thing, I would have demanded the car stop and climbed out on the side of the road. Yuri's offer came with no strings-attached. He wasn't going to use his money to control me. It occurred to me that he took great pleasure in doing outrageously expensive things for the people he cared about—and I was one of them.

"Yes."

"Good girl." He kissed me long and hard, his tongue darting into my mouth and dancing with mine. Our tender, sensual moment was interrupted by the car rolling to a stop. Reluctantly, he broke our kiss. A flash of uncertainty crossed his face. "There's something I should tell you before we go inside."

My gut clenched. "What is it?"

"I have a dog."

I blinked. "Um—okay."

"No, you don't understand. Sasha is—well—he's big. He was bred to be my four-legged bodyguard. I haven't ever introduced him to a girlfriend so I'm not sure how he's going to react. He's incredibly protective of me so he may be a bit...testy. He barely tolerates Jake and Derek and he hates Nikolai and Ivan. The only people he hasn't tried to bite are Feodor and Dimitri. If I think he can't handle your presence in the house, I'll have him put in his kennel."

Anxiety raced through me. "Maybe I should just stay in the car."

"It's better for him to meet you now. I want him to grow accustomed to you."

Putting an end to the discussion, Yuri opened his door. A moment later, the door on my side opened. Jake offered his hand and helped me out of the backseat. After showing him some hospitality, he'd been nothing but smiles and sweetness with me. "I take it the boss told you about the hell hound?"

His description of Yuri's dog had me glancing nervously at the front door. Yuri held out his hand and I hesitated before walking around the car to join him. He brushed his knuckles across my cheek. "Don't listen to Jake. He's just teasing you."

Looking back at Jake, I wasn't so sure. He didn't look like he was teasing.

With a gentle tug, he led me up the front steps to his door. Before Yuri could grasp the handle, it opened to reveal an elderly man. He didn't seem the least bit surprised to see me standing with Yuri. With a broad smile, he stepped aside. "Welcome home, sir."

Yuri started to make introductions but the most terrifying bark tore through the house. My eyes widened in a panic at the deep, shockingly loud woof. I heard the thumping footfalls on the gleaming hardwood floors before the great beast came into view. Gasping, I stepped back and nearly lost my balance. Only Yuri's tight grip on my wrist kept me from falling.

"Stand still." I wasn't sure if he was talking to me or Feodor because we were both trying to bolt.

Stepping forward, Yuri bellowed at the dog in Russian. His short, sharp commands brought the bear-sized beast to a sliding stop. The dog plopped his big bottom down and sat perfectly still. The ferocious looking monster was almost eye-to-eye with me even sitting.

Keeping me in full view of Sasha, Yuri moved closer to his guard dog and ruffled the spot between its ears. The dog whined and licked his jowls as Yuri spoke softly. I couldn't understand a word he was saying but I prayed it was something along the lines of *don't eat my girlfriend*.

"Lena, come here. It's time for you to meet Sasha." Yuri held out his hand.

I gawked at him and shook my head. "No, thank you."

"Lena." He spoke sternly and wiggled his fingers. Not wanting to look like a total wimp in front of everyone, I mustered my courage and took a tiny step toward him. When I placed my palm against his, he pulled me even closer. Holding my hand, he guided me toward the dog's head. I cringed as the soft fur touched my fingertips but didn't dare jerk back. I didn't want the beast to misinterpret any quick movements.

When the dog pushed against my petting hand, I held my breath. *Please don't eat me.*

Instead, the dog whined and made a happy sound as he nuzzled my stomach and rubbed his huge head all over me. Realizing the dog wasn't going to bite my hand off, I relaxed and continued to gently pet him. "Hello, Sasha."

The dog lifted up its massive paw and smacked my

arm. I gripped his paw for a quick shake and let it drop. When I tried to stop petting him, he pushed against me again, the force of it enough to make me stumble backward. After communicating his desire for me to continue, I didn't dare stop.

"I think he likes me." I smiled at Yuri, my grin one of pure relief and amusement.

"Likes you?" Yuri studied his dog. "I think he's smitten. I've never seen him take to anyone so quickly."

Scratching behind both ears, I said, "You just have very good taste, don't you, Sasha?"

Chuckling, Yuri snapped his fingers and gave the dog an order. Sasha hurried to comply and moved to his master's right side. Yuri slid an arm around my waist. "Come. Let me show you the house."

I glanced back at the car. "My bag—"

"I'll handle it, Miss Cruz," Feodor assured me.

"It's Lena." I extended my hand and shook his, noting the subtle signs of arthritis in his swollen knuckles. "And thank you."

At Yuri's side, I got the grand tour of the place. As he pointed out the architectural details here and there, I realized how much of himself he'd put into building the place. I saw such excitement in his eyes as he showed me the fireplace he'd reclaimed from a Russian dacha and the limestone he'd chosen from a Texas quarry.

"You look bemused, Lena." He leaned against the door frame of the sumptuous library and watched me as I ran my fingers along the deep but empty shelves. "Is the house not to your liking?"

"It's beautiful, Yuri."

"But?" He shot me a teasing smile. "You look as if you expected something different."

"Maybe."

"Maybe?"

"Okay. I did," I finally admitted. "You know how these mega mansions can be with their gold leaf and more marble than a mausoleum. They're often rather gauche."

He feigned offense by touching his chest. "Me? Gauche?"

"No," I said with a laugh. "Pretentious? Yes."

"Ouch!" He chuckled at my playful barb. "Since you haven't seen the upstairs, I think you should reserve your judgment on that account."

"Why? Is your bed made of pure gold?"

His eyes darkened with need. "You'll have to wait and see."

I swallowed hard at the implication. After the way he'd rocked my world in the shower, I didn't know if I'd survive a tumble between his sheets.

He held out his hand. "Dinner?"

I nodded and joined him at the door. "Does Feodor cook?"

"Not tonight," Yuri said. "I wouldn't want him to feel the stress of making everything perfect for you so I made other arrangements."

"Is he seeing someone about his hands?"

Yuri glanced at me in surprise. "You noticed?"

"Of course."

"He's going to the best man in Houston. Feodor says his hands and knees feel better but I try not to let him take on too much. This is supposed to be his retirement."

"Then you should get this place staffed, Yuri. Put him in a managerial position but make sure he's well-supported. You'll have peace of mind and he'll be happy knowing he's looking after your home."

Regret tightened his expression. "You're right. I shouldn't keep putting off the hiring of new staff. My priorities lately—"

"Are out of balance?" I interjected carefully.

Yuri stopped walking and turned to look at me. He gave a reluctant nod of his head. "Very."

Stress radiated from him in waves. I rubbed his arm. "Don't you have an assistant?"

"For the business, yes, but not personally." He made a face and slashed his hand through the air. "I don't want someone I don't know poking around in my personal and home life."

"Well, you can't do it all. A man in your position has a million things on his plate. I can only imagine how many things you've put on hold to spend the day with me." I cupped his jaw and ran my thumb over his bottom lip. "You have to find someone you can lean on, Yuri."

He gripped my hand. I trembled under the intensity of his piercing gaze. "Help me, Lena?"

I reared back with shock. "What? *Me?*"

"You." He ran his finger down my cheek. "It has to be you. I trust you to help me find some balance in my life."

I opened my mouth to decline the offer but then slammed my lips together. What else did I have going on right now? A whole lot of nothing. My blog had always been something I'd updated on the fly and dedicated an hour to in the morning and another two hours or so in the evening. Without a job to fill in my daytime hours, I had a lot of empty time to occupy.

"Okay," I agreed softly. "But," I held up a finger, "I do this my way. I won't have you micro-managing me and standing over my shoulder. If you give me a set of tasks to accomplish, you have to trust that I'll accomplish them efficiently and to your standards without your involvement."

"All right. I can pay—"

I put my hand over his mouth. "No."

"Yes," he replied, his answer muffled my palm.

We both smiled as he tugged my hand away from his face.

"Lena, you can't work for free. That's insulting."

"Here's the thing, Yuri. I have a pretty good feeling that if I'm hanging around your house doing this personal assistant thing, you're probably going to seduce me every chance you get—and I'm going to let you. Taking your money while we're involved would be distasteful. I won't give people a reason to talk about our private business."

He grumbled but didn't disagree with me about inviting gossip. "Let me make you a deal."

"I'm listening."

"Work with me until you find new employment. When you make the move into a new position, we'll settle up with what I owe you for the hours you've worked for me. That way you won't be my paid employee *and* my girlfriend at the same time."

Even though I didn't want to violate my principle of taking money from a man who was also heating up the sheets with me, I recognized that it was fair to be paid for my work. This wasn't a perfect solution but it was elegant enough for me to accept.

Glad the he understood my concerns of mixing money and pleasure, I acquiesced with a nod. "Okay. I can live with that."

"Good." He kissed my forehead. "Tonight, over dinner, we'll draw up a contract so it's entirely legit."

"On a napkin?" I asked playfully.

"Only the very best for you," he replied with a smile.

I rolled my eyes and wound my arm around his. "So where's this dinner you promised me?"

"Probably waiting for us in the dining room," he said

matter-of-factly. "I hired a private chef for the evening."

"Ooh! Fancy!" I gave his arm a little pinch. "A gourmet meal sure beats my offering of cold cereal any day."

"I'm sure Feodor would be delighted to trek down into the cereal cellar to pick out a box of our very best vintage. I hear 2010 was a particularly good year for marshmallows."

"Really?" I giggled at his silliness. "A cereal cellar?"

"Well, I *am* pretentious after all."

"Yes. Extremely," I added with a grin. "And me? What am I?"

Yuri considered me for a moment. His lips pressed against my temple. "Perfectly perfect."

I wasn't so sure about that but I wasn't about to contradict such a lovely compliment. "Thank you. That's sweet."

He wrapped his arm around my shoulders and gathered me close to his side. I kept pace with him as we made our way into a cozy dining room just off the kitchen. It was smaller than the larger formal dining he'd shown me and fully furnished unlike most of the rooms I'd seen.

A moment after we'd taken our seats, Feodor appeared with a decanter of wine. As he filled my glass, he smiled at me. "I placed your things in the guest room, Miss Cruz."

"Okay. Um—thanks."

With a nod, he left the dining room. I glanced across the table at Yuri who sipped his wine and eyed me carefully. "What is it, Lena?"

I dragged my finger along the edge of the table. "The guest room?"

"I didn't dare presume."

I understood what he meant. Whatever happened tonight, it was my choice.

And I had already made my decision.

CHAPTER NINE

After a delicious dinner and delectable dessert course, I found myself curled in the corner of a cushy sofa in Yuri's office. It was the only other room on the first floor that had been furnished and decorated. We'd fallen into a discussion about the European pipeline he wanted to construct. With his long legs stretched out in front of him, he sat on the opposite end of the couch. I still couldn't believe how damn sexy he made a pair of jeans look.

"So that's the problem with the pipeline in a nutshell." He wiped a hand down his face and shook his head. "Every time I think I have the project nailed down, something pops up and there's a setback."

"Is that a problem for the funding?" I asked the question without thinking. "Sorry. It's none of my business."

He shrugged. "The backers of the pipeline are public knowledge. I hold the largest interest, obviously, but there are others—and yes. They're nervous."

"Maybe one of them is sabotaging you. After that

mess in Cyprus and the ongoing recession fears, it's possible one of your backers needs to pull out of the deal. If they want to save face and not have to expose their shaky financials, tanking the pipeline deal is a sneaky way to do it."

His gaze snapped to my face. His expression convinced me he hadn't even considered that yet. "Shit."

He was off the couch in an instant and digging his black phone out of his pocket. I'd seen the white one back at my apartment. The black seemed to be his business phone and the white his personal one. It wasn't the first time I'd worried about the way he had so much to juggle.

"I've been so focused on environmental groups protesting the pipeline and rivals and the political angle that I didn't even *think* about that possibility"

I watched him pace back and forth and talk hurriedly to Anna, the executive assistant who had botched the email about our postponed date. If she was that bad with personal correspondence, I hated to think what else she'd let slip through the cracks in that office.

Because they conducted the conversation in Russian, it was impossible for me to follow. He seemed curt and to the point. It was odd to see him so focused. His demeanor totally changed as he gave his orders. I realized then that the way Yuri was with me was so completely different than he was with others.

As he finished his conversation and set aside his phone, he leaned back against his desk and held my gaze. "What's that look, Kitten?"

My eyebrows arched. "Kitten, huh?"

"Would you prefer sweetheart or perhaps something in my own language?" His lips twitched with amusement. "How about *zaychik moy*?"

I narrowed my gaze. "Do I even want to know what that is?"

"I'm sure Vivian would be thrilled to translate for you."

"No doubt." I rose from my comfy spot and crossed the distance. Resting my hands on his hips, I gazed up at him. "You're different with me. It was strange to see the ultra-focused business version of you pacing back and forth in here."

"I'm relaxed with you. At ease," he said and cupped my face. Our lips met in a gentle kiss. "I would love to stand here and promise that my business dealings won't bleed over into the time we spend together but I won't lie to you. That," he gestured to his black business phone, "comes with me as a package deal."

"I know." I rose on tiptoes to kiss him. "I can handle it." I stroked my hand down his chest. "I wish I could help you with this pipeline thing. It sounds like it could really turn into a tangled mess."

"It might," he conceded. "Your suggestion of sabotage isn't one I'd considered but it's one I'm reluctantly willing to admit might be correct."

"Earlier, when we came in here, you told me that the details of the environmental report were part of a private assessment. Who else would have that information, Yuri? If it's not a backer, it's someone from the *inside*." I traced my thumb along his chin. "I got totally screwed by my crew at 716. Don't let the same thing happen to you."

"I won't."

"Good." Standing there, pressed up against his solid heat, I became intensely aware of how desperately I wanted to feel his naked skin against mine again. Our shower had given me a taste of the exquisite pleasure he offered.

My gaze fell to his phone. "Are you expecting another call from Anna?"

He nodded. "Later."

I picked up his phone and tucked it into the pocket of his jeans. "Then we'll leave this on the bedside table."

Desire darkened his eyes. Without giving me a chance to change my mind, he grasped my hand and dragged me out of the office. I scurried to keep up with him. Excitement fluttered in my belly. I *so* wanted this. I wanted *him*.

We ran upstairs and took a right down a long gallery hall. Startled by the sight of one of Vivian's paintings, I skidded to a halt. He snapped back when I was an arm's length behind him. Glancing at the wall, he smiled. "Oh. That."

"She'll stroke out from pure elation if she sees that you nestled her painting between a Basquiat and a Galán."

Yuri shot me a surprised look. "You know your art."

"I didn't have much of a choice. Until Nikolai moved Vivian into her own studio in that warehouse of his, I was surrounded by her paint and sketches and books for years." I took a step back to get the full effect of the wall. A smile played upon my lips. "She looks good there."

"Not as good as you're going to look in my bed," Yuri said before bending down to sweep me up in his arms.

I squealed with surprise as he tossed me over his shoulder. "What are you doing? Put me down!"

"I've waited long enough. No more stalling." He strode down the long corridor with me over his shoulder like a sack of potatoes. The sound of Sasha barking and bounding upstairs echoed in the still house. I lifted my head to see the massive, furry beast racing toward us. No doubt my squeal had alerted and confused him.

At the end of the hall, Yuri spun around and gave

Sasha a stern command. The dog slid to a stop but whined pitifully when he realized Yuri was leaving him in the hallway. I felt bad for the dog but the idea of having a canine audience wasn't one I particularly relished.

Safe inside his room, Yuri carried me to the bed and dropped me on it. Giggling, I bounced twice before he crawled over me. With his knees on either side of my thighs, he pinned me in place. Our gazes clashed as he loomed over me and interlaced our fingers. He trapped my hands overhead and captured my mouth in a punishing kiss.

Trembling with anticipation, I wound my legs around his waist and surrendered to the erotic swipe of his tongue. His fingertips drifted down my cheek and along the curve of my throat. Yuri shifted his weight so he had unimpeded access to my body. I shuddered as his masterful hands outlined my breasts and followed the slope of my tummy.

Our rapidly exhaled breaths mingled as Yuri unbuckled the thin belt I'd paired with my dress and tugged down the side zipper hidden along my ribcage. When he pulled me into a sitting position, I went willingly. He peeled the dress down to my waist and unhooked my bra.

Already my nipples had formed dark, tight peaks. He palmed my breast and brushed his thumb over my sensitive flesh. "God, you're so beautiful, Yelena. Such silky, warm skin…"

I gasped and fell back to the bed as he suckled my nipple. He eased the sharp arcs of delight caused by his suckling mouth with slow drags of his velvety tongue around my puckered flesh. I ran my fingers through his hair and lightly scratched my nails against his scalp. "Yuri."

He kissed his way down my belly and nipped playfully at my belly button. Grasping my dress, he dragged it down my hips. I answered his silent plea and lifted my bottom. With a couple of pulls, my dress and panties were whisked away and tossed to the floor. I felt a little silly for choosing my sexiest pair of undies when Yuri hadn't even paid them notice.

When he stood and started to undress, I pushed up onto my knees and crawled to the edge of the bed. I shoved his hands out of the way and flicked through the buttons lining his shirt. He toed out of his shoes and yanked off his socks before unzipping his jeans. I licked my lips as he stepped out of his jeans and boxers. That thick cock jutted forth so proudly.

He shrugged out of his shirt and let me run my greedy little hands all over his sexy chest. I couldn't get enough of his ripped physique. "You're so damn fine."

He laughed and kissed me, sliding his arms around me and taking me down to the mattress again. "No need for the compliments, Kitten. I'm already out of my pants."

I giggled at his lighthearted remark and then moaned with need as his wicked mouth found that spot on the side of my neck that made my toes curl and my tummy clench. He caressed my naked body with such reverence. His big hands teased and squeezed and stroked until I was so hot I felt sure that any moment I would spontaneously combust.

Only then did he slowly, teasingly, walk his fingers down my belly. Our gazes held as he cupped my bare mound. He nuzzled our noses together and nipped at my lower lip. "Spread your legs for me."

I inhaled a shaky breath but complied with his order. He brushed his fingers up and down the seam of my pussy. I ached so badly down there. My clit throbbed mercilessly. I could feel the evidence of my arousal seeping from my core.

Even so desperately aroused, I was clearheaded enough to think about consequences. Benny and Dimitri's impending parenthood was proof enough of what happened when a couple got caught up in the heat of the moment. For those two lovebirds, the unexpected surprise of a baby was a welcome one but for me? I wasn't ready for that responsibility.

I touched Yuri's jaw. "I'm on the pill but I won't have sex without a condom. Do you have protection?"

He kissed me long and hard and deep. "I would never put you at risk. I've got it covered."

"Thank you."

With the necessities out of the way, I closed my eyes and enjoyed the erotic caress of Yuri's hand between my thighs. He kissed my neck and cheek before sliding down a little lower in the bed so he could use his mouth to sensually torment my breasts. While he traced my nipples with his tongue, he parted the tender folds of my pussy and explored me with his fingers.

Head thrown back, I tried to calm my racing heart but it was impossible. Yuri's talented fingers discovered my pulsing clitoris. Every tug of his lips around my nipple was punctuated by the gentle pressure of his finger swirling over the throbbing pink pearl. I curled my hands into the fluffy white comforter and tightly gripped the fabric. His fingertip alternated between those lazy circles and a side-to-side motion until I was panting and pleading.

"Please, Yuri." I arched off the bed and into the heat of him. "Please."

"Soon," he whispered and abandoned his sensual torment of my nipples. Ruddy and swollen, they throbbed without his soothing tongue. I cupped my breast, supporting the weight of my aching flesh, but it wasn't the same as having Yuri's strong, masterful hands on me.

He zigzagged down my body, peppering ticklish kisses along my ultra-sensitive skin. I knew exactly where he was headed and dragged short, almost panicked breaths into my lungs. Sliding off the bed, he knelt at the edge and grasped my waist. Showing his impressive strength, Yuri pulled me toward him and used those big hands of his to spread my thighs wide open.

I trembled violently inside as he gazed at my pussy. He murmured something in Russian, his voice so incredibly husky, and then dipped his tongue between my dusky lips. I cried out and clawed at the bedding. The wild sensation threatened to make me scream so I stifled my moan with a hand pressed tightly to my mouth.

Yuri's head popped up at the stifled sound. He clasped my arm and tugged my hand away from my mouth. "Don't you dare hold back with me. I want to hear it all." He nuzzled his face against my hot pussy. I could hear the grin in his voice as he added, "Stroke my ego."

When he lapped at my exposed clit, I decided to do exactly as ordered and let loose a loud groan. Yuri pushed my labia apart with his fingers and coaxed my clit from beneath it protective hood. His skilled tongue fluttered over the little nub. My hips started to move as the wild urgings took hold.

I wanted to come so badly. Submitting myself totally to Yuri, I closed my eyes and concentrated on the feel of his tongue gliding over me. I reached down and threaded my fingers through his thick hair. His free hand moved across mine. The intimacy of the moment hit me hard.

Yuri hummed against my clit. The delicious vibrations rattled through me. The hand that had been clutching mine drifted away. Two fingers speared me and I gasped at the wonderful intrusion. He worked them in and out of my soaking channel at a leisurely pace, awakening all the nerve-endings in their path.

Overcome with ecstasy, I writhed atop his bed as his tongue found the perfect rhythm. He drove me crazy with his talented mouth and those thrusting fingers. Rocking my hips, I climbed the heights of ecstasy. My tummy fluttered and clenched. "Yuri. Oh. *Yuri*!"

I shouted his name as the rapturous waves of my climax tore through me. He groaned with excitement and forced my thighs even wider apart with his broad shoulders. Totally exposed and open to him, I had no choice but to surrender completely to the wicked ministrations of his mouth. He feverishly flicked my clit until I screamed a second time.

Head throbbing and body pulsing with the sheer delight of two incredibly powerful orgasms, I sagged against the bed. It wasn't until I heard the sound of a bedside drawer opening and closing that I also became aware of the pitiful, high-pitched whine Sasha made on the other side of the door.

"Ignore it," Yuri said as he tossed a strip of condoms onto the bed and climbed on top of me. "He isn't used to the sounds of lovemaking." With a mischievous grin, he kissed me. "I'm sure by the end of the week he'll have acclimated to the sound of you shrieking with pleasure."

My cheeks grew hot. "Sorry."

"Kitten, don't you dare apologize for that." He grabbed my hand and dragged it down between our bodies. "Feel how hard you've made me."

I gulped as I clasped his stiff erection. Hard was an understatement. I stroked my hand down the rigid length of him. His eyelids drifted together and his jaw clenched as I teased him with my hand. Wanting to show him the same pleasure he'd just given me, I asked, "Do you want me to suck you?"

His eyes flashed open. He traced my lower lip with his thumb. "I can't even tell you how many nights I've fantasized about you kneeling at my feet and taking my cock between these silky, pouty lips."

His heady admission made my tummy wobble. The idea that Yuri had been fantasizing about me in the same way I'd been dreaming about him made it all so much hotter. I nipped at his thumb. "Show me how you want me."

Yuri rolled off me and stood next to the bed. He pointed to the spot in front of him. "Kneel there."

I scampered off the bed like an overeager puppy and knelt at his feet. I'd never really been enthusiastic about giving a blowjob—it was simply part of the quid pro quo of relationships—but I couldn't wait to get my mouth on Yuri.

"Hands behind your back," he said in a voice tight with desire.

Apprehensive, I glanced up at him. He must have read the worry on my face. He cupped my cheek. "I wouldn't dare do that to you."

Reassured that he wasn't going to make this into something ugly, I clasped my hands behind my back. I noticed the way my new position thrust my breasts forward. Yuri gazed down at me with such appreciation. He swept his palms down my neck and across my breasts before taking his cock in hand and rubbing it from the tip to the base.

When I opened my mouth without being asked, he smiled down at me. Stepping forward, he brushed the head of his dick against my lips. I flicked my tongue out and swiped at him. I heard air hissing between his teeth as I sucked him gently, just the tip of him, and swirled my tongue along the sensitive underside of his cock.

He groaned and sifted his long fingers through my hair. Gathering a handful in one hand, he started to slowly pump his hips. I gazed up at him and was shocked to see such utter adoration etched into his face.

Relishing the way he looked at me, I bobbed up and down on his shaft. I painted his skin with my tongue and sucked him deeper and harder. The subtle rock of his hips pushed his cock against my tongue. Humming around him, I took more of him into my mouth.

He grazed his fingertips along my jaw. "Do you want me inside you now?"

I let his hard cock slip free from my mouth. "Yes."

"I can't promise that I will be gentle. I'm on the edge, Lena."

I sucked him into my mouth again and held his gaze as I took him long and slow and deep. When I released him, he shuddered. Nestling my cheek to his thigh, I whispered, "I don't need gentle tonight. I just need you."

He reached for my hand and helped me stand. With his fingers still tangled in my hair, Yuri claimed my lips in a possessive kiss. I could feel his trapped cock throbbing against my belly as he plundered my mouth. When he guided me down to the bed, I went willingly.

He knelt on the edge of the mattress and ripped open a condom packet. After he sheathed himself, Yuri moved between my open thighs. Planting his hands on either side of my head, he dipped down to kiss me. I wiggled my bottom until our bodies were perfectly aligned. With one rough thrust, Yuri entered me.

"Ah!" Head tipped back, I bared my neck to him as he rocked in and out of my slick channel. I was so damn wet and excited that it eased the sudden thrust of his huge cock. He took advantage of my bared neck and gave me a love bite that drew a yelp from my lips. My pussy clenched around his massive shaft. The tight squeeze amplified everything I felt down there.

Sweeping the hair from my eyes, Yuri captured my gaze. No man had ever looked at me like that. His ravenous gaze seared my skin. He cupped my face as he drove into me. The intimacy of our coupling was raw and powerful. It occurred to me that until this moment I'd only been *fucked*.

But this? *This* was lovemaking.

And it was splendorous.

I gripped his shoulders and wrapped my legs around his waist. Yuri's powerful strokes hit all the right spots. I shivered beneath him. When he shifted the angle of his penetration, I saw the proverbial stars. My nails dug into his tanned skin and I cried out as the first euphoric waves hit me.

"Come with me," he urged and kissed my neck. "I want to feel your tight pussy milking me."

I loved the way he spoke such dirty words with that sinfully sexy mouth. Yuri's pace quickened. Snapping his hips, he slammed his cock deeper and faster. When he reached between us to rub my clit, I gasped. "Yuri!"

"Come, Yelena." His lips touched mine. "Come with me."

And I did. There was nothing I could deny this man. I came so hard I saw spots dancing before my eyes. The blissful bursts started in my core and spread through my belly and up into my chest. I cried out his name again and again, no longer caring who heard me or how my loud shrieks ricocheted off the walls and ceiling.

Yuri hammered into me one last time. His forehead

touched mine as he shuddered violently. I could feel his cock, thicker and even harder, throbbing inside me as he climaxed. My name left his lips on a pleasured sigh.

As we clung together and shared tender kisses, poor Sasha lost his doggy mind outside in the hallway. His outrageously loud barks rattled the walls. When he started to scratch and throw his weighty body against the door, Yuri grunted with annoyance and reluctantly pulled away from me. He pecked my cheek and gestured to the door. "I'm sorry."

Laughing, I shook my head and smiled. "It's fine. He doesn't understand."

Yuri grumbled something in Russian as he stood. I expected him to head for the door but he made his way toward the master bathroom. By now, Sasha made such a terrible ruckus I worried the bodyguards would come to investigate. "Do you want me to let him in, Yuri?"

He paused at the entrance of his bathroom and glanced back at me. "No. He needs to learn our routine."

"But the door—"

"Can be replaced," he said matter-of-factly and disappeared into the bathroom.

Sitting up against the mound of fluffy pillows, I slipped under the covers and tugged them over my lap. The way Yuri spoke of Sasha learning our routine convinced me that he was in this relationship for the long-haul. I wasn't simply a diversion to him.

The idea that he saw a future with me filled me with such giddiness and hope. It had been a long time since I'd felt excitement like this. Right now, with Yuri, anything was possible.

When he emerged from the bathroom, he remained stark naked. Sweat glistened on his gorgeous body. I slipped out of bed to take care of necessities. Yuri finally opened the door—and Sasha bounded into the room like a bolt of furry lightning.

"Sasha!" Yuri shouted the beast's name as he narrowly escaped a nasty fall. Sasha swiped him again with his big tail and pushed Yuri into the door. "Sasha!"

When the dog caught sight of me, he rushed toward me. I put up my hands, certain he was going to bowl me over, but Sasha shocked me by stopping in time. He nuzzled my belly with his wet nose and walked fast circles around me as if trying to assure himself I wasn't injured.

Yuri gave a stern command and Sasha finally obeyed. He sat down right at my feet and leaned his big head against my ribcage. Bemused, I glanced at Yuri. "May I pet him? Does that send the wrong signal?"

Yuri shut his bedroom door and strode toward us. His lips settled into an irritated line. "I'm not thrilled by the way he ignored my commands. It's dangerous for him to be so excited and unresponsive. He could have hurt you."

"I thought he was going to hurt you." I reached out and touched his shoulder. "Are you okay? He slammed you into that door pretty hard."

He waved his hand. "I'm fine. You can pet him. I suppose I shouldn't be angry with him for wanting to protect you." Yuri ran his fingers through Sasha's fur. As if murmuring to himself, he said, "He must be able to sense how much I care for you."

My gaze flicked to Yuri's face but he was focused on Sasha's head. I scratched between the dog's ears. My fingers grazed Yuri's and we smiled at one another. "Maybe you should teach me the commands tomorrow. I know they're in Russian but I'm sure I can learn them."

"I don't think you'll have a choice. If you're going to be working here as my assistant, you're going to be alone with Sasha and Feodor. You'll need to be able to get him under control or I'll have to kennel him while I'm away since he gets so overly excited with you."

Even though I hated the idea of Sasha being in a kennel, I recognized that he was bred to tear intruders to bits. If someone innocent like a package delivery guy got too close, I didn't know what Sasha might do. Until I was confident in my ability to keep him calm and under my command, I didn't dare put other people or him at risk.

When I stepped toward the bathroom, Sasha whined and moved in front of me. With a nudge of his head, he pushed me against Yuri. Chuckling, he slid his arms around me and kissed my neck. "I like the way he thinks."

"Funny," I said and patted his arm.

"Sasha." Yuri snapped his fingers. He gave another Russian command. I watched the dog's face. He stared at me and gave a moment's hesitation before finally obeying his master and trudging to the big, comfy bed in the corner. He flopped down and heaved a dramatic sigh.

Stifling a smile, I ducked into the bathroom. I couldn't believe how much personality Sasha possessed. When I emerged a few minutes later, Yuri had already climbed into bed and turned off all the lights except for the one on his side of the bed. He patted the empty space next to him. I crawled onto the bed and slipped into his waiting arms.

As we kissed, I heard the jingle of Sasha's tags and the strangest dragging sound. Breaking away from our goodnight kiss, we glanced toward the dog. I couldn't help but laugh at the sight of Sasha dragging his fluffy bed across the room. He pulled it all the way to my side of the bed before stopping.

"My God," Yuri said with a groan. "He is really laying it on thick!"

Giggling, I rolled onto my belly and reached down to

ruffle his fur. "Don't listen to him Sasha. He's just jealous of your mad skills with the ladies."

Laughing, Yuri snuggled up against my back and caressed my naked skin. "We'll see how much you enjoy those mad skills of his when he starts to snore."

"Do you snore, Sasha?" I scratched under his chin and received a happy yowl from the bear-sized beast.

"Like a chainsaw," Yuri said and kissed my shoulder.

When Sasha settled down, I turned into Yuri's comforting warmth and draped my leg across his. There was so much I wanted to discuss with him but this wasn't the time. Right now, I was content to drift off in his protective embrace.

Lulled to sleep by the soothing repetition of his fingers combing through my hair, I had no idea that I was enjoying my last few moments of blissful ignorance.

CHAPTER TEN

Yuri came awake to Sasha's low growl. Pulled from a deep sleep, he blinked rapidly and tried to focus. Those years of training in Special Forces never really left him. In the space of a few heartbeats, he was totally alert.

Moonlight silhouetted Sasha's hulking frame near the door. In all the years he'd had his beloved guard dog, he'd never seen Sasha react in that way. That response meant one thing—an intruder.

Yuri didn't like to doubt Sasha but after his reaction earlier with Lena he wasn't sure if he could accept the dog's response with confidence. It was possible he was acting this way because he heard a mouse or some other nocturnal animal moving around in the big, empty house.

Whether he was on edge because of his newfound infatuation with Lena or because there was real danger, Yuri couldn't say. With her sleeping peacefully next to him, he wasn't about to take a chance with her safety.

He reached over and slid his hand under the bedside table. Two powerful magnets kept a pistol and loaded magazine concealed from prying eyes. Sitting up, he slammed the magazine into place and racked the slide. The sharp sound woke Lena. Before she could say anything, he put his hand over her mouth and brought his lips close to her ear. "Sasha hears something. Stay put."

He felt her head move up and down as she silently acknowledged her understanding. After a quick kiss to her forehead, he slid out of bed and found his jeans on the floor. Once they were zipped, he moved with stealth to the door. Sasha didn't have to be commanded. He did exactly as he'd been trained and assumed a ready position at Yuri's side.

Holding his breath, Yuri listened intently. At first, he heard nothing—but then the faintest tap of footsteps against the solid wood planks hit his eardrums. Jake and Derek often did a walk-through during their night shifts but Sasha never reacted like this. After the way Sasha had tossed him into the door to check on Lena, Yuri couldn't be absolutely sure his dog wasn't protesting the close presence of another male, even a friendly one.

Whispering to Sasha, he gave a firm command and sent him back to Lena at the bed. The dog didn't hesitate. He trotted to her, ready to guard the woman he'd claimed with his life.

Yuri flipped off the safety on his gun and cracked the door. The floor to ceiling windows at the end of the gallery hall illuminated the space. Movement near the paintings caught his attention. At first, he couldn't believe what he was seeing.

A man dressed in black lifted one of his paintings from the wall. The alarm sensors attached to the wall and the frame should have activated but there was no screeching noise. It occurred to Yuri that this thief had managed to bypass the alarm system without interrupting the electricity running through the rest of the house.

Derek and Jake wouldn't have been alerted to the presence of a prowler yet.

Stepping into the hall, Yuri used the shadows to his benefit. Aiming his pistol, he cleared his throat. "Put the painting against the wall and your hands on your head. One stupid move and I'll have no choice but to fire."

Everything happened so quickly after he issued his warning. The idiot threw the painting and the sound of it clattering against the floor startled Sasha. In a heartbeat, the dog raced across the bedroom and into the hall. Before Yuri could call him off, Sasha had the intruder by the arm. A gut-wrenching scream echoed in the stillness of the house. Sasha flung the man side-to-side like a ragdoll.

"No!" The intruder screamed. "NO! Stop! Stop!"

"Oh my God! Yuri, make him stop!" Lena shoved by him and rushed down the hall. "Make him stop!"

Her shriek further agitated Sasha who must have bitten down harder because the man let loose a guttural scream.

"Yuri!" Lena screeched at him. "Make Sasha stop! It's my cousin!"

Her words hit him like a slap to the face. *Her cousin?* "Sasha! *Lyezhat!*"

The dog let loose instantly and the man stumbled backward and flat onto his ass. Sobbing, he held his arm to his chest and cursed a blue streak in Spanish. "My arm! That dog ripped off my fucking arm!"

When Lena tried to get close, Sasha barked at her but Lena stood her ground. "NO!"

Cowed, Sasha whined but didn't try to interfere as Lena crouched down next to the man she'd claimed as her cousin. In a stupor, Yuri flicked the safety on his pistol and tucked it into the back of his jeans. He called off Sasha and forced him to the opposite end of the hall.

"Yuri, we need light. Hurry. *Please.*"

Even though he wanted to demand answers, he found the nearest light switch. Thankfully it worked. Whatever this thief had done to bypass the alarm system hadn't affected the lights.

Wearing only his shirt, Lena knelt next to the bleeding thief. She tugged the black ski mask off his head to reveal his face. The two clearly recognized one another. Her gaze fell to the man's mangled arm and she squeaked. Eyes wide, she paled with fear. "Yuri, we need towels and an ambulance."

"Like hell," he interjected meanly. "He tried to steal from me. He's getting cuffs and a perp walk."

"Yuri!"

"Don't *Yuri* me, Lena." He ran a hand through his hair and tried to get a hold on his wildly vacillating emotions. Betrayal gnawed at him. "What the hell is he doing here?"

She glared at him. "How the hell should I know?"

He wanted to believe that this was a coincidence but it was too neat. "The first night we sleep together your cousin tries to steal from me. How do you explain that?"

Her expression hardened. Those dark eyes glittered with fury. "What are you saying, Yuri? If you want to accuse me of something, man up and fucking do it!"

He caught the hitch in her voice. She blinked rapidly before turning her attention to her wounded cousin. His chest ached at the realization he'd hurt her with his angry outburst. He had no proof and shouldn't have gone there.

Racing footfalls echoed downstairs. "Boss! Someone scrambled the alarm. I've got Derek on it but we heard the commotion! You okay?"

"Lena and I are fine. The intruder...not so much."

Jake appeared on the top step. He took in the scene

with a quick scan. "Who the hell is this?"

Yuri's jaw clenched. He gestured to Lena. "Ask her."

Shock filtered across his bodyguard's face. "Lena?"

She gulped nervously and finally confessed, "He's my cousin. His name is Tommy Cruz."

White as a sheet, Tommy glanced from face to face. He licked his lips and kept his good hand pressed to his bleeding arm. He made no attempt to explain his presence.

"Jesus," Jake said with a shake of a head. "We're going to need an ambulance. I'll call 9-1-1."

"No!" Tommy finally spoke. "No. Please. If you get the cops involved, they'll kill him."

Yuri's gut clenched. "Kill who?"

Tommy swallowed and turned a regretful gaze Lena's way. "Your dad. They have your dad."

Her face slackened and she fell back hard on her bottom. "Who?"

"The Guzman Cartel," Tommy answered in a shaky voice. "I'm sorry, Lena. I'm so sorry. It's all my fault."

"What did you do?" Her broken voice gnawed at Yuri. "Tell me!"

With a tearful exhalation, Tommy explained, "There was this painting and I thought I was doing the right thing. I did, Lena. I really did. It was *so* much money. The *feria*—I couldn't turn it down, you know? I fenced it—but there was a bounty on it. It belonged to Lorenzo Guzman. I didn't know." He started to sob pathetically. "Your dad was on the wrong side of the border unloading some inventory and they grabbed him."

"You stupid jerk!" She smacked her cousin hard. Yuri winced at the loud crack of her palm against his cheek. "It's always money with you! *Always*! You greedy bastard! If anything happens to my dad, you're going to wish

Sasha had finished you."

Feeling the situation spiral out of control, Yuri stepped forward. "Jake, please go back to the staff quarters. Keep Derek there. I'll handle this."

"But, sir, I—"

"No." Yuri cut him off with a slash of his hand. "What you've heard doesn't leave this room, understood? Under no circumstances are you to contact Dimitri. No one else gets dragged into this mess."

Jake's lips settled into a grim line. "Okay, Boss."

He didn't like it but he would do as told.

As Jake headed for the stairs, Yuri added, "There will be another car or two arriving within the next hour. Pay no attention to them."

When Jake was out of earshot, Yuri addressed Lena. "Go get some towels from my bathroom." He touched his pocket but it was empty. "Find my white phone. It's probably on the floor."

Lena held his gaze before finally nodding and pushing off the floor. As she passed him, he grasped her hand and dragged her close. Cupping her face, he kissed her tenderly. Later, in private, he would apologize for jumping to conclusions. She seemed to understand and returned his kiss with the gentle affection he'd come to expect from her.

Alone with Tommy, he fixed him with a glare. "I'm only going to say this once so listen carefully. If you lie to me and it causes Lena or her father to be hurt, I will make sure that the rest of your miserable life is excruciatingly painful. *Me entiendes?*"

Tommy nodded. "Yep."

When Lena reappeared, she pushed his phone into his hand and rushed to Tommy's side with the towels. She wrapped them tightly around his injured arm but she was anything but gentle with her cousin. Yuri dialed the only man who could help him.

"Do you know what fucking time it is?" Nikolai grouched at him.

"I need your help." He caught Tommy glancing at him. No doubt the conversation the younger man couldn't understand left him uneasy. *Good*, he thought angrily. He wanted the little prick to sweat.

The sound of rustling fabric came across the speaker. "What's happened?"

"Not over the phone," Yuri replied. "I need you here. At the house," he added. "And bring Kostya." Without saying the words, he'd told Nikolai how serious this was.

"Twenty minutes," Nikolai said and hung up the phone.

As he pocketed his phone, Yuri grew aware of Sasha's continued whining. The dog had blood matted around his mouth. The sight of it made his gut churn. Even though he'd bought the dog specifically for protection, he'd never really imagined Sasha would ever have to bite anyone.

Glancing at Lena, he said, "Nikolai will be here soon. Keep that arm wrapped. We'll get him medical attention as soon as I have all the answers I need."

"Okay."

"Sasha." The dog clambered to his feet and followed him through the master bedroom and into the bathroom. He grabbed a wash cloth, got it wet and soapy and made quick work of cleaning the dog's face. Later, when he had more time, he would brush his teeth. For now, this would have to do.

With Sasha clean, Yuri led him to his bedding and gave him a stay command. Sasha whined, no doubt because he wanted to keep Lena in full view, but obeyed nonetheless. Yuri shut the door, closing the dog safely inside. He didn't want to take any chances with Nikolai and Kostya coming.

Out in the hallway, he discovered Feodor kneeling next to Lena. It wasn't until that moment that Yuri realized how scandalously underdressed she was. She had his shirt tucked around her thighs but he doubted she had anything at all on under the thin cotton.

Crouching down behind her, he rubbed her back. "You should get dressed. It's going to be a long night."

She didn't argue with him. She took a step away from him but then hesitated. It finally occurred to him that she had no idea which guest room Feodor had given her. The older man gestured to the door right next to Yuri's master suite.

After she entered the room, he caught Feodor's questioning gaze. With a shake of his head, he silently communicated that this wasn't the right time. Feodor didn't push. Instead, he said, "We should take him downstairs."

Yuri agreed and helped secure the towels firmly around Tommy's bleeding arm. The skinny bastard hissed in pain as they got him to his feet but Yuri didn't feel any compassion. If the Guzman Cartel, one of the most notoriously violent gangs south of the border, had Lena's father in their custody, he was probably feeling a great deal more pain than this.

They were halfway down the stairs when Lena caught up with them. She'd thrown on a pair of hot pink shorts and gathered her hair in a high ponytail. An expression of fear and worry twisted her beautiful features. Yuri's heart ached for her. He could only imagine what she was feeling right now.

Down in the kitchen, Feodor draped a tablecloth over a chair and put another on the floor to protect it from any dripping blood. Tommy sat down and anxiously eyed them as they waited for Nikolai to arrive.

Clearly needing to feel useful, Lena asked Feodor, "Where do you keep the cleaning supplies? I'll tackle that mess upstairs."

"Leave it," Yuri said with a wave of his hand.

"But—"

"Nikolai's man will take care of it, Lena."

Her eyes widened slightly. Whether she knew of Kostya or not, he couldn't say. It was likely Benny had spoken of him but he couldn't be sure. Either way, she seemed to understand what he meant.

The doorbell chimed loudly. Yuri shook his head as Feodor shuffled toward the arched kitchen doorway. "I've got it."

He crossed the house and unlocked the reinforced double doors. Smoking a cigarette, Nikolai stood on the top step. He'd come alone in his sleek black car but Kostya was pulling into the driveway behind him.

Nikolai took his final drag and lifted his shoe to snuff out the cigarette. He pocketed the butt instead of tossing it carelessly into Yuri's landscaping. "So?"

"It's bad." Yuri watched Kostya climb out of his SUV. Raising his voice, he said, "Bring your cleaning bag. There's a lot of blood."

"Disposal?" Nikolai asked as he trailed him into the house.

Yuri shook his head. "He's still alive. He needs a doctor."

Nikolai frowned. "Is it one of your bodyguards? Was there a botched hit?"

"No." Sadly, he said, "That would actually make this whole situation so much simpler. No—it's Lena's cousin."

Nikolai's eyes narrowed. "The fence?"

Yuri shrugged. "I don't know. He was trying to steal from me."

"Why? Lena's father and the nephew deal with high-end fencing. I've never known them to dabble in the B-and-E end of things. Joe Cruz is extremely careful."

"Apparently he wasn't careful enough. Hiring idiot nephews to work for you appears to have its drawbacks. "

Kostya appeared in his scrubs and looked like a surgeon. He had his red bags in hand. "Where am I going?"

Yuri motioned to the grand staircase. "Top of the stairs. You can't miss it. And don't open the bedroom doors. I've got Sasha closed in and he's incredibly agitated tonight."

Kostya nodded and headed upstairs to do what he did best.

With a flick of his fingers, Yuri indicated Nikolai should follow him to the kitchen. His voice lowered, he admitted, "I'm out of my depth here. This is cartel shit and I don't know how to help her."

"Her? You mean Lena?"

"Her father is being held by the Guzman Cartel."

Nikolai wiped a hand down his face. The heavy ink on his fingers and the backs of his hands drew Yuri's gaze. With an irritated sigh, Nikolai said, "I can't promise anything, Yuri. I need the facts first. Then I'll do what I can."

Side by side, they entered the kitchen. Tommy took one look at Nikolai and jumped off the chair. Stumbling backward, he knocked over two chairs and held up his uninjured arm. "No. No. No." He shot a pleading look at Lena. "Don't let them kill me."

"They're not going to kill you!" Swallowing nervously, she glanced at Nikolai. "You're not, right?"

Showing his dark sense of humor, Nikolai chuckled. "No, Lena." He flicked his attention to Tommy. "Not tonight, at least."

Her cousin went ghostly white. "Look, I didn't have a choice. I needed that painting."

Yuri held up a hand. "Sit. Then start from the beginning."

Tommy did as instructed. Gulping, he licked his lips and told the whole sordid tale. "We had these paintings, right? Like—we were holding onto them until the heat died down so we could fence them. They were supposed to be Tio Joe's retirement. He's getting out of the game and these paintings were *mega* cash."

"Retiring?" Lena sounded shocked. "When did he decide that?"

"A few months back," Tommy said. "He didn't want to tell you until it was a done deal. He said this was going to be a promise he wasn't going to break."

Yuri witnessed the pain flashing across her face. He thought of the way he'd stood her up at the restaurant. Her reaction made so much more sense. He vowed then and there he was never going to break another promise to her.

"So Tio went down to Matamoros to unload a shipment of shit that we've had accumulating in the warehouse," Tommy continued. "While he was gone, I got this call about one of the paintings. This chick was offering big bucks for it, way more than Tio thought he'd get for it through his connection in New York. I wanted to surprise him. I wanted to show him I was serious about taking over the business and producing a profit. I made the deal, got the cash drop and left the painting in one of the empty warehouses near that old gas plant where your dad likes to make transactions."

Lena cursed angrily and rubbed her eyes. "You fenced a hot painting to some chick in a warehouse and it never occurred to you that it was a bad fucking idea?"

Tommy grimaced. "I know. It was stupid."

"Yeah, it was, Tommy. You know the rules. You only fence art to another fence. Layers of protection, Tommy. That's the only thing that keeps you safe."

Yuri stared at Lena. He'd known she was street smart but apparently she possessed a wealth of criminal knowledge.

Feeling his stare, she rolled her eyes. "Let's just say dinnertime conversations around my house didn't revolve around the weather or the upcoming elections."

"Clearly," he muttered and turned back to Tommy. "This painting you fenced? How did a cartel painting get into your hands?"

Tommy shrugged. "I don't know. We don't touch the cartel business. Like *at all*. That shit is crazy dangerous. I guess the fence who sold to Tio Joe lied about the painting's provenance."

"Obviously," Lena grumbled. "But why come here tonight? Why try to steal one of Yuri's paintings?"

"The one I sold was a Galán. I tried to get a hold of the buyer but her phone was a burner. It's dead. So I went online and tried to find out everything I could about the painter. I read that the last one sold at an auction was sold to him." He gestured to Yuri with a tip of his chin. "A record price, too. So I figured maybe they would take this painting as a fair trade for your dad's life."

"Figured?" Yuri asked. "You don't know for sure?"

Tommy shook his head. "They won't let me talk to him. They've shut me out."

"I talked to him on Sunday morning." Lena spoke so softly Yuri barely heard her. She glanced up at him with shimmering, watery eyes. "He called and it was so early. I thought he sounded strange but it never occurred to me that he was in trouble."

"What did he say?" Nikolai wondered. "Maybe he was trying to give you a message."

She shook her head. "He told me he loved me and asked me if I had my gun close. That was it."

"He was trying to warn you," Nikolai replied.

"Yes." She made another face. "God, I'm so stupid. The other night, at 716, I busted a dealer called Chains in one of the back rooms. He told me that Tommy had screwed up a job but I didn't ask which one because I didn't care."

Yuri heard the anguish in her voice. He pulled her close and kissed her temple. "It's okay, Lena. I'll fix this."

Hope filled her gaze but she shook her head. "You can't fix this. These people? The cartel? They are not going to simply trade my father for a painting."

"No," Yuri agreed. "I'm sure they'll want more."

"Yuri," she said softly, "you can't—"

He silenced her with a kiss. "I can, and I will."

"But—"

He kissed her again, putting an end to the protests. "Go upstairs and wait for me. I'll handle this."

She glanced at Tommy. Even though she was angry with him, her concern for her cousin won. "You won't hurt him?"

"No. I think Sasha taught him a lesson." He pressed his lips to her forehead. "Go."

With a nod, she pulled out of his embrace and left the kitchen. Without needing to be asked, Feodor followed her. He didn't worry about the older man repeating anything he'd heard. He trusted Feodor with his life.

When they were alone with Tommy, Nikolai asked,

"What do you want me to do with him?"

Lena's cousin looked like he was about to piss his pants. Although he rather enjoyed making him squirm, he showed mercy on the would-be thief. "Get him patched up and stow him in a safe place. I want him under lock and key until this is over and no phone or internet access. I don't trust him. He might throw my Lena to the wolves to save his own ass."

"I wouldn't! I promise. I won't hurt her."

"You've already hurt her."

Nikolai gestured for him to come closer. Turning his back on Tommy, Nikolai slipped into their mother tongue. "Look, Guzman is going to want that painting back. For a high-end item like that, I'd typically go to Joe Cruz for information. Unfortunately…"

"I can handle that end of things. I have a friend who knows everyone in the art world. He's the one who helped me start my collection."

"The Dane?"

Yuri nodded. "If anyone can find a hot Galán, it will be Niels."

"Good luck on that front." Nikolai glanced back at Tommy. "You understand that this could get messy. That shit that Ivan went through to save Erin will look like child's play by the time this is over." Nikolai slashed his fingers across his throat. "They're probably going to want a head for the original theft of the painting."

Yuri felt Tommy's intense stare but didn't give the man the satisfaction of acknowledgment. "Let's hope it doesn't get that far."

"And if it does?"

"It won't."

Nikolai's jaw tensed. "You've been in this glamorous world of yours so long you've forgotten what it's like down here in the rotten shit with the rest of us."

Yuri rubbed the back of his neck. He bristled at Nikolai's assertion that he'd gotten soft but maybe his dearest friend was right. "Look, one thing this *glamorous* world has taught me is that *everyone* has a price—even a man like Lorenzo Guzman."

"But are you willing to pay it? This won't come cheaply."

Lena's smiling face flashed before his eyes. "I'll do it whatever it takes to protect her and to save her father."

Nikolai studied him. "I'll see if I can arrange a meeting. It might be difficult with my history."

Yuri frowned. "Your history?" And then it hit him. "Shit! Vivian's father?"

Nikolai nodded. "That outlaw motorcycle club he rides with runs protection, guns and drugs for the Guzman Cartel."

"Hell!"

"It's probably going to add a considerable premium to the cost of doing business with them."

"It's fine. I'll cover it." Yuri considered what his terms should be. "I want proof of life and a daily phone call between Lena and her father until we get this mess sorted out to my satisfaction. Let them know I want him in one piece and as unharmed as possible." He considered the mayhem and barbarism so often in the papers and on the news. "No beatings, no starvation, no torture."

"Yeah. Okay."

Yuri grasped Nikolai's shoulder. "Thank you. I know how much you're risking by helping me."

"You've risked more for me. I'm happy to do this for you."

Yuri was surprised Nikolai had brought up the ugly episode from their childhood. It was a thing none of them ever discussed. For Nikolai to bring it up now...

Kostya entered the kitchen with his heavy bags slung over his shoulder. The knees of his scrubs were stained red. "It's done." His gaze jumped to Tommy. "Should I take care of him now?"

Yuri's lips twitched at the horrified expression on Tommy's face. "Yes. Get him to the doctor. I'll settle up the account tomorrow."

Kostya crossed the kitchen for a better look at Tommy. He peeked under the towel and winced. "The doctor is going to charge more for that. Do you want to pay the extra fee for anesthesia?"

Tommy looked like he was going to pass out at the very idea of going through the surgery required to put his arm back together without any pain relief. Yuri showed some pity and nodded. "Whatever it takes. Make him comfortable."

Tommy's shoulders rounded as he fell forward in a relief. "Thank you."

Yuri ignored him. Nikolai clapped him on the back. "We've got this. You should go upstairs and talk to her."

Nikolai's romantic notion surprised him. He expected that kind of thing from Ivan or Dimitri. Maybe he wasn't the only one getting soft...

He shook Nikolai's hand and hugged him quickly. "Thank you."

Nikolai made a dismissive gesture and stepped toward Tommy and Kostya. "Get up. Keep that towel wrapped tightly. I won't have you bleeding all over my damn car..."

After leaving the kitchen, Yuri found Feodor sitting on the stairs. He sat next to the old man he'd long considered a mentor and leaned back on his elbows. It had been Feodor who had taught Yuri the art of street economics and Feodor who had pushed him to be ambitious once he'd finished his time in the military. Everything he had today, he owed to this man.

Side by side, they watched Nikolai, Kostya and Tommy leave. The situation struck Yuri as being so surreal. He'd always managed to insulate himself from the seedier side of life but now it was right here in his home. He wasn't sure how he felt about that.

With a heavy sigh, Feodor finally spoke. "This is very serious."

"Yes."

"One night with this woman and now you've got a cartel knocking on your front door."

He heard the warning loud and clear. "To be fair, I've already had the Russian mob walking in and out of that door since I broke ground here."

Feodor made a *humph* noise. "That's different. That's something you understand. That's *your* history. This? This is all new—and very violent."

"This isn't her fault. She didn't ask to be born into a family of criminals any more than I asked to be abandoned in a public park."

"You care about this girl." It wasn't a question. Feodor stated it as fact.

"Yes. Very much."

"She's like you." Feodor held his gaze. "I can see it in her eyes, in her face. She knows where you come from because she's been there. She's a good match."

"Yes." Feodor wasn't saying anything that Yuri hadn't already recognized for himself. Lena felt like his other half, a kindred spirit that understood him in ways no other woman possibly could. "She's the one for me."

Feodor didn't seem the least bit surprised by Yuri's assertion. "Then you'd better get this mess cleaned up quickly. Don't let her out of your sight. That cartel has long arms and they'll have no problem reaching her here."

Fear clutched his gut. There was quite a bit of protection that came from being Nikolai Kalasnikov's best friend but would that protection extend to Lena? Would the cartel honor those unspoken rules?

Without another word, Yuri stood and helped Feodor to his feet. The old man's creaky joints made him wince. He watched Feodor shuffle down the hallway before locking up the house. He noticed the alarm had been reactivated and made sure to punch in the code once the front doors were locked.

Wanting to know how Tommy had gotten into the house and bypassed the alarm, he popped into his office and used the house phone to call the staff quarters. Derek got him up to speed on the alarm issue and assured him that a technician would be out in the morning to bolster the system. Jake explained that Tommy had come in through one of the glass doors of the solarium. He'd secured it and had a contractor lined up for the morning to replace the broken pane.

"This shouldn't have happened, Boss. Derek and I should have caught the problems in the security system. We shouldn't have spaced out our rounds tonight."

"I think we should view this as a learning opportunity." Yuri knew that Jake and Derek took their jobs so very seriously and didn't feel the need to chastise or berate them for the break-in. "Tommy exploited the weaknesses in my home security. Now we know that we need backups of the backups and so forth. I'll want a report and an action plan by tomorrow evening."

"Already on it."

"Good."

With Derek and Jake squared away, Yuri left his office

and headed upstairs. The sharp scent of Kostya's cleaning solutions lingered in the hallway. Yuri cast a critical eye around the space. There wasn't a single hint that anything terrible had happened here. Even the painting had been returned to its spot.

When he stepped inside his bedroom, he saw Lena's purse and overnight bag sitting on the end of his bed. His stomach pitched as he realized she planned to leave. He followed the sound of her voice to the master bathroom where she sat on the edge of the tub and tended to Sasha.

Unlike his earlier quick tidy, she worked diligently to clean the blood from the dog's paws. She'd removed his collar and had it soaking in one of the sinks. The silver tags had been washed and were drying on a hand towel on the counter. Sasha happily allowed her to scrub him clean.

"I don't know where you keep his toothpaste or toothbrush. He let me wipe his teeth clean with a wash cloth but he could still use a good scrub." She lovingly petted the dog. "You should probably take him in to see his vet. He might need, like, dog therapy or something after biting Tommy."

He sensed she wanted to talk about anything but the real issue at hand. Not wanting to push her away, he obliged. "I'm sorry you had to see that and I'm sorry Sasha had to use his training to protect us. If Tommy hadn't thrown the painting—"

"I know." She stood up and dropped the soiled cloth into a hamper. Sasha shadowed her movements as she stopped at the second sink to wash her hands. "Has Tommy left?"

He nodded. "Nikolai and Kostya took him to the doctor. He'll be stowed in a safe house until this is sorted out."

"You don't have to do that."

"It's not a big deal."

As she dried her hands, she shot him a look of disbelief. "You know it is."

Yuri felt the tension between them growing tauter. Running his fingers through his hair, he exhaled roughly. "I saw your bags. Are you leaving?"

"I think I have to go."

Frowning, he asked, "Why would you think that?"

She let loose a noisy breath. "My cousin just tried to rob you. Now I've got the Guzman Cartel breathing down my neck?" She shook her head. "No, Yuri. I'm not doing this to you. I saw what a risk Ivan took helping Erin. He could have been killed that night they broke into his house. I'm not doing that to you."

"Lena—"

"No," she cut him off. "You're not putting your neck on the line for me. You have enough of your own problems with the pipeline."

"*Fuck* the pipeline," he stridently replied. "That pipeline means nothing to me. *You* are my number one concern, Lena. *You.*"

"You don't mean that."

"Don't," he retorted carefully. "I'm a grown man and I know what I feel. When I say something, I mean it."

Still refusing to believe him, she insistently added, "But that pipeline is your future."

Grasping her waist, he dragged her close and slid a hand behind her nape. "*You* are my future. That pipeline is metal and gas and money and easily replaceable—but you?" He teased his mouth across hers. "You, my sweet Lena, are irreplaceable. You're my one-of-a-kind girl."

Her pouty lower lip began to quiver. She inhaled a shaky breath and tried to speak but nothing came out but a pent-up sob. "I'm so-sorry."

"Hush," he whispered as she continued to stammer her apologies. "It's all right. You've had a frightening night."

He embraced her tightly and caressed her back. She clung to him now, her hands gripping his arms, and buried her face against his chest. "Yuri, you don't have to do this. You don't have to get tangled up in my personal nightmare."

"It's too late." He tilted her head back and gazed down into those pretty brown eyes. "I'm all tangled up in you, Lena." He kissed her tenderly. "And I have no intention of cutting myself loose."

She stared up at him with such wonder in her eyes. "I've never wanted to believe a man more but—"

"I know," he whispered gently. "I know you've been hurt in the past by your father and your mother and their broken promises." He claimed her mouth in a loving, easy kiss. "Give me time, Lena. I'll prove I'm a man of my word…"

CHAPTER ELEVEN

I jerked awake to the sound of my cell phone ringing on Yuri's bedside table. When I stretched out to grab my phone, Yuri inhaled a surprised breath. I felt his body tense and quickly reached back to soothingly pet his chest. After our crazy night, I wasn't surprised that he was on edge.

Rubbing my face, I sat up and answered my phone. "Hello?"

"Lena!"

"Dad!" My heart raced as his voice registered in my ear. "Are you okay? Oh my God. Please tell me you're okay."

"I'm okay, *mi'ja*." He cleared his throat. "I guess you know."

"Yeah." Sadness crept into my voice. "Why didn't you tell me the other morning? I would have done something to help you then."

"I thought that was my last call." His voice wavered. "I didn't want to scare you."

"Dad…"

"Listen, they're going to let me call you every morning at this time until they get their painting and the money. Apparently your boyfriend has friends in some very interesting places. He got them to agree to a deal for my safety." He hesitated before finally asking, "Why didn't you tell me you were dating this Yuri guy?"

"I didn't tell you because we weren't actually dating until very recently. Like, you know, yesterday." My cheeks grew hot as I imagined what my father was thinking. "It's not like that. I mean—this thing between us has been a long time coming. It just wasn't the right time until yesterday."

Yuri's big, warm hand idly stroked my leg. I found his touch incredibly reassuring.

"I understand. He must care about you a lot to get dragged into this."

I glanced down at Yuri and smiled. "Yes, I think he does."

"I'm glad."

A gruff voice shouted in the background.

"I've got to go, *mi'ja*. I'll call you tomorrow."

"Same time?"

"Yes."

"Okay."

"I love you, Lena."

"I love you, too, Dad."

The line went dead. Still clutching my phone, I let my hand drop to my lap. The crushing weight of my fear and sadness engulfed me. I didn't want to cry in front of Yuri again—I'd been *mortified* when it had happened last night—but I couldn't stop the painful sob clogging my throat.

"Kitten," Yuri whispered and dragged me down into

the bed. He slid his arms around me and cradled me against his chest. "It's going to be all right. We'll track down the painting and Nikolai will help me make the arrangements to do a swap."

I nuzzled my nose against his neck and inhaled his comforting scent. "You make it sound so easy."

"I'm not going to lie to you." He wiped away the wetness clinging to my cheeks with his thumbs. "It's probably going to be a complex process, and it may take longer than either of us like but I'll get it done."

"How?" I didn't know how anyone could do what he'd promised. "Finding a hot painting like a Galán isn't going to be easy. Especially if word has gotten out that it was stolen from a Mexican drug lord!"

"I have a friend who knows everything that happens in the art world—on both sides of the law. If anyone can find this painting, it will be him."

"And then what, Yuri?" I caressed his cheek, the raspy stubble on his skin pricking my fingertips.

"And then I make an offer on the painting." He brushed hair away from my face. Our gazes met in the dim, purplish light streaming in through the balcony windows. "Once the painting is in my hands, it will be a very simple, straight-forward transaction."

I burrowed closer to his soothing heat. "I hope you're right."

"I am."

All I could think about were the ways it could all go badly. If Yuri couldn't find the painting or if the new owner refused to sell it, what would Lorenzo Guzman want? Drug lords weren't known for being the most honorable of men. What if Guzman double-crossed Yuri? What if he killed my father to send a message to other people who thought they could rob from him?

"I should have asked Tommy which fence sold them the painting in the first place. I bet Lorenzo Guzman would like to know the name of the person who originally stole it from him."

Yuri hummed with agreement. "It was probably an inside job. These kinds of things usually are."

"Like your pipeline sabotage?"

He let loose a deep sigh. "Yes."

"Did Anna ever call back last night?" After we'd made love and fallen asleep, the commotion in the hallway had started. Once Yuri had calmed me down in the bathroom, he'd carried me to bed and held me until I'd drifted off in his arms.

"If she did, I didn't hear it." He yawned and stretched an arm overhead. "I should probably get up and touch base with her."

I snuggled closer, not wanting to be away from him just yet. "But it's so early."

He laughed and placed a noisy kiss on the top of my head. "Sweetheart, this actually qualifies as sleeping in for me."

I glanced at the clock again. "Wow! And I thought I was an early riser."

"I like to get up, work out, shower, dress and have breakfast by six."

"Ugh." I threw my arm over my face. "If I stagger out of bed and down a cup of coffee by seven, I feel like a champion. If I manage to wade through a page of my social media alerts, I feel like I can conquer the world."

Chuckling, Yuri threw his leg over mine and pushed up onto his hands. He peppered ticklish kisses along the side of my neck. "Maybe I can use some positive reinforcement to convince you to move onto my schedule."

I sifted my fingers through his hair. "You're going to have to be awfully persuasive."

His sexy grin made my tummy flip-flop. "I have a few tricks up my sleeve."

"I bet you do." I couldn't help but smile as his lips descended toward mine. The idea of waking up like this every morning was so incredibly tempting. I knew Yuri wasn't offering that—yet. Someday…

A loud snort and a whine interrupted our morning kiss. We both looked over to see Sasha sitting impatiently at the bedside. He looked rather annoyed by the sight of Yuri on top of me and made his displeasure known with a smack of his massive paw to his master's side.

"All right," Yuri said with a frustrated huff. "I'll let you out."

I sat up and enjoyed the view of Yuri's ridiculously hot body as he strode to the door to let Sasha out of the room. That was another thing I wouldn't mind waking up to see and feel pressed against me every morning.

"I'm going to have to rethink Sasha's sleeping arrangements."

I giggled as Yuri slid back into bed with me. Just when he started to kiss me, his phone rang. Groaning, he kissed me hard and deep before shoving out of bed again and grabbing the black phone rattling across the bedside table. He answered a bit gruffly and instantly started speaking Russian. I had a feeling it was Anna and whatever she was telling him was something he didn't want to hear.

Certain that our amorous moment had just been tanked, I climbed out of bed, grabbed my overnight bag and made my way to the bathroom. The walk-in shower with its gorgeous aqua blue and turquoise glass tile beckoned me. The showerheads mounted in the ceiling and the walls provided such a luxurious experience. It was like showering in a warm rainfall.

I used my travel kit of toiletries to scrub and shave. I took my time, hoping Yuri would join me for another shower like the one we'd shared at my place, but eventually there was nothing else for me to do. I was stepping out of the shower and wrapping a towel around me when Yuri finally entered the bathroom.

"Take off the towel."

My surprised gaze flicked to his face. That hungry, intense gaze made me break out in goose bumps. I unwrapped the towel and bared my damp body to him. "Now what?"

"Go about your morning routine. I don't have time to properly make love to you this morning but I'm damn sure going to enjoy the view while you get dressed."

"Really?" I had to laugh at his request. "You want to watch me moisturize and put on my makeup and style my hair?"

"Very much," he said before dropping a kiss right on the sensitive spot where my neck curved into my shoulder. "There's a hair dryer in that drawer, if you need it."

"Thanks."

Feeling a little self-conscious, I started my normal after-shower routine. I could feel Yuri's gaze following me as he showered. Emboldened by his obvious desire for me, I embraced my inner sex kitten as I slathered on my favorite lotion. I caught him staring at my bottom as I rubbed the thick lightly-scented cream into my legs.

"Tomorrow I'm helping you with that," Yuri announced as he stepped out of the shower and fastened a towel around his waist. "If anyone is going to rub their hands all over you, it should be me."

As I shimmied into my panties, I laughed but accepted

his offer. "Deal."

Standing side-by-side at the double sinks, we brushed our teeth. While I worked moisturizer into my face, Yuri started to shave. As I applied my makeup, I kept stopping to watch him methodically scraping the razor over his skin.

"What?" He shot me an amused smile. "You've never watched a man shave?"

"No."

"Not even your father? I thought that was something little girls did. Watch their father's shave."

I shook my head. "My dad actually had a pretty crazy beard when I was younger. He only went for the clean-shaven look when I was, like, fifteen or sixteen."

Yuri swished his razor around in the sink of water he'd prepared and then held it out to me. "Here."

My eyes widened. "Are you serious?"

"Sure. Why not?"

"I don't know. What if I nick you?"

He glanced at my legs. "You didn't cut your legs while shaving in the shower. That's infinitely more difficult that standing here at the sink and shaving my face."

He had a point. Intrigued by the offer, I moved closer and accepted the razor. Yuri grasped me by the waist and placed me on the marble counter. It put me at a comfortable height to shave him. I studied his foamy face and tried to figure out how to begin.

"Start here." Yuri touched the spot where he'd last swiped. "Hold the skin taut for the closest shave."

Feeling a little nervous, I did as instructed and dragged the razor across his skin. I expected him to jump or shout with pain at any moment but he held incredibly still until I'd finished my first pass. As I rinsed the razor in the hot water, he gave me another set of directions.

"A little more pressure this time and a bit faster," he suggested. "Do this piece again. Run your fingers over it to make sure it's smooth."

With a nod, I tried again, following his directions to the letter. While I rinsed the razor a second time, Yuri checked the patch I'd shaved and smiled approvingly. "Very good."

Renewed with confidence, I continued to shave his handsome face. There was something oddly soothing about sharing this morning ritual with him. The trust he'd put in my hands spoke volumes. I very carefully shaved around his mouth, holding my breath as I drew the razor across his skin as steadily as possible. His neck was easier and less nerve-wracking.

As I wiped away the traces of shaving cream with a damp wash cloth, I ran my fingers over his skin to ensure it was nice and smooth. "What do you think?"

"That I've found the perfect job for you every morning. What do you say?"

"Well, I guess I am technically your personal assistant."

"And what's more personal than shaving a man?"

"I suppose there isn't much that would qualify."

"Exactly." After kissing me, he lifted me off the counter and set me on my feet. All the playfulness fled his demeanor as he finished up his morning routine. "Listen, you shouldn't talk about this mess with your father to anyone."

I glanced at him with surprise. "I don't want to worry Benny but I can't keep this from Erin or Vivian."

He frowned. "Why don't you want to worry Benny?"

It suddenly occurred to me that Dimitri hadn't told him about Benny's condition. Playing it off, I shrugged. "She has a lot going on with the launch of the bakery. I wouldn't want her to stress out over me."

Yuri narrowed his eyes. I could tell he didn't believe me but he didn't push for the truth. "I suppose you can tell Vivian and Erin. I'm sure Ivan will have heard and I know Nikolai will likely put an armed guard on Vivian, just in case." He snapped the lid back onto his antiperspirant. "Which reminds me—you'll be taking Jake or Derek with you from this point forward."

"What? No! I don't need a bodyguard."

Yuri fixed me with one of his no-nonsense stares. "This isn't up for discussion. You will take a bodyguard or you won't leave this house."

"Look, I agreed to work for you but that doesn't mean you can order me around, Yuri."

"With me," he corrected. "You're working *with* me, Lena. And I'm not trying to order you around because you're an employee. I'm trying to keep you safe. After what happened last night, I absolutely cannot allow you to go anywhere alone. Now that the cartel knows I'm willing to go to bat for your father, they're going to realize how incredibly important you are to me. They'll see dollar signs."

My gut clenched painfully. "You think they'd kidnap me?"

"It wouldn't be the first time those monsters tried something like that. They're already holding your father hostage. They know I'd move heaven and earth to get you back."

He said it so easily. I was reminded of what he'd said last night about proving that he would always be there for me. He meant every word he said—and it scared me. The very thought of giving into the hope he inspired frightened me. I knew how badly it hurt when my father broke a promise. My soul would be crushed if Yuri hurt me.

But a wisp of bravery invaded my chest and wound its way around my heart. I would never know if Yuri was all the things he promised if I didn't give him a chance. If he proved me wrong, I'd be the happiest girl in the whole world. If he proved me right and shattered my trust in him, I'd probably never crawl out of bed again.

"All right, Yuri. I'll do what you've asked. I'll take the bodyguard."

He visibly relaxed. Taking a step toward me, he opened his arms. I slid into his warm embrace and enjoyed the feel of his strong arms wrapped around me. "Thank you for not fighting me on this. I only want to keep you safe."

"I know." Looking up at him, I asked, "How the hell am I supposed to go about my day pretending nothing has happened?"

Yuri cupped my face and traced my mouth with his thumb. "Do you remember yesterday when we talked about feeling like frauds? About wearing masks and faking it to fit in?"

"Yes."

"That's what we do until this mess is cleared up and your father is safely home. We pretend everything is fine. We don't need outsiders poking around in our business."

Secretly, I was thrilled by the way he said *our* business. For the first time in so long, I didn't feel alone. I didn't have to face something scary on my own. I had Yuri to lean on and help me through it.

"So—what are you doing today?" I kissed his freshly shaved cheek and unwound myself from his embrace.

"After breakfast, I'll head into the office. I promised Vivian I'd stop by her studio this afternoon to sit for some photographs for new painting series."

"Have you seen any of the finished pieces yet?"

He shook his head. "Have you?"

"Yes. They're amazing. I've been lucky enough to watch her grow as an artist since we were in high school together and this collection is—well—it's awesome. I can't wait until the show next year." I touched my finger to my lips. "But I won't spoil the surprise for you."

He chuckled. "I'll be out of the house all day. I was hoping we could have lunch but I don't think it will be possible. We'll have a nice dinner instead. Is that all right with you?"

"Yes, but it should be something simple if you're going to ask Feodor to cook. He had a rough night."

Yuri snapped his fingers. "That reminds me. I'll make sure to contact the staffing agency I've contracted and tell them you'll be handling the selection of my full-time staff."

"Do you have specific criteria for your employees?"

"I've already narrowed the field by answering a questionnaire from the agency about personal habits, credit scores, that kind of thing."

"Credit scores? Really?"

He shrugged. "They seem to think that high scores equal trustworthiness and responsibility."

I rolled my eyes. "Oh give me a break! What if someone gets laid off and has a few months of late bills while they try to get back on their feet? That doesn't mean they're not trustworthy. It just means they've hit a rough patch."

"I'm not disagreeing with you. I'm simply telling you how the agency works."

"Yeah, well, remind me not to apply there if I run out of PR job options."

Yuri shot me a sexy grin. "You don't need to worry

about that possibility. I have a feeling your career options are going to open up when word gets around that you're a free agent."

I wasn't so sure about that but it was nice that Yuri thought it.

"So what are your plans for today?"

"I'll sit down with Feodor and chat with him about staffing the house. I'm supposed to meet with Benny around ten to talk about her business launch and make some adjustments to the marketing and publicity moving forward. I might try to do some networking at lunch and put out some feelers. Oh and I'm helping Erin do some shopping for Ivan's birthday this afternoon."

"Good luck," Yuri said with a laugh. "He's as difficult to buy for as Nikolai."

"Any recommendations?"

"Books," Yuri called out as he entered the master closet attached to the bathroom. "You can't go wrong there."

"Are you giving him books for his birthday?"

"Not this year. I'm giving the two of them a three-day weekend in Vegas to watch one of the big fights. Ivan will enjoy that and I'm sure he'll spoil Erin rotten at all of the high-end shops and boutiques there."

"He'll love every minute of it. Making Erin smile seems to be his favorite thing in the world." I followed him into the master closet and nearly fainted at the sheer size of the space. It was easily as big as the apartment I shared with Vivian. It was a stark reminder of the differences in our income levels.

"Erin loves him. That much is clear to anyone who watches them together. I worried about them in the beginning, that they were moving too fast, but now I see they're simply perfect for one another." Yuri selected a suit and laid out a shirt. At the large marble-topped island in the center of the closet, he pulled out a drawer that contained cuff links and watches. Glancing at me, he asked, "Will you pick a tie from the rack?"

"Sure." I made my way to the section of his closet dedicated to ties and pocket squares. By the time I'd chosen the perfect steel blue tie, he was half dressed. I stood nearby and watched him button and tuck in his shirt and slip on his belt. When he fiddled with his cuff links, I reached out to touch one. "These are beautiful."

"*These* are beautiful." He palmed my bare breast and brushed his thumb over my nipple. "We may have to institute a new rule."

"Oh?"

"You aren't allowed to get dressed until after me. That way I get to enjoy the sight of your gorgeous body while I get ready." He leaned down and lavished kisses on my breasts.

When he suckled me gently, I moaned at the delicious tingle his lips evoked. My breath hitched as he stroked my belly. "Yuri, you said there wasn't time this morning."

"Fuck it," he swore roughly. "I own the damn company. They can wait for me."

"But—"

He captured my mouth in a demanding kiss that left me shaking and breathless. Those insistent hands of his roamed my curves. I surrendered to his caresses and let him stoke the flames of my desire. Gripping his shoulders, I widened my thighs as his knee nudged them apart.

"Oh!" I gasped when his hand dipped inside my panties. Though his kisses were insistent and rough, his fingers were gentle as he explored me. Our tongues tangled as he parted my delicate folds and swirled his fingers around my throbbing clit. "Ah!"

"I want to hear you," he whispered against my lips. His skilled fingers coaxed a cry from my lips as he penetrated me with one finger and then two. Pressing his forehead to mine, he groaned, "You're so wet."

"It's you. It's all you." I moaned as he started to fuck me with his long, thick digits. Wanting to touch him, I jerked on his belt and yanked down his zipper. I slipped my hand under the waistband of his boxers and grasped his massive shaft. He growled as I clasped him even tighter and started to stroke him.

Frantic with desire, we worked one another into a frenzied state. He rubbed his thumb around my pulsing clitoris while plunging his fingers in and out of me. I cried out in shock when he used his other hand to torment my breasts. Pinching and rolling my nipples, he caused the most wonderful shocks to arc through my aching, needy body.

I scratched my nails across his forearm as that first shudder gripped my core. Head thrown back, I climaxed. "Yuri!"

"Yes," he urged, his fingers thrusting into me again and again.

"Yuri! *Yuri!*" I cried his name like a litany as he pushed me higher and higher. When I couldn't take anymore, when I was sure I'd collapse from the sheer bliss of it all, I grabbed his wrist and forced those magnificent fingers of his to go still. "No more. I can't take anymore."

Laughing, he noisily kissed my cheek and carefully removed his hand from my panties. He brought his glistening fingers to his mouth and licked my slick nectar from them. The sight made my knees weak.

Sliding down to the floor, I pulled open his pants and yanked down his boxers. Grasping his cock by the base, I painted his hot flesh with my tongue before sucking him into my mouth. Already he oozed pre-cum. The taste of it blossomed on my tongue and made me greedy for more.

He sifted his fingers through my hair and started to pump his hips. "I'm so close."

Licking my lips, I sat back and begged, "Come for me. Let me taste your cum."

A guttural growl escaped his throat. I welcomed that steely shaft as it started to thrust against my tongue. I tightened my lips around him, sucking him hard and letting him know just how badly I wanted him.

He groaned my name a split-second before his hot seed blasted my tongue. Moaning excitedly, I took him deeper into my mouth. Refusing to waste even one drop, I lapped at him until there was no more to be had.

Yuri exhaled loudly and slumped back against the island. He held his arms wide. "Come here, Kitten."

Smiling, I let him pull me into my embrace. It seemed the kitten nickname was going to stick. From anyone else, such a term of endearment probably would have grated on my nerves but from Yuri it felt so intimate and sweet.

He swiped my lower lip with his thumb before kissing me. "I don't know how I'm going to concentrate today. You're driving me crazy."

"Then I guess I better cross my afternoon plans to text you dirty pictures off my list," I teased.

The mischievous glint in his hazel eyes made me smile. "I suppose that means my plans to sext you are off the table too."

I giggled and kissed him. "Sadly, yes."

With his hand tangled in my hair, he said, "When you're done running your errands, take Jake to your apartment and get your things. You can have that side of the closet."

My eyes widened with surprise. I convinced myself he was thinking only of the short-term and didn't dare let myself think that he meant anything else. "Thank you. That will be much more convenient." I glanced at the wide open space he'd offered. "I'll only need a few things to tide me over until my dad is free and I'm off house arrest."

His piercing gaze seared me. "You may as well bring it all. If I have my way, you're never getting off house arrest."

Uncertain how to respond to such a bold statement, I reached for the tie that had been forgotten in our passionate tryst. Looping it around his neck, I whispered, "We'll see."

His mouth curved in a sinfully sexy grin. "Yes, we will."

CHAPTER TWELVE

"Have you read this one?" Erin flashed a high-octane thriller at me.

I shook my head and took the book from her. "Not yet, but it looks good."

"I'm just not into the thrillers and science fiction like Ivan." She added the book to her towering pile. "I like my urban fantasy and paranormal romances. Space travel and all that science bore me to death. Serial killers and terrorists and bomb plots?" She shivered. "Not my thing."

"I like the fast-paced reads." I made a mental note to pick up a digital copy of that thriller later. "They're exciting."

"I prefer a different kind of exciting." She sidled closer and bumped me with her hip. "Speaking of…how did it go last night?"

"You mean before my cousin broke in, tried to steal Yuri's painting and got mauled by a dog the size of a grizzly bear?"

Erin winced. "Yeah. That's pretty awful but I think I probably have you beat when it comes to home invasions. Ivan fought off two armed thugs with his bare hands while I hid in a closet. I'd take a huge dog and two bodyguards any day."

She had a point. "I guess Benny really wins, though. Dimitri fought off, like, five guys and got stabbed and shot in the process. They even burned down her bakery."

"She's pretty kickass though. She had a baseball bat and took out, like, three of those guys. Me? I curled into a ball and pretended I was invisible."

I shook my head. "Man, we have had some terrible luck this year. Maybe we should get smudged or something. We need to get rid of this bad juju that's following us around."

"Right?" Erin laughed and plucked another book off the shelf. She added it to the growing pile in her arms and nearly dropped all the books when the weight shifted.

"Why don't you just get him an ereader for his birthday?" I took half of her armload.

"He doesn't like them. His library collection is so incredibly valuable to him. When he was a child, reading was the way he escaped from the hell of his everyday life." She touched the tower of books in her arms. "These are comforting to him."

I trailed her to the long line snaking around the front of the book store. Even though Yuri had suggested a book for Ivan, I decided to choose something else. Erin had bought half the store anyway so he'd be set for books for a while. I thought about the trip Yuri was planning to gift them. A nifty idea started to sprout.

"So how was Benny this morning?"

"Puking," I said with a grimace. "It seems she's getting hit a little harder with morning sickness. Remind me never to get pregnant," I added with a shudder.

"Poor thing." Erin made a sad face. "We should put together a small gift basket for her. We'll tuck in some ginger ale and crackers plus some nice feel-good stuff so Dimitri can pamper her."

"That's a sweet idea. I'll see if Vivian wants to go in on it with us."

"Did I tell you that Ivan sat for her last week?"

"No. How did it go?"

"He was nervous about showing his tattoos to someone other than me. I think it was even harder for him because Vivian can read all of them and she knows so much of the symbolic history behind them. She made him very comfortable and it didn't take long. She only snapped a handful of photographs, all from the neck down, and then she was done with him."

"Yuri is supposed to drop by her studio this afternoon. His sitting won't take long." I touched my chest. "He only has one tattoo."

"Really? Just one?"

I nodded. "He seems downright conservative compared to Ivan and Nikolai."

"Vivian still hasn't told Nikolai about the series she's doing. She specifically asked Ivan not to mention it. I could tell it made him uneasy but he agreed." She eyed me carefully. "Do you know why she's being so secretive about it with Nikolai? I don't think she's ever kept anything from him."

"She tried talking to him about his tattoos when she first became interested in them but he shut her down like hardcore. It rattled her badly and she's never brought the subject up with him again." I let loose a sigh. "She knows that he's going to flip his lid when he finds out what she's been doing."

Erin looked worried. "Do you think he'll get angry with her?"

I shrugged. "Will he grouch at her? Probably. But Nikolai get angry with Vivian?" I laughed. "Please!"

"True. He's almost as bad as Ivan when it comes to me." Her gaze jumped to the entrance of the bookstore. Stepping toward me, she hurriedly whispered, "Detective Santos is headed this way."

"What?" I glanced over my shoulder just in time to see the dark-haired detective step through the crowd of teenage girls lusting over a mountain of werewolf romance paperbacks. "Shit."

Detective Eric Santos, a member of Houston's gang unit and Vivian's cousin, sauntered toward me. He smiled pleasantly. "Hello."

"Hi," we replied in unison.

"Lena, when you're done here, would you mind if we had a quick chat?"

"Not at all," I said with a smile.

"Great. I'll grab a coffee and wait for you."

I kept that smile plastered in place until he'd turned his back. Looking toward Erin, I let it slip. "Now what?"

"Just talk to him. He's a good guy."

"Yuri was really specific about not letting anyone know about my dad. I got the feeling the negotiations Nikolai had undertaken on his behalf were contingent on keeping the police out of it."

"We're just having coffee at a bookstore with our friend's cousin. It's no big deal."

I scanned the bookstore and found Jake hovering nearby. In the span of a few hours, I'd become shockingly accustomed to Yuri's bodyguard shadowing me. Our gazes met across the store. He glanced at Eric Santos and then back at me. I gave a little shrug to let him know I didn't have a choice.

The line started moving faster. Before I was ready to face him, I made my way to see the detective. He'd taken a corner table. Erin sat with me. I noticed Jake moving to the closest book display.

Santos didn't miss him. "I see you've got protection now."

"My boyfriend worries." It felt weird to call Yuri my boyfriend but I wasn't sure how else to describe our relationship.

"He should." Santos sipped his coffee. "I heard about your cousin."

My heart skipped a beat. Did he know everything? How much of my family's situation was already public knowledge on the streets? "Oh?"

He nodded. "I heard he fenced a stolen painting. A painting that belonged to a certain Mexican gentleman who isn't known for leniency or mercy."

"Well," I said cautiously, "Tommy isn't the smartest of criminals."

Santos snorted derisively. "That's for damn sure."

"So is that all you needed? To warn me that my cousin had blundered into another mess?"

He ran his finger around the lid of his cup. "I went by your dad's warehouse to check on him but he wasn't there."

I swallowed nervously. "He's on a business trip."

Santos studied me intently. "A business trip, huh?"

"Yes."

"Okay." He glanced at Jake again. "You keep that shadow of yours tight. These people? They will make the Hermanos and the Albanians look like choirboys." Coffee in hand, he rose from his chair. "You let Nikolai know that I'm keeping a close eye on Vivian until whatever this is gets cleared up. I can see that you've got the best protection money can buy so I'll focus on keeping my cousin safe."

"I'm sure Vivian will appreciate it." She wouldn't but Santos wouldn't care. Like Nikolai, he could be overbearing and paranoid when it came to protecting her.

With a nod, Santos left our table and disappeared into the crowd.

Erin touched my arm. "You okay?"

"I'm fine. I think he probably knows everything."

"So do I. You'll have to tell Yuri."

"I hope this doesn't cause problems for my dad."

"I don't see how it will. Eric Santos has no jurisdiction in Mexico and that's where your dad is now. He can't get involved in anything down there or mess up the negotiations and the deals that are in place. Even if he could, he wouldn't."

"How can you be sure?" I so wanted to believe her.

She glanced at the wall of windows overlooking the parking lot. "When my sister was in trouble, he gave Ivan a clear signal that he'd hang back and let him find a way to keep her safe in prison and me safe on the outside. I'm sure they would have executed a search warrant on our house that night but Santos let Ivan get there first so he could make a deal with the Hermanos and Albanians to save my life."

"Let's just hope he shows me the same consideration…"

* * *

Yuri fished his ringing phone out of his pocket. One glance at his phone's screen and he knew this wasn't going to be a call he enjoyed. Glad for the privacy of the backseat of his car, he answered. "Dimitri."

"What the hell do you think you're doing keeping something like this from me?"

"Why, yes, Dimitri, I am having a nice afternoon—and you?"

"I don't think this is funny."

Yuri pinched the bridge of his nose. "I assure you the situation isn't funny on my end either."

"You should have called me immediately. I should have been told that you were facing off with a damn cartel!"

He wasn't sure how Dimitri had found out but it didn't much matter now.

"I didn't want to put you or Benny at risk. It's the same reason I didn't call Ivan last night. Vivian is already involved by her association with her father and Lena so calling Nikolai seemed the best possible move. He has the connections I need, and he'll want to keep a close eye on Vivian, especially with her father getting out of the pen any day."

Dimitri sighed loudly. "Listen, you need to let me set you up with another bodyguard or two. I don't like the idea of you and Lena having only one guard watching your movements. It's exhausting for the guards and it puts you at a higher risk."

Yuri conceded that Dimitri knew his business well. "Fine—but I want one of us watching her."

"A Russian?"

"I need someone I can trust not to be in the Mexican's pocket."

"The only one I have on my roster is safely tucked into Nikolai's pocket."

"That's fine. I'll take him. He'll be more afraid of him than of any cartel drug lord. Who else do you have available to watch her?"

"What about Kelly?"

"The bouncer at my club?"

"He's a highly decorated Marine and a solid guy. His father is sick and he needs the money. I trust him."

"Okay. I'll take Kelly."

"I'll send them to her apartment to keep an eye on her."

"Send them to my house. She's staying with me."

Dimitri seemed to perk up at that tidbit. "Oh?"

"Yes."

"It's about damn time you made your move with her. I worried that someone else was going to sneak in and take her from you before you'd worked up the courage to even ask her out on a date."

Dimitri's worries mirrored his own. Feeling comfortable discussing his relationship with his friend, he admitted, "I royally fucked it up the other day. I very nearly lost her but she gave me a second chance. I'm not messing this one up."

"Make sure that you don't. If you hurt her, Ivan, Nikolai and I will never hear the end of it from Erin, Vivian and Benny."

Yuri laughed. "No doubt."

"Are you sure that bodyguards are all you need? I'd be happy to come by and watch her personally."

"No." Yuri firmly declined the offer. "You need to take care of Benny. I won't have you putting yourself at risk, not now when everything is coming together for you." Before Dimitri could argue with him, he added, "I've handled the docking arrangements for the big yacht. Everything is squared away on my end for your wedding."

"Benny will be relieved to hear that. And Johnny?"

"He's already transferred to that yacht's crew. There

shouldn't be any problem bringing him in for the wedding."

"Good. That will make her so happy."

"I'm sure it will." His car pulled up to the curb outside the renovated warehouse where Vivian kept her studio. "Listen, I'm running late for a meeting. Can I call you later?"

"Yes. I'll touch base with you as soon as I have my two guards on their way."

Yuri hesitated before asking, "Are we okay?"

"We're fine—but don't keep things like this from me again. We've been through a lot together. There's no reason to start keeping secrets now."

"You're right. I apologize."

"Yeah. Okay. I'll talk to you later."

Yuri pocketed his phone and stepped out of the car. Derek's gaze jumped between a sleek black car across the street and a maroon sedan down the block. "Those cars are making me nervous, Boss."

Yuri glanced at the cars in question and laughed. "They should. If I'm not mistaken, that sedan is probably holding a couple of plainclothes police officers. I'm sure they're enjoying their staring contest with Kostya."

Still laughing, Yuri strode toward the locked entrance and hit the buzzer. A few moments later, Vivian came across the intercom and unlocked the door for him. Derek kept close as they made their way to the second floor. Nikolai used the ground floor as storage but the second he'd converted into a massive studio space for Vivian's twentieth birthday. It was the kind of gift a man gave to a woman he loved but Nikolai maintained that he only viewed Vivian as his ward. Yuri wasn't convinced.

"Hey!" Barefoot and wearing a paint-splattered apron, Vivian greeted him at the entrance. She glanced at Derek.

"I see you've brought reinforcements."

"This is Derek. He's one of my private guards." Yuri gestured toward the windows. "I see you've got two sets of babysitters on you."

Vivian rolled her pale eyes. "Is that ridiculous or what? I stepped outside of my apartment this morning to go run and walked right into Kostya. I came home from the run and found two of Eric's off-duty buddies watching me."

Yuri didn't like the idea of Vivian's detective cousin sticking his nose in where it didn't belong but he couldn't blame the man for wanting to look out for his family. The detective had saved Dimitri and Benny's life and had given Ivan a chance to make things right with the Hermanos and Albanians so Yuri hoped the man would stay out of it this time around as well. Lena's father's life depended on it.

"Derek, why don't you have a seat over there?" Vivian pointed to a cozy corner with a couch and reading material. "The small fridge has water and soda if you're thirsty."

"Yes, ma'am."

Vivian crooked her finger. "Yuri, this way."

He followed her to a corner of the warehouse she'd set up for photography. There was a simple stool sitting against a gray backdrop. "I suppose I'm sitting here."

She nodded. "I doubt you have as many tattoos as Ivan or Kostya so this won't take long. You can put your jacket and shirt on that table."

A quiver of discomfort pierced his belly as he started to undress in front of his girlfriend's best friend. Clearing his throat, he asked, "May I see the other pieces in the collection?"

"Sure." She shot him a playful smile. "Would you like me to turn around while you take off your shirt? I promise I won't peek."

He chuckled. "Funny."

"Sorry. You seem tense."

"The last few days have been rather intense."

Vivian's expression turned sad. "I couldn't believe it when Nikolai called me this morning to tell me about Lena's dad. That's just awful. She tried to play it off when we talked earlier but I can tell she's terrified." Picking up her camera, Vivian added, "I'm really glad she has you in her corner, Yuri."

His eyebrows rose with surprise. "Are you? Even after the way I messed things up on Monday?"

She shrugged. "I realize you made a mistake. I know you'd never deliberately hurt her. I've seen the way you've watched her over the past few months. I know that look."

Yes, I'm sure you do, he thought silently.

"I know Lena is really good at projecting this tough, badass bitch character when she's scared but a lot of it is bravado. Yes, she's more than capable of taking care of herself, but she needs someone to lean on, Yuri."

"I want to be that someone. I've made it clear that I'm in this for the long-haul with her."

"But she's giving you that mistrusting, uncertain vibe?"

He nodded. "I can tell she's been hurt badly by her parents. Her father seems to have broken so many promises to her and her mother ran off and died."

"Yeah," Vivian said, her voice unnaturally tight. "She definitely has some issues that you'll have to work out together."

"She's worth it. Hell," he said with a self-deprecating laugh. "I'm not exactly baggage free here. I've got my own hang-ups."

"We all do, Yuri." She pointed to the stool. "Ready?" Naked from the waist up, he sat down and straightened his back. "Like this?"

"Yes. Just so you know—I'm not doing any face captures. I'm only interested in your tattoos." She moved closer and held the camera up to her face. "Do you have a story behind this tattoo?" The camera came down to reveal her smile. "Obviously it's about brotherhood."

"I had it done while I was in the military. Dimitri and I were stationed in different areas. Nikolai and Ivan were in prison." He absentmindedly touched the tattoo as Vivian crouched down to snap a photo from a different angle. "It made me feel close to them again. It reminded that our bond could survive anything."

Vivian finished her quick photo session. "I like that description. I'm going to find a way to incorporate that feeling into the painting."

His part finished, Yuri grabbed his shirt and slipped back into it while Vivian uploaded the pictures and made some notes in a spiral notebook. She glanced over at him as he fixed his cufflinks. "Thank you for doing this. I've been so lucky to have such great friends willing to sit for these photos."

"I'm happy to do it. I'm glad you consider me a friend."

"Well, you are my best tipper at the restaurant," she said with a cheeky grin.

He laughed and teased, "I think you're setting the bar for friendship a bit low."

"Probably."

"Since we're friends, perhaps you wouldn't mind helping me with something?"

"That depends. What kind of help?"

"It's for Lena." He slid his arms into his suit jacket. "She was wearing this really beautiful blazer this morning—"

"The poppy red one with the black piping?" Vivian interjected.

"Yes."

"I love that color on her. Isn't it great?"

"Very," he agreed. "I noticed that her left wrist looked a little bare. I wanted to get her something pretty."

"Something pretty?" Vivian leaned back against the table. "Like jewelry?"

"Yes. Gold, I think."

"And you want me to—what? Recommend something?"

"I thought you might know if there's a piece she's had her eye on or maybe a certain style she prefers."

She reacted with mock shock. "You're asking me for advice on how to woo a woman? I thought you were supposed to be some internationally renowned playboy."

Yuri took her playful jabs in stride. "It's different with Lena. She's not just any woman. With anyone else, I'd go to my jeweler and ask for something bright and gaudy and obscenely expensive. I want to get it right with her. I want something that's special to her." Letting some vulnerability into his voice, he said, "I want this to be perfect for her. Please?"

Vivian's expression softened. "We went window shopping a few weeks ago. I'll make you a list and some recommendations."

"Thank you."

She picked up a pen and her notepad and gestured to the far wall. "Why don't you look at the paintings while I make this list?"

Yuri crossed the warehouse to the horizontal racks storing her canvases. The unit had swinging arms that allowed the canvases to be flicked through one by one. He couldn't help but wonder what Nikolai had spent on this little contraption.

Studying the first canvas, he finally understood what Lena meant. This series of paintings staggered him. He leaned back as he gazed at the canvas so he could take it all in and digest it. The haunting portrait showcased a torso marked in prison tattoos. They weren't the Russian tats he was so used to seeing but the kind a man would get in a place like Mexico or Central America.

A few more canvases flicked by and he found Dimitri's phoenix. She'd painted the broad expanse of his back and the fine detail of his tattoo in the foreground but the background was a swirling mass of flames and smoke with fine ash littering the bottom edge of the canvas. If Dimitri didn't make an offer on this one after her show, Yuri intended to snatch it up for his gallery wall.

At the very back of the collection, he spotted a canvas covered with a cloth. Curious, he lifted the cloth and took a peek at the painting underneath. His heart stuttered in his chest as the sight registered.

The painting depicted an eerie night scene with a dilapidated two-story house and broken window along the top story. Bloody streaks marred the pointed shards of shattered glass. There, in the shadowy background, a tattooed chest was barely visible.

Yuri's gut clenched as he realized what she'd painted. It was the night she'd been shot while breaking into a house for her father. It was the night Nikolai had saved her life. It was the night the two of them had been inextricably bonded.

It was the night the lies between those two began.

Hearing her approaching footsteps, he hastily covered the painting. He tried to look nonplussed but she wasn't fooled.

"I don't mind you looking at that one. I prefer to keep

it covered because it's an ugly memory." She touched the covered painting. "Sometimes I think I remember more of the man who shot me but it's never enough."

Yuri eyed her carefully. "What do you remember about him?"

"Just that he had that strange tattoo in the center of his chest," she said while touching her shirt. "He didn't speak. He just shot me." She had a faraway look in her eyes. "And then I was falling and I hit the ground so hard. When I woke up again, Nikolai was standing over me. He had a hand on my stomach and he was whispering so softly." She inhaled deeply. "And then I blacked out again and woke up in the hospital."

"They never had any leads?"

She shook her head. "Nikolai said that he'd seen a dark-haired man running from the house after the gunshot. For a while, the police suspected my father had accidentally shot me. Then the theory was that one of the many men he'd crossed had done it." She shrugged. "It doesn't really matter anymore. It's in the past."

How Yuri wished that were true! He cast one final glance at the covered painting before asking, "Has Nikolai seen this collection?"

"No." She held out the folded sheet of paper but didn't let go when he tugged on it. "I'd prefer that you didn't tell him. I want the collection to be a surprise when he comes to the show. I want him to see what kind of beautiful art I'm able to create because of this wonderful space he gave me."

Yuri saw such excitement in her eyes. She clearly hoped to knock Nikolai off his feet—but Yuri worried his old friend would be reeling with a different kind of shock when he got a good look at the tattoo-inspired pieces.

"I won't ruin the surprise but perhaps you'd prefer to show him before everyone else? Maybe a quiet, private viewing for the two of you?"

Interest flashed in her eyes as she released the folded sheet of paper. "Maybe."

He prayed she'd choose that route. Yuri didn't know what would happen if Nikolai walked into that downtown gallery and spotted *that* painting hanging on the wall.

Yuri pocketed the list. "Thank you."

"Anytime, Yuri." She walked at his side as they crossed the warehouse. "Would it be all right if I dropped by your house to see Lena tomorrow? She mentioned that you've got her on house arrest to keep her safe."

He snorted with amusement. "Yes, I'll be a good warden and allow my prisoner to have some visits."

Smiling, Vivian said, "I'll have to bring my babysitter."

"Just Kostya or the Houston PD too?"

"I'm pretty sure your house is outside their jurisdiction."

"I highly doubt your cousin is going to let a little thing like jurisdiction keep him from watching you like a hawk."

She didn't argue that point. "I'll let you know when your painting is done so you can take a peek before the show."

"You realize I'll want to buy it, right?"

"Yes—and you realize I'm going to add a special billionaire's premium to the price, right?"

He laughed. "I expected nothing less."

"Tell Lena I'm coming to see her tomorrow."

"All right."

Walking out of the warehouse, Yuri couldn't shake the feeling that sweet Vivian was playing with fire—and Nikolai would be the one who felt the heat.

CHAPTER THIRTEEN

I knew the moment Yuri arrived at the house that evening. Sasha had been quietly sleeping at my feet in the kitchen as I discussed the staffing issues with Feodor but he jumped to his feet and raced to the front door with a loud, excited bark. Feodor started to follow him but I held up my hand and slid off the stool. "I'll go."

As I hurried to catch up with the beastly dog, I heard his growl change from that higher pitched excited whine to a lower, menacing growl. The fine hair on the back of my neck stood on edge and goose bumps broke out on my arms. Jake appeared from a nearby doorway, the one leading into the second living room, and gestured me back away from the door.

Trotting over to my side, Sasha pushed against my belly with his big head and forced me behind him. With his bottom just inches from my feet, Sasha used his body to shield mine. I put a gentle hand on the back of his head and brushed my fingers through his fur. Moving my hand lower, I gripped the back of his collar, just in case.

When the doorbell rang, Sasha let loose a series of barks so loud they made my ears ache. With a hand on the weapon holstered at his hip, Jake opened the door. A tall beautiful blonde woman came into view. Her panicked gaze jumped to Sasha who snarled and snapped at her.

I tugged on his collar. "Sasha! No!" I tried to remember the words Yuri had taught me during breakfast but blanked. I used the only Russian word I could remember. "*Nyet*!"

Sasha glanced back at me and grumbled before plopping his bottom down again. He wasn't going to attack but he didn't like having the door open or that woman standing there.

She raised her voice so I could hear her. "My name is Anna, and I work with Mr. Novakovsky. I've brought some paperwork for him. He was already out of the office when I finished it and I'm headed out for a personal trip." She flashed a glossy folder. The movement made Sasha bark and Anna took a nervous step backward. Extending the folder toward Jake, she said, "I'll just leave it here."

"I'm sorry," I called out as she backed down the steps. "Sasha isn't good with people. I'll make sure Yuri knows you stopped by this evening."

She flashed me a tight smile before scurrying down the steps and out of view. Jake closed and locked the door and engaged the security alarm again. He waved the folder. "I'll put this on Yuri's desk."

"Okay." I let my grip on Sasha's collar loosen. The dog looked up at me with gleaming eyes. He seemed so proud of himself for protecting me. I didn't have the heart to scold him for being so over-the-top. "You and I have to work on our obedience training."

He made a yowling sound and smacked my leg with

his paw.

"You're a big boy and you could really hurt someone. Again," I added, thinking of Tommy. "You're supposed to defend Yuri's house but that doesn't mean you have to scare the piss out of *everyone* who comes to the front door."

My phone started to ring so I fished it out of the pocket of my skinny jeans. I recognized the number as Ty Weston's. We'd exchanged some texts but hadn't spoken at length since our wild night cruising Houston's gay bars.

"Hello?"

"Hey, sweetheart! How are you?"

"Good. You?"

"I'm damn fine as always. Listen—you have a few minutes to talk?"

Just then, Sasha tried to lick my face but I blocked him with my hand. He didn't take rejection well and slobbered all over my hand. "Sasha! No!"

"Uh—did I catch you at a bad time?"

"No." I couldn't stop the giggle burbling in my throat as Sasha continued to beg for attention. "It's Yuri's dog. He's sort of infatuated with me."

"Just like his master, if my spies around town are right."

I didn't dignify that with a response. Wagging my finger at Sasha, I managed to get him to calm down. "What did you want to discuss?"

"You're not going to confirm or deny your relationship with your moneyed Russian honey?"

"Are you asking as a friend or a tabloid blogger?"

"Both."

"Then no comment."

"Uh-huh."

"Look, I have the right to some privacy."

"Okay. Okay. No need to be so touchy."

I rolled my eyes. "You have ten seconds to tell me what you wanted to discuss or I'm hanging up."

"*Rawr*!" He playfully growled at me. "Now I know why the bouncers at 716 called you the Dragon Lady."

"Really, Ty? I'm hanging up now—"

"No! Wait. I have a business proposal I wanted to discuss with you. Your social media cover-your-ass blitz last night pushed a ton of business toward the bars and clubs we'd visited. Apparently, they had bachelorette party bookings like crazy! They were really pleased. They wanted me to see if you'd like to do some promos for them. You know—waving cover charge for your followers if they have a QR code at the door. They're willing to kick a nice fee your way."

I was taken aback. I'd hoped to salvage my pride by showcasing the fun I'd had and making it very tongue-in-cheek but to make money off it? "Seriously?"

"Yes—and it got me thinking, Lena. We have some skills and strengths that play well off one another. Maybe we should consider throwing in together."

"A gossip columnist and a PR girl?"

"I know. It sounds crazy but what do you do best?"

"Um…"

"You rescue businesses, baby girl! You took 716 from the toilet to the top of the Houston club scene. You helped Tai and Chuy launch their food truck to save their restaurants. Your friend's bakery relaunch is a huge hit."

Was he right? Was *that* my real talent?

"And me? Girl, I understand how a crisis and a scandal play out in the media better than anyone."

"So what are you suggesting? That we form some kind of crisis management firm?"

"Something like that," he agreed. "I've got a lawyer in

mind for the legal end of things. Can we meet for drinks to chat?"

"I'm busy tonight."

"An early lunch? Say eleven?"

"I can swing that."

"Great. I'll text you the details. I'm really excited about this, Lena. I hope you'll give it some real consideration. I think we have something here."

"I'm open to all possibilities right now."

"Wonderful! Until tomorrow!"

"Bye."

Pocketing my phone, I tried to wrap my head around Ty's proposal. Everything he'd said really resonated with me. Was this why I'd been so unhappy at my old job?

Sasha suddenly spun toward the door. His ears perked and he let loose a rough growl. He moved in front of me again and continued to rumble warningly.

But this time the door opened to reveal his master. Overcome with excitement, Sasha bounded across the entryway to meet Yuri. Unlike me, Yuri got him under control with one sharply worded command. Tail wagging, Sasha sat and waited for Yuri to acknowledge him.

As Yuri petted Sasha, I spotted the three men trailing him. Derek came through the door first and gave Sasha a wide berth. The two men who followed Derek went wide-eyed at the sight of the behemoth dog. The first of the two strangers through the door I didn't recognize but the second face I knew very well.

"Kelly?"

The Faze bouncer and former Marine grinned at me. "Hey, Lena!"

I glanced at Yuri who tightly held Sasha's collar. "What's going on?"

"Dimitri thought it would be safer for us to have two

extra guards. I see that you already know Kelly Connolly." He gestured to the other man. "This is Vasya."

The giant Russian nodded at me. "Miss Cruz."

"Call me Lena. I prefer that." Catching Yuri's gaze, I smiled sweetly. "Can I see you in the office really quick? You had a visitor while you were out and she left something for you."

Yuri saw right through my ruse but he smiled and nodded. "Sure." He glanced at Derek. "Get them set up in the staff quarters and run them through the security program. I'll touch base with you later this evening."

"Sure, Boss."

As the men left the foyer, Sasha relaxed but kept close to Yuri who joined me as I headed for his office. Once we were safely inside, Yuri shut the door and leaned back against it. His pleasant expression slipped. "What's wrong?"

"Two more guards, Yuri?" I rubbed the back of my neck as the stress of the situation made my stomach clench. "That's so *expensive*."

His expression turned comical. "Is *that* what this is about? Money?"

"Of course it's about money." I couldn't believe how blasé he was about the situation. "I know the going rate for Dimitri's security guards. When you told me that Jake was going to follow me around, I didn't make a fuss because he's already under contract but adding two more guards? Yuri—it's too much."

"It's a small price to pay for my peace of mind."

"A small price? No, it's a huge—"

"Enough," Yuri cut me off. His curt tone surprised me. Softening the harshness of his interjection, he reached for my hand and dragged me closer. His palm curved against my cheek. "You agreed that you would let me spoil you."

"When I made that promise yesterday, I thought we were talking about the occasional trip abroad or a handbag or something. I didn't agree to let you spend tens of thousands of dollars to hire me another babysitter."

I tried to pull away from him but he slid his arm around my waist and kept me right where he wanted me. "Your father is being held hostage in exchange for a painting. I need to know that you're safe. Kelly and Vasya are here to make sure that nothing happens to you."

"Yuri, please," I whispered, my throat tightening.

"Help me understand what bothers you so much, Lena. I'm trying to see things from your point of view but it's difficult."

I tried to find the right words. "Money makes us unequal, Yuri. It makes me *less* than you. I want us to be equals. I want us to be partners—and I can't be your partner if I'm running a mental tab on what I owe you."

"You don't owe me anything. Everything I give you I give freely. There are no strings attached to any of this."

I could hear the hurt in his voice. My chest tightened as I realized how I was making him feel by constantly harping on the money issue. "I'm sorry. I didn't think—I don't want you to think I'm ungrateful."

"I don't think that." He kissed me with such tenderness that the prickly heat of tears irritated my eyes. "I know you're struggling to feel equal with me in this relationship." He cupped my face. "You are my equal. I see you as my equal. The numbers in our bank accounts don't matter to me. They shouldn't matter to you."

I swallowed hard and placed my hand against his strong jaw. "I promise I'll try to let it go, Yuri."

"I realize it won't be easy for you and I appreciate that

you're willing to try." His lips touched mine briefly. "In fact, why don't we start with this?"

He reached into the pocket of his suit jacket and retrieved a box. The cheery hue, that telltale robin's egg blue, made my heart stutter.

My shocked gaze jumped to his face. "What's this?"

He pressed the box into my hand. "It's a just-because gift."

Biting my lower lip, I studied the box. "This is probably one hell of a just-because."

He chuckled. "I hope you like it."

I didn't think that would be a problem. I had a feeling I was going to love whatever the box held. With trembling fingers, I untied the bright white ribbon and lifted the lid. My lips parted and a soft gasp escaped them as I uncovered the gleaming gold cuff I'd been lusting over a few weeks earlier. Interwoven leafy vines stretched from one end of the delicate, airy cuff to the other.

Lifting my gaze to Yuri's smiling face, I asked, "How did you—"

And then I remembered where he'd been this afternoon.

Narrowing my eyes, I murmured, "Vivian?"

He grinned and gingerly lifted the obscenely expensive cuff from the box. Holding my hand, he slipped it around my wrist. "I wanted this first gift to be perfect."

As I admired the gorgeous cuff, I caught exactly what he'd said. "The first gift?"

His sexy grin made my tummy wobble. With a flourish, he produced a second box from another pocket. He whisked away the empty box and tossed it on the nearby sofa before thrusting the new box into my hands. Even though I wanted to exclaim at how much he'd spent on his shopping spree, I didn't dare. I could see how much he enjoyed giving me these gifts. His eyes damn near sparkled with excitement.

Inside the second box, I found the matching earrings. They were the same vine motif but dotted with dozens of tiny shimmering diamonds. I fingered them with such awe. "Oh, Yuri!"

"Let me see them on you." He swiped the box from my hands.

I slipped the simple studs from my ears and dropped them into my pocket. Yuri stepped closer and carefully threaded the posts through my lobes. The gentle, cautious way that he held my earlobes set my skin alight. Breaths quickening, I gazed up into his smiling face.

Yuri touched my cheek. "What's that look, Kitten?"

Blinking back tears, I confessed, "I'm just thinking how ridiculously lucky I am to have stumbled into your life." Lest he think it was the beautiful jewelry that had inspired my thoughts, I added, "It's not about the earrings and the bracelet. It's just—it's everything. Any other man would have thrown me and my cousin out the front door last night. Any other man would have told me to take my cartel problems and my ex-con dad and hit the streets." I gulped down the painful knot blocking my throat. "But not you."

"Not me," he whispered and lowered his mouth to mine.

I rose on tiptoes to meet his seeking kiss. Winding my arms around his neck, I darted my tongue between his lips. He answered the invitation to deepen the kiss by sifting his fingers through my hair and tilting my head back for better access.

Just as the kiss started to get really interesting, someone knocked at the door. Sasha leapt up from his spot on the rug and marched to the door to woof loudly.

With an irritated groan, Yuri ended our kiss. He brushed his knuckles down my cheek. "Between that dog, the staff and our phones, we may never make love again."

Giggling, I patted his chest. "Maybe we should check into a hotel."

"At this point, I'm willing to *buy* us a hotel to get five minutes alone with you."

He said it jokingly but I could see him actually going through with such an outlandish thing. Trying to rein him in, I suggested, "How about a bed and breakfast?"

Yuri tossed back his head and laughed. Glad the money tension between us had dissipated, I reached for the door and discovered Feodor on the other side.

"Dinner is ready."

"We'll be right there."

I glanced back at Yuri. "Dinner?"

He strode to his desk and picked up the folder sitting there. "I thought you were telling a white lie earlier to get me alone in here. Who brought this?"

"Anna." I stepped aside so Sasha could escape the office. No doubt his dinner had been placed in his bowls too. "She said it was important but that you'd already left the office. She was on her way out of town, I guess."

He nodded. "I'm sending her to Europe to tamp down the environmental protests. They voted to give me permission to build but it's not playing so well in all the papers. She's going to help Jameson, the pipeline project VP, get the situation under control. After that, she's going to spend some time with a sick relative."

"Do you still think it's an inside job? The sabotage, I mean?"

"Yes." A frustrated sigh erupted from his lips. "I had my financial team vet our backers again and they swear everyone looks good. I hate to think someone who works for me is causing these problems but I'm starting to become very suspicious."

"I'm really sorry that all this crap with my family got dropped on your doorstep when you're trying to save this pipeline deal."

He waved his hand. "If the pipeline doesn't come off the way I want, I'll find a new way to make it work. We may have to change the route or come up with a better design, one that will placate the environmentalists, but I'm getting this pipeline built."

I raised an eyebrow. "Come hell or high water, huh?"

"Absolutely." He dropped the folder onto his desk and strode toward me. After pressing a kiss to my temple, he said, "But no more business talk for a while. Let's have dinner like two normal people and try to forget everything else going wrong in our lives."

I didn't know if it would be that simple to go an hour without thinking about my father's precarious situation, my dumb cousin's criminal blunder or my job prospects—but if any man could make me forget my troubles, it was Yuri.

* * *

Later that night, Yuri sat at his desk and finished up the last of his nightly correspondence. He'd been reading through the day's reports while enjoying a drink and the light notes of *Scheherazade* over the office's sound system.

Across the office, Lena lounged on the sofa and quietly tapped away at her laptop. She'd already had her evening bath and had changed into a tiny pair of striped shorts and a tank top. Though he'd wanted to join her in that bath, work had beckoned him. As much as he wanted to blow it off to spend an evening enjoying her supple curves and pleasured sighs, there were hundreds of employees who depended on him to maintain focus.

Soon, he promised himself, and picked up the next stack of paperwork that needed his attention.

The folder Anna had dropped by the house caught his eye. He shifted aside the geology reports from the newly proposed mine and picked up the folder. Inside, he found a thick stack of papers and a cover sheet with Lena's personal details and a quick synopsis of the contents of the dossier.

Feeling suddenly uncomfortable, he glanced at her but she remained none the wiser. His heartbeat kicked up a few notches as he quickly perused the file. She had a clean credit report and surprisingly high balances in her checking and savings accounts. He had a good idea of the salary she'd earned at the PR firm so he now understood just how frugal she truly was.

Her father's photographs from his driver's license and passport didn't show the hardened criminal he'd expected but a tall, lean, clean-cut Latino man in his fifties who could have easily passed as a white-collar type. The rap sheet attached to an older mug shot wasn't nearly as long as others he'd seen. Joe Cruz had nothing on Ivan or Nikolai.

"Yuri?"

He slammed the folder shut. Hoping he didn't look as guilty as he felt, he met her questioning gaze. "Yes?"

"What do you know about crisis management firms?"

Setting aside the folder, he chuckled softly. "That if I had one on retainer I wouldn't be dealing with this pipeline bullshit. Why do you ask?"

She closed her laptop and put it on the cushion next to her. "Ty Weston called me earlier, before you came home."

"Oh? And what did Houston's biggest mouth want?"

"To talk to me about going into business with him."

Yuri blinked a few times before his brain processed what she'd said. "*You* go into business with *that* gossip columnist?" He laughed harshly and put his metaphorical foot down. "I absolutely forbid it."

Now she was the one laughing and rolling her eyes. "Oh please. Like that works with me!"

"It does with Erin whenever Ivan says it," he grumbled.

"Well, I'm not Erin and I don't find the alpha caveman thing as hot as she does."

Ignoring her remark, he asked, "Why in the world would you want to go into business with a man who has a reputation like Ty Weston?"

She snorted. "Did you really just ask me that? You the billionaire playboy infamous for his high-profile, love 'em and leave 'em romances? You with an inner circle of friends that includes two felons and mob connections?"

He held up his hand. "All right. Point taken."

"Look," she rose from the couch and came toward his desk, "I haven't agreed to anything. We're meeting for lunch tomorrow to discuss his idea."

Walking around his desk, she leaned back against it and exposed those sexy legs of hers to his approving gaze. Running his hand down her thigh, he asked, "And what exactly is his idea?"

"He made the point that what I seem to do best is rescue businesses in trouble. Tai and Chuy's restaurants, Benny's bakery, 716, the restaurants and two clubs I worked with when I first started interning at the firm." She ticked off the locations on her fingers. "It's like my whole career has been built around that one area of expertise."

"That explains why you felt stagnant and bored in your old position." He let his fingertips drift down the smooth curve of her knee. "You only find excitement in being challenged and once the businesses are doing well your work is done. What does Ty plan to bring to the table?"

"I'm damn good at working social networks but Ty understands how scandals and crises play out in the media in ways I never will."

"Because he exploits them and uses them for link bait to increase his page hits and drive advertising dollars into his bank account," Yuri retorted with some disgust.

Her eyes brightened. "I'm surprised you know the term link bait."

He dragged his fingers along the inside of her thigh, creeping right up to the first touch of cloth before stopping. "When I first became aware of you, I got to know you via your social media platform. You actually had a post that first day I started following you making fun of link baiting."

"Really?" She seemed oddly touched. "I can't believe you've been paying attention to me that long."

"I couldn't help myself. From the first moment you came into my view, I couldn't think of anyone else."

"Not even Tanya?"

He smiled at her catty tone and lifted her tank top a few inches, baring the sloping pane of her belly. "Tanya Who?"

She smacked his arm. "Nice save."

"Hardly," he whispered and leaned forward to press his lips to her naked skin. "I intend to have you here. On my desk," he added, in case she had any doubts. "Every time I sit here to wade through reports from my staff, I want to be inundated with the memories of you riding my cock."

As he snaked his hand under her shirt to cup her breast, she reached down and plucked an expertly hidden condom from the waistband of her shorts. With a mischievous grin, she tossed it onto his desk. "Take me."

He nipped at her navel. "I love a girl who is always prepared."

Giggling, she raked her fingers through his hair. The sensation of her short nails scratching at his scalp sent a tingling shiver down his spine. His cock throbbed to life. The memory of her soft lips wrapped around his cock last night made his balls ache and his groin tighten.

"You make me crazy." He grasped the waistband of her shorts and dragged them down her hips. She wore no panties and he appreciated it immensely. Dotting kisses alone her soft skin, he whispered, "I keep telling myself to go slow, to make love to you gently and take my time, but then I see you like this and I lose control."

Gripping his hair, she widened her stance and offered him access to the place he most wanted to visit. "I like it when you lose control. I like the way you make me feel."

Sliding to his knees, Yuri shoved his chair out of the way and nuzzled his face between her thighs. "Right now, I plan to make you feel very, *very* good."

He pushed her shorts all the way down her legs so she could kick them off. The moment the restricting fabric was out of his way, he grasped her thighs and shoved them apart. With one long lick, he swiped the seam of her sex. She inhaled sharply and then mewled like a kitten when his tongue probed her folds and found her clit.

She said his name on a low groan. "*Yuri.*"

He loved to hear her enjoying his wicked ministrations. Unable to get enough of her, Yuri lashed her sweet cunt with his tongue. He alternated swirling movements with long, slow tugs of her clit. She gripped the lip of his desk so hard her knuckles had gone white.

When he penetrated her with one finger and then two, Lena cried out and pushed her pussy against his mouth. He attacked her swollen clit, determined to make her shatter and to hear her shouting his name. Thrusting his fingers in and out of her wet channel, he curved them just so and found that spot that made her knees wobble. Suckling her clit, he pushed her over the edge.

"Oh! *Oh*!" She came hard, her clit pulsing against his mouth as he continued to torment her. "Oh God. *God*!"

When she rose on tiptoes to escape his fluttering tongue, he decided to show some mercy and let her come down easily. She still panted and shuddered as he stood and spun her around to face his desk. Tangling his hands in her hair, he pressed his cheek to hers. "I'm going to fuck you now."

"Yes. *Please*. Fuck me, Yuri. Fuck me now."

He doubted she'd ever begged any man to take her. The heady knowledge that he affected her in ways no other man ever had left him reeling. He quickly freed his cock from his pants and rolled on the condom.

Enthralled by the sight of her wiggling ass, he swept his palm up and down the plump curves of her bottom. She spread her thighs even more and displayed that pink pussy that felt so damn good squeezing and enveloping him. Unable to delay a moment longer, he pressed the head of his cock against her entrance and slowly slipped inside her.

She moaned and pushed back encouragingly. "Yes."

Certain she wanted exactly what he desired, Yuri clasped her waist and began a hard, fast rhythm. She clawed at his desk, shoving papers and pens out of the way as he pounded into her from behind. The sexy sound of their bodies noisily meeting in the throes of passion echoed in the office. He could only hope that the classical strains of music flowing out of the speakers muted their coupling for the staff in the rest of the house.

Running his hands down her back, he leaned forward and kissed her neck and shoulders. She shivered and reached back to cup his hip. He picked up his pace and depth, taking her roughly and making her cry out with excitement. The desk vibrated beneath them. A stack of bound reports sitting on the corner of his desk rattled too close to the edge and fell to the hardwood planks with a noisy *thwap*.

Heat ripped through his lower belly as those first fluttering waves heralded his impending release. Biting back the need to come, he focused on Lena's needs and ignored his own. When her breaths hitched and grew more frantic, he reached for her hand and dragged it down to her side.

"Touch yourself," he growled urgently. "Make yourself come for me."

She whimpered but did exactly as commanded. Lifting her bottom, she reached between her thighs and started to flick her clit. The heavenly fit of her snug pussy grew impossibly tighter as she chased her own climax. The first spasm broke his tenuous hold and he surrendered to the blissful bursts tearing through him.

He cursed under his breath as the waves of ecstasy made him rock on his feet. He caught himself at the last moment and managed not to fall forward on top of Lena. Flopping back into his chair, he dragged her onto his lap. Panting and shuddering, they clutched at each other and made out like teenagers in a steamy backseat.

"I'll be right back," he said finally and untangled himself from her nubile body. Leaving her in his chair, he leaned down and kissed her tenderly. "And then we'll take this upstairs."

He ducked into the private bathroom. Though sex had always required the use of condoms, Yuri found himself loathing the damn things. When it came to Lena, he wanted nothing between them, not even that thin sheath of latex. How would she react if he subtly suggested they have the necessary testing done to rid themselves of the nuisance? He trusted her to be faithful and he damn sure wasn't interested in any woman other than Lena.

Still thinking of the best way to approach that rather sensitive subject, Yuri stepped out of the bathroom and spotted Lena standing behind his desk. He noticed the floor had been tidied. The jumbled papers on his desk were now in neat stacks.

And there, clamped in her hand, was the dossier he'd asked Anna to prepare.

When he saw the betrayal and hurt etched into her beautiful face, Yuri experienced the most brutally painful clenching of his gut. Suddenly, he was reminded of the words she'd spoken that morning at her kitchen table. She'd given him one more chance—and there was no doubt in his mind he'd just royally fucked it up.

CHAPTER FOURTEEN

"What the hell is this, Yuri?" Chest tight and heart racing, I glanced down at the incriminating paperwork for a second time. I'd been tidying the mess we'd made during our fantastic romp when my gaze had flicked across the folder. As I'd picked it up, the papers had fallen onto the desk. It was the sight of my father's mug shot that had stricken me cold.

Jaw clenched, he took a tentative step forward. "It's nothing, Lena. It's simply a dossier on your background. It doesn't mean anything."

I couldn't believe what I was hearing. "Are you serious? Are you really going to stand there and lie to my damn face?"

"I'm not lying." He put his hands together in front of him. "I don't care what the file says about you or your father or any of that."

"Then why the hell have it done? Huh?" Anger bubbled violently in the pit of my stomach and I tried to keep my temper under control.

"The night you called me in Berlin, when you were drunk, Nikolai made an offhand comment about you having a gun because of your father. I didn't know what that meant—who he was or what he did. I asked Anna to put together this file so I could understand you."

"Understand me?" Betrayal gnawed at my heart as I rifled through the nearly two-inch thick file. I jerked out the sheet with my bank account details and waved it angrily. "You think this helps you understand me?"

The paper fell to the floor as I pulled out another sheet, this one my high school transcript. "Or what about this one? Huh? Is my C in AP Calculus that fucking important to you?"

He ran his fingers through his hair, leaving the ends sticking up wildly. "God, I didn't think—"

"What? You didn't think I would find out? Because that's the problem, isn't it, Yuri?" I stabbed an accusing finger in the air. "You're only upset because you got caught."

"That's not true."

"Bullshit." Feeling so stupid, I gestured to the sofa where I'd been researching and reading email earlier. Balling up my father's mug shot, I threw it at Yuri and hit him in the chest. "I was sitting right there while you were over here reading all about my family's dirty little secrets."

"Lena, please," he pleaded.

"No, Yuri. You started this. Now let's see how good an assistant your sweet little Anna is."

"You don't have to do this. Please." He came closer. "Let's just shred the whole damn thing and forget this ever happened."

I gawked at him. "Do you really think it's that simple? Do you think I'll just forget how awful you made me feel? How embarrassed and stupid and betrayed I feel right now?"

"Yelena," he said, his voice husky with regret.

"You wanted to know everything about me, right?" I started to dig through the dossier in search of the sealed juvenile court record I was sure Anna had uncovered. The evidence of one of my deepest shames popped into view. I slapped it against his chest. "Well, there you go, Yuri. Now you know something I've only ever shared with Vivian. Go ahead. Read about what a messed up thirteen-year-old vandalizing freak show I was."

He refused to look at the page. Instead he crunched it in his big hand and dropped it. "No."

"What? *Now* you have a conscience?" I tried to hold back the tears burning my eyes but it was impossible. Fat, hot tears splashed onto my cheeks. Confused and hurt, I asked, "Why?"

"I don't know," he admitted finally. "I did what I always do when I want an answer. I assigned the task to someone else."

"I would have told you everything in here if you'd only asked."

"I know."

"Do you?" I shook my head. "I don't get you, Yuri. I really don't."

He tried to touch my face but I smacked his hand away from me. Gulping, he whispered, "I'm sorry, Lena. I didn't mean to hurt you."

"But you did."

Tossing the folder into his chair, I made my way to the French doors overlooking the back patio and lushly landscaped yard. Desperate for some space, I walked out of the office. The flagstone pavers were cool beneath my bare feet. Hugging my arms, I tried to figure out what the hell I was going to do now.

Through the open doors, I heard Yuri shut off the music before shoving paper into a shredder. The machine whined noisily as it chomped and chewed up the sordid and mundane details of my life. Rubbing my face with both hands, I fought the urge to scream my frustration.

Even as angry as I was with Yuri, I sensed he hadn't done this maliciously. He was so aloof when it came to things like this. I didn't doubt that he'd simply given Anna an order as a quick afterthought before jumping onto a plane. It was so like him—and he had to change.

Our relationship couldn't be conducted like a business. If he wanted answers, he needed to come to me and ask the damn questions. In the same way I was trying to become more aware of my hang-ups with money, he had to stop thinking of our relationship as a neatly boxed transaction.

Sasha's frantic barks met my ears. They were muted but nearby. I realized he was in the solarium. No doubt, he needed to be let out. I decided that if Feodor or one of the guards didn't let him out to do his business in the next minute or so, I'd go get him myself.

Behind me, Yuri continued to shred the file he'd had prepared. Not wanting to think about that anymore, I descended the steps and walked a few dozen feet across the patio. The burbling fountain in the middle of the yard drew my attention. The grass was cold and damp against my toes as I walked farther away from the house.

Overhead, the tiny sliver of a moon didn't lend much light. The old timey gas-style lamps dotting the backyard cast a warm glow on everything. The white limestone and marble sculptures looked so incredibly beautiful out here, almost ethereal.

From the far left, I heard the solarium doors open. Sasha's ear-splitting woof seemed even louder out here. I could hear him bounding toward me and rolled my eyes at his overprotective nature. Turning toward the sound of his barks, I tried to hush him. We were far away from Yuri's neighbors, but with a bark like that, there were sure to be complaints.

"Sasha! Sh!"

His barks grew more frantic and almost panicked. I realized something was wrong the moment he launched himself into the air. Sure I was about to be crushed, I turned my back on him and screamed. "NO!"

Sasha hit my shoulder with his front paws and took me to the ground. My head narrowly missed the beveled lip of the fountain. I screamed again as Sasha's snarling face crashed toward mine. I braced for a nasty bite but he simply nuzzled me quickly.

Before I could try to process what was happening, Sasha started to bark again. His quick, panicked barks rang through the night. With his paws on my chest and his big body covering me, I could hardly breathe.

What the hell is wrong with him?

The snap of a bullet ricocheting off the fountain made my blood run cold. Another bullet hit the fountain and then another.

Sasha wasn't trying to kill me. He was trying to save my life.

Grasping the dog's fur, I jerked him down against me, desperate to put as much of his body below the fountain's profile as possible. The last thing I wanted was for the big beast of a dog to catch a bullet.

Praying that I would survive this ordeal, I shouted the only name that mattered. "YURI!"

*

Yuri had just discovered an interesting piece of information in the dossier when Sasha's incessant barking got his attention. Even over the noisy whir of the shredder, he heard Sasha losing his mind in another part of the house. Moments later, Sasha's barks sounded like they were coming from outside. Apparently someone had let him out of the house.

When he heard Lena shouting at the dog, Yuri groaned with irritation. The dog had to learn to treat Lena with more care. She was much too small for him to be jumping all over.

But when she screamed, the sound so high-pitched and terrified, Yuri dropped the folder and rushed to the still-open doors. He scanned the backyard and found Lena on the grass next to the fountain with Sasha on top of her. At first he thought it was the dog hurting her but then he saw the unmistakable red flash of a sniper rifle's laser sight.

His heart damn near stuttered right out of his chest. "*YELENA!*"

A bullet ripped through the door next to him. The glass and wood shards splattered his neck and arm. The door behind him burst open and one of his new bodyguards raced into the room. Kelly slapped the light switch, plunging the room into darkness, and hurried across the room to Yuri's side. The sometime Faze bouncer pushed a gun into his hand as they crouched behind the slim safety of the doors.

"It's loaded. Jake is working on killing the lights. When it's dark, you provide suppressing fire and I'll get her."

"Like hell," he growled. If anyone was grabbing Lena, it was going to be him.

Leaning out the door, Yuri took aim at the closest

lantern lighting up the backyard and popped off a round. He hit his target and killed that ball of light. Following his lead, Kelly stepped out just long enough to fire at another lamp. Two by two, they picked them off until the yard was dark.

As if reading his mind, Kelly shoved him forward. "Move."

The former Marine moved to a better position and fired into the trees where the sniper was probably hidden. Yuri took advantage of the suppressive fire to dart from one sculpture to the next. When Kelly whistled, Yuri stopped and took over shooting into the trees so the bodyguard could get closer.

He caught Kelly's gaze. The Marine gave a series of hand signals that Yuri easily interpreted. When Kelly was done switching out his empty magazine, he gave a silent countdown. Three, two, one...

As Kelly started to fire again, Yuri darted the twenty or so yards to Lena and Sasha. He flattened his body to the ground next to her and slid his arms around her small body. Sasha dropped to his belly and crouched low against the fountain's curved edge. Yuri put a loving hand on the dog's side. "Good boy. Such a good boy."

Touching Lena's face, he wished he could see her but there wasn't enough light. "I've got you. Just hold onto me."

Sobbing hysterically, she gripped his arms and pushed her face into his chest. The rapid fire of high caliber sniper rounds and smaller caliber handgun fire continued all around them. He didn't know how the hell they were going to get out of here but he didn't care as long as she was safe in his arms.

To his utter shock, two headlights came into view. One of his SUVs equipped with the very latest in defense technology bounced as it raced across his beautifully landscaped yard. The SUV maneuvered onto the far side of the fountain, effectively blocking the sniper's attack.

A door popped open and Jake appeared. "Boss! Let's go!"

Snatching Lena by the waist, he dragged her to her feet and tossed her over the fountain's ledge. "Run!"

She sloshed through the knee-deep water and scrambled into the idling SUV. The vehicle continued to take heavy fire but Yuri felt confident it would allow them to escape their precarious position. Sasha bounded after him as he slogged through the chilly water to reach Lena and the SUV.

Once they were all safely inside, Vasya punched the gas. Yuri pulled Lena onto his lap and put a steadying hand on Sasha's neck. The dog's incessant growl covered the snap and pop of bullets hitting the racing SUV. Lena continued to sob against his throat. He squeezed her tightly and silently vowed to never let her out of his sight again.

When they were safely inside the garage, they poured out of the SUV and into the house. The guards rushed them into the ground floor panic room where Feodor already paced nervously. Seeing them uninjured, the older man relaxed but his I-told-you-so expression didn't bode well for the conversation Yuri was certain they would soon be having.

Not caring about his mentor's opinion at the moment, Yuri ignored his censorious look and carried Lena to a chair. He carefully placed her on the seat and ran his hands over her body in a desperate attempt to convince himself she was okay. There were scratch marks on her shoulder and thighs from Sasha's paws but she looked otherwise unhurt.

"I'm sorry. I'm sorry. I'm so sorry." The words spilled from her mouth. "This is all my fault. Oh God. I almost got you killed."

He clasped her sweet face in his hands and captured her frantic gaze. "Stop. *Breathe*. You're fine. We're both fine." He glanced at the dog resting next to her. "Sasha is fine. Everyone is okay."

"It's not okay. It's not." She roughly wiped at her wet face. Streams of tears left her skin glistening. "This is all because of me. Because of my stupid family."

"We don't know that." Even though he suspected this was cartel related, he wasn't going to jump to that conclusion yet. He used his shirt to wipe her face clean and then kissed her tenderly. "Don't you dare apologize for something you didn't do."

"But—"

"No." He kissed her again. The reality of why she was out there in the first place hit him hard. "It's my fault you were out there tonight. I'm the one who hurt you. I'm the one who betrayed your trust and sent you running from the house." His throat became painfully tight. "If it hadn't been for Sasha—"

She leaned forward and wrapped her slender arms around him. With her face buried in the crook of his neck, she whispered, "Sasha deserves a steak dinner for, like, the rest of his life."

Yuri laughed softly. "At the very least."

"Boss?" It was Derek. "It's all quiet. We think the threat is gone—and the cops are on their way. We're about to have every police officer and sheriff's deputy within fifty miles up our asses."

Though Derek put it more colorfully than he would have, he didn't disagree with the sentiment. Kissing Lena's cheek, he gave her a direct order. "You are to stay here in this panic room with Feodor and Sasha until I come to get you. Understood?"

She nodded dutifully. "Yes, Yuri."

Feodor brought over a blanket and bottle of water from the supply cabinets. Certain she was in safe hands, he exited the panic room to find Derek and Vasya waiting for him. He touched the giant Russian's arm. In their shared language, he gave one command. "Watch her."

Vasya placed his huge body between the rest of the house and the door. Walking with Derek, he left the small hallway.

"What's the party line, Boss?"

He knew what Derek was asking. How much did he want them to reveal to the investigators who would soon be traipsing over every inch of his home?

"I trust your discretion."

Derek understood. "I'll pass the word along."

"Do that."

Heading to his office, he grabbed his phone and made two quick calls before the police began to beat down his door. He needed two men at his side tonight if he was going to survive this scrape and keep Lena's father alive—his lawyer and Nikolai.

CHAPTER FIFTEEN

It was after one in the morning before Yuri got the last detective out of his house and walked his saint of a lawyer to the door. Craig and his legal team would more than earn their retainer over this mess.

He'd already sent Lena upstairs with Sasha, Kelly and Vasya to guard her. Feodor was still puttering around in the kitchen but he would turn in eventually. Derek and Jake had taken the first shift. With the cop cars sitting on the house, Yuri wasn't worried about a repeat performance of the nightmare they'd just survived.

In his office, he found his closest friends waiting for him. Dimitri had arrived soon after the first police officers. Apparently he'd given Vasya strict instructions to call him with updates. Yuri hated that Dimitri's new businesses was being dragged through his shit-storm but he hoped they could find a way to spin it positively. Lena would know just how...

"We're alone." He shut the door and leaned against it. The stress of the last few days left his shoulders slumping and his stomach churning.

"How is Lena?" Concern colored Ivan's voice.

"Shaken," Yuri answered.

"And you?"

"Now that the fear and panic has finally subsided, I'm starting to feel an immense amount of rage," he admitted. It was all he could do to keep his shaking hands clenched at his sides.

"Was it the cartel?" Dimitri finally dared to ask the question they were all thinking.

Nikolai shook his head. "I received assurances that this was absolutely not the cartel. Guzman made the point that he gains nothing from trying to kill Lena and everything from keeping her alive and Yuri happy. This is all about the money and saving face for him."

Ivan started to pace. "What about this pipeline, Yuri? Erin said there some major protests in Europe. Those protestors outside your downtown headquarters were all over the news tonight. Would they be crazy enough to go after you? To go after Lena?"

He shrugged. "At this point, anything is possible." Reluctantly, he admitted, "There have been problems with the pipeline. Someone is leaking negative stories to the press. They're trying to tank the deal. I thought it might be one of the investors trying to back out in an underhanded way but that's looking less likely. It might be someone on the inside."

Dimitri blew out a noisy breath. "And if it's not related to the pipeline?" He seemed hesitant to ask but did it anyway. "You've made a lot of enemies building your empire. What might seem insignificant to you could be a life-changing moment to someone else."

Yuri wanted to argue with Dimitri but he stopped himself. Even though he'd never done a competitor dirty in business and had always tried to be fair in his dealings, there had been times during his early years running his private equity firm that hadn't been particularly pleasant. He'd built his early wealth by swallowing up failing businesses, slashing their workforces, jettisoning the failing sections and selling them for big profits.

Dragging a hand across the back of his neck, he unhappily admitted, "There is probably a long list of people who hate me for business reasons."

"I think this angle that Dimitri has suggested is the most likely one for this mess," Nikolai stated. "Give it to the police and let them run with it. You'll keep them busy and out of this *other* thing."

Ivan fervently agreed with Nikolai's advice. "Listen to me, Yuri, the last fucking thing you need is detectives digging around in Lena's problems. The surest, fastest way to get her father killed is to get them nosing around where they don't belong. One stumble on their side and that guy?" He shook his head and drew his finger across his throat. "I wouldn't chance it."

"I won't." He hated the anxious feeling riding along his spine. How Nikolai managed to always look so calm when he was living on the wrong side of the law, Yuri would never understand. He finally comprehended the reason Ivan had been so desperate to escape that life. The stress of keeping the authorities at arm's length while trying to protect Lena and her family was going to give him a heart attack.

"What about Vivian?" Ivan addressed Nikolai. "Erin is beside herself with worry. She's terrified that the cartel will do something to hurt Vivian because of her father's connections."

Nikolai's jaw twitched. "I have Kostya on her. That cousin of hers has someone babysitting her around the clock. Of all of us, she's probably the safest right now."

"Erin would feel better if Vivian came to stay with us until this whole mess blows over. Kostya is welcome to stay with us too." Ivan clearly understood the two were coming as a package deal.

"I'll see if she'll agree to it."

Ivan smiled. "She won't have a choice. Erin has quite a gift for guilting the people she loves into doing the things that are best for them."

Yuri didn't doubt that for a moment. Erin seemed to be the mother hen of the group of women. Not that Vivian or Lena or Benny seemed to mind. They appeared to understand it was Erin's way of showing them how much they meant to her.

Their late night discussion came to its natural end. As the men left, Ivan gave him a bear hug that threatened to burst his lungs and Dimitri clapped him on the back so hard he was sure he'd have bruises in the morning. Only Nikolai stayed behind.

Alone with his friend, he took in Nikolai's tense expression. Expecting the worst, he asked, "What is it?"

"Guzman has a new timetable, Yuri. He wants the painting and the ransom you agreed to pay in seven days—or he wants the cousin."

Irritation blazed through him. He didn't like this cartel asshole putting the squeeze on him, especially not with the *obscene* amount of money on the table. If it had been anyone else, Yuri would have called him personally and told him to go fuck himself.

But the man had Lena's father's life in his hands. One wrong move and Yuri would sentence Joe Cruz to death—and a very violent, very traumatic one at that.

"Can you get the painting?"

"Niels is working on it. He'll come through for me but

I can't possibly predict when that will be. It could be tomorrow or two months from now."

"Two months from now, Lena is going to be mourning the death of a family member." Nikolai's eyes showed such sadness. "Unfortunately, you'll be the one to decide which one needs a gravestone."

Aghast at the very thought, Yuri shook his head. "I can't do that."

"Then find the painting." Nikolai squeezed his shoulder. "Or I'll have to make the decision for you."

The coldness in Nikolai's voice stunned him. He'd always known that his friend didn't blink at such ugliness but to hear him say that he would decide whether to send Lena's cousin to the cartel or leave her father to die there? It drove home that Nikolai lived a life Yuri couldn't ever truly fathom.

Without another word, Nikolai left the house. Yuri locked up behind his friend and trudged upstairs. Vasya sat in a chair outside the open master bedroom door. He heard the soft voices of Kelly and Lena drifting out of the room. The two ran in the same night club circles and knew enough of each other to be friendly. He didn't mind in the least and was honestly relieved that she had a familiar face around her right now.

When he stepped into the room, Kelly hopped to his feet. Showered and changed into a nightshirt, Lena remained on the cozy couch in the reading nook. Kelly looked a little nervous so Yuri instantly put the younger man at ease with a smile. Even so, Kelly bid Lena a quick goodnight and beat a hasty retreat from the master suite.

Finally alone with her, Yuri settled onto the couch next to her and stretched out his tired, aching legs. Closing his eyes, he dropped his head back against the cushion and inhaled a long, slow breath. Lena clasped his hand and dragged it onto her lap. She ran her fingers over his knuckles, the movement surprisingly soothing.

He didn't want to talk about the shooting or the cartel but they had to discuss that awful episode in his office. It was the last damn thing he wanted to talk about this late night at night but it had to be done.

Holding her gaze, he stated the obvious. "I crossed the line. I'm so very sorry for hurting you and I'm going to try my very hardest to never make you cry again."

"You did hurt me," she said softly. "I wish I could make feel you how embarrassing and painful it was for me to find that stupid file."

"I have a damn good idea of how terrible it was for you." He brushed his fingers down her cheek. "Can you forgive me?"

"Yes."

"*Will* you forgive me?"

"I already have." She squeezed his hand. "That doesn't mean I don't have conditions."

"Anything."

She arched one of those perfectly shaped brows. "That's a dangerous offer to make for a man with your deep pockets."

He chuckled at her playful reply. Showing her he was serious, he brought her hand to his lips and pressed a kiss to every single one of her fingertips. "Anything, Lena."

"You have to stop treating our relationship like a business transaction. If you need to tell me that you're running late or you're going to have to reschedule a date, pick up your phone and call me. Even texting me would be better than handing it off to your assistant. If you want to know something about me, open your dang mouth and *ask* me."

"Agreed. Absolutely."

Holding hands, they settled into a comfortable silence. Yuri gave consideration to their developing relationship. He wondered if it was time to lay all his cards on the table. He'd been so hesitant to tell her *exactly* how he felt about her because he feared spooking her but right now it seemed silly to hold back. He was going toe-to-toe with a fucking cartel for her. If she didn't already suspect how he felt, he'd be shocked.

"Lena, we can't keep doing this."

She went rigid. Eyes wide, she asked, "You're breaking up with me?"

"What? NO!" He slid closer and placed his palm against her cheek. "No. Of course not." He silently cursed himself for being so clumsy. "What I should have said is that we can't keep treating this relationship like it's in a trial phase."

"I don't understand."

"We're going through the motions like this is a normal, run-of-the-mill relationship when it's anything but. There's no hot and cold here or on and off. I know you're afraid to take the plunge into something serious so quickly but I'm not."

She gulped nervously and her grip on his hand tightened. "What are you saying, Yuri?"

"I'm saying that right here, right now, you have to decide what it is you want with me." Cupping her face, he gazed into those big, beautiful brown eyes. "Because— God help me, woman—I'm in love with you. I'd do *anything* for you."

She blinked rapidly but couldn't keep the tears from spilling onto her lashes and cheeks. Voice husky, she said, "You don't have to do *anything* for me but love me. That's all I need."

"Do you want me?"

"Yes. So much," she whispered. "I'm falling in love with you and it scares me." She made her confession in a shaky voice. "I'm so scared to put all my trust and love in you. I've been hurt so many times but you? God, Yuri, if you broke my heart, it would crush me."

"Never," he vowed. "*Never.*"

"You say that now but I have so much baggage. I'm not an easy person to love."

The shame filling her voice made his heart ache. He thought of the mother who had walked out on her and the gaping hole in Lena's confidence and self-worth that one act had left behind.

"Look at me." He forced her to meet his gaze by tilting her head back. "That is not true. I'm finding it incredibly easy to love you, Yelena Cruz." He brushed the tears from her face. "And you're not the only one with baggage, Kitten. Together, we'll figure out a way to fix each other."

She smiled sadly. "That might take a long time."

"I don't mind." He kissed her then, claiming her mouth with all the love and passion he felt for this brilliant, beautiful woman. "Because I have all the time in the world for you."

With a joyful sob, she threw herself into his arms. He happily caught and embraced her. Burying his nose in her still damp, freshly washed hair, he breathed in that scent he loved so much. Despite the terrible turn of events they'd just lived, Yuri had never felt closer to her.

Sensing that she needed to be held and soothed after her traumatic experience, he coaxed her into bed and shut off the lights. Cradling her against his chest, Yuri sifted his fingers through her hair and caressed her arm and back until her breaths grew deeper and more relaxed. It filled him with such a strong sense of pride to know that she felt safe and secure in his arms.

For him, sleep didn't come so easily. His mind raced as he tried to remember every person he'd ever done business with in any capacity. There were more angry outbursts and tense negotiations than he'd remembered earlier when talking with his friends. A few long-buried memories made him uneasy. Had he really been such a dick?

But who would hold a grudge so long? And over a business deal?

Yuri couldn't quite explain it but this felt personal. If someone he'd crossed in business wanted to hurt him, the natural response would be to go after his money. Sabotaging the pipeline deal? Now *that* made sense from a business revenge angle.

Trying to kill Lena? That was personal. That had the feeling of someone who wanted to hurt him.

He had to agree with Nikolai on that count. The cartel wouldn't gain anything from killing Lena and crushing his soul. Lorenzo Guzman wanted his painting and his money. He didn't have a beef with Yuri.

So why target Lena? Why try to take the most important thing in the world from him?

The troubling thought perplexed him for most of the night. He fell into a fitful sleep but jerked awake every half hour or so. It was impossible for him to shed the eerie feeling that things were only just beginning to get dangerous. Suddenly four bodyguards and Sasha didn't feel like nearly enough.

When Lena rolled onto her side, he shifted and spooned her from behind. He lifted his head high enough to see the clock and groaned softly. It would be time to wake much too soon. He still hadn't figured out what the hell he was going to do about keeping Lena safe. She couldn't leave the house—that was for damn sure. He wasn't even sure he wanted her passing by the windows.

He'd just dozed off when Lena's phone started ringing. She bolted upright and started slapping at the bedside table. Putting a comforting hand on her belly, he silently urged her to relax. She threaded her fingers through his and answered the call. "Dad?"

Yuri listened to her side of the conversation. From the sounds of it, her father had no idea what had happened and Lena didn't trouble him with the details. He sensed she wanted to spare her father the gut-gnawing worry.

His chest tightened as he thought about the very important details he'd kept from her. What Nikolai had told him about the deadline and the terms Guzman demanded had to stay secret between them. He wouldn't burden her with things beyond her control.

As Lena wrapped up her phone call, Yuri wiped a hand down his tired face and decided he wouldn't go into the office downtown today. Everything that needed his attention could be taken care of from home.

"Yuri?"

Lena's gentle voice interrupted his thoughts. He glanced over and discovered her holding his ringing white phone. He hadn't even heard it. Taking it from her, he sat up and studied the screen. That international dialing code belonged to the only person he desperately wanted to hear from this morning.

"Niels?"

The amused chuckle on the other end confirmed it was the Dane in question. "I debated calling so early in your time zone. I'm sure I woke you."

"I don't mind." Yuri didn't dare hope for good news. "Well?"

"Relax. I've found your painting."

Yuri's stress levels plummeted. "And?"

"It won't be easy to pry from its owner's greedy little hands. I made an offer but he refused. Don't worry—I've got an idea. We'll have to call together our poker club and I think we're going to need a very big boat."

Yuri and Niels belonged to an exclusive group of high-rolling billionaires and millionaires who got together to play poker a few times a year. Their games were rarely open to outsiders so naturally everyone wanted a chance to play.

"Lucky for me, I happen to know where to find a very big boat."

Niels laughed. "Yes, I thought you would. So shall we say Saturday evening?"

"Yes."

"I'll make some calls and get this set up for you. It will look better if you're not the one who arranged the tournament."

Niels would want a favor someday but being indebted to the Danish tycoon was worth it. "Thank you."

"Believe me. It will be my pleasure to see this pompous ass knocked down a few pegs."

The call ended and Yuri dropped the phone onto the sheet twisted around his hips and Lena's thigh. She stroked his upper arm. He couldn't see her face in the darkness but he felt the concern radiating from her. "Is everything okay, Yuri?"

"That was Niels. My friend who knows the art world," he clarified in case she'd forgotten. "He found the painting."

"What? Really? Oh my God!" She exhaled a sigh of relief. "What happens now?"

He rolled onto his side and caressed her cheek. Using his fingertips for guidance in the dark, he found her mouth and gave her a kiss. Nuzzling her neck, he murmured, "Right now, I'm going to make love to you."

She shivered as he nipped at the sensitive curve of her neck. "I see."

"When we're finished," he slid his hand down her side and along her hip, "you're going to pack a bag and I'm going to take you to Monaco."

"What's in Monaco?" She made a soft whimpering sound as his hand slipped between her thighs.

"One of my yachts," he explained while probing her hidden depths. "Actually it's anchored in the sea there."

"Ah!" She clutched his shoulders as he penetrated her slowly and dragged his thumb across her clitoris. "Oh! But—ah! What about Sasha?"

Yuri nipped at her lower lip. "He's staying here. The last thing I need is that dog running wild on a yacht."

"No," she said with a laugh. "I meant right now. He's got his head on my hand and it's sort of freaking me out."

Yuri tore his mouth away from her neck and glanced over at the edge of the bed. He could feel the big dog's heavy breaths wafting across his arm. Refusing to be cock-blocked by the dog this morning, he pecked Lena's cheek. "I'll be right back."

Snapping his fingers, he hopped off the bed and called Sasha to follow him. He opened the bedroom door and ordered the dog into the hallway. Kelly jumped out of his chair as Sasha trotted by him. Surprised to see the former Marine still awake, he hid his nakedness with the door. "Shouldn't you get some rest?"

"Sleep isn't something I particularly enjoy these days."

Yuri understood what the younger man meant. He'd never seen the kind of ceaseless hell the Marine had on his multiple tours but he could imagine how difficult the effects were to manage after leaving the service.

Clearly understanding why Yuri had put the dog out in the hall, Kelly cleared his throat. "I think I'll, uh, go get some coffee."

"You really should." Yuri shut the door and turned the lock. He didn't want anyone bothering them this morning.

As he crawled over Lena, she giggled furiously. "I don't know how I'm going to look him in the face later."

"The same way I do." He grasped the hem of her nightshirt and dragged it up and over her head. Tossing it over his shoulder, he planted his knees on either side of her thighs. "Now—where was I?"

He skimmed his lips across the swell of her breast. "Here?"

"Um...a little bit lower," she replied playfully.

"Hmmm," he hummed just as playfully. "Was I here?" He dotted kisses up and down her bare tummy.

"Um..."

"No," he said definitively. "I'm fairly certain I was right down here."

Sliding onto his stomach, he pushed her thighs apart and planted a noisy kiss right on top of her clit. She purred and lifted her hips.

Remembering how beautifully—and loudly—she reacted to his oral attentions, he mischievously instructed, "Kitten, try not to wake the whole neighborhood..."

CHAPTER SIXTEEN

I had to give it to Yuri. The man had promised me an unrivaled travel experience and that was exactly what he'd provided. Flying on a privately owned jet was so incredibly pleasant compared to the long, slow-moving security lines at airports and the cramped seating.

Jake, Derek, Vasya and Kelly had come with us and were in another section. They were kicked back in their reclining seats reading or watching television with headphones.

On the jet, I'd had an entire seating area to myself while Yuri conducted business in the mobile office in the rear of the plane. The comfy seats and scrumptious snacks had been heavenly compared to the bruised knees and stale pretzels from my last commercial flight.

But the very best part? I'd been able to nap with my head in Yuri's lap while he studied stock reports and forecasts. When he'd invited me to curl up against him, I'd declined out of embarrassment. Some of his employees were travelling with us and I'd already gotten quite a few looks. Then it occurred to me that I didn't really give a shit what those people thought. Yuri wanted me to relax and he wanted to stroke my hair and remind me how much he loved me. That was permission enough for me to enjoy myself.

When we'd finally arrived at the French airport closest to Monaco, I'd been surprised to learn that we would be taking a helicopter to the yacht. The realization that his yacht had a helipad drove home just how huge this boat was. At my first glimpse of the gleaming white mega yacht, I nearly fainted in my seat. Hearing something described as four-hundred-feet long conjured up certain images but *seeing* it with my own eyes was something totally different.

The damn thing looked like an aircraft carrier floating on the Mediterranean. Stunningly, it wasn't even the biggest boat anchored out there. I spotted two other yachts that made Yuri's luxury vessel look rather modest—and that was saying something.

Yuri leaned closer, pushing his shoulder against mine, and pointed at the big boats that had left me awestruck. His voice was crackly in my ear as we used the in-flight communication system to talk. "That one is owned by a sheikh from Dubai. Nice guy. Fantastic polo player."

"And that one?" I gestured to the other massive yacht.

"Oh, that's the Pyxis. It's Mikhail's pride and joy." He must have seen the curiosity in my eyes. "We were in the military together. He made a fortune in metals and minerals."

"I've got to get my hands on some aluminum or nickel," I muttered.

Beside me, Yuri laughed. "If only it were that easy."

The helicopter began its descent. On instinct, I gripped my hands together in my lap. My belly lurched as

I prayed the helicopter wouldn't plunge into the sea. Always alert to my needs, Yuri pried my hands apart and held them in his own. He interlaced our fingers and smiled warmly.

The helicopter set down without incident. When the rotors finally stopped spinning, staff in spiffy navy and white uniforms rushed out to greet us. Yuri reached over and unbuckled my safety harness before dragging the headphones from my head and hanging them on their hook.

Holding my hand, he led me out of the helicopter and onto the helipad. We were quickly taken to a reception room where the rest of the staff stood in lines as if waiting to be inspected. Jake and Derek had come with us on the helicopter and were whisked away by two men who seemed to be the security officers on the ship.

As Yuri introduced me to the captain and crew, I heard the helicopter firing up again. A handful of Yuri's staff, Vasya and Kelly were waiting at the airport. I tried to concentrate on the names rapidly ticked off by the captain of the vessel but I had a feeling I was going to forget half of them. Thankfully every member of the staff wore a nametag.

One face in the second row caught my eye. I'd never met him in person but his face was familiar to me because of the photographs I'd seen around Benny's house and the bakery. "Johnny?"

He smiled at me. "Miss Cruz."

His respectful reply surprised me. He seemed so different from the mental image I'd created of him from the different stories I'd been told. I noticed the gang tattoo from some of his pictures had been covered with angel wings. The collar of his polo shirt hid most of it but the very tips of the wings peeked over the top.

Apparently he was making a conscious effort to leave that old, dangerous life of his behind.

Even though I wanted to talk to him, I sensed this wasn't the time. Later I would track him down, but, right now, Yuri seemed intent on showing me some more of his yacht. The mindboggling tour left me reeling. The sleek, modern design elements gave the boat a five-star hotel feel.

"What is it?" Yuri asked as we took our seats in the private dining area overlooking the beautiful, calm sea. A champagne breakfast awaited us.

"I just realized it probably costs more to fill up this boat with fuel for one trip than I made in, like, an entire year."

He seemed to be mentally calculating the costs. "It's probably closer to two years."

"Ouch."

He blanched. "I'm sorry."

"It's fine. I know what you meant." I unfurled the perfectly pleated napkin and draped it across my lap. "Don't get me wrong. It's a little disconcerting to think of the disparity in our incomes in such real-world terms."

"But?" He waved off the crew members hovering nearby. "We'll let you know if we need anything."

"Yes, Mr. Novakovsky."

When they were gone, I answered Yuri. "But—I agreed to try to not let the money stuff bother me so I'm going to smile and pretend I'm not cringing inside at what it's costing you to help me."

Yuri leaned over and cupped the back of my neck. Holding my gaze, he asked, "What's the use of all this money if I can't do good things with it?"

"I'm not sure giving money to a cartel to ransom my father back is such a good thing," I whispered in embarrassment.

"Will it make you smile to see your father safe and sound?"

"Yes."

"Then I'd gladly spend ten times what this weekend is costing me to see you smile."

He meant every word of it—and I loved him for it. "Thank you."

He tapped his lips. "Kiss me and we'll call it even."

Happy to oblige, I leaned forward and pressed my mouth to his. "I love you."

With a teasing smile, he pushed the wispy ends of my hair behind my shoulder. "You're only saying that because you want me to hand over my credit card and unleash you on those high-end shops in Monte Carlo."

"You know me so well."

He teased his mouth across mine. "I'm not completely joking. I am taking you out for a shopping trip after lunch."

"What? Why?"

"Because I want to spoil you." He lifted one of the covered dishes and started to serve himself. "After last night, you deserve it."

I wasn't so sure about that but I wasn't about to argue with him. He derived immense pleasure from showering me with expensive, beautiful things and I rather enjoyed receiving them. Running my finger over the gold cuff adorning my wrist, I decided this was one of those compromises that I was happy to make for him.

Last night's terrifying experience had shown me that life was too short and too damn unpredictable to be constantly second-guessing everything. Yuri and I were going to have the occasional arguments and there were subjects we'd probably never agree upon—but that was simply part of being in a constantly evolving and growing relationship.

And he was worth it. God, he was *so* worth it.

"Eat. It's getting cold."

I selected portions from the yummiest looking dishes and sipped the crisp champagne. As I nibbled on some crispy bacon, I caught Yuri watching me. Feeling self-conscious, I dabbed at my mouth with a napkin. "What?"

Shaking his head, he leaned back in his chair to observe me better. "I'm simply thinking about how very perfect you look here."

"I don't know about perfect..."

"You are." He picked up his fork and tucked back into his breakfast. "You have no idea how many times I've been on this yacht—"

"With other women," I hazarded a guess.

He had the decency to look chagrined. "Yes—but it never felt like this. With you, this all feels...natural." He paused and seemed to be thinking of the perfect words to describe what he felt. "It all finally feels *right*."

I understood him perfectly. "I know this is going to sound sappy and overly romantic so don't laugh."

"Never," he promised with a tiny smile playing upon his lips.

"I honestly can't imagine going through this with anyone else. I finally understand why Erin and Ivan were bonded together so quickly. I know why Benny jumped in with both feet when it came to Dimitri."

"Yes. In fact, I suspect I owe Ivan an apology. I wasn't exactly easy on him when he told me he'd asked Erin to move in with him after knowing her for a month."

"It was five weeks."

He chuckled at my correction. "All right. *Five* weeks."

"And you made me move into your house after a late

night taco truck dinner and a bowl of cereal!"

He grunted and stabbed a slice of melon with a fork. "It was a little more complicated than that."

Thinking of our wild week together, I nodded. "Just a little."

As we finished our lovely, private breakfast, I yawned. We'd left Houston around noon on Thursday but had arrived here on Friday morning. The time difference and the lack of good sleep over the last few days was starting to take its toll.

"Let's get you settled in so you can have a long nap," Yuri said as he led me across the public rooms of the yacht to the private corridors.

I rubbed his chest. "What about you?"

"I caught a nap on the flight. I'll be fine."

I studied him. "Are you sure? I can feel the stress radiating from you."

He nuzzled my ear. "You'll have to do something about that later."

I blushed. "Yes, I'm sure I can think of something."

"I'm confident you will."

We entered the spacious master suite. The view of the sea took my breath away. I hurried across the room to stand before the squeaky clean glass so I could take it all in and really enjoy it. "This is so beautiful, Yuri."

Coming up behind me, he embraced me and pressed his cheek to mine. "We'll go sailing in the summer. There are so many gorgeous ports of call I want to show you."

I wasn't quite sure how we were going to make a vacation like that mesh with our work schedules—I assumed I'd be fully employed by the summer—but I trusted we'd find a way to make it gel. "I'd really like that."

"All of your bags have been unpacked. Tatiana, the

head maid, will see to any of your needs. There's a card on the bedside table listing the crew member extensions."

A quiver of guilt shook me. "I shouldn't be enjoying this so much."

Yuri stepped in front of me. Hands on my shoulders, he frowned down at me. "Why would you say something like that?"

"My dad is being held hostage by a crazy drug lord and my cousin got his arm nearly ripped off by a dog the other night. They're both hoping they won't be next on the hit list of some cartel assassin—and me?" I gestured to the glittering blue sea. "I'm floating in the middle of the Mediterranean and enjoying the kind of luxurious life most people can only dream about, Yuri."

"I don't particularly care what your cousin thinks of all this but your father? I'm sure your father would want you to enjoy what little pleasures you can find right now. He loves you and he wants you to be happy." Yuri dragged his fingertips down my cheek. "He knows we're doing everything we can to get him home."

"I know."

Yuri tipped my chin and traced his thumb across my lower lip. "When we have all of this ugliness behind us, we'll take your father with us on a long cruise of the Caribbean. How does that sound?"

"Like a lot of fun," I answered with a smile.

"Good. Then it's settled. Now you can enjoy this trip guilt-free."

I had to smile at the simplistic way he sometimes viewed things. It wouldn't be that easy to flip my guilt switch off but I appreciated his advice. I couldn't imagine my father being disappointed or resentful or angry with me about any of this.

"Did Derek fix your phone so you can receive and

send calls from here?"

"Yes. I'm hopeless with the time change. When will I hear from my dad again?"

He glanced at his watch. "He calls around seven, yes? So that will be one o'clock in the afternoon here."

"Okay."

Yuri began plucking free the buttons lining the front of my blouse. "I want you to get comfortable and rest. Understood?"

"Yes." I glanced around the room in search of the closet where they'd probably stowed my things. "I should probably dig out my pajamas."

"No." He dragged my shirt off my shoulders and draped it over a nearby chair. "The images of you naked in my bed are the only things that will get me through my day in the office."

I worried about the pipeline deal. While we'd been flying to Paris, the news of the shooting had hit the press. I wanted to apologize for the mess I'd dragged to his door but I recognized that it wasn't going to help. He didn't want an apology from me anyway. He'd made the perfectly clear.

Standing still, I let him undress me. He made sure to cup and squeeze and pinch every inch of plump flesh that interested him. I giggled as he swept me off my feet and put me to bed. Crawling over me, he grasped my wrists and dragged them over my head. I experienced the most deliciously illicit thrill at being held in place my by him.

He must have read it in my face because he quirked his head to the side. "How would you feel if I tied you up some night?"

I licked my lips. "Just tie me up? Nothing weird like spanking?"

He laughed softly. "I take it Benny's been telling you

stories of Dimitri's dirty little penchants."

I squirmed uncomfortably. "She's told me a few things."

"Relax, Kitten. I'm not into that sort of thing. I wouldn't pass up the chance to tie you down and worship this sexy fucking body—but that's as far as I want to go."

The description of what he wanted to do to me left my mouth dry. "We should really try that soon."

He laughed harder and kissed me long and hard and deep. "You little vixen! You're trying to keep me away from my business meetings."

I wrapped my thighs around his waist and tugged him down against me. "I wouldn't dare do such a sneaky, underhanded thing."

Yuri captured my mouth in a sensual kiss. His tongue swiped mine a few times. Sucking my lower lip, he nibbled it gently and left me vibrating with lust. "Later," he promised. "But right now I really do have to take care of business matters."

I smiled up at him and let my legs slide back to the mattress. "If there is anything I can do to help, please let me know."

He moved off of me and tugged the thin sheet over me. "Would you mind looking over some of the materials my PR team is putting together? I know that energy and environmental concerns are outside your area of expertise but you have good instincts."

"Sure. Of course. I'm sure your team has it under control but I'd like the chance to get to know your business better. It would be nice to have a better grasp on the issues you're facing when we sit down at the dinner table every night."

"See?" He said with a pleased grin. "Now you're talking as if we really are partners."

Rolling on my side, I watched Yuri leave the room. The giddy smile tugging at the corners of my lips couldn't be suppressed. I hoped this was one partnership that never ended.

* * *

Later that evening, I reclined on a comfortable chaise lounge stationed in the secluded and totally private balcony off the master suite. The sliding door between the two spaces was wide open. Yuri had already slipped into his pajama bottoms for the night but paced back and forth as he chatted on the phone with Niels. I hadn't met this elusive Danish friend yet but he seemed to be one hell of a guy for putting this mini-poker tournament together for Yuri.

After an afternoon of shopping and the most delicious dinner at one of the top restaurants in the world, I wanted nothing more than to prop up my tired, aching feet and enjoy the gentle sea breeze. A stack of the public relations materials and the prospectus for the pipeline sat on my lap. The lamp next to me provided enough illumination to read through the detailed information provided.

Reading through the spiral-bound reports, I spotted Yuri's notes in the margins and on the actual copy. It was clear that he was extremely hands-on and had very strong opinions when it came to the business. It also became clear to me how many levels of management and acquisition there were between Yuri and the rest of his workforce. Even so, the firm ran as one well-oiled machine.

"Has that bored you to sleep yet?" Yuri had a smile in his voice as he came out onto the deck.

"Not quite," I said and shifted the stack to the small table near me. My lustful gaze roamed his sexy chest. Shirtless and awash in the warm glow from the lamp, he looked so damn hot. "I'm very impressed with the organizational setup you have. If I ever start my own company, you'll have to give me pointers."

"If?" He turned to face me and leaned back against the high railing. The position exposed the corrugated plank of his finely-toned abdomen. "Is there any doubt that you won't be going into business on your own or with Ty?"

I shrugged and pulled my knees toward my chest. "I'll have to see what he has to offer at our rescheduled meeting."

"How did he take that?"

I snorted indelicately. "He made sure to send me some rather melodramatic texts earlier after I posted pics of us shopping together. I let him know that he's not in your league and if he wants a minute of my time he has to up his game."

Yuri chuckled. "I'm sure he found that amusing."

I thought of the colorful text he'd sent me. "Sure. We'll go with amusing."

"Do you think you can work with him? And be honest with yourself, Lena. There's nothing worse than being in business with someone who grates on your nerves and tries your patience."

"Honestly, I really like Ty. I think he can be difficult at times but the same can be said for me." Dropping my gaze in embarrassment, I confessed, "The bouncers at 716 called me the Dragon Lady."

Yuri's belly laugh got my attention. Head thrown back, he practically guffawed at that embarrassing tidbit. "Dragon Lady, huh?"

Rolling my eyes, I fought the urge to smack him with

one of the thicker reports. "So I could be a little testy at times."

"Testy?"

I thought of the first few run-ins I'd had with Yuri, before we'd been friends and when he'd totally offended me. "Yes, I guess you have seen me at my worst."

"Sexiest," he clarified. "You have no idea how sexy you are when you cross your arms and tap that foot."

I gawked at him. "You're joking."

"No." He crossed the deck and nudged my thigh with his bare foot. "Move over."

I happily slid to the side of the wide, low chaise lounge so he could join me. When he was resting on his back, I curled up against him. "Is everything set for tomorrow night?"

"Yes." He threaded his fingers through my hair in that soothing way I'd come to love. "Niels has already spoken to the rest of the gang—Archer, Misha, and Tari—so they're fully apprised of the situation at hand and the necessity of me getting back that painting."

"Why can't you make an offer on it?"

"Niels already tried. He even tried again with an anonymous buyer but Jerry—the man who has the painting in his possession—knows the painting is hot. He doesn't want the wrong kind of attention right now."

"So what's the plan?"

"In a lucky coincidence, Jerry has been asking to join our poker games for years. Niels offered him a spot but only if he buys-in with the painting."

I thought of all the ways this setup could go wrong. "How good are you at poker?"

"I'm not as good as Mikhail or Tari but I'm all right."

"What if you lose?"

"It doesn't matter. As long as Jerry doesn't win—and

he won't—the painting will end up in my hands tomorrow night."

"You sound very confident."

"I refuse to go into that game feeling anything less."

That was one strategy for keeping his head in the right place. "Are all of your friends already in town?"

"I saw a helicopter flying out to Misha's yacht a while ago. Tari came with him apparently. Archer and Niels are at a hotel in Monte Carlo. They invited us to a party they're having but I declined."

"Because of me?"

"No." He rubbed my back. "Because I'm tired and because I don't think you'd like the kinds of parties those two throw."

My curiosity wouldn't let me rest. "Um…what kind of party is that?"

He hesitated. "Let's just say those two are deeply into a certain lifestyle that involves a lot of leather and collars and riding crops."

Pushing up on my palms, I stared down at him. "No way! You have super kinky friends?"

He laughed. "These two make Dimitri's restraint fantasies seem like child's play."

"Wow." I started to put my head back down on his chest but another thought gripped me. Holding his gaze, I asked, "Have you ever been to one of their parties?"

He reluctantly nodded. "Once, seven or eight years ago, I went to the private club the pair owns in London. It was an eye-opening experience."

Feeling fluttery with excitement, I drew my initials on his bare chest. "Did you like what you saw?"

"Some of it aroused me but most of it was too far outside my comfort zone to make feel anything but distaste. I had my ass beat enough as a child to associate only pain and suffering with canes and paddles and whips. It does nothing for me."

I sensed he didn't want to take a trip down memory lane to his childhood in that rotten orphanage so I let that comment go. Instead, I focused on the part that interested me most. Walking my fingers down his tummy, I asked, "What did you see that aroused you?"

As if reading my mind, he shifted his hips. "Niels showed me to a private room. It had one of those one-way mirrors like you see on cop shows. You know, for interrogation rooms? I could see the group in the room but they couldn't see me."

My heart started to race as he described the risqué scene. I swept my hand over the tented fabric rising higher and higher just below his navel. "What were they doing?"

"There were four of them. Three men and a woman," he clarified. "They'd set up this kinky interrogation-themed fantasy. By the looks of it, the woman was supposed to be a hooker. The men were police officers. They were making damn good use of their cuffs."

I slipped my hand into his pajama bottoms and encountered his hot, naked skin. My fingertips brushed the steely heat of his erection. "Tell me more."

His breath hitched in his throat as I grasped his cock and stroked him slowly. "It was the first and only time I'd ever seen a real woman take more than one man. Not a porn star, you understand. It was—intense."

I let my hand move lower and cupped his heavy sac. Not sure I'd like the answer, I asked the question that had me a little worried. "Is that something you want to try in real life?"

His chuckle rumbled through his chest and into my cheek. "No. I think that there are some fantasies that are best left in that realm." Reaching down, he covered my hand with his. "I think I'd probably end up in jail if I had to watch another man touching you." He paused. "Unless you wanted to—"

"No," I hastily interjected. "I'll admit the idea of it is rather sexy. Maybe I'd even enjoy watching it from afar but actually letting two or three men go at me? No. It's not for me."

"I'm sure that has something to do with the places we came from, Lena. What others find illicit and titillating loses some of its erotic appeal when you've watched pimps force prostitutes into cars to be used and debased."

What he said made sense. The sort of violence I'd been forced to witness at such a young and tender age hadn't been a good thing. No doubt it had colored my outlook on all aspects of my life.

"But I don't want to think about those ugly things," Yuri decided. "I want to make love to you here in the middle of the Mediterranean."

"What? Out here?"

"Where else?"

"But someone might hear or see us!"

"This section of the ship is very well hidden." He dragged me onto his lap. "As for the other, you'll simply have to try to be a little quieter than usual."

I moaned as Yuri's lips moved across that ticklish spot on my neck. "I'm not sure I can do that. You make me lose all control."

"Oh, you know how to stroke my ego." He pushed my hand against his erection. "Now be a very good girl and stroke my cock."

"Like this?" I clasped his rock-hard shaft and stroked from the very base of him to the tip.

He groaned loudly. "Just like that…"

"Before you get too relaxed, you might want to remember that I'm not carrying a condom tonight. So unless you've got one hidden away somewhere in these pajamas of yours…"

His frustrated growl sent shivers through me. "Wait here. I'll be right back."

We untangled ourselves. While he darted into the bedroom, I stood up long enough to peel off my night clothes and place them on the pile of paperwork. Resting on my tummy atop the chaise, I placed my cheek against my arm and waited for him to return. The cool breeze washed over me. The sound of waves crashing against the boat provided the most wondrous soundtrack.

"I wish you could see yourself right now."

I glanced back at Yuri and found him staring down at me with such love and hunger burning in his pale eyes. "How do I look?"

"Delicious." He put a knee onto the chaise. "Sexy. Like some otherworldly creature." He kissed his way up my calf and thigh to the curve of my buttock. I inhaled a shocked breath as he gave me a love bite on my plump flesh. "You look like a dark-haired siren."

A pleasured sigh escaped my lips as Yuri caressed my back and crawled over me. With his hand planted next to my shoulder, he held most of his weight off of me. His other hand moved between my thighs. "Lift your ass for me."

I happily complied. When his hand applied gentle pressure to my thighs, I widened them even more. As he nipped at my nape and whispered the dirtiest things, Yuri used those skilled fingers of his to make me so wet. I clawed at the all-weather fabric of the chaise and rotated my hips as he worked me into a frenzied state.

"Do you want me to fuck you now?" His thrusting

fingers kept me hovering right on the edge. "Do you want my cock, Yelena?"

"Yes! I want you. I want you now."

His throaty groan filled me with such anticipation. He backed off just long enough to sheath himself and then grabbed my hips, hauling me up onto my knees. "You'd better hold onto something because I'm burning up for you. I can't hold back."

That was all the warning I received before he thrust roughly into me. Moaning, I urged, "Don't hold back. I want you. All of you."

He tangled his hand in my hair and found a hard, fast rhythm that made my damn toes curl. Gripping the back of the chair and the cushion, I held on for dear life as Yuri pounded into me from behind. The perfect angle of his penetration hit all the right spots. I pressed my face into the thick cushion and howled with sheer delight as the first waves of ecstasy punched through my core.

But that wasn't enough for him. He seemed determined to make me come again and again. His hand slipped around to my front and down to the spot where our bodies joined. My inflamed clit still pulsed from that first powerful orgasm when he started to roll his fingertips across the swollen bud.

I shrieked his name into the cushion and prayed the French or Monegasque version of the Coast Guard wasn't about to swarm the boat. My aching breasts brushed against the rough fabric of the chair. The rasping sensation left my nipples tingling. Every nerve-ending in my body seemed electrified now.

When I climaxed for the third and final time, I hardly made a noise. A high-pitched squeak was all I could manage as Yuri jackhammered my pussy. The rapturous waves crashed over me again and again, dragging me down in the blissful undercurrents until I could hardly pull a breath into my lungs.

With one final, powerful thrust, Yuri found his release. He jerked rapidly and groaned my name over and over before collapsing against my back. We fell down onto the cushion. After a few moments, Yuri found enough strength to roll off of me and onto his side. I felt him move away just long enough to deal with the necessities before spooning me.

Panting and shaking, we interlaced our fingers against my belly. He pressed a loving kiss to my cheek before laughing softly. "We'll be lucky if Vasya doesn't bust that door down in the next ten seconds." He pinched my backside. "I thought you were going to be quiet?"

I reached back and smacked his hip. "I thought you were going to go easy on me."

"Never," he whispered. "I intend to make every time that we're together one you'll remember."

I was confident he'd have no trouble achieving that goal.

CHAPTER SEVENTEEN

"Are you ready for this?"

Yuri finished fastening his cuff link and enjoyed the sight of Lena in only a fluffy white towel. Her pouty lips were still slightly swollen from that wickedly perfect blowjob she'd just given him. He tried to burn that erotic image of her into his mind.

Grinning mischievously, he said, "Kitten, after that *good luck charm* you just gave me in the shower? I can face anything."

She giggled and slid her arms around his waist. He closed his eyes and enjoyed the feel of her small, warm body pressed against his. "I really love you for doing this."

He smiled warmly. "I know you do."

Certain she was already worrying, he caressed her arm. "I want you to stay in the master suite tonight. I've already arranged a special dinner for you—but I gave orders to cut you off after two drinks," he teased. "I remember what happened the last time you were upset with me."

She rolled her eyes and whacked his arm. "You're never going to let me forget that I drunk-dialed you."

"Never," he said with a grin and pecked her cheek. Rather somberly, he added, "I'm sure that stupid dossier I ordered will probably be something you never let me forget."

A sad smile played upon her lips. "I want to say that I'll never bring it up but I won't make promises I can't keep. I'm sure that at some point you'll piss me off and I'll whip that out to verbally smack you with a few times."

"I know how shallow it makes me sound but I truly didn't think it would hurt you when I ordered it done. I simply saw it as the quickest way to get the information I wanted so I could understand you."

Simply talking about his colossal mistake made his stomach churn painfully but Lena soothed the ache with a gentle squeeze of his hand. "I know why you did it and I do believe you when you say that you didn't realize how it was going to blow up in your face. I trust that you won't do something like that again."

"I learned my lesson."

"Good." She hopped up onto the marble vanity and watched him finish his dressing routine. "That's an awfully spiffy outfit for a poker game."

"Niels sets the dress code. I'd prefer to kick back in a polo shirt and jeans but Niels prefers that we play as *gentlemen*."

"Uh-huh," she said dryly. "This Niels guy sounds rather pretentious."

Yuri laughed. "You have no idea."

"But he's a good friend to do this for you."

"A very good friend," he agreed. "Outside of Nikolai, Dimitri and Ivan, he's one of the few men I truly trust."

"Even though he's a dirty, kinky bastard?" she asked with a cheeky grin.

"Especially because he's a dirty, kinky bastard," Yuri replied before swooping in for a kiss. "Promise me you won't sit down here and worry all night. I have this under control. We'll get the painting tonight. Nikolai will arrange everything once the painting is secured. Tomorrow we'll fly straight to Mexico to get your father."

Hope flared in her dark eyes. "I won't worry. You just concentrate on playing a damn good hand of poker."

"Done."

When he claimed her mouth this time, he gave her towel a tug. As the damp ends of the plush cotton fell away from her body, he ran his hands all over her luscious curves. He cupped her breast and lightly pinched her darker nipple between his fingertips. She hissed but not with pain. The way she arched into his touch and sprouted goose bumps told him she liked the little bite of discomfort. Bending down, he soothed the reddened peak with his tongue.

She ran her fingers through his hair. "Yuri…"

He bit down gently and made her yelp. "No time to finish this I'm afraid."

"What?" She glared at him. "Are you really going to get me all hot and bothered and take off?"

He grinned evilly. "It's a damn good way for me to ensure you'll be thinking of me all evening."

She smirked. "Oh, I don't know about that. I'm sure that with one quick phone call I could have a dozen crewmen lined up at that door begging to give me a little one-on-one service."

He knew she was playing but the pang of jealousy twisting his gut was real. "The first man who touches you had better be a damn good swimmer because I'll throw his ass overboard myself."

She rolled her eyes and patted his chest. "There's that alpha caveman again."

"I didn't hear you complaining about this alpha caveman when we were on the balcony last night." He let his hand drift down her bare belly to the seam of her thighs. When she kept them squeezed tightly together, he raised an eyebrow. "Am I being shut-down?"

Her sexy little smile sent his heart racing. She reached down and grasped his erection through his pants. "You said we didn't have time to finish what you'd started. I'd rather wait here in breathless anticipation until you have the time to do it right."

He bit back a groan. "This game had better not go until sunrise."

Abandoning his throbbing cock, she reached up and straightened the collar of his shirt. "You know I'm going to have Johnny spy on you, right?"

He chuckled. "I assumed. Have you had a chance to speak with him?"

She shook her head. "He's supposed to stop by later so we can discuss Benny's wedding. Erin emailed me a list of, like, thirty things I'm supposed to take care of including measuring him for his tuxedo."

"She's taking this wedding planning rather seriously."

Lena shrugged and slipped off the vanity. "She's always been good at that kind of thing. You've been to some of the dinner parties and barbecues she's thrown at Ivan's house. She's like a Martha Stewart clone."

He took one last look at Lena's gorgeous curves before heading into the closet for his shoes. "Why didn't Erin go into event planning instead of accounting?"

"Job security, I guess."

Yuri slipped on his shoes and wiggled his toes. "But

she got laid off from the firm right around the time she moved in with Ivan, yes?"

"Yes."

"So much for job security," he grumbled.

"I'm not sure that exists anymore. Most of the people I graduated college with are already on their second or third jobs. That's kind of crazy when you consider that most of us are still under twenty-five."

Yuri kissed her cheek on the way out of the bathroom. "All the more reason for you to work for yourself. Don't let someone else decide if you're getting a paycheck next week."

He caught her rolling her eyes in the mirror's reflection as she followed him. "Says the billionaire."

"Says the billionaire who started with nothing but a loan from an old man who believed in him," Yuri reminded her.

"Old man?" The penny dropped. "Feodor?"

He nodded. "After I paid back the loan and interest, he refused to take another dime from me unless he was employed by me. I even tried to get him to invest but he was happy living his comfortable, quiet life."

She leaned against the door frame. "I need to find me an old man with cash to loan."

Smiling, Yuri trapped her right there and brushed his mouth against hers. "You've already got an old man right here willing to loan you whatever you need."

Her eyes widened. "Yuri, I was joking."

"I wasn't."

"But—"

"We'll discuss it later. Once you've made up your mind about what you want to do with your future," he amended.

"Yes, we'll definitely discuss it later." She seemed to

understand there was no winning this round.

As far as Yuri was concerned, there would be no discussion. When she was ready to strike out on her own, he would be the one funding her new venture. The last thing he wanted was for Lena to start her new business with the weight of all that debt on her shoulders. There was no doubt in his mind she'd make a success out of whatever she attempted so he considered the risk minimal. Not that any amount of risk would have stopped him from supporting her.

"And you are not an old man." She ran her thumb across his mouth. "Older? Yes. Old? No."

"I'm staring forty in the face."

"Wow. Could you be a bit more dramatic?"

"Probably."

She patted his chest. "Why don't you haul your creaky old behind upstairs and win that painting?"

He smiled indulgently. "Yes dear."

* * *

"Well?" I ambushed Johnny when he appeared at the door for the second time that night.

He slipped inside the master suite and shut the door behind him. His tight expression told me everything. "It's not going so well for Yuri but the other Russian dude? He's got a good hand, I think."

"Crap."

"Don't worry. Yuri will come through for you. The guy didn't even *know* me but he saved my damn life by getting me out of Houston. If he'd do that for me just to help out Dimitri, you've got nothing to worry about, Lena."

Johnny had a point. Feeling calmer, I motioned for

him to follow me into the suite. "Tatiana brought me a measuring tape while you were running down there to spy on the game. Let's get you measured so Erin will get off my case."

He laughed. "Benny keeps texting me, too."

I picked up the small leather notebook I kept in my purse and opened it to the page I'd scribbled together according to Erin's instructions. Measuring tape in hand, I started at his shoulders and worked my way down while we chatted. "So do you like working on the yachts?"

"It's only been a couple of months but I'm starting to really enjoy it. I'm visiting places I never imagined I would ever see and learning useful stuff." Dropping his voice a few notches, he admitted, "I've been talking to the captain about going to a maritime academy."

"Really? That's great."

"It looks like the police aren't going to file any charges against me so I'm legally clear." He shifted his arms so I could measure him properly. "Sometimes I can't believe how damn lucky I was to escape that car alive and without ending up in jail."

"I'm sure it helped that the men who shot up you and your friends got caught red-handed attacking your sister and Dimitri and burning down the bakery. From what Benny's told me, they all flipped on one another and tried to make deals. It's one of the reasons Jonah Krause was so screwed."

"Do you think he'll go to prison for what he did?"

"Yes, but I doubt it will be for very long or in a very tough place. He knows a lot of people in the right places."

"Yeah. I guess."

"Hold this end of the tape measure." I handed it to him and gestured to his inseam. "I'm not about to put my hand anywhere near my friend's brother's junk."

Johnny laughed and held the tape firmly in place. "I don't want your hand there either. Seriously, Yuri would kick my ass out into the ocean if he found out about it."

I snorted and took the measurement. "He talks big but I doubt he'd actually throw you overboard."

Johnny tilted his head. "He's not the kind of guy who makes empty threats—and I'm not about to find out. I'm an okay swimmer but I'm not good enough to make it to the beach."

Laughing, I finished his measurements and jotted down his shoe size. "Erin says she'll handle everything. All you have to do is show up with the yacht."

"I can do that." He hesitated. "Um—you know my sister is…" He pointed to his stomach.

I nodded. "She hasn't made it public knowledge yet. Yuri doesn't seem to know yet. I only know because I was there when she realized she was pregnant."

"Is she okay? I mean—is she healthy and all that?"

"She seems fine. Tired and nauseated but that's normal." I rubbed his shoulder. "Dimitri will take care of her. You don't have to worry."

"She's all the family I've got left. I'm going to worry. But I know what you mean about Dimitri. There's no other guy I trust to really take care of her. Hell—he's taken better care of her than I ever did."

I was sure agreeing with him would only make him feel worse. Instead, I said, "Dimitri loves her so much and she really loves him. They're going to have a wonderful life together."

"They both deserve it."

I thought about how hard it must have been for Johnny to be halfway around the world from his sister. The two siblings had a rocky history but it was clear they loved one another.

"You know, maybe in a year or so, all of this Hermanos bullshit will be water under the bridge and you can go back to Houston for longer visits."

"I hope so." He handed the tape back to me. "Are we done?"

"Yeah."

"Do you want me to keep updating you tonight?"

I glanced at the clock and shook my head. "It's already really late. You should go to bed. Your day starts a lot earlier than mine."

Johnny nodded and headed to the door. "Thanks for measuring me. I'll see you around, Lena."

"Night, Johnny."

Alone in the suite, I decided to take a glass of wine onto the balcony and enjoy the sea breeze. As I got comfy on the chaise, I had flashbacks to the sinfully sexy memories of Yuri ravishing me. The things he did to me!

A sound from the master suite interrupted my steamy thoughts. I held still and listened. Was that the door closing?

Setting aside my glass of wine, I stood and made my way to the open sliding door. I glanced around the spacious room but didn't see anyone. "Yuri?"

When I stepped into the bedroom, the fine hairs on the back of my neck stood on edge. I could *feel* someone's presence in the space. Gulping nervously, I took another step into the room. "Hello?"

There was no answer.

I made my way to the phone, fully intent on calling for one of the bodyguards to come up and check out the room. As I reached for the phone, a large brown envelope on the bed caught my eye. My name was printed on the front in bright red Cyrillic letters. *Where the hell did that come from?*

Now I knew someone had been in here—and it creeped me the hell out.

I picked up the phone and dialed the extension for the security team. One ring later, a gruff male voice answered. "Yes?"

"Kelly, will you please come up to our room?"

"Is everything okay?"

"Um—I'm not sure. Just—hurry."

The line went dead. I dropped the handset into its cradle and gingerly picked up the envelope. I was still staring at the damn thing when there was an insistent knock at the suite's door. I raced to the door and yanked it open.

His face a mask of concern, Kelly rushed inside. He gripped my shoulders. "Are you okay? What's wrong?"

I closed the door and waved the envelope at him. "I went out on the balcony to have a drink and I heard a noise. Like someone was in here. When I came to investigate, I found this envelope on the bed."

He tapped the front. "What does that say?"

"It's my name."

"Did you open it?"

"No."

"Are you going to open it?"

"Maybe."

"Someone was willing to risk being caught to put it in here. They obviously wanted you to read it."

"Who would do that?"

"I don't know," Kelly admitted. "It's got my alarm bells ringing. After someone tried to shoot you in Yuri's backyard, I'm not thrilled by the idea that someone was able to get this close to you."

"It had to be someone in the crew." I glanced at him as another terrifying thought struck. "Or one of you security guards."

Shock turned his expression slack. "You don't think—I mean, no fucking way. Vasya and I have been together all day and all evening in a different section of the ship."

I chewed my lower lip. I hated to even go there but I had to ask. "And Derek and Jake?"

"Derek was handling the arrival of the poker guests and Jake's been playing liaison with the guards that follow the other VIPs." Kelly slashed the air. "There's no way it's one of us."

"Who else is onboard?"

"There are a five people from Yuri's firm in the guest section. They're the ones you were working with over lunch, the PR crew and the pipeline guys."

"Have they been moving around the ship tonight?"

"Not in this section," Kelly said confidently. "The only way to access this area is with a keycard or a thumbprint. Everyone who comes into this private section is logged into the security system."

"That's a good place to start."

"Unless someone stole a keycard," he warned. "I'm not going to accuse someone unless I have real proof." He glanced around the room. "Let me check the rest of the suite. Maybe there is some other evidence."

While Kelly started snooping around the suite, I sat down on the edge of the bed and examined the folder. It was flat and light. My curiosity got the better of me. Carefully, I opened the folder and retrieved the single sheet of paper and a glossy photograph from inside.

I stared at the picture. It was a black and white print of an incredibly bleak scene. Was it a factory? An abandoned warehouse? I couldn't really tell. The writing and logos visible on broken boxes and crates and empty tanks told me the photo had been snapped somewhere in Russia.

The letter proved impossible for me to decipher. What little Russian I'd picked up from Vivian was of no use to me. I could read a couple of words but nothing useful. I spotted Yuri and Nikolai's names in the neatly printed passages but nothing else.

"Well?" Kelly stood nearby. I sensed he was hanging back so he wouldn't accidentally see the contents. Like me, he understood there were simply some things that couldn't be unseen.

Even though I had an idea of what this note was about—it was clearly something to do with Yuri and Nikolai's past—I lied to Kelly. "I don't know what it means."

"Should I get Vasya?"

"No." I couldn't trust the guard with information I couldn't even read.

"Should I get Yuri?"

I wanted Yuri so badly but it wasn't the right time. Yes, someone was trying to scare me and doing a damn good job at it, but I wasn't in imminent danger. "No. He's got enough on his mind. This can wait."

Kelly didn't seem to like that answer. "I'm not sure that's a good idea. He's going to tear me a new one when he finds out I've kept this from him all night."

"I'll deal with him. You just figure out who the hell was in our room."

"I'm putting Vasya on the door. That big ole Russian tank will keep you safe."

I smiled at his description of the gigantic man. Still, I had to be sure. "You're positive Vasya was with you all evening?"

"We haven't been out of each other's sight since we arrived on this yacht."

"Okay."

"Listen to me, I promised Dimitri I would have your back and Yuri's. I don't my break my promises."

"Thank you."

Kelly stayed right outside the door until Vasya lumbered down to take over as my guard. I heard them speaking quietly in the hallway. A few moments later, Vasya knocked and opened the door. "I can come in?"

He hadn't quite mastered the finer parts of English but I had no doubt he would. Anyone who could speak and read two different languages with two different alphabets had earned major respect from me.

"Sure." I waved him inside.

He crossed the room and shut and locked the balcony door. "No more balcony tonight. Okay?"

"Okay."

"And I check on you every half hour."

"That's fine."

Finally alone, I did the only thing I could think of to solve the mystery of the letter. I snapped a picture with my cell phone and sent it to Vivian.

Some freak just left this on my bed. What the hell does it say?!

After I sent the message, I calculated the time difference. Vivi was probably gearing up for the evening dinner service at Samovar. If she saw the message before I went to bed, it would be a miracle.

Feeling uneasy but secure with Vasya so close at hand, I slipped into bed and turned on the television. I found an international news channel that broadcasted in Spanish and turned up the volume just high enough for me to hear. I tried to pay attention to the news stories but I couldn't get my mind to stop racing.

There was something seriously wrong here. I'd been convinced the shootout at Yuri's Houston home had been related to the cartel. Lorenzo Guzman was a nasty snake who wouldn't think twice about using that type of intimidation tactic.

But now I realized how wrong I'd been to go with my first assumption.

I started to wonder if there wasn't some bigger plan at play here. The cartel, my dad's kidnapping, Tommy getting the phone call about that painting? It was too neat. Throw in the attempted sabotage of Yuri's pipeline and it had the makings of a plot from one of those thriller novels I loved so much.

My gaze fell to the envelope next to my hand. I ran my finger over the innocuous looking item and considered the photo and letter it held. Those were the keys to this whole thing.

I jumped as my cell started to ring. With a hand over my thudding heart, I picked up the phone and glanced at the screen. Relieved, I quickly answered, "Vivi!"

"Have you shown that letter to anyone?" Her panicked voice made my heart race even faster.

"No. Why?"

"Listen to me and listen very carefully. Delete that picture you took. No one can ever see it. Do you understand?"

"Vivian, you're scaring me."

"We should be scared. That letter—it says things, Lena. Things that neither of us have any business knowing about the men we care about most. Terrible things. Awful things. Just give it to Yuri and forget you ever saw it."

"And you?" I asked as I tucked the envelope under my pillow for safekeeping. "Can you forget what you read?"

"No, but it helps me understand certain things."

"It doesn't help me understand anything. Is Yuri in trouble?"

"I don't know," she answered honestly. "Someone is trying to rattle his cage. I'm sure they're going to succeed."

Dishes crashed in the background and Vivian swore softly. My eyes widened at the sound of a cuss word leaving her sweet little mouth. If she was dropping *that* word, she was really upset.

"Lena, please, I'm begging you. Be safe. Don't go anywhere without Yuri. Like don't even turn your back without him there to watch you. That letter? It's ancient history—and anyone who has been carrying around a grudge that long is seriously dangerous."

"I'll be safe. I promise."

"Remember what I said about the picture."

"I'm deleting it as soon as we hang up."

"Okay. I love you, Lena. Be careful."

"I love you, too, Vivian."

Our conversation ended with me even more confused and upset than I had been when I'd discovered the envelope. I quickly found the photo in question and deleted it without hesitation.

Feeling so conflicted and anxious, I dropped my phone on the bedside table and rolled onto my side, facing away from the door. I ran my hand over the spot where Yuri usually slept. "Baby, what secrets are you hiding from me?"

CHAPTER EIGHTEEN

"I told you we'd pull this off." Grinning, Niels smacked Yuri on the back. "It cost us a small fortune but we did it."

Yuri rubbed the back of his neck and stretched his aching shoulders. He glanced around the bar at his friends' smiling faces. There had been a few times during the night when he'd been sure the painting would stay in Jerry's hands but Mikhail and Tari had come through in the end. After Archer had gone bust, Yuri had quickly followed. Niels had made it another round in the game.

Just as Yuri had started to feel real desperation, he realized that Mikhail and Tari were working their own game. They beautifully maneuvered Jerry right into their trap. He'd caught the subtle signs between Archer and Niels—a nose rub, an earlobe tug, a stretch or a yawn— that were easily interpreted by Mikhail and Tari. In that moment, Yuri had recognized how incredibly lucky he was to have friends like these.

After Mikhail had cleaned out Jerry and taken

ownership of the painting, he'd laughingly asked Jerry to a rematch and offered to spot him the same amount of cash he'd just lost from the house bank. It hadn't taken Yuri long to realize that Mikhail was purposely allowing Jerry to win back everything but the painting. When Jerry had left ten minutes earlier, he'd done it with a smile on his face.

"I will admit to feeling guilty about playing Jerry that way," Yuri confessed as he sipped his drink.

"Don't," Tari interjected. "Do you realize what would happen to him if that cartel found out he had the painting? Getting fleeced by us? That was a favor."

Sadly, Tari was probably right.

"I don't understand it." Archer stood in front of the painting in question and stared upon it. "What the hell am I looking at here?"

Niels snorted and downed the last of his beer. He slapped his best friend on the back. "Come on. Let's get back to the hotel. Maybe Juliette is still hanging around our suite."

Archer perked right up and glanced at his watch. "It's a bit late."

"It's never too late for what I have in mind."

Yuri tried not to imagine what shenanigans those two were about to get into this late at night. Instead, he shook their hands, thanked them profusely and promised a favor in return. Mikhail and Tari finished their drinks a few minutes after Niels and Archer departed.

"We should go," Mikhail said. "I'm sure your girlfriend misses you."

Yuri thought of Lena and hoped she was sound asleep. Everything would be all right now.

"Listen," Mikhail said and slipped arm around his shoulders. At nearly six inches over six feet, Mikhail was quite a bit taller than Yuri and had to lean down to speak softly. Tari spoke excellent Russian so Mikhail kept his voice low. "I asked Jerry where he acquired the painting. He told me he got it from a woman—a Russian woman."

Yuri remembered Tommy Cruz telling him that he'd gotten a call from a woman about the painting. He'd neglected to mention her nationality. "A Russian? You're sure?"

Mikhail nodded. "A bit strange, yes?"

"Yes."

As Yuri waved goodbye to Mikhail and Tari, he couldn't stop thinking about this new bit of information. The woman who had called Tommy asked for that painting specifically. How would she have known the painting was in Lena's father's warehouse if she hadn't known the person who stole it or the person who originally fenced it? The idea of a Russian connection to this cartel mess started to feel...personal.

Turning back to the painting he'd just purchased from Mikhail, Yuri stared at it. The piece was a thing of strange beauty. It was the sort of painting he would have loved to have on his walls but tonight it inspired only distaste. He *never* wanted to see this painting again.

"Boss?" Derek stood near the doorway looking very irritated. He gestured with a flick of his fingers and Kelly stepped into the room looking guilty as hell.

Yuri's chest tightened. "What is it?"

"Something happened while you were playing poker. Apparently, Kelly decided not to tell me until the game was over. He says Lena asked him not to get you involved but I reminded him that he works for you, not her."

Yuri didn't like stepping on toes and chose not to set Derek straight in front of his subordinate, but later, in private, he would remind his head bodyguard that the moment Lena walked in his front door they began working for her.

Sighing, Yuri asked, "What happened, Kelly?"

"She called me a little before midnight and sounded scared. I ran up to the master suite and found her looking really shaken. Someone had been in the suite while she was on the balcony. They left an envelope with her name on it."

"WHAT?" Stomach seized with panic, he fought the urge to run to her. "Is she all right? Who was it? Are they still on the boat?"

Derek shot Kelly an annoyed frown. "The jarhead says no one without clearance was in the private section."

Kelly looked like he wanted to gut-punch Derek for the jarhead remark but he kept it professional. "Actually that's not what I said. I said that there were two keycards used during the time in question. Johnny Burkhart was up there getting fitted for a tux and talking about his sister."

Yuri nodded. "Johnny's sister and Lena are good friends. That's why he was asked to serve our rooms."

"There's no suspicion he was involved. At the time your suite door was being opened from the outside, Johnny was swiping his card to get into the staff quarters. He was seen coming in the main door by seven other guys."

"So who came into my room?"

Kelly glanced at Derek. "It was his card that opened the door."

"Which is impossible," Derek snapped back, "because I've been *here* all night."

Yuri's mind raced as he tried to recall Derek's location during the night. "He's right. He wasn't out of my sight once."

Kelly shrugged. "So someone stole his card or made a

copy. Either way someone was in that room—and we don't know who it was."

The realization that he couldn't keep Lena safe made him sick. "Who is with her now?"

"Vasya," Kelly said. "She's been asleep for the last hour or so. He's got the door propped open so he can watch her."

"Get the painting," he ordered and headed for the door. "It's not leaving my sight until we hand it over."

"When do we leave?" Derek asked.

"Soon," he said, no longer certain he could trust anyone on this ship. Kelly seemed like a straight-shooter and Vasya had Nikolai vouching for him. He'd never once doubted Derek or Jake or any of the crew on the ship but maybe he'd been too trusting. His gut soured at the realization that he really didn't know any of these people he employed.

He found that great big bull of a guard watching over his Lena. Vasya rose from the chair he'd placed in the open doorway. "Boss."

Yuri nodded at him before entering the suite. The television screen cast an eerie glow around the room. Lena was rolled on her side, facing away from him. She slept on top of the covers and looked uncomfortable. Already familiar with her sleeping habits, he reached down to lift her up as Kelly arrived with the painting. Yuri gestured to the far side of the room. "There."

"Yes, sir."

After Vasya set up the easel, Kelly carefully propped the painting in place. The two guards left the suite and shut the door behind them. Yuri finished moving Lena under the covers. She stirred but he quieted her with a tender kiss and the soft caress of his hands upon her back.

As he stood, his hand brushed something jutting out from under her pillow. He felt the sharp edge of an envelope and tugged it free. Unable to read in the dim light of the television, he carried the envelope into the bathroom, shut the door and flicked on the light.

The sight of Lena's name in Cyrillic surprised him. He shook the contents onto the counter. His gaze flicked across the angry looking letter and the black and white photo. Almost immediately, his stomach lurched painfully. That warehouse…

The old, painful, disgusting memories rose to the surface of his mind along with bile from his stomach. He barely made it to the toilet before retching. Everything about that night—the smells, the sounds, the sensations—coursed through him as fresh as if they were happening right now. He retched violently, his stomach seizing with pain as the long-buried memory of the thing he'd discovered, of the thing he'd *done*, overwhelmed him.

Crawling to the counter, Yuri grabbed the note and photo. He flopped down on his ass and stared at them. *How?*

He read the note twice before the words finally started to make sense. Someone *knew*. Someone knew every sordid detail of what he'd done. Of what he'd done to save Nikolai.

Hands shaking, he fished his phone out of his pocket and dialed Nikolai.

Always business, Nikolai answered with the all-important question. "Did you get the painting?"

Yuri cleared his throat. "Yes. It's safe."

"I'll make the arrangements. Do you want to go tomorrow or should I—"

"Someone knows," he interrupted.

"Knows what? About you and the cartel?"

"Someone knows about Pasha." He spoke the name that hadn't left his lips in more than twenty-five years.

Dead silence stretched on the other end of the line. Yuri hated himself for bringing up the nightmare that Nikolai had survived.

"Someone left an envelope addressed to Lena on our bed. It held a note and a photograph—of the warehouse," he added reluctantly. "The writer put details in the letter, details only someone who was there that night would know."

"Are they threatening to turn us over to the authorities?" Nikolai's voice had taken on a gruff tone.

"No, the writer says we'll get a different kind of justice." He thought of the shooting Lena had barely survived. "This is why someone tried to shoot Lena. They wanted to hurt me."

"No jury would ever convict us for what happened that night. That man was a monster. The things he did to—" Nikolai's voice abruptly cut out. "I'm not a little boy anymore and a letter isn't going to scare me."

"It's not just the letter! Someone tried to kill Lena. Someone that I trust enough to be on this ship came into the room tonight. Do you understand how it feels to be unable to protect the woman I love?"

"Yes."

Yuri realized that was the closest Nikolai had ever come to confirming his feelings toward Vivian. Blowing out a noisy breath, he asked, "What the fuck do we do?"

"You get that painting to Mexico and make the trade for Lena's father. Then we regroup in Houston and figure out who is after us. I'll touch base with my contacts back home. This has to be someone close to that monster. Only a friend or relative would hold a damn grudge this long."

265

"That makes sense."

"I'll call you later with the details about the exchange." Nikolai hesitated. "Did Lena read the letter?"

"She might have tried but her Russian is terrible. I doubt she showed it to anyone else." He understood Nikolai's desire for privacy. "I'll ask her in the morning."

"I'll talk to you soon."

Yuri placed his phone on the counter and shoved up off the floor. Desperate for a shower and to feel clean again, he stripped and turned on the hot water. He stood under the spray for at least ten minutes before giving himself a mental shake. Lathered up, he scrubbed his skin until it was pink and raw. The memory of all the blood that night still haunted him. That had been one hell of a thing for a twelve-year-old to process.

As he dried off and brushed his teeth, his thoughts turned to Nikolai. God, how he loathed the idea of his best friend having to relive that experience. With palms flat on the marble countertop, Yuri stared at his reflection in the foggy mirror. *What the hell do I tell Lena?*

She was going to be curious about that letter and the picture. If he lied to her, she would know—but he couldn't tell her everything. Not yet. How much did he dare reveal?

* * *

I came awake to the comforting sensation of Yuri's strong arms wrapped around me. Content to feel his big, warm naked body pressed against mine, I remained perfectly still and enjoyed the silence of morning. The privacy shades had been lowered on the windows but pale rays of sunlight still streamed into the room. It was going to be a beautiful day.

My fuzzy brain finally cleared enough for me to remember that weird letter and Vivian's cryptic, worried advice. Even though there were a million questions I wanted to ask Yuri, I decided to let him sleep in. He'd been running himself ragged lately. Everything I wanted to know could wait. I had a bad feeling the discussion that letter would entail wasn't going to be one I would enjoy.

Carefully, I slipped out of bed and tiptoed to the bathroom. I showered and brushed my teeth but didn't put on my makeup or fix my hair. After working in some moisturizer, I threaded my arms through the sleeves of the silky dressing gown I'd brought with me and returned to the bedroom. The thought of crawling back into bed with Yuri tempted me.

Crossing the room, I became aware of something on the far side of the room that had been hidden in the shadows when I'd first awakened. I damn near tripped over my own feet when I realized I was looking at *the* painting.

I hurried across the room and gazed upon the piece of fine art. It was a strange, haunting scene depicted on the canvas. Definitely not the kind of thing I'd want hanging in my house but clearly drug lords had different tastes.

Excitement bubbled within me like fizzy champagne. He'd done it! Yuri had done it!

"As lovely as that painting is, I'd rather stare at you without that robe."

Turning toward the bed, I grinned at Yuri and tugged on the silken belt keeping it closed. The fabric pooled around my feet. Overcome with joy, I ran across the room and leapt onto the bed. Yuri laughed and pulled me onto his naked body until I straddled his hips.

Cupping his handsome face, I whispered, "You big,

sexy, wonderful Russian! How will I ever repay you?"

Tangling his fingers in my damp hair, Yuri captured my mouth in a passionate kiss. "I have a few ideas."

His stubble rasped my face as he nuzzled me in between sensually erotic kisses. He ran his hands over my bare skin like a sculptor admiring his work. Palming my breast, he tweaked my nipple and pressed his face against the crook of my neck. "You're so damn beautiful, Yelena. Every time I touch you I find something new that I love."

I looped my arms around his strong, muscled shoulders. "I love you, Yuri."

"I love you, Kitten."

His nickname earned a smile from me. I gasped as he started to nibble my throat and play with my nipples. My sensitive flesh puckered to tight peaks that Yuri tormented with his tongue and fingers. Every tug of his mouth around my breast sent erotic shivers straight to my clit. The pink pearl pulsed to life. My pussy started to ache with need.

Yuri's hard cock rubbed against my inner thigh. When I shifted on his lap, the thick, blunt tip bumped my clit. I hissed at the delicious sensation and rubbed against his shaft, stimulating myself on his steely length.

Grasping my bottom with both hands, Yuri aligned our bodies and breached my slick, wet sheath with just the crown of his cock. Our gazes held as he rocked into me a little deeper before pulling back. We both knew what was different this time.

Shaking with arousal and excitement, I whispered, "I've never—"

"I'll stop. Tell me to stop."

His husky voice did crazy things to me. I didn't want him to stop. I wanted to share this experience with Yuri. Biting my lower lip, I sank down on his hard, thick cock, taking every last inch of him into my pussy. We both moaned and breathed a little faster as the heady experience of making love without a latex barrier between our bodies gripped us.

"You feel so good." Yuri's shaky breaths buffeted my cheek. "So damn hot and wet." He fell back on the bed and grasped my hips. "Ride me, Yelena."

With my hands on his chest, I swiveled my hips until I found the perfect rhythm. He watched me with such awe. I felt so incredibly beautiful and desired. Yuri's hand swept up and down my front before settling on the spot where my neck and shoulder curved together. He thrust up into me and I cried out at the exquisite delight. "Ah!"

Back and forth, I rocked my hips. This position felt so damn good. My clitoris remained in constant contact with him. Every thrusting motion he made left me gasping. "Oh. *Oh.*"

His thumb brushed my mouth. "Yes."

My pace hastened. The first curls of pleasure unfurled in my core. That blissful knot of shuddery vibrations grew and grew. My pussy clenched Yuri's cock tighter and tighter. He urged me on and thrust into me harder and faster until I hovered on the edge. Closing my eyes, I tried to draw out those wonderful flutters as long as possible but one more thrust broke my control.

"Yuri!" I clawed at his chest and gyrated wildly atop him, desperate to wring ever last ounce of pleasure from that orgasm. When I fell forward against him, Yuri gathered me close and flipped our positions. He grasped my legs and dragged them up higher until my knees rested against those broad shoulders of his.

"*Unnnhhh.*" I let loose a guttural groan as his cock slid deeper. Clinging to his rippling arms, I gazed into his hazel eyes while he started to chase his own pleasure. I didn't think he'd ever looked sexier or more handsome to me than in that moment. My heart threatened to burst in my chest as I realized how much I loved this man.

As if having the same moment of clarity, Yuri dipped his head until our breaths mingled. He pounded into me now, his cock gliding in and out of me faster and harder. Every plunging thrust made me grip him tighter. I watched his face with fascination as he climbed closer and closer to his climax.

"I love you, Lena." He slammed into me with enough force that I slid up the bed. His cock swelled inside me as he shuddered in my arms and filled me with his blazing hot seed. "I fucking love you so much."

I caressed his face as he shuddered again. "I love you, Yuri. *Always.*"

His mouth found mine in a demanding kiss that branded me with his passionate love. My legs fell from his shoulders, and he rolled onto his side, dragging me with him. With his spent cock still buried inside me, I relished the sensation of being so intimately joined to him.

After a few minutes of sensual kissing, Yuri pushed the damp hair away from my face. He ran his thumb down my cheek. The serious look in his eyes worried me. "I have to tell you something."

My tummy twisted with fear. "What?"

"I read the letter."

"Oh." My hand slipped under my pillow but the envelope was gone.

"I destroyed it early this morning. I couldn't risk anyone else reading it. Did you show it to anyone else?"

I couldn't lie to him. "I snapped a photo and sent it to Vivian." The horrified expression on his face scared me. Quickly, I explained, "She told me to delete the picture and to keep the letter hidden until I gave it to you. She wouldn't tell me what it said, just that I needed to be careful and not go anywhere without you."

He seemed to relax. "I trust Vivian to understand that what she read must never be spoken aloud to anyone."

"And me?" I tried not to sound hurt. "Don't you trust me?"

"I do. I truly do." He touched his forehead to mine. "I can't tell you everything. Some of the details in that note—" He swallowed and shook himself. "I can't. I will tell you this much. When I was a child…" He dropped his gaze as if ashamed to look at me. "When I was a child, I killed a man to save Nikolai."

For a long moment all I could do was stare at Yuri. The pain and shame radiating from him shook me from my stupor. I rubbed his arm and forced him to meet my gaze. "Tell me."

His eyes shimmered with unshed tears as he made his confession. "We were boys, so young, and I was jealous of Nikolai, of the treatment he received at the orphanage. I didn't understand then…" His voice trailed off and he shook his head again. "I followed him one night and…and he was being hurt. I reacted like any twelve-year-old boy would at discovering that terrible, terrible thing. I picked up a pipe and hit Pasha across the back of his head. I didn't know my own strength. He hit the floor and—and there was so much blood. So much blood." He gulped as if he might be sick. "Nikolai and I ran back to the orphanage, grabbed Ivan and Dimitri, and we left that night."

My eyes grew hot as I processed his confession. The few details he'd given were enough for me to piece together what young Nikolai had endured. I could only imagine how horrifying it would have been for a twelve-year-old boy to stumble upon his friend being hurt like that.

"So you see—I'm a murderer."

"You are *not* a murderer. You were a child trying to save your friend." I grasped his face in my hands and held his gaze. The pain reflected in his eyes left me breathless with sympathy. "What happened was an accident. It was manslaughter at the very worst. No jury in their right mind would have convicted a little boy for saving his friend from a...*monster* like that."

"Maybe," he said, blinking rapidly. He cleared his throat and tried to get a grip on his painful emotions. "But someone knows and someone wants to make me pay for what I did."

"By trying to kill me?" The pieces began to fit together.

"I'm starting to think this whole thing—from your cousin to your father to the pipeline—it's all a setup."

"Last night, I wondered the same thing. It's too convenient, you know? Too neat." I hesitated. "But this thing with my dad and my cousin started before we were officially together. How would someone know you were attracted to me? How could they know that hurting me would hurt you?"

"Lena, I was more than simply attracted to you. People close to me would have been able to see the difference in the way I reacted to you and the way I reacted to every other woman."

"So it is someone close to you," I whispered, suddenly uneasy.

"Yes."

"What are we going to do?"

"We stick together until we get your father home safely to Houston. After that, I'm honestly not sure where to begin. Nikolai is digging into Pasha's history. We think it might be a friend or relative of his that's playing this ugly game." Reluctantly, he added, "I think it's best that we stay away from our friends to avoid collateral damage."

"Yes. Absolutely." I thought of Vivian. "If someone is trying to hurt me because they want to cause you pain, what about Vivian? Nikolai may not be willing to come right out and say that he feels strongly for her but it's evident to anyone who sees them that he cares deeply about Vivian."

"She's still with Ivan and Erin and has Kostya shadowing her constantly. I assume that cousin of hers, the detective, is watching her like a hawk. She's probably safe, but at the first hint that she isn't, Nikolai will hide her away where none of us can find her."

"Should we think about doing that? Going into hiding, I mean?"

"I considered it last night but I feel safer in public. For now," he amended. "This is a highly dynamic situation and we'll have to adjust on the fly." Pulling me into his embrace, he kissed the top of my head. "Right now, let's focus on getting your father safely home."

Suddenly, saving my father from a cartel seemed like the very least of our worries…

CHAPTER NINETEEN

"Relax," Yuri urged and put a comforting hand on Lena's back. She fidgeted non-stop next to him as the private jet made its final approach and descent toward the private airstrip.

They were arriving in Mexico after dark. He didn't like coming into what he considered enemy territory in the dark but the thought of leaving Lena's father in the cartel's hands another night wasn't one he could stomach. Too much could go wrong. He wanted the exchange done quickly.

"Sorry." She chewed her lower lip as the jet touched down and slowed to a stop.

"Don't," he whispered and brushed his fingers across her pout. "This will go smoothly. Everyone gets what they want tonight."

She gripped his hand but didn't say anything. He read her easily. She didn't believe him but she didn't want to call him out on it while surrounded by their bodyguards. He didn't blame Lena for feeling uncertain or doubtful.

After everything they'd been through in the last week, it was expected.

Leaning closer, he pressed a comforting kiss to her cheek. A look passed between them that said it all. Despite her fear, she trusted him to handle this. "Wait here, Kitten."

Unlatching his seatbelt, he rose from his seat and made his way to the front of the jet where Derek and Jake were discussing the security situation while Kelly chatted with an impromptu recon team. The Marine had a couple of friends who happened to be in the area on a vacation. They'd been only too happy to come in to scout the area for them. Yuri imagined the men found it a bit fun to use their dormant soldiering skills again.

Kelly finished his phone conversation and quickly filled them in on the situation on the ground. From the sounds of it, the men had staked out the airstrip for hours. Kelly's phone dinged again and again as texted recon photos were sent to him. They crowded around the small screen to study them.

"You should put these two in touch with Dimitri," Yuri suggested. "I realize they're doing you a friendly favor but that is damn impressive groundwork."

"That's a Marine for you, Boss." Kelly pocketed his phone and reached for the thin jacket he would be wearing to hide his shoulder holster. Glancing back at Lena, he asked, "Is she still coming off the plane?"

Yuri nodded. "I don't think I could keep her on here if I tried."

"No," Kelly agreed, "but Vasya sure as hell could." Lowering his voice, the gruff Marine said, "Let me handle it. She'll be pissed at me, not you."

Realizing it was the easy way out but also recognizing it was the best way to keep her safe, Yuri acquiesced.

"Thank you."

While he stepped closer to Derek and Jake and listened to their game plan, Yuri allowed his gaze to jump to Kelly and Lena. Her frosty body language prompted a surge of sympathy for poor Kelly. When she crossed her arms and snapped her gaze to the window, Yuri made a decision to stay right where he was. The last thing he needed was a verbal wallop from that beautiful mouth.

Jake came back from the cockpit. He gestured to the door and sent one of the attendants to unlock and secure it. "The crew will keep the plane ready to go."

Kelly's phone rang. He fished it out of his pocket and pressed it to his ear. "Yeah? Okay." With a nod, he lowered his phone. "They're coming. Two SUVs. My guys haven't seen anything else. So far, so good."

Yuri's chest tightened as they prepared to meet the cartel for the handoff. Turning back to Lena and Vasya, he walked down the aisle to the giant guard. With a flick of his fingers, he indicated the taller man should dip down. In their shared language, he whispered, "If anything happens out there, you tell the pilot to take off and get Lena to safety. I've already spoken to him. He has my orders. You get her to Nikolai. Understood?"

Vasya's silent nod assured Yuri Lena would be safe. Holding her gaze, he winked. A smile cracked her tense expression. She mouthed three words. *I love you.*

Feeling the weight of the upcoming transaction on his shoulders, Yuri followed Jake and Derek out of the jet. Kelly shadowed him down the stairs to the tarmac. The darkness left him uneasy but the knowledge they were being surveilled by men Kelly trusted bolstered his confidence in the mission.

The two parked SUVs were still running. Their headlights illuminated a small space on the tarmac. Yuri remained just outside of the bright circle of light, refusing to make himself a clear target. Doors started to open. His anxiety skyrocketed as silhouetted men poured out of the vehicles. Scanning the men, he didn't see one visible weapon. Maybe Lorenzo Guzman was a man of his word.

The drug lord in question strode forward into the circle of light. "Yuri."

Outmaneuvered, Yuri reluctantly crossed into the light. "Lorenzo."

"You have the painting?"

"I want to see Joe Cruz first."

Lorenzo made a gesture and a door on the closest SUV was opened by one of the cartel minions. A hooded and cuffed man was produced from a rear seat. Joe Cruz shuffled forward under the guidance of the cartel muscle. He was left at Lorenzo Guzman's right side. The cartel leader plucked the hood from Joe's head.

The shock of light left Joe Cruz blinking and ducking his head. Yuri looked him over to make sure this was the man in question. He looked exactly like the driver's license photo in the dossier. From the looks of him, he'd been beaten badly when first kidnapped but he looked well into the healing process now.

"I kept my word. No one has touched him since we made our deal." Lorenzo Guzman pointed to the fading bruises on Joe's face. "He's been fed, showered and provided with clothing."

"On my tab, I'm sure," Yuri replied dryly.

Lorenzo laughed sharply. "Of course."

"My accountant has deposited the balance of the funds we agreed upon in the escrow account. Once we land safely in Houston, I'll give word to release them to you."

Lorenzo waved his hand. "I wouldn't be here if my accountant hadn't already assured me that the money was there." He shoved Joe forward. "Take him."

Yuri reached out to steady Lena's father. He held the other man's gaze for a moment before gently pushing him out of the way. Looking to Kelly, he gave a curt nod. "Get the painting."

"I suppose you won't tell me who had it."

Yuri shook his head. "No."

"It matters very little to me now. I caught the man who stole it from me." Lorenzo's eyes narrowed. "He was working with someone from your side of the fence. You wouldn't know anything about that."

"No."

Lorenzo studied him. His gaze jumped behind Yuri to the painting being carried down the stairs by two flight attendants. "Well—I suppose this concludes our business."

Yuri stared at the hand Lorenzo extended. A silver handcuff key rested on the man's palm. Though it made his stomach pitch, he grasped the kidnapping drug lord's hand. "This ends here. Tonight."

"Don't worry, Yuri. You're too high-profile for my tastes. I prefer to keep things quiet."

With the handoff complete, Yuri turned away from Lorenzo Guzman. He placed his hand between Joe's shoulders. "Let's go."

Jake, Derek and Kelly surrounded them as they crossed the tarmac. He sent Joe up the stairs and into the jet first. When they stepped into the jet, Lena jumped to her feet. The relieved and excited expression that lit up her beautiful face made all of this hassle worth it. Knowing that he'd been able to give this to her filled him with the strongest sense of happiness and pride.

Standing back, he watched the tearful reunion as the doors were secured and Kelly gave his friends one final phone call. Lena led her father to the private seating area in the rear of the jet. Yuri turned to Jake. "Let's get the hell out of here."

*

"Sit, Dad."

He dragged me close and looped his cuffed arms around my neck. "I'm so glad to see you, *mi'ja*."

Swallowing the sob clogging my throat, I whispered, "I'm so glad you're safe."

Shaking with relief and adrenaline, I helped my dad into one of the cushy seats. Yuri tapped my shoulder and presented me with the handcuff key. I wanted to throw my arms around him and kiss him until he was breathless and panting but my father's presence put the kibosh on that urge.

After unlocking the cuffs, I unwound them from his wrists. The sight of raw, reddened patches upset me. Yuri obviously sensed my anger. "There's a first aid kit at the front of the jet. We'll patch him up here but I'll have the doctor come by the house tonight."

My father's grateful gaze settled on Yuri. "Thank you. For everything."

"It was my pleasure to help Lena." He reached down and grasped my hand. "We're about to takeoff."

I took a seat across from my father and buckled my safety belt. Yuri sat next to me. On instinct, he reached for my hand but pulled it back at the last second, almost as if he felt uncomfortable. I gripped his hand and dragged it onto my thigh. His sweet smile made my tummy flutter and we interlaced our fingers.

Soon we were in the air and racing back to Houston. There were so many questions I wanted to ask my father but I suspected a barrage of them was the last thing he needed right now. When it was safe to remove our belts, I stood up and excused myself. "I'm going to grab the first aid kit. I'll be right back."

"Ask one of the attendants or Jake. He always knows where these things are." Yuri made his way to the private bar. "Would you mind closing the door?"

I shook my head and glanced at my father. It was clear the two men had things they wanted to discuss. "I'll take my time."

Yuri's almost imperceptible nod was my answer. Slipping out of the private section of the jet, I shut the door and slowly walked down the main aisle.

Kelly looked up from his comfortable kicked back position. "How's the old man?"

"I don't think he's really processed that he's free yet."

"Give it time. He's probably going to crash when we get him back to Houston. He may be difficult to be around for a few days. Just give him some space."

Kelly seemed to be speaking from experience. "I will."

"If he seems to be struggling, I'll talk to him." Kelly sat up in his chair. "Did you need something?"

"Do you know where the first aid kit is? My dad has some bad bruising and raw stripes on his wrists."

"Sure." Kelly headed for the flight attendant station at the front. He opened a couple of cabinets before finding the bright red box. "Here you go."

"Thanks." Armed with the kit, I returned to the private area Yuri typically used as his in-flight office. At the door, I hesitated. Apparently, I hadn't closed it firmly because it was ajar enough for me to hear my father and Yuri talking. Even though I knew better than to eavesdrop, I couldn't help myself.

"So what happens to Tommy now?" my father asked.

"He can leave the safe house as soon as he likes. Whether that's a smart idea, I can't say. He absolutely is not welcome anywhere near my home."

"And me? Am I welcome?"

"Of course you are. Why wouldn't you be?" Confusion colored Yuri's voice.

"After all this trouble I've caused, I'm sure you want to see me far away from Houston."

"Make no mistake, Joe. I'm not a fan of trouble and I won't have Lena dragged into this sort of mess again. But—you're her father and she loves you. As long as you keep out of trouble, I will welcome you into *our* home with welcome arms."

My heart stuttered at Yuri's mention of his home as *ours*.

"I'm not doing this again." Dad sounded beaten and emotionally exhausted. "I was planning to retire from fencing before the end of the year. That timetable has been accelerated."

"What do you plan to do?"

"Landscaping."

My father's answer seemed to stun me as much as it did Yuri.

"Landscaping? Do you mean a small business?"

"I used to do yard work and construction in between jobs, before I built a reputation as a high-end fence. I always loved that work. It's calming. It's *quiet*."

"I think quiet is a very good idea. In fact, I'm happy to help with whatever it takes to get you into your retirement."

I held my breath as I waited for my father's reply to Yuri's offer. I wasn't the least bit surprised that Yuri wanted to help him into something legal.

"And what strings come attached to that offer?"

"No strings, Joe. I'll do whatever it takes to give Lena peace of mind. I don't want her worrying about you."

"Are you sure you're not making this offer because you're concerned about the way a criminal father-in-law will make you look?"

Eyes wide with shock, I pressed my fingertips to my lips and waited for Yuri's answer.

He laughed. "If I was worried about the way my association with ex-cons looked, I would have walked away from two of my friends years ago. I'm not embarrassed by your history but I'd rather not have it rubbed in my face. I can see you want out—and I know Lena wants you out."

"It seems you'll do anything to make her happy."

"Anything in my power to give is hers."

"You haven't been dating her very long."

"That's true, but when a man knows, he knows."

"Is this your way of asking for my blessing?"

"When it's time, I'll ask properly. I don't think Lena is ready to even discuss that step yet."

"And you?" my father asked.

"I'd marry her tomorrow morning at the courthouse if she'd have me."

Yuri's steadfast answer sent me reeling backward. I bumped into a hard male chest and barely managed to smother a yelp of surprise.

Spinning around, I came face-to-face with Jake. He had a teasing smirk on his face. "It's not very nice to eavesdrop."

I smiled at him. "I trust you to keep my secret."

A fleeting look of sadness flashed across his face. "You'd be surprised at the secrets I'll keep."

As Jake backed away and returned to his seat, I wondered what secrets burdened him. Working in the private security business probably entailed a great deal of secret-keeping. What secrets of Yuri's was he keeping?

"There you are!" Yuri pushed the door open and held out his hand. "I was starting to worry."

After hearing how much he loved me and how serious he was about our relationship, it was all I could do not to grab the front of his shirt and jerk him down for a passionate kiss. He was right. I wasn't ready to have *that* discussion but there was no doubt in my mind that he was *the one* for me.

Patting his chest, I explained, "I got sidetracked talking to Kelly and Jake. Is everything okay with my dad?"

Yuri leaned down to kiss me. "Everything is going to be just fine."

For the first time in days, I believed it.

CHAPTER TWENTY

"Dad, are you sure you want to go home today? Yuri really meant it when he said you're welcome to stay as long as you'd like."

I sipped my coffee as we finished our breakfast in the kitchen. Sasha nudged my leg with his big furry head and silently begged for some of the bacon left on my plate. Even though Yuri had asked me not to feed Sasha from the table, I couldn't deny those wide dark eyes gazing up at me so adoringly. From the moment we'd walked through the door last night, Sasha hadn't let me out of his sight.

Feodor puttered around in the background, always ready to offer a refill or more of the scrumptious muffins he'd thrown together. I cast the older man a concerned glance. He'd been waiting for us when we'd arrived a little before midnight. I'd urged him to sleep in but I was positive he'd been ready with Yuri's coffee when he'd been called out a few hours earlier to deal with some last-minute negotiations to secure the final approvals on the pipeline.

"I know he meant it." My father ran his finger around the rim of his coffee cup. "I'm thankful for the offer—for all his offers of help—but I should get home and get things sorted out with Tommy."

Even though my curiosity begged to be satisfied, I didn't ask how things would shake out between my father and my cousin. "Is there anything else in that warehouse of yours that I should be worried about?"

Dad looked chagrined. "I've always been so careful but this time?" He smoothed his hand over the wooden tabletop. "I'm done." He reached across the table to take my hand. "If it wasn't for you, I would be dead."

I didn't even want to think about that. "But you're not. This is your chance to go legit."

"I won't waste it. I'll make you proud of me."

Gripping his fingers, I confessed, "I may not have always been thrilled to have a criminal father but I've always been proud to claim you as my dad. I know that you made big changes when you got out of prison and again when she left."

His eyes darkened with sadness. "She would have been proud of the successful young woman you are."

Bitterness crept into my voice. "No, she wouldn't."

Dad held tight to my hand, refusing to let me pull away and retreat emotionally. "You have to forgive her for leaving. She's gone now and there's no use hating a dead woman."

I swallowed hard as the old guilt started to gnaw at me. Instead of telling the truth and shaming the devil, I simply nodded. "You're right. I should forget her."

Because I damn sure wasn't ever going to forgive that woman for leaving us.

He let go of my hand but tapped my fingers gently.

Looking uncomfortable, he cleared his throat. "You love Yuri."

"I do."

"I'm glad. I want you to be happy." He pulled back his hand and drank the last of his coffee. "Don't let the mistakes I made with your mother and the mistakes she made hold you back, Yelena. *Me entiendes?*"

"Yes."

"Good." He stood up and Sasha instantly jumped to his feet. Thankfully, the overprotective dog didn't growl at my father but he pushed against me, reminding me that he was right there to defend me. My dad shook his head and gathered up the empty dishes. "I can't believe Tommy was dumb enough to break into a house where a dog like that lives."

"I don't think Tommy realized Sasha lived here."

"How did he miss a dog that size?" Dad asked as he carried the dirty dishes to counter near the dishwasher. "You said he figured out a way to bypass the alarm system. If he studied the house that much, he wouldn't have been able to miss that dog."

I glanced at Feodor who looked to be following my train of thought. Yuri's fears that this was more of an inside job than he'd first suspected seemed more likely. I tried to remember exactly where everyone had been that first night. Hadn't Derek been the one in charge of the alarm?

"Will you give me a ride back to my place?"

"I'll have Kelly or Jake drive us." I crossed the kitchen to the phone mounted on the wall. "My car is still in the parking lot at my apartment."

"Uh-huh," my dad said slowly.

I knew that tone but I had already dialed Jake so it would have to wait.

"Jake here," he answered a bit breathlessly.

"Hey, Jake, can you drive my dad home and take me to run some errands?"

"Yes for your dad but the errands are a maybe. Where did you want to go?"

"By my apartment to get some things."

"All right. We'll make it work. Give us a couple of minutes."

As I hung up the phone, I caught my dad's eye. "What?"

"I'm not trying to tell you how to live your life—"

"But?"

"But," he said carefully, "you've worked damn hard to earn an education. Don't throw it all away on being a kept woman."

Feodor choked on his hot tea. Rolling my eyes, I stepped closer to him and patted his back while he dabbed at his mouth with a napkin. He waved me away with an amused smile on his face. "I'm fine."

I fixed my dad with a glare. "I'm not a kept woman. Right now, things are very dangerous and uncertain and I'm staying here because it's safer for me, for Vivian, for my friends. And, yes, technically I am unemployed right now but I have no plans to mooch off Yuri. I have plenty of money saved to get me through my unemployment and I'm already looking into starting a new business with a friend of mine."

Dad exhaled with relief. "Okay. That's all I needed to hear."

The side entrance off the butler's pantry opened and Sasha rushed off to inspect the newcomer. Certain it was Jake or Kelly, I didn't call him back. I started to ask Feodor if Yuri had mentioned anything about dinner plans but a high-pitched yelp from Sasha stopped me cold.

Terrified, I hurried to the arched pantry entrance. "Sasha?"

Skidding to a stop, I discovered poor Sasha collapsed on the tile floor with a dart sticking out of his neck. My panicked gaze jumped to the side door but the gun muzzle pointed right at my face was all I could focus on in that horrifying moment.

"Walk backward slowly and don't try anything stupid…"

* * *

The intercom on his desk buzzed. He grunted at the annoying interruption and dropped the stack of faxed paperwork from the final pipeline negotiations onto his desk. Punching the key, he growled, "What?"

"Ty Weston is here to see you, sir."

The last thing Yuri wanted to deal with today was that gossipmonger. No doubt he'd come here to ask if Yuri intended to support Lena in the proposed business. "Tell him I don't have time. Ask him to make an appointment."

He hit the button and ended that discussion. The pile of notes and email backing up in his inbox irritated him even more. Anna's last-minute trip to deal with an ailing family member had been extended another couple of days, and he desperately needed her help.

The door to his office burst open and Ty strode into the room with that over-confident swagger that grated on Yuri's nerves. Impeccably dressed, he smoothed a hand over his hair. "We have to talk, Yuri."

Mary scurried in after Ty. "I'm so sorry, Mr. Novakovsky. He got around me and your guards."

Yuri leaned to the side and spotted Vasya panting in

the open doorway. With a flick of his hand, he sent his staff retreating. "I'll deal with him."

Once the door closed, Ty crossed the room and tossed a flash drive onto Yuri's desk. "That showed up with my morning paper."

Dread chilled him. "Do I even want to ask what's on it?"

"You're not going to be happy." Ty dropped into a chair near his desk. "I thought about taking it to Lena but she would be humiliated if she knew what was on it. I brought it to you because I assumed you have ways of dealing with this kind of blackmail."

Stomach churning, Yuri plugged in the flash drive. The moment it loaded he spotted the video file. Though he had a sinking feeling what the file contained, he clicked it anyway. Twenty seconds into viewing the tryst he'd shared with Lena on the desk in his home office, he closed the window.

Cold with shock and the surge of betrayal, he clicked through the photos on the drive. Someone had taken snapshots of him shaking hands with Lorenzo Guzman and making the exchange for Lena's father.

Yuri cleared his throat. "Who else has seen this?"

"A reporter at the paper received those same pictures of you in Mexico making whatever fucking deal that is with the cartel."

Yuri's gaze snapped to Ty's face. "How do you know?"

"Carson is an old boyfriend of mine. He was an embedded journalist in Iraq and Afghanistan but he's moved to the business beat here. Before he took the job here, he did some time following the cartel violence in Juarez and Sinaloa so he understands what those pictures mean."

"Why didn't he call me first?"

"He recognized Lena immediately. He's worked with her before and he knows that we're friends. He won't run the story because he's afraid it might get people killed. That's not the kind of journalist he is."

"Thank God for that," Yuri murmured. He unplugged the drive. "Do you know who sent this?"

Ty shook his head. "If I had to guess it's an assistant or one of those linebackers you hire to watch your back. The only people who get close enough to you to plant a camera and reveal all those dirty details are the people who work for you and have some level of trust."

Yuri wiped a hand down his face. Mind racing, he asked, "What did they want you to do with them?"

"Embarrass you. I read that you've got your pipeline deal nailed down. I've been following that saga for the last couple of weeks. It was pretty obvious that someone was trying to stall that deal or fuck you over completely. When that didn't succeed, they went for the old standby—personal humiliation."

"I'm not embarrassed to be caught making love to Lena."

"I'm sure you're not but do you think she wants a blown-up screencap of her orgasm-face all over the damn internet? There goes her credibility. Suddenly she's that jumped-up skank from the projects who earned her new business on her knees."

Yuri cringed at the awful way Ty described the situation. He recognized that Ty didn't believe those things but the gossip columnist understood how others would perceive Lena's position. He shoved out of his chair and slammed both hands on this desk. "*Fuck*."

"Hey," Ty said loudly. "Don't freak out. We'll keep a lid on this."

"We?"

"Me and you."

Yuri narrowed his eyes. "What makes you think I trust you?"

"You don't have to trust me," Ty replied matter-of-factly. "You need me. The first thing I learned in this business is that you always have to have the bigger, uglier secret. There isn't a gossip blog or business journalist who will touch these stories once I make it known that I'm working with you. They know I won't hesitate to take them out at the knees to protect a client."

Yuri's estimation of Ty climbed a few notches. "We don't have to do anything quite so drastic yet."

"I agree but it's always good to be frank with people."

Yuri couldn't argue with that. "I need to get home and sweep my office. It's apparent from this," he picked up the drive and pocketed it, "that I've been bugged."

"I've got a private investigator on my payroll who knows his way around surveillance. I'd be happy to loan him to you."

"I appreciate the offer but no. I'll handle this on my own."

Yuri gathered up his things and headed for the door. Ty trailed him to the door. "Keep me in the loop."

Yuri wasn't so sure he wanted to tie himself to a man who made his millions with an empire of gossip blogs but there wasn't much of a choice here. He needed Ty's help. "I will."

Out in the lobby, he motioned for Derek and Vasya to follow. "We're going home. Now."

Derek frowned with concern but didn't say anything. Yuri's jaw clenched and unclenched during the elevator ride down to the garage. Safe inside the backseat of the car, he made sure the partition was safely in place and then called Nikolai to quickly relay the situation.

Nikolai cursed obscenely as the news of the attempted blackmail using Lena registered. "We have to find this man. *Now*."

"I agree. Do you have any leads?"

"I'm waiting to hear back from a friend I keep in contact with but it doesn't seem promising. Ivan swears that Pasha talked about a kid of his own but I don't remember it."

"A boy?"

"Ivan says it was a girl named Katya. He remembered seeing her once in the old man's office at the orphanage. She had dark hair."

"A dark-haired Russian girl named Katya? That narrows it down," he grumbled.

"Don't be an asshole, Yuri. It doesn't suit you."

He grunted and picked at his jacket. "I don't know what to do anymore. I never feel lost or out of control like this."

"That's the point. The person doing this wants us to feel helpless. It's part of the thrill."

He ran his fingers through his hair and scratched at his head. "I can't live like this, Nikolai. I don't know how you do it. How you can stand the constant checking over your shoulder."

"I don't check."

Yuri heard the coldness edging into Nikolai's voice. "You're a braver man than me."

"You have something to lose. I don't."

Yuri understood what his friend meant. If he was the only one at risk, it would be easier to take all of this in stride but he wasn't. It was the thought of Lena being caught in the crosshairs, of Lena being hurt, that sickened him and filled him with dread and fear.

Nikolai's decision to keep everyone at arm's length

seemed smart now. The life Nikolai had chosen entailed a great deal of risk and collateral damage. Keeping the people he loved at a safe distance was the only way he could ensure that his choices wouldn't hurt others.

But it had to be a lonely life.

Yuri thought of the way Lena had brightened and filled his life. It was the same for Dimitri and Ivan—but Nikolai?

Whether it was right or wrong, Nikolai had obviously fallen in love with sweet Vivian over the last few years. Yuri remembered that evening in his office when they'd scared the piss out of Jonah Krause and forced him to sell his retail development as punishment for trying to kill Benny and Dimitri. What had Nikolai said? That someday Vivian would make a very nice man a good wife.

What must that feel like for Nikolai to stand back and watch the woman he cared for so deeply living a life he could never truly be a part of?

"I'm coming to see you." He heard a chair squeak and then the noise of a kitchen. "I'll be there in twenty minutes."

As usual, Nikolai abruptly ended the call. Yuri texted Lena to let her know he was on the way and to stay out of that damn office but she didn't immediately reply. He decided she was probably busy with her father.

It wasn't until he entered the front door of his home that he realized something was wrong. For the first time ever, Sasha didn't bark or run to the door. His heart raced as he took in the eerie silence. "Lena? Feodor? Sasha!"

"Vasya, go check the staff quarters," Derek gave the order in hushed tones. "Find Jake and Kelly."

With Derek hot on his heels, Yuri raced to the kitchen, the place where he expected to find Feodor at this time of day. The sight of the old man sprawled on his back and snoring deeply struck fear in his heart. Derek knelt down next to Feodor and rolled him onto his left side. The movement revealed a syringe sticking out of his arm and cuts on his hands. The bruising on his face proved the man had put up a fight.

Yuri spotted the bloody streaks on the tile and followed them into the mud room. Lena's father had crawled that far before passing out. The knife lodged in his upper shoulder had slowed him down but he'd obviously tried to chase after his daughter. Very gently, Yuri rolled his future father-in-law onto his side. He found Joe's pulse and exhaled roughly. Despite the blood loss, he was breathing steadily and his heartbeat was strong.

Yuri grabbed a towel from a nearby cabinet and placed it around the knife in an attempt to stabilize the weapon and help with the bleeding. "Call 9-1-1. Joe has been stabbed."

"Already on it, Boss!" Derek shouted back. "Sasha's alive but barely. They hit him with a damn tranquilizer dart."

Banging and cursing echoed loudly in the kitchen. Yuri glanced over his shoulder and watched Vasya carting Kelly's heavy body. The Marine was bloodied and snoring like Feodor. No doubt he'd also been drugged.

"The staff rooms are destroyed. He was handcuffed to a sink and left for dead. I couldn't find Jake."

Suddenly the pieces fit together. Jake had bugged his office. Jake had snapped those photos in Mexico. Jake had delivered the threatening letter to Lena.

As he pressed on Joe's bleeding shoulder, he noticed the door leading to the garage was slightly ajar. A bloody streak on the edge caught his attention. Yuri shut the door and discovered the message Joe had left in his own blood.

Jake. Anna. 916 Ord—

He clearly hadn't been able to finish the message but it was enough. He'd started to scrawl the address of the hellhole where Lena had lived with her mother while her father was in prison.

He didn't know the roles Jake and Anna played but there wasn't time to investigate. They had Lena—and he was going to get her back.

There were several sets of keys in the wall box mounted by the door. He grabbed the set for his fastest sports car and quietly slipped into the garage.

Where he was headed, he needed no bodyguards. This was something he had to face alone.

CHAPTER TWENTY-ONE

The walk from the broken curb where he'd parked to the front door of the ramshackle, dilapidated home on the corner was the longest of Yuri's life. Unarmed and uncertain as to what he faced, he walked right up to the front door and shoved it open. As long as these two monsters held Lena, he would do whatever it took to keep her alive. Because the pair hadn't called or texted him with instructions, it was clear they expected him to come find them.

He wrinkled his nose at the musty, moldy scent of the abandoned house. Like the others in this forgotten neighborhood, the house had been condemned and marked for demolition. He chose his steps carefully, uncertain whether the rotting floorboards would support his weight.

The sound of irritated voices sniping at one another echoed at the rear of the house. He followed the sounds to the kitchen. Lena came into view as he drew near. She had her wrists bound together in front of her and her ankles roped too. Her bloody nose and busted lip infuriated him. She noticed him a heartbeat before her captors. The look of relief and love on her bruised face bolstered his courage.

"Stop right there," Jake ordered. Holding a gun on Yuri, the bodyguard slid behind him. "Hands on your head."

Yuri did as commanded. He stared at Anna as Jake frisked him for weapons. His long-time assistant had dyed her platinum blonde hair a dark walnut shade. Gone was the pretty smile he expected. Her features seemed twisted with rage, with revenge. "Katya?"

Her pale-thin lips twitched with sad amusement. "Do you remember me now?"

Yuri shook his head. "No, but Ivan did."

She gritted her teeth. "All these years I've waited for you to recognize me, to remember what you animals did to my father."

Yuri's gut clenched as Katya snatched Lena by her long, beautiful hair and dragged her to a standing position. She was quite a bit taller and manhandled Lena easily. He winced as Lena was jerked roughly. When Katya produced a sharp-edged knife from the counter behind her, his heart stuttered in his chest. The wicked piece of steel nicked Lena's throat as Katya held it in place. The sight of Lena's blood dripping onto Katya's hand enraged him.

"Lena has nothing to do with this. Let her go."

"This is *your* fault. You shouldn't have fallen in love with this one. I let you have the others. I let them live but this one? This one you loved and so now you have to pay."

Lena's eyes squeezed shut as Katya jerked her back and pushed the knife against her throat.

"No!" Yuri took a step forward but Jake caught the back of his shirt and held him back. He slammed his elbow into the guard's stomach but Jake's hold only loosened for a brief moment. The muzzle of the gun jammed into his side, warning him not to do anything stupid. He wouldn't be any use to Lena dead. "Tell me what you want. I'll give you anything."

"Anything?" Katya laughed acidly. "Can you bring my father back from the dead?"

Anger flared in his gut. "Bring him back? That disgusting pedophile and rapist?"

Jake's grip lessened. "Pedophile? But Katya—"

Yuri laughed harshly. "Let me guess, Jake. She didn't tell you that her father used to pick boys from the orphanage to sell to high-paying pedophile clients? She didn't tell you that her father used to rape little boys in that house of fucking horrors behind the orphanage?"

The gun pressed into his side fell a few inches before being shoved roughly against his ribs. "Katya, is that true?"

"He's *lying*," she spat angrily. "All those boys were lying little bastards who wanted to ruin my father. They wanted to take him away from me and make me orphans like them. Unwanted. Unloved. Forgotten. They were *jealous* of me because I had a real family." Katya slammed her knuckles into the side of Lena's head. "Until *you* took him from me!"

Dazed, Lena blinked rapidly and tried to recover from the unexpected blow. Yuri desperately tried to draw Katya's attention. "I did take him from you. *Me*. I was the one who killed him."

"Why?"

"Because he was raping my best friend," Yuri shouted. "He was hurting my best friend."

"*LIAR!*"

"I wouldn't lie about that. Your father was a monster—and I'm glad he's dead." Yuri purposely taunted her in the hopes she'd fly at him and leave Lena alone. Something told him Jake wasn't onboard with Katya hurting an innocent woman.

"You're the monster!"

"Maybe you're right," he conceded. "I'm the one who picked up a pipe and bashed his fucking head in like a rotten apple. And I'd do it again in a heartbeat."

Katya screamed with anger and pointed the knife at him. The mad gleam to her eyes chilled him to the very core. "Maybe that's how I should kill her. Jake, find me a pipe."

"Now, wait, Katya," Jake said hurriedly. From the sound of his wavering voice, the bodyguard was quickly losing his will to carry out this brutal attack. "You never said anything about hurting Lena. You promised we were going to use her as bait to lure him here to make him pay for attacking and robbing and killing your father. You said they used the mob to cover it up, to get away with murder but—"

"Don't be stupid! She was never going to leave this house alive."

"She's innocent." Jake's composure faltered. "This isn't about justice anymore. This is about something ugly— and I won't be part of it."

The gun fell from Yuri's side but Jake kept his tight grip on Yuri. Katya raised her knife and pointed it at her partner in crime. Screaming like a Russian demon, she lost her fucking mind on Jake. The knife swung wildly in front of Lena's face. If her hands and ankles hadn't been bound she might have had a chance to escape…

Lena's tearful gaze met his. For a few heartbeats, the

world slowed to a near standstill. Without saying a word, she telegraphed her intentions with a single look. Silently, she mouthed one simple, beautiful phrase. *I love you.*

In the next instant, Lena chomped down on Katya's arm. The shock of witnessing his sweet Lena perpetrate such a barbaric act froze his limbs. Blood spilled around her lips as she bit down even harder. Katya shrieked with agony and ripped her arm free. The wild movement brought the knife dangerously close to Lena's neck but his brave woman threw up her bound wrists and blocked the knife's blade with that wide gold cuff he'd given her. The very tip of the knife bounced off the cuff and sliced her jaw.

Lena's pained shout pulled him from his stupor. Throwing back his head, he slammed his skull into Jake's mouth and nose. A solid kick to the balls dropped the bodyguard. Scrambling forward, Yuri reached Lena in time to snatch her by the shoulders and toss her out of the way.

Katya flew at him with the knife. There was nothing to do but block her slashes with his forearms. He hissed as the blade plunged into his arm again and again. The stab wounds hurt like hell but he refused to let this deranged woman anywhere near Lena again.

As the knife slashed at his chest and ripped open his shirt and the flesh beneath, two gunshots startled Yuri. Like him, Katya jumped with surprise. Terrified Lena had been hurt, he glanced at her but her gaze was fixed on the doorway behind them all. Looking back, he found Nikolai standing there with his pistol still raised. Jake had fallen to the floor, a gun gripped in his hand and blood pooling around his chest and arms.

"*Aaarggh!*" Yuri's guttural burst of pain exploded from his mouth as Katya jammed the knife into his right shoulder. The blade became stuck as he twisted away from her and fell forward. Before she could rip it free and stab him again, Nikolai fired two more times, hitting her square in the chest. The weight of her body dropped onto his back and drove him to his knees.

In an instant, Nikolai had reached him. He pushed Katya onto the floor where she gasped and clawed at her bloody chest. Yuri reached back to touch the knife sticking out of his back but Nikolai gripped his hand. "Leave it alone. This is for the surgeons to handle."

Huddled against the wall, Lena sobbed loudly. Nikolai crouched near her and produced a knife from his boot. He quickly cut the ropes binding her wrists and ankles. Once she was free, she scuttled across the rickety floor. "Yuri!"

Bleeding profusely, he crawled toward her and rested his head in her lap. The throbbing pain of the knife embedded in his shoulder was easy to ignore when her soft hands touched him.

"Oh, baby, you'll be okay." She ran her fingers through his hair. "Just hold still, Yuri."

He reached up and touched the spot just below her bloody jaw. The wound would scar and serve as a reminder of all they'd survived. "I'm sorry."

"Don't," she whispered and bent down to brush a kiss across his temple. "I love you so much—and you came for me. That's all that matters."

A terrible rattling breath interrupted their declaration of love. Katya gasped for air as her lungs filled with blood. Yuri had seen enough chest wounds during the campaign in Chechnya to know the woman had only minutes. He wanted to hate her for what she'd done but he felt only the most supreme sadness. Her mind had been been twisted by that terrible, vile man she called a father and then filled with hatred when she'd been left orphaned and alone.

Showing the depth of her kindness and forgiveness, Lena grasped Katya's hand, the same hand that had wielded the knife that sliced her face, stabbed her father and her lover. Voice shaking but calm, Lena said, "You're all right. You're going to be all right."

It was a lie—and Katya knew it. Even so, the woman's expression softened. She dragged the final gurgling breaths into her destroyed lungs. Lena kept a tight grip on Katya's hand even after it was all over.

Dizzy from the blood loss and awash in adrenaline, Yuri started to fade. As he fought to stay conscious, he watched Lena hold out her now bloody hand toward Nikolai. "Give it to me."

Nikolai couldn't hide the shock on his face. "No."

"I'm not asking. Give me the damn gun and go."

"It's a clean gun." Nikolai hesitated for a moment before handing over the weapon he illegally possessed. He crouched down and gripped Yuri's hand. "I'll stay close by—just in case."

"Go," Lena urged.

As Nikolai fled the scene, Lena expertly unloaded the weapon and made sure to wipe down every inch of it— even the shiny rounds—before marking the gun and bullets with her fingerprints. The way she expertly handled the weapon would have impressed him under different circumstances. Today, it saddened him.

"You don't have to do this." He stayed on his side as she slid away from him and started to rifle through the drawers in search of another knife. When she found one, she used it to slash at the ropes that had been binding her wrists and ankles. She dropped the knife on the floor there.

"I do. He saved us. I know he's done some shady shit in his life but I won't throw him to the wolves. We'll tell them this was the gun you brought. If Nikolai's DNA or fingerprints show up on it, you tell them that Nikolai took it away from you because he didn't want you to go after Jake and Katya on your own. We'll tell them I was able to get to the gun when it was knocked off the counter after I cut the rope cuffs. I got behind Jake and shot him. Then I shot Katya."

Yuri cringed at the ugly idea of letting Lena take the fall for the shootings. "No. I won't let you do this."

"It's too late. This is happening." She reached into his pocket and withdrew his phone. "No one is going to charge me for defending the man I love and saving my own damn life."

He tried to stay awake as she dialed 9-1-1 but the blood loss made him weak and cold. There were so many questions racing through his mind. How Nikolai had come to be here still perplexed him. Listening to Lena take the blame for what had happened here soured his gut. He wanted to cry out that she was innocent but the numbness took hold.

For now, Lena was safe—and that was enough for him.

* * *

"It's not that bad. Really," Erin added with a reassuring smile. "That plastic surgeon did a really nice job."

Sitting in the hospital waiting room, I studied the swollen area along my jaw that had been sewn and glued shut in the reflection of the mirror she'd produced from her purse.

"Erin is right." Vivian comfortingly patted my arm. "It

will heal nicely."

Closing the mirror, I handed it back to Erin. "I guess a faint scar is better than the alternative."

Erin hugged me from the side. Teary-eyed, she whispered, "I don't even want to think about that. I'm so glad you're all okay."

Okay was probably the best way to describe everyone. Kelly and Feodor were being kept overnight for observation after having the unknown sedative injected into their systems. Sasha's vet had made a house call to check on him and now Dimitri and Benny were staying over to watch him as he slept off the tranquilizer.

"Your dad looked pretty good," Vivi remarked. "From what I could see from the hallway, I mean."

I nodded and sipped cold water from the bottle Ivan had handed me before taking up a strategic seat across the room. He had the best view of everyone coming and going. No doubt he'd been tasked with watching over all of us.

"For someone who took a boot to the face and a kitchen knife to the back? Definitely."

"At least they'll be on the same floor," Erin said, clearly trying to find a silver lining to all this. "Yuri and your dad, I mean. It will make visiting easier for the next few days."

"How long do you think they'll keep them?" Vivi wondered.

"The doctor said Dad will probably go home in two days. I hope they won't keep Yuri very long. He won't be able to handle sitting still and doing nothing."

"Maybe it would be good for him to learn to enjoy a slower pace," Erin suggested. Lowering her voice, she said, "Ivan was a real workaholic before we got together. He still puts in some crazy hours but he's definitely learned to cut back and enjoy life more. That might be good for Yuri. All that stress can't be healthy for him."

"It might be good for both of you to slow down," Vivi remarked. "You two are exactly alike when it comes to work. In all the years I've known you, the last week has been the first time I've ever seen you take some time for yourself—and it took a dang cartel threat and some blackmailing nut to make you do it!"

When she put it like that...

"Miss Cruz?" A nurse in bright blue scrubs smiled at me. "Mr. Novakovsky is in his room now."

Even though I wanted to jump up and run down the hall to see him, I rose slowly as instructed by the doctor who had seen me in the ER for my smacked up face and the surgeon who had sewn me back together. Vivian gave my hand an encouraging squeeze. As I left the waiting room, Ivan winked at me and smiled.

The nurse walked me to Yuri's private room. Desperate to see him, I entered quickly and shut the door. The setting sun filled the room with a pinkish hue.

Yuri's tense expression relaxed as his gaze fell upon me. "Kitten."

Joy bubbled inside me like the fizzy champagne we'd enjoyed on his yacht. I couldn't get to him fast enough. Standing next to the bed, I visually examined him. Both of his arms were bandaged. The gaping neck of his hospital gown revealed another bandage on his chest and the top edge of the bandage on his back. An IV line snaked out of his right arm.

Cupping his strong jaw, I whispered, "How are you feeling?"

"Buzzed," he answered honestly.

I giggled. "I suppose that's a good thing right now."

"Very good," he agreed. His smile faded and he

brushed his fingers across my cheek. "Are you all right?"

"The bruises will fade and my lip will heal. This too," I added while gesturing to the cut.

"And what about this?" He touched my head. "And this?" He touched my heart. "Are these going to heal so quickly?"

"I don't know. I don't think it's really hit me yet." I swallowed hard. "I'm sure it will later, when I'm alone."

"I don't want you alone. You need to be around the people you love and the people who love you."

Thinking of Erin, Vivian, Benny and their men, I nodded. "I don't think that will be a problem. Dimitri and Benny are already at our house taking care of Sasha. I guess Vasya was able to carry him into his kennel after the vet saw him. And Ivan brought Erin and Vivian to the emergency room. They haven't left my side."

"Good." He hesitated. "Have you spoken to the police?"

"Yes. Have you?"

He shook his head. "Not yet but I assume they'll be here soon. Did you call my lawyer?"

"No but Nikolai did. Craig was at the house before the paramedics even had you loaded into the ambulance. He shielded me from the more aggressive questioning."

"Are you sure you want to stick with this story?"

"Yes." I still didn't know where my instinct to protect Nikolai came from but I trusted it. "Everything would come out, Yuri. *Everything.* If Nikolai wants to tell people about the abuse he suffered as a child, that's his business. I won't have that admission forced on him. Regardless of who shot Jake and Katya, there was no other way out of that situation. We were both going to die today, Yuri. Whether I take responsibility or Nikolai does, it doesn't change the reality."

Yuri looked like he wanted to argue. "I don't want you to suffer for more of my mistakes."

"And I didn't want you to suffer for the mistakes of my father and my cousin but you did. You risked so much to save them both, to save the people I love. This is my way of saving someone you love."

His eyes shut briefly. "I wish it wasn't so sordid, so dirty."

"So do I."

He tried to squeeze my hand but winced. "Sorry. They said there isn't any bad nerve damage but it may be a few weeks before my grip and dexterity returns."

"I guess it's a good thing you don't work with your hands."

Yuri grinned and his eyes gleamed impishly. "Oh, I don't know about that. I think I've done some of my best work with these hands."

Thinking of all the ways he'd sensually tormented me with those masterful hands, I blushed. "Yes, you have done some rather amazing things with them."

He chuckled. Eyes shining with love, he murmured, "I want to hold you."

I studied the bed. "Don't move. I'll just squeeze right in here."

After kicking off my shoes, I gently climbed onto the bed and insinuated myself between his side and the safety rail. I made sure not to put any pressure on his chest and watched his face for any signs of discomfort. He draped his bandaged arms around me. "I love you, Yelena."

"I love you, too."

"You realize I'm going to marry you someday."

Smiling up at him, I kissed his cheek. "I figured."

He snorted with amusement. "I suppose that answer will have to do for now."

"For now," I agreed.

"While the doctors were sewing me back together, I decided that we're going on a very long vacation after Dimitri and Benny's wedding."

"Is that so?"

He laughed quietly. "It is. You aren't fighting me on this one. You need some relaxation and rest as much as I do."

"Erin and Vivian just said the same thing to me. Apparently, they all think we're workaholics."

"We are. It's probably why we get along so well but life is about more than work and money and success." His arms tightened around me. "I've waited years to find you, Lena. I intend to enjoy every damn minute we have together."

His sweet vow touched me. "Ditto."

"You pick out the places you want to visit and we'll do them all."

My eyebrows shot up. "All of them?"

"Why not?"

"Maybe the top five," I said, thinking of how long it would take to visit all the places on my bucket list. "We have our whole lives ahead of us to get to the rest of them."

"Then top five," he agreed indulgently. He kissed the top of my head. "And add a stop to Los Angeles to that list."

"Los Angeles?" I scrunched up my face. "Why? Do you have business there?"

"No, but I thought you might like to see your mother."

His words hit me like a speeding truck. Voice shaking, I reminded him, "My mother is dead, Yuri."

He swept his fingers down my hair. "I don't know

who told you that but it isn't true. She's alive. Her address was in the dossier that I shredded."

Suddenly nauseated, I bolted upright and off the bed. The awful truth, the one thing in the whole world I'd been willing to lie to him about, had been uncovered.

"I'm sorry." Yuri tried to sit up but fell back when the pain wouldn't let him. He pressed a hand to his shoulder. "I shouldn't have told you like this. I wasn't thinking about what a shock—"

"I already knew," I said, my voice scratchy and my eyes burning.

Yuri blinked with confusion. "What do you mean? But you told me—"

"I know what I told you. I told you the same thing I tell everyone." Humiliated to admit the truth, I dropped my gaze to the floor. "I found her when I was seventeen. I saved money all summer and bought a bus ticket to Los Angeles the week before my senior year of high school began."

"You rode a bus? All the way to Los Angeles? At seventeen?"

I could hear the distaste in his voice but didn't dare lift my gaze to his. "Yes."

"Why didn't your father give you money for a plane ticket?"

"He didn't know I was going. We never talked about her after she left."

"You went across the country *alone*? Yelena, you could have been killed or kidnapped or—"

I held up my hand. "I know how stupid it was."

Still unable to meet his gaze, I wiped at the tears rushing down my cheeks. Realizing there was no way to keep the awful, ugly truth a secret, I let it all spill out of me. "I was so excited. The whole way there I kept dreaming of all the wonderful things that would happen. I thought we would hug and laugh and stay up all night talking and go to fucking Disneyland."

My painful sob echoed in the quiet hospital room. "But she wasn't happy to see me after all. She looked horrified—*horrified*—to see me standing on the doorstep of her big, beautiful new house."

I managed to force down the bile rising in my throat as the humiliating memories assaulted me. "When her husband asked who I was, she said I was a solicitor selling magazine subscriptions and slammed the door in my face. She had a whole new family. A perfect family," I added. "And she didn't want me poisoning it."

"*Lyubimaya…*"

"I went back to the bus station and bought a ticket home. Dad didn't even realize I'd been gone. He'd been fencing some stuff in New York. Right around Christmas, he found the address and asked me about it. I didn't know how to tell him the truth so I told him she was dead because we were already dead to her."

"*Angel moy…*"

"So I lied to you, too, Yuri." I sobbed into my hands, the broken gulps of air making my lungs burn. "I lied because there's no way you could love me if you knew that my own mother didn't want me."

Yuri's strong, loving voice cut through my sobs. "Come here, Lena. I would come get you myself but I can't. Now come here, Kitten."

I forced my feet to move even though I wanted to run out of the room in embarrassment. Yuri grasped my hand and tugged me closer. "Onto the bed. Now."

I did as he commanded, sliding back into the small space I'd earlier occupied. Yuri shifted enough to gaze down at me. It wasn't pity or disgust reflected in those warm hazel eyes of his. No, it was love, the brightest, fiercest love.

"You listen to me, Yelena. That woman is a fool and there's no help for a person like that." He kissed me tenderly. "I'm no fool and I see what's right here in front of me. You are loved by so many people—by your father, by your friends and by me." He claimed my lips with such love. "I will never abandon you, Lena. You are precious to me."

Yuri's words started to fill that raw, gaping hole inside of me. For the first time in so long, I actually began to feel a glimmer of wholeness.

"I'm going to spend the rest of my life showing you how much you're loved." With a teasing smile, he added, "And I'm going to take you to Disneyland."

Still crying, I laughed at his playful remark. Though it was said teasingly, I had no doubt we'd both be sporting mouse ears in goofy pictures someday soon.

After Yuri wiped my face with his hospital gown, he urged me to snuggle closer. Huddled close to the man I loved, I relished the flare of hope burning so brightly within me. If any man in the world had the audacity to be everything he promised, it was my Yuri.

CHAPTER TWENTY-TWO

FOUR WEEKS LATER

"I've got to hand it to you, Erin. This is one hell of a wedding!" Champagne in hand, I took the open seat next to her.

Grinning, she looked rather pleased with herself "It was fun to plan. Of course, having full access to Yuri's yacht and all the secret handshakes from Nikolai and Ivan's business relationships around town helped." She leaned closer. "You wouldn't believe how affordable this bash was. Like—seriously."

"I've seen you haggle when we go thrifting," I reminded her with a laugh. "I'm not at all surprised you got all this for less."

And it was a beautiful wedding. It was a mid-sized gathering of Dimitri and Benny's friends and family. Ivan had taken the role of best man and Benny had asked me to be her maid of honor. Johnny looked fantastic in his tux and watching him give away his sister had been a bittersweet moment to watch.

Because Ivan hated speaking in public, Yuri had given

the best man's speech—and he didn't disappoint. We'd all been rolling with laughter and smiling as he delivered a poignant but witty speech, but it was Dimitri who had us wiping our eyes and cheering when he finished his heartfelt speech with an announcement of Benny's pregnancy.

I watched the happily married couple as they swayed on the dance floor. Safely out of her first trimester, Benny seemed to be over the worst of the morning sickness and the exhaustion. The cut of her wedding gown, an empire sheath, made it possible for her to keep their secret through the ceremony, but out on that dance floor, the fabric twisted just enough to show the rounded curve to her belly. Without even realizing it, Dimitri had been placing his hand across her tummy in a protective, shielding way all night.

"We should start a pool," Erin said with a giggle. "Due date. Boy or girl. Weight. All that."

"I'm so in."

"Maybe we should start a pool on that," Erin suggested with a slight gesture of her head.

Following the subtle lift of her chin, I spotted Vivian dancing with Kelly Connolly. The sight of the two laughing and swaying surprised me. Out of habit, I searched the crowd for Nikolai. He stood with Yuri and a couple of men I didn't recognize. His dark gaze was fixed on the dancing couple.

As if he could sense me watching him, his attention flicked my way. Our gazes clashed but I didn't look away. After the harrowing experience I'd shared with him, I no longer felt as nervous or scared around him. We would never be friendly—I wasn't sure he was capable of being friendly with any woman other than Vivian—but we were warm acquaintances.

Turning his back on Vivian and Kelly, Nikolai signaled that he was okay with whatever she wanted. But as I watched Vivian and Kelly dancing, I got the feeling that the two weren't attracted to each other in the least. There were no lingering touches or intense flirty looks exchanged between the pair.

I sipped my champagne. "I don't think that's going anywhere. It's just a dance."

"Pity," Erin said with a little frown. "They make a hot couple."

"I don't think Vivian wants anyone but the one man she can't have."

"I don't know about *can't*. I think if she went after him, he'd be defenseless against her." Erin drummed her fingers on the table. "What's the story with Kelly? I thought he'd given up his bodyguard post."

"He's not doing long-term jobs anymore. Apparently he told Dimitri that he worried he would become too attached to his clients. He's lost enough people that mattered to him while he was in the Marine Corps so he doesn't want to do that in civilian life. The last I heard he's doing short private security jobs. You know, a weekend here or there."

"I was so worried that Dimitri's new venture was going to take a hit after that mess with Jake but I guess it's turned out okay."

"Ty and I worked overtime to spin the hell out of that situation. Honestly, Dimitri has dozens of bouncers and bodyguards working for him and only one turned out to be rotten. It's very clear that he's super careful about vetting the men he hires. I think Jake was basically a great guy who got taken in by a beautiful psychopath with a sob story."

"At least that's all over now."

A few days earlier, I'd been cleared of any charges. I suspected the DA and the detectives on the case didn't fully believe my version of events. There were inconsistencies in some of the forensics, after all, but nothing to prove that Nikolai had ever been in that house. As far as I could tell, no one but the three of us knew that secret—and it would stay that way.

"Has Vivian decided what she's going to do once you totally move in with Yuri?"

"She's looking into a smaller apartment at the same complex." A quiver of guilt pierced my chest. "I still feel torn about moving out but she says she's happy for me."

"Vivian is happy for you. She always means what she says."

"Still..."

"Let it go, Lena." Erin shot me a knowing look. "Don't think this to death. If you want to move in with Yuri, move in with Yuri. Vivian wants you to be happy. She's a big girl and she'll be fine. Frankly, I think she's getting annoyed with the way we all treat her like our little sister."

"She's the closest thing I've ever had to a sister and she is younger than us."

"She's also survived more than the three of us," she gestured between the two of us and toward Benny, "can even imagine. Maybe it's time we step back and give her some space."

I grinned at Erin. "Damn, you are sexy when you go all mama-bear like that."

She rolled her eyes. "I've already got a date for tonight so the flattery is wasted on me."

"Speaking of your date..." I watched Ivan striding toward us. When he reached the table, he bent down and swept Erin into his brawny arms. He took her seat and settled her across his lap. From the way he kissed her, it was clear he was starting to feel the effect of all that vodka. His inhibitions had definitely been lowered and his libido was raging. Judging by the way he devoured her mouth, Erin would be lucky to make it to the room they'd been given on the yacht with all of her clothes intact.

"Ivan!" Giggling, Erin grasped his big hand and pushed it down to her waist. "Later."

I couldn't hear what he said in that gruff voice of his but Erin's face turned bright red. She nibbled her lower lip and tried not to smile. "Okay," she said a bit breathlessly. "We can go now."

He started to stand with her in his arms but she wiggled off his lap. "I'll walk."

Ivan looked like he wanted to protest but she grabbed his hand and tugged him after her. With a quick smile my way, she excused them with a wave.

"Jesus!" Ty exclaimed before dramatically falling into the chair Erin and Ivan had just vacated. "These Russians know how to throw a party!"

I couldn't help but laugh at him. He looked rather frazzled without his tuxedo jacket and his shirt gaping open at the top. His cheeks were ruddy from the exertion of dancing and he seemed to be sweating, something I'd never seen him do. "How much have you had to drink?"

"I don't know," he admitted with a brash laugh. "Too much probably."

"You have a ride home?" I was sure he had a driver but wanted to make sure my new business partner got home in one piece.

"Actually," he slid his chair closer, "I'm hoping that sexy beast takes me home."

Sexy beast? I followed his boldly pointing finger and nearly fell out of my damn chair. "Vasya?"

YURI

"Is he fucking hot or what?" Ty rested his chin on his hand and openly flirted with the behemoth bodyguard. When Vasya's lips briefly curved in a smile, I realized how blind I'd been. No wonder Vasya was always volunteering to babysit me. He wanted to spend time around Ty!

Recovering from the shock, I asked, "Are you two an item?"

"Not yet but I think this might be my lucky night."

"He's on duty."

"Well—maybe I'll follow him home. Do you think Yuri would mind if I spent the night in your guest house?"

"It's not Yuri I'm worried about."

He scrunched up his nose. "Oh, right. That awful dog."

I took offense. "Sasha is the sweetest, gentlest baby of a dog."

Ty guffawed. "Sweetheart, you need a new dictionary. That genetic experiment you call a dog looks like the bastard son of a grizzly bear and a gorilla."

I rolled my eyes. "Whatever."

Ty's smiling gaze jumped back to Vasya. His eyes lit up and he practically jumped out of his chair. "Oh, I think I'm about to get that quickie I've been craving."

I glanced at Vasya who was slowly heading away from the crowd. No doubt he was going to take Ty to some private room where they could indulge in some late-night loving. I considered the size difference in the two men. "He's going to break you in half."

"Sugar, I'm counting on it." With a spring in his step, Ty disappeared in the crowd.

Vivian appeared next to me and playfully bumped me with her hip. "Did I really just see Ty Weston chasing after Vasya?"

"Apparently, they're sort of a thing."

"Nice." She put a hand on my back. "I thought your dad was coming."

"Benny and Dimitri invited him but he changed his mind."

"Hey," Vivian said and crouched down next to me. "Don't sound so sad. You did what you thought was the right thing when you lied about your mom. He'll get over it."

"Maybe," I said uncertainly. The memory of our shouting match in Yuri's library remained raw and real. "He was really angry. I don't blame him."

"He's your father. He'll forgive you."

"I lied about my mother being dead. That's a huge thing. It might even be unforgiveable."

"Lena, I've forgiven *my* father for the awful things he did to me. If that wasn't unforgiveable then neither is the lie you told. You were hurting and you were humiliated so you did the easiest thing you could to protect yourself— and your dad will see that."

"Maybe."

Vivian sighed. "Look, we are carrying around so much baggage from our parents. The last thing we need is to heap more guilt onto our own shoulders." She squeezed my hand. "Let it go."

We became aware of the DJ announcing the bride was about to throw her bouquet before they escaped on their honeymoon. Vivian tugged me out of my chair and to the dance floor. A few dozen unmarried women jostled for the best spot already.

"Where is Erin?"

I laughed. "Let's just say Ivan decided they were going to turn-in early."

Vivian giggled and then jokingly said, "I'm shocked."

The DJ's countdown pulled my attention to the small stage where Benny stood with her back to the crowd. When Benny launched the gorgeous bouquet into the air, the women around us started to rush forward. I barely managed to stay upright but Vivian was dragged along with the crowd. Her hands flew up in the air—and the bouquet smacked her open palm.

She snatched the bouquet and waved it around with a shocked grin on her face. I couldn't stop laughing at the priceless look Vivian wore. While the other women glared daggers at her, Vivi scurried over to meet me. "I got it!"

"I see that." I fingered the luscious roses. "I didn't think you were the bouquet-catching type."

She shrugged. "It's the competitor in me, I guess. I'll give it to Erin for good luck. I'm sure she'll be the next one of us to walk down the aisle."

"Probably," I agreed.

Two familiar arms slipped around my waist. Yuri's lips touched my neck. Laughing, he addressed Vivian. "I saw you throwing out your elbows to catch that bouquet."

Her jaw dropped with mock outrage. "I did not!"

We were still laughing when Nikolai joined us to see off the newlyweds. We moved into the line forming along the path they would take to the helipad. The beaming couple stopped for lingering hugs and well wishes from all of us before rushing off to begin their honeymoon.

After watching the helicopter fly away, the rest of our guests returned to the party. Yuri tugged me away from the packed dance floor. "But our guests—"

"Are all grownups," he interjected. "The staff hired for the wedding has everything under control."

When he had that gleam in his eye, there was no arguing with him. Yuri led me down to the private section of the yacht and into the master suite. The privacy shades had been lowered and he locked the door behind him. "Strip for me."

My tummy trembled wildly but I followed his command. While I slipped out of my heels and peeled out of my dress and undergarments, Yuri began to remove his tuxedo. "Leave on the diamonds."

I touched the exquisite necklace and earrings he'd left on my pillow that morning. As he took off his shirt, I caught sight of the brand new tattoo adorning the left side of his chest. It looked so starkly beautiful among the pinkish scars now dotting his skin. My lips parted with surprise as I realized what he'd had tattooed over his heart.

"For me?" I crossed the space between us and ran my hands around the freshly tattooed area, being careful not to touch his healing skin. He'd placed our interlaced initials inside a circle of vines. The design reminded me of the golden cuff he'd given me, the one I wore nearly every day.

"For you." He kissed my fingers. "I left some space here, over my heart, for later."

"Later? Oh." I blushed as his meaning hit me. For when we were married and had children... "It's always good to plan ahead."

He chuckled softly. "As much as I enjoy keeping you in my bed, I may end up running this tattoo down my arm."

He was teasing but I shook my head. "Let's not get crazy. If—when—we decide to take that step, I think three is a good number."

"Four or five is a better number." He nuzzled my neck and gently grazed his teeth over the sensitive patch there.

"When you can carry and deliver them, we'll discuss four or five."

Laughing, Yuri plucked the pins from my hair. The silky waves fell around my shoulders. "We'll table that discussion until next year."

My eyes widened. "Next year? But we—"

"Later," he murmured and silenced me with an erotically charged kiss. When he crouched down and grasped the backs of my thighs, I hopped up and wrapped my legs around his trim waist. He carried me to the bed and placed me in the center.

Pinned beneath him, I breathed excitedly. Already my pussy throbbed and ached to be filled by his big cock. I wanted his masterful hands and that wicked mouth on me. Arching up against the hard heat of him, I silently begged him to ravish me.

Grinning with mischief, he dragged two long silk straps from under the pillows. "Do you remember that night outside Monaco when I asked if you wanted me to tie you up?"

"Yes." I vibrated with arousal and anticipation.

"Do you still want me to do that?"

"Yes." My trembling voice betrayed my enthusiasm. "Tie me up. Take me."

He wasted no time in binding my wrists and securing them overhead. A frightening memory tried to resurface but I refused to let that ugly thing intrude upon this wonderful, intimate experience. He must have seen the flash of panic on my face.

Cupping my face, Yuri kissed me with such tenderness and love that it brought tears to my eyes. "You're safe with me."

"I trust you." There was a time when I never could have imagined saying those words to any man. With his love and patience and willingness to risk it all to save me, Yuri had proven that he was worthy of that trust. He'd shown me the depth and strength of his love.

His eyes shimmered suspiciously as he caressed my naked skin and claimed my mouth with sinful kisses. "I know what it means to earn your trust. I will never—*never*—take that for granted."

And he wouldn't. He'd spend the rest of our lives together proving to me that he deserved that trust. I would spend the rest of our lives together basking in the glow of his love and endeavoring to show him every day how much he meant to me.

"You've made me so incredibly happy, Yuri."

"I know, Kitten." He placed a noisy kiss on my breast. "Tonight, I plan to make to make you very, very happy."

"Oh?"

"Yes." He playfully walked his fingers down my belly. Closing my eyes, I spread my thighs for him and sighed with pleasure. "And I think I'll start right about here…"

YURI

AUTHOR'S NOTE

I hope you enjoyed the third installment of the *Her Russian Protector* series! The series continues with full-length novels featuring Nikolai and Sergei. Upcoming books in 2014 include sequels for Nikolai and Sergei as well as new tales for Kostya, Alexei and Danila.

ABOUT THE AUTHOR

When I'm not chasing after my wild preschooler, I like to write super sexy romances and scorching hot erotica. I live in Texas with a husband who could easily snag a job as an extra on History Channel's new Viking series and a sweet but rowdy four-year-old.

I also have another dirty-book writing alter ego, Lolita Lopez, who writes deliciously steamy tales for Ellora's Cave, Forever Yours/Grand Central, Mischief/Harper Collins UK, Siren Publishing and Cleis Press.

You can find me online at www.roxierivera.com.

ROXIE'S BACKLIST

Her Russian Protector Series
Ivan (Her Russian Protector #1)
Dimitri (Her Russian Protector #2)
Yuri (Her Russian Protector #3)
Nikolai (Her Russian Protector #4)
Sergei (Her Russian Protector #5
Nikolai Volume 2 (Coming 2014)
Sergei Volume 2 (Coming 2014)
Kostya (Coming 2014)
Alexei (Coming 2014)

The Fighting Connollys Series
In Kelly's Corner (Fighting Connollys #1)
In Jack's Arms (Fighting Connollys #2)—Coming January 2014!
In Finn's Heart (Fighting Connollys #3)—Coming March 2014!

Seduced By…
Seduced by the Loan Shark
Seduced by the Loan Shark 2—Coming Soon!
Seduced by the Congressman
Seduced by the Congressman 2

Erotica
Chance's Bad, Bad Girl
Halftime With Craig
Tease
Eddie's Cuffs 1
Eddie's Cuffs 2
Eddie's Cuffs 3
Disturbing the Peace
Quid Pro Quo
Search and Seizure

ROXIE RIVERA